Ragged Claws

by
John Guy Collick

The second volume of The Book of the Colossus

Published by John Guy Collick

Copyright © John Guy Collick 2014

John Guy Collick asserts his moral right to be identified as the author of this book.

ISBN: 978 0 9576439 5 6

I should have been a pair of ragged claws
Scuttling across the floors of silent seas.

T.S. Eliot - *The Love Song of J. Alfred Prufrock*

At the end of time all directions are given in relation to the body of God. His head lies to the north, and his feet point south.

AT THE EDGE of the new universe a door rose through swirls of gas and collapsing dust. The sides of the portal sliced through the fabric of the cosmos, scissor cuts in quantum tissue - a narrow gap rising up for half a light year. Young star systems studded its outer surface. It opened inwards onto darkness. On the other side lay nothing but an infinity of emptiness.

Near the bottom a hand extended into the new universe. It wasn't human - two square thumbs flanked three stubby fingers and the skin had the texture of cracked plastic. Something was stepping through the door, groping blindly. Light filtering back through the portal fell across a shoulder covered in barbs thousands of miles long and a wedge of solid bone that was the head. With its body still encased in the icy darkness of the old universe the being sensed the warmth of fresh suns on its finger tips.

In its other hand it held a carved box sixty-five thousand miles deep. Lights speckled its surface - the citadels and fortresses of an entire species stored in planet-wide layers and compartments within the intricate carpentry. In a few millennia, when the being had stepped over the threshold between the old reality and the new, it would open the case and scatter its worshippers across the plains and valleys of countless worlds.

Behind it walked a second god, this one a mass of scales and tendons, bearing its people in a necklace of fused glass, each bead the size of one of the long-dead planets of the ancient cosmos. After that came another and another, each god different, each carrying worshippers - in sacks, on trays, cupped in alien hands or suspended in clouds of energy. Most, like the roiling fountain of darkness that was the deity of the Black Roses, resembled the creatures they carried towards the God Door. Others bore no similarity to their acolytes. Humanoids worshipped titanic clusters of crystal and filaments, squat beings slithering on multiple limbs prayed to vast gold-skinned hominids swathed in gauzy fabrics that billowed in their wake for thousands of miles.

The line of gods stretched into the old universe. Far beyond, in the darkness, a mannequin half a million miles from head to toe lay on a singularity five light years square. Using materials plundered from wormholes driven back to a time when lights filled the universe the last remnants of humanity struggled to fashion their own god in the hope that one day he too would carry them through the God Door. Deep in the Heart and Skull the Machine Men wove the energies needed to give him life. On and around the Body humans fashioned the titan out of metal, wood, glass, cloth - from the heaviest alloys to the most delicate ceramics. Across the singularity, covered in the soil of ground-up worlds, and within the dark interstices of this colossal puppet, empires rose and fell over the long aeons. Many forgot why they built, retreated into the shadowed caverns of the Body and changed. Others found the immediacy of power and conquest more to their taste than fanciful promises made for distant descendants. As the Great Task reached its conclusion only a few remembered the

God Door and the purpose of this immense figure they'd constructed out of the bricolage of the past.

No creature can make thoughts greater than its own so the Machine Men divided the Mind of God into eight spirits, gave them the bodies of giants and sent them out into the world of men to study the beings God would one day save. In the forgotten town of Metacarpi, in the shadow of the Thumb, treachery slew one of the titans and left the city a ruin. Six months later, deep within the Forearm of God, a survivor of that battle walked through more dark streets, hunting for a clue to show him how to repair the shattered mind of the colossus.

CHAPTER ONE

THE INSTANT MAX Ocel heard the girl scream he sprinted down the alleyway. After five steps caution kicked in. He ignored it, he understood the difference between an ordinary cry and a desperate call for help. The pitch changed, rising higher and higher, no longer human. He clattered to a halt, a chill settling on his heart as the noise shifted beyond the animal to an alien note of such ferocity he grimaced in pain and almost clapped his palms over his ears. His hand went for his gun. Damn it, he'd left it at home, not wanting to frighten the sage he'd been hunting for weeks. He was unarmed, and in this pit of a town. The shrieking stopped. Somewhere a creature howled in reply. *It's still screaming, it's gone ultrasonic. What in God's name is ahead of me?*

He forced himself to calm down, pacing along the passage as he glanced upwards. The locals used the giant faces painted on the ceiling far above to work out where they were, but the buildings leaned so close that after dark the sky was nothing more than a line flanked by jagged eaves. To Max it appeared as if someone had hacked at the air with a bread knife. He could be anywhere. He dared to shut his eyes and listen. It felt as if the cry silenced the whole city. His own heart argued back as he tried to soothe it into a more manageable rhythm. The sounds of scuffling erupted from the darkness - breaking glass, a body thumping into a ramshackle door, nailed boots on stone.

Max counted four attackers and two victims as he entered the courtyard. A man knelt on the ground, his arm raised in defence. A robed figure lay behind, slumped at the bottom of a crooked tower. The assailants hunched over them, cruel silhouettes in trench coats. Max spotted a curved sabre in one fist, an automatic pistol in another. He targeted the gun owner, ignored the whimpering coward in his head and padded across the square. He kicked the man in the side of the knee. A sound like splintering wood echoed off the walls. The attacker screamed and fell, the firearm rattling over the stones. As the next one turned, blade lifted to strike, Max ducked and drove his elbow up into the woman's jaw - a trick Abby taught him long ago - but his feet caught on the edge of her coat as she collapsed and he stumbled. A foot slammed into his side and he flipped over onto his back. Through the flaring pain he struggled to grasp what was happening. Was he that out of practice? God, if only Abby were here, but she'd stayed at home playing with that damn toy, tapping out plays to impress her new friends. A sword flashed across his field of vision. He pulled his knees up ready to kick out, hoping to deflect the blow. A white flash detonated to his right and the enemy staggered away, clutching her stomach. The scimitar rattled on the cobbles as she crumpled in a heap, blood pooling around her legs. The two uninjured thugs retreated, supporting the crippled survivor between them.

Max got to his knees. *God almighty, I'm winded already*. The fight had lasted barely a minute. The man who'd fired stared at him in horror, both hands clasping the gun's grip. Max guessed he was in his late twenties. Black curly hair framed a sharp face that bore a goatee and waxed moustache. The barrel shook, clearly he'd never shot someone. Not wanting to be next Max stood up and wrenched the weapon out of his fingers. The man looked relieved to be rid of it. He turned and peered under his companion's hood. Max saw his shoulders slump in relief.

"She's OK, just shaken."

A woman then, maybe the man's wife or lover. Max guessed the robbers jumped the pair, thinking them an easy target. Neither were fighters. Even under that voluminous cloak Max sensed a child-like delicacy in the man's partner. Why the hell were they abroad at night? Anyone with any sense stayed behind locked doors, or even better, fled this wretched hole forever.

Shouting filtered between the houses. The man coaxed his companion to her feet.

"Pell." The hood moved and Max caught a glimpse of blonde curls and a pink cheek.

"Pell, they're coming, we have to go."

Max knew the passage was the only route out and if they went that way they'd run into the reinforcements thundering towards them. He fought the urge to panic and looked at the tower. Once, frustrated with the endless maze of the city, he'd climbed onto the roofs, picking his way home across the jumbled wilderness of slate and wood. With the faces in the sky above to guide him he'd found it much easier than trying to understand the streets below. The only problems came from people objecting to a stranger clambering over their houses. He'd been shot at three times, once with a machine gun, and caught in a vicious dagger fight in a forest of washing. This time he saw no other choice. The tower rose up among the buildings, bending back and forth like an arthritic finger. No lights shone in its windows. Max threw his shoulder against the door. The other man joined him and on the fourth lunge it burst inwards in a cloud of splinters.

As he thought, no-one had entered the tower for years, perhaps decades. Dust coated the floor of the corridor, stacks of crates lined the walls. Most had collapsed and shattered remnants blocked the passage to their right. Max smelled the odour of rust mingled with rotten wood and camphor. The man and his companion ran round the curve to the left, their feet echoing on stairs. Idiots. They'd no clue what might be up there and they'd left the entrance wide open. He tried to push the door back into its frame. They'd smashed the latch so he piled the sturdier boxes against the broken planks. A shout echoed from the other side of the courtyard, muzzle flashes sparked from the shadows and bullets thumped into the lintel above his head. He began to realise what he'd done. His father's old curse, stone-headed duty, had dragged him into this. He had one gun and two helpless victims against a gang of armed footpads. Cursing his own stupidity he fired a few rounds at the mouth of the alleyway, hoping to buy enough time to climb to the level of the adjacent rooftops. He hurried after the couple, finding them huddled on the first landing.

"Don't stop," he hissed, pushing them up the steps. He paused to tip a pile of barrels down the stairwell, watching with satisfaction as several punched holes through the wood. That should slow the bastards. The pair climbed on ahead. As Max followed he glimpsed an empty room the width of the tower. Pale light from the cityscape fell across oak paneling. It reminded him of his father's room at the top of the Carceral Archipelago - cold, shadowed and inhuman.

They'd gained the fourth floor when the sound of splintering wood told him their pursuers had summoned the courage to break into the building. He toyed with the idea of firing down the stairs but didn't want to reveal their position. With any luck their attackers would waste minutes searching the lower floors.

Max reckoned they'd reached the same height as the neighbouring roofs and wanted to find a way of crossing the gap between the tower and the next house. They ascended one more flight for good measure and found themselves in a bedroom with a decaying four poster bed. Beyond it he could see glass doors opening onto a balcony. The man started to walk towards it. Max grabbed his arm and pulled him back. The fool hadn't seen the loose boards, another step and he'd fall into the room below.

"Follow me round the edge, stay in the shadows," he whispered.

"Berthold," said the man with a brief smile. He stuck out his hand. Max stared at him thunderstruck, what was he doing? *This isn't a bloody cocktail party!* Ignoring the others he crept along the wall towards the window. Relief washed over him as he spotted a building just yards away.

"Pell?" a voice called out from the floor below. Max froze. He hadn't heard the enemy on the stairs, they were nimbler than he thought. He cursed under his breath.

"Pell? Are you there my dear?" came the sing-song chant of an owner summoning a pet cat.

"Return to us, sweet Pell. That fuck-wit Berthold has nothing to offer you, nor that foolish man with the gun. Sarracinte is kind. He understands and he will forgive."

Sarracinte. It nudged at Max's memory - a name to whisper, a man to avoid, maybe a local pimp or crime lord. There were so many in this stinking city. Max hadn't paid much attention. He and Abby originally planned on staying here for a few days at most so he'd never bothered to study the town and its hidden ways. He had bigger things to occupy his thoughts. Three weeks later, with gunmen stalking him through a ruined tower, he wished he'd taken more notice of the local gossip.

"Come down Pell, and we'll let Berthold and the stranger live. If we have to come up there it'll be blood and screaming and death."

Max glanced at the girl. She'd stepped back into the shadows and all he saw was darkness on darkness. In shock or deliberately silent, she didn't speak or move. Berthold watched him with an expression of panic. Max missed Abby so much. She'd be jogging on the spot with excitement by now, desperate for a fight or a mad leap through those windows into the night.

Lamplight flared through the gaps in the floor. *Damn.* Max wanted to explain his plan to his companions so they could co-ordinate their escape but the slightest noise risked alerting the hunters. He leaned forwards, peering through the spaces. Sarracinte's thugs were as stupid as they were overconfident. The lantern showed them pacing back and forth, rummaging through the clutter below. The remainder must still be on the first few levels. He held up four fingers for Berthold who just looked confused. He mouthed *on the count of four*. The man shrugged. *For God's sake.* He'd have to cause a diversion and make a run for it, praying the others would follow. He counted in his head and fired through the cracks.

Howls of pain erupted from below. Max pulled the trigger again. Silence for a second. The planks in the centre of the room burst apart in a hail of bullets. God's cock, they had a machine gun.

"Stop firing you morons," screamed one of the attackers. "She's not to be harmed, no. NO!"

"Two seconds," said a woman's voice.

Something that looked like a tennis ball flew up through the smoking hole, landed on the boards between Max and his companions and rolled a few inches, hissing. He leapt over it and yanked Berthold and Pell towards the windows. It wasn't until they were on the balcony, surrounded by shattered glass and about to leap, that his terrified mind caught up with his instincts.

Grenade, they've thrown a grenade.

It felt as if the city itself hit him in the small of the back with a flame-wreathed fist. He yelled in fear as the shock wave carried him over the gap, hurling him ten yards across the neighbouring roof. Fragments of wood showered onto the tiles. Max hadn't a clue where the others were or if they'd had time to jump before the explosion took out their hiding place. He bumped against the ridge and managed to hook an arm around a rusting chimney. He saw a churning mass of soot and dust envelop the tower. Orange flashes punctuated the smoke. The cretins had set it on fire and now he heard shouting and screaming. He guessed the blast had wrecked the stairs, trapping the men in the upper stories.

His companions lay a few feet away. The girl stirred, propping herself up on her arms. Max still couldn't see her features and when he called down she didn't answer. He nudged Berthold with his toe. The man coughed and swore. That was good enough for Max. He grabbed him by the scruff of the neck and hauled him out of sight. Pell crawled after them.

Max looked up. The city sat on the floor of a cavern a hundred miles wide. In the last stages of syphilitic madness the original ruler had painted the distant ceiling with immense faces, a gallery of vast grotesques leering down on the citizens. Over the centuries each ward came to identify itself with the expression in the sky above, descending into a fierce tribalism divided by the competing emotions twisting the features of the imaginary gods. Narrowed eyes stared into his. They were beneath the face called *Searching*. Max laughed in relief. The house he and Abby rented stood a mere two heads further on.

As Max had hoped the next one crumpled in tears and the one after that roared with silent mirth. *Laughter*, that was their ward, on the edge of the main canal running through Interosseous. If they were quick and clever they'd be home in less than an hour. With any luck Sarracinte's idiot thugs would think they'd perished in the destruction.

He got Berthold and Pell to their feet and led them over the rooftops. All around rose twisted eaves, skyscrapers, clusters of crooked chimneys and sloping walls that seemed to have no purpose. The skyline of Interosseous was the scribble of a mad child. Crazy angled windows shone with red and yellow lights. Once in a while Max noticed movement behind ragged curtains. When that happened he increased his pace.

Interosseous spooked him. Darkness and strange shapes filled the metropolis. The bustling sounds of day to day business always came from another street or just around the corner, never the narrow, empty passageways Max walked. It was a villainous pit without laws, rules or controls, built from a shifting patchwork of deals, fixes, stings and alliances. Max wondered if the anarchy spilled out into the very fabric of the reality that held the town together. How else could he explain the peculiar shifts in perspective or the visions he glimpsed in the corner of his eye when he walked between the crooked buildings?

They were supposed to be making their way north through the Arm but a string of bad luck had brought them to this thousand-mile-long dead end and now they were lost. Max knew they'd lingered too long, not wanting to retrace their steps back to the Wrist. They hoped instead to find a route through the littered confusion of shadows and shattered chambers that filled the Forearm. After weeks of hunting Max had learned of a sage living in the city who knew the path. It was the first piece of good news they'd had in ages and he'd been hurrying back to tell Abby when he'd heard the scream.

As he picked his way across broken slates and cracked gutters he mulled over the events of the night, recalling the cry that brought him to Berthold and Pell's aid. Had the girl uttered that alien howl? To begin with it sounded like a woman screaming for help but it changed into something monstrous and skittered beyond his hearing. He tried to catch a glimpse of Pell's face but she kept her head covered. The brief vision of yellow hair and smooth skin told him she was human. How did she make that god-awful noise?

They crested the roof of an abandoned factory. Max saw a mile-wide stretch of concrete stained with pools of oil and water, leading to the canal. To his left decaying houses clustered beside a line of jetties - watermen's offices converted into homes as the barge trade died and the warehouses emptied. At the end of a causeway he spotted a light in the first floor of a ramshackle three-story cottage. He grinned despite himself. She was up, no doubt hammering at that stupid typewriter - Abby the Time Scavenger turned playwright, just about the strangest image he could conjure out of this insane universe. She'd even befriended a troupe of actors lost like them in this treacherous realm.

Max fought against the urge to run across the open space and checked the surrounding cityscape. After a quarter of an hour he took a gamble. The gang in the tower hadn't followed them and he was sure they'd made the trek back undetected. For all his initial helplessness Berthold padded with a soundless grace through the shadows. Pell never appeared to move but each time Max checked behind him she'd switched position. He nodded, they climbed onto the concrete and slipped between the hills of scrap and debris littering the wharf.

Abby's new typewriter sounded like a machine gun. In her mind it was a wonderful treasure she'd unearthed at the back of a junk shop at the end of their first week in Interosseous. It drove Max insane. She jabbed at the keys as if trying to drill holes in a metal plate with her fingers, and the constant rat-tat-tat made him feel trapped in the middle of a never ending firefight. It was all he could do not to flinch at imaginary bullets. The problem was she looked so happy when she typed that he hadn't the heart to tell her to stop, though he fought the urge to hurl the bloody thing into the canal. Once, after she'd hammered her way through a three day epic non-stop, he'd suggested she put it on a high shelf and do something else for a while. She'd been so lost and miserable for the next two hours that he'd had to relent. Now, as they approached the cottage, the incessant rattling filled him with relief. He'd survived a battle in the foul streets of Interosseous. He just wanted to go home to Abby, even with a couple of refugees in tow. He suspected he was putting himself and his partner in danger but saw no other choice.

She sat cross-legged on a stool in one of his baggy shirts and a pair of knickers. She'd attempted to tame her wild red hair into a pony tail to stop it falling over her eyes and into the space between the type bars and the ribbon. The effect was alarming, as though she'd attached the rear end of a startled hen to her head. She typed with her tongue stuck out, still hunting for the keys despite two weeks of constant practice and hitting them as hard as she could when she found them.

Abby Fabrice turned. Her green eyes went wide at the bruises and soot on Max and wider when she spotted Berthold and Pell in the doorway. She snatched a revolver out of the desk drawer, killed the lights and pressed herself up against the window, scanning the terrain between the jetties and the town. Max was impressed. She hadn't forgotten the old routines. In fact she looked more on form than he'd been in the fight beneath the tower.

"How many?" she asked.

"They didn't follow us."

Max pulled Berthold and Pell into the room and locked the door.

"Sure?" Max bristled at the insinuation. *She thinks I've gone soft.* He hefted the gun he'd taken from Berthold and took position by another window, if only to prove to her that he hadn't lost his edge. Beyond the concrete plain the houses of Interosseous cut broken shapes out of the air. At this distance they looked like theatre scenery, punctuated by those odd-angled windows. Nothing moved.

They waited. Max counted out the minutes. He checked behind him a couple of times. Berthold hovered by the table, looking scared. Not an inhabitant of this city, then, no-one that frightened lasted long in this place. Max's knowledge of the geography of God's forearm was hazy at best. He'd heard of isolated kingdoms scattered throughout but knew nothing of their people. He couldn't see Pell. The bathroom door was shut. She must have locked herself inside. That made sense if Sarracinte's thugs were after her. He got the impression she was hardly more than a terrified girl. He and Abby exchanged glances. Her eyes glowed jade in the darkness. She nodded and backed into the room. Max stayed, giving the landscape a last sweep.

"I think we're good," he said.

Silence.

"Abby?"

The light came on. Max froze, fury welling up inside him. Berthold's arm circled Abby's neck. His other hand held a vicious knife at her throat. He watched Max, his eyes two shards of calculating hatred. Abby whimpered in terror. Berthold tightened his grip and she dropped her gun, her hands flailing.

"I saved your life, you bastard," said Max.

"For which I'm eternally grateful," replied Berthold with an easy smile. The frightened victim had left his face, replaced by arrogant confidence. In the light Max saw elegant clothes and a couple of expensive rings. A cravat spilled over the collar of his soft leather jacket.

"Please, please don't let him hurt me," begged Abby. She started crying, her legs trembling as fear took over. Berthold chuckled and a bead of blood appeared at the point of his dagger. Max looked into Abby's eyes. He'd make the smug bastard suffer for this.

"Bring your money and your weapons and place them on this table," said Berthold.

"What are you planning?" asked Max as he started to go through his own pockets. Abby was on the verge of fainting, her body slumped in Berthold's grip. He struggled to keep hold of her.

"You're going to get us out of this city or I'll gut your woman."

Max burst out laughing. He couldn't help himself. Abby straightened her legs and smacked the back of her head against Berthold's nose. She twisted and slammed his face into the typewriter. He fell to the floor. She kicked him hard. Out of the corner of his eye Max spotted the knife quivering in the far wall, the point an inch deep in the wood. Abby picked up her new toy and peered at it, swearing to herself.

"The fucker's bent the W," she said, giving Berthold another outraged kick. She hefted the machine in her hands, clearly tempted to drop it on his head. Thinking better of it she put the typewriter back on the desk and pointed the gun at him. She cocked the hammer. Max understood it was all for show but Berthold squealed and covered his face with his hands.

"If you kill him who will take me home?"

Max turned and felt his mouth open in stupefied astonishment. An alabaster statue of a naked woman stood in the bathroom doorway. Blank eyes without iris or pupil watched him. Clearly she wasn't blind for that gaze held a fierce intelligence that burned like a long-dead sun. When she spoke the hairs on the back of his neck rose up - her teeth, tongue and palate were as white as the rest of her. She was bald, although it looked as if someone had glued a handful of shredded paper between her legs. Struggling to master his shock he looked beyond her. On the tiles a yellow wig and mask lay next to a crumpled robe.

"A Philosopher," whispered Abby. "You've found a real Philosopher."

CHAPTER TWO

ABBY HAULED BERTHOLD onto a chair and gave him a rag for his nose. He flinched when she went near him. *Yes, snivel away you smarmy bastard*, thought Max. *You've just met Abby Fabrice.*

"Speak," she commanded, sitting down with her gun on her knee.

"I rescued her from Sarracinte's brothel," Berthold mumbled thickly, nodding towards Pell. "I'm taking her home."

"Where's home?" asked Max. He couldn't take his eyes of Pell though he realised he was gawping at a naked woman.

"Back to the Abdomen, via the Glass City, to the north."

Max and Abby swapped glances. God's stomach lay forty thousand miles north west. To get there you had to cross the space between the Arm and the side of the deity's body. Before that stretched thousands of leagues of forearm, a honeycomb of chambers, tunnels, shattered buildings, empty abandoned citadels and cities in vaults as big as worlds. From what Max had discovered during their time in Interosseous the wilderness towards the Elbow held little civilisation. People muttered about creatures living in endless night, buried deep in the titanic structures of the limb. Yet Berthold seemed nothing more than a louche sophisticate. Max knew they had to make their way up the Arm to reach his ultimate destination, the Kingdom of the Machine Men in the Heart or the Head. This Glass City of Berthold's sounded a possible stepping stone. He saw Abby's interest perk up as curiosity overcame anger. She glanced at Pell.

"Go put something on," she said to the girl, giving Max a glare. He closed his mouth. *Sorry.*

"How did you get here?" he asked, sitting on the other side of Berthold. Stuck between the two of them the man looked like a trapped rabbit.

"There are ways through the Forearm past the dangerous places. They're risky but I know the path. I wanted to take Pell to the Glass City. There's an old transit system. It still works and it leads to the Elbow. From there I can get her across to the Abdomen."

Max looked at Abby expecting to find the old hunger for adventure in her eyes but to his surprise he saw sadness instead.

"And your story?" she asked Pell. The girl joined them at the table, her head a ball of chalk sticking out of the coarse robe. Max noticed how the shadows avoided her, making it hard to see her face, as if she glowed with a soft light that chased away the gritty darkness.

"My people were heading towards the Umbilical Ocean," her voice sounded like two sheets of paper rubbed together. It made him shiver. "We stopped at the city of Costae Fluitantes. Men kidnapped me. I remember being flown over a vast sea littered with destroyed ships."

The Ocean of Forgotten Guns, thought Max. Abby grinned at him. That got her attention. It was a place they'd dreamed of long ago, a name conjuring up sinister mysteries. *One of the reasons we stepped through the door into the Thumb.*

"They locked me up most of the time until we reached Interosseous. They sold me to Sarracinte." Her gaze dropped to her lap and two ghost hands plucked at threads in the cloak.

"I found her there. I was doing business with Sarracinte." Berthold swallowed. *Doing business? Screwing his whores more like*, thought Max.

"I spotted Pell and decided to rescue her."

"Why?" said Max.

"Sarracinte's a cruel, evil bastard," Berthold nodded in the direction of the wharf. "Dredge that canal and see how many of his ex-whores you find. That's what'll happen to her when she's outlived her use."

It sounded too glib. Max doubted the man was solely motivated by honour. God knew how much a Philosopher was worth, whether a whore or not. He reckoned Berthold planned to sell her on to the highest bidder. Be that as it may, the girl had no business in a place like Interosseous.

"What do we do?" asked Abby.

Berthold looked at them, panic in his eyes. Pell continued to stare at her fingers, seemingly unaware of her surroundings.

"Lock them in the spare rooms. Handcuff this bastard to the bed," he said. He spotted Abby's frown.

"I'm not kicking them out, not out there," he nodded towards Interosseous. "We'll decide what to do with them in the morning."

Berthold shot him a look of pathetic gratitude. He'd the sense to realise by now that Max was the gentler of the duo and Max couldn't help feel sorry for him. Out of his depth, his attempt to kidnap Abby was as amateurish as it was desperate. If what he said was true and he came from a Glass City to the north, navigating his way through the treacherous landscapes of the Forearm, he could prove useful.

"Fine, you can stay here for the night," said Abby. "But if you try and pull any more stunts I'll break your arms."

After sex Max and Abby lay in a soft tangle. Her head rested on his chest and red hair filled half his vision. He traced her name in the sweat on the small of her back with his fingertip, wondering why he needed to summon up the courage to tell her.

"I'm meeting a sage tomorrow."

She stirred against him, saying nothing. It amazed Max how easily their bodies fit together. With other women he'd always found an elbow, hip or chin digging into him, perfumed hair up his nose. He and Abby were two pieces of a matched puzzle and sometimes they'd wake mid-fuck without realising. *I don't deserve this. It's too perfect. I betrayed my father and let the giant Bassandis die. I fear the future of mankind rests with me.*

"With the sage's knowledge and Berthold as a guide we can find a way out of this city at last, aim for the Elbow and then the Abdomen," he said.

They'd locked Berthold in an attic room, chaining his feet to the bedstead and tying his hands. Pell appeared less of a threat. She sat on her bed and stared through the window at the lights of the city flickering red in the distance. Max wanted to ask her a thousand questions but she'd closed in on herself, turning into a mute figurine. He guessed the escape, and whatever had happened to her in Sarracinte's whorehouse, had left her in shock. When they talked she answered in monosyllables, only speaking out once for a glass of water. In the end they let her rest, locking the door behind them.

As they lay in bed Abby reached up and cupped Max's chin in her hand. He had his father's long jaw, crusted with bleached stubble.

"The players are leaving the day after tomorrow," she said. "They want to try and go north as well, to risk the canals. Thaisa thinks there're cities towards the Bicep where they can perform. Safer places than this shit hole." That didn't sound right. If Abby's actor friends thought easier pastures lay elbow-wards they were the only ones.

"Perfect. We can journey with them and you can keep writing your plays," said Max but he knew that wasn't the real reason for Abby's silences and sad looks, more frequent as the days in Interosseous crept by. Six months ago a giant had looked into his eyes and seen something that gave the titan hope. He'd told Max to speak to the Machine Men, the creatures who lived deep in the Heart and Head. But humans couldn't withstand the forces that knitted the core of the deity's being. Even if Max reached their kingdom how would he enter it and what would happen to him when he did? Max's own father caused the destruction of part of God's mind. He doubted they'd greet him with open arms. If they let him live it'd be a miracle.

They were both frightened. Love made them cowards, terrified for each other. Abby didn't want to go anywhere near the Kingdom of the Machine Men. She thought he'd die there or change into something monstrous. But Max had to go if it was the only chance to save mankind. He remembered piloting a flyer between wormholes in the Wasteland, visiting ancient worlds to bring back treasures stolen from temples and cities, Abby charging ahead, him racing to keep up. He ached to return to that life. They still could but at what price?

He looked around the room. Abby had hung cloth from the walls, painted the floorboards rainbow colours and covered the shelves with bizarre ornaments. He wondered at this parody of domesticity. Were Abby's eccentric attempts at interior decorating an attempt to redefine themselves as a normal couple, like the bourgeois families from the suburbs of Metacarpi? Kids playing at grownups, no, demented mercenaries with a death wish playing at grown ups. Did she actually want to stay in this place? Was that why they were stuck here, because Abby was trying to recreate her lost home? In the old days she'd be heading north regardless of whether they knew the way or not. *That's why you spend every day hammering those plays out on that typewriter. You're pretending you're back at the Theatre of Angels.*

They came to the Thumb filled with wild elation at this new realm and in the first heady weeks they forgot what they'd left behind. It was easier for Max. The remnants of his life lay in a line of rubble in the sea and the ashes of a father he'd hardly known. Abby missed her sister Rebecca and the permanent bohemian revelry of her theatre. As their wonder at the Body of God faded over time the memories stole up on them. Abby never admitted she hankered for what she'd lost but occasionally Max felt her shoulders shaking in the night, and all he could do was gather her to him and let her sob out her regrets onto his chest.

He kissed her on the head and on the lips when she tilted her face towards him.

"They say the Philosophers have commerce with the Machine Men," she said. He loved her for her bravery, saying the very things she feared would tear them apart. "Pell might be able to help."

Enough. He pulled her up so her hair fell about them in a cloud. She gave him a wistful version of her mad grin and nipped him on the nose as she threw her leg over his waist, lowering herself onto him.

Max left the house early as the morning began to spread a pallid light over the concrete wharf and the mirror surface of the canal. Berthold sprawled half out of bed, clamped to the frame by the ropes and handcuffs and snoring with his mouth open. Pell sat in her room with her hands folded and her eyes closed, a statue guarding a forgotten tomb. Max and Abby scanned the space between the jetties and the distant houses. Nothing. Max dared to hope he'd got away from their attackers. He'd started to realise what the rescue meant. Berthold claimed to know a safe way as far as the Elbow. He obviously boasted or fabricated lies to save his life but Pell was a Philosopher, a creature from the Skin of God. She'd been born in the darkness beneath an empty sky to creatures who studied the rarest wisdom and who spoke to Machine Men. The germ of a plan formed in his mind. Return her to her people in exchange for contact with the Heart and Head. Abby stayed to guard their prisoners. He recognised the unspoken fear in her farewell kiss and tried to ignore the guilt as he turned his back on the cottage.

Max walked through Interosseous, tracking his progress by the faces in the sky. The houses rose on either side, their crumbling roofs leaning towards each other. Dead windows bellied out from greasy brick walls that looked swollen with decay. No matter where he stood it was as if he were at the bottom of a valley, the thoroughfares and alleyways ribbons of grey rising through slopes forested with rotting buildings. He hoped it was a peculiar quality of the light. Air filled the entire Body of God, carrying alien energies that caused it to brighten and fade during the day. But there were other forces inside the sleeping titan. Max guessed they held the whole insane patchwork together. Occasionally, to his dismay, gravity shifted beneath his feet and the level floor he'd been standing on became a slope. Interosseous was a nexus of warped spaces filled with whispers, forever teasing at the edges of his perception.

In the gaps between the gutters Max spotted the faces on the roof - an eye, a sneering mouth, a pallid cheek. He kept checking the scrap of paper in his hand, trying to match the expressions miles above with the directions he'd bought for a hundred coins from a fixer in a back alley two days ago. *Lust - Contempt - Rage - Weeping.* He trod shadowed ways through the districts in a silence punctuated once in a while by the slamming of a shutter or the sound of feet running over cobbles. After a while he realised the path really did slope downwards. The houses around him gave way to ruins. At last he came to the edge of a pit half a mile wide and filled with rubble and detritus. *The forgotten things, all the debris, it's ended up here. This is the bottom of the city.* He peered through the haze. There, near the centre, between hills of junk a lone chimney poured a thread of smoke into the air.

To his surprise the man who answered the door looked more a builder than a sage. Although half a foot shorter than Max he was heavy set with a square clipped beard and a swift, intense gaze. The only part of him vaguely scholarly was his bald head and the stubby pencil tucked behind a blue and green patterned ear. Chiomedes the Sage folded beefy arms smothered in tattoos and looked Max over. Scorch marks and stains covered purple dungarees.

"You found me then," he said, stepping to one side to let Max enter.

Walls vaulted upwards to where light filtered from filthy windows set under the eaves. The daylight faded half way down to be replaced by the oily glow of half a dozen lanterns hanging above a circular staircase leading into darkness. It filled the ground floor. Chiomedes pushed past, picked up a lamp and descended. Max noticed the disturbing fractals cast into the wrought iron stairs digging into the soles of his boots. He followed, grateful for the weight of the automatic at his waistband.

They climbed down for an age, the light above shrinking to a disc no bigger than a coin. Max realised they must be below Interosseous itself, stepping into the lightless vaults far beneath the city. He shuddered despite himself. Chiomedes stopped at the foot of the stairs, raised his lantern and looked up at Max.

"It's cold here. There are air currents, from below."

Max caught the amusement in his voice but chose to ignore it. A sloping passageway brought them to a domed chamber a good twenty yards across. Max reached out and touched the wall - lead, oily under his fingers. The plates, each as tall as he, arched over his head like fish scales. Another set of stairs fringed a pit twice the width of the one they'd descended. Desks, machines, bookshelves, cabinets, consoles, chemical apparatus, orbs, gnomons and astrolabes filled every inch of the space between the shaft and the walls. Models of mathematical structures and molecular lattices lay scattered over the tables and floor. Max stared dumbfounded at the hole in the centre of the hall. For one astonished instant he thought the sage had a wormhole, here in the Body of God. He looked over the rail expecting to see the familiar infinite void, glowing mist and landings leading to ancient worlds. With disappointment he saw nothing but a spiral staircase disappearing into gloom. The sage stood beside him holding the lantern above the blackness.

"Three hundred miles deep," he said. "I descend to learn. Everything you see here comes from the darkness."

"You found these things down there?"

Chiomedes looked at Max as if he was the biggest fool in the universe. Max bristled, feeling his ears redden.

"Found? I didn't find anything. It was brought to me."

Max stepped carefully back from the edge. The sage gestured around him.

"We are surrounded by creatures, beings, spirits forged in the wooden and iron cells of God. A million years in the building, imagine what such ancient shadows engender or what they attract to this tiny desperate realm we've built for ourselves. They bring me things of interest, we strike bargains and deals."

Beings, creatures. Max remembered the tales of monsters crawling up from wormholes. That's what they'd thought the giants were when they first met Ragaleis in the Wasteland. He wondered about the sage's bargains, what he gave his donors in return. He had a brief image of things boiling over the edge of the pit filled with the promise of fresh meat. The sage noticed his expression, slapped him on the back so hard it stung and laughed, a rich booming yell that surged around the dome and poured into the vault.

"Don't worry, I trade in knowledge, ideas, concepts. Nothing in those depths is interested in something as gross and physical as you."

Max wasn't so sure but he managed a smile to show the man's jokes didn't faze him. Chiomedes jerked his head and Max followed him to a cabinet. The sage pulled out a slim book and dropped it with a thump on a table. Waves of dust spread over the cracked wood.

"What do you know of the Machine Men?" he asked.

"We created them to build the parts of God we can't enter, the Heart and the Head," said Max.

"That was a million years ago. They aren't our children any more," said Chiomedes with a frown.

Max remembered the vision he'd seen in the Giant's house, becoming one of the eight titans himself. Glittering insects crawled over his hands - Machine Men. He imagined they looked like bugs crafted by a mad jeweller.

"Why do you want to meet them?"

"That's my business," he said, damned if he was going to tell the sage about the death of Bassandis. Chiomedes grunted and let it pass.

The sage opened the volume. Max's heart thudded in his chest. A proper map book. He looked in wonder at the outline of the colossus. Chiomedes jabbed at it with a stubby finger.

"The Machine Men are retreating into their own kingdoms, the Heart and the Head where Theuderic their king holds court. If you want to speak with them that's where you need to go. How you'll make contact with them once you come to the boundaries of their realm is another matter unless you can find one still in the empires of man. They used to send ambassadors to the mighty - your best bet is the Steel Queen. She's closest." He pointed at God's stomach. "If any tarry in our world they're most likely to be there. Her kingdom is one of the few true civilisations left. She keeps the light of knowledge burning, though for how much longer who knows?"

"What do you mean?" asked Max. Something in the man's tone of voice chilled him.

"God's waking up, but it's too late," the sage said. The shadows in the pit lengthened. Max suppressed a shudder. Did Chiomedes know about the ruined mind of God after all?

"When you came from outside did you expect the Body of God to be filled with wisdom?" Max heard mounting anger in the man's voice. "Noble men and women crafting wonders for the new universe? It's taken too long. You've journeyed through the Forearm, you've seen it. Those of us left at the end of time huddle in our petty towns - pockets of villainy built out of desperation." He gestured towards the hole in the centre of the floor. "The darkness changes us, empties us of our souls, our purpose. Even if the deity is waking, when he steps through the God Door he will be empty, a god of nothing but shadows and the raving echoes of the mad."

Max wondered if he was wasting his time, if he'd ended up in the cellar of an embittered maniac looking to foist his own lunacy on anyone prepared to listen. He cursed himself. He was an idiot to think he could learn from the inhabitants of Interosseous. The sage jerked the book around to face Max. He flicked through a few pages until he found a picture of the Forearm with half a dozen cross sections spaced out between elbow and wrist. Max leaned forwards. It was the first map of the inside of the limb he'd ever seen. *At last, a way onwards.*

"Take it, I don't need it - and I wish you luck, the little good it'll do you."

CHAPTER THREE

MAX WALKED BACK through the streets of Interosseous, the book tucked into his lizard skin waistcoat. It showed a path of sorts, though unclear and threaded with danger. He mulled over their journey. It had taken them half a year to get this far. Although the lower Forearm held less than a dozen cities they were linked by long tunnels snaking through the interstices of the body, large and clear enough for the high-speed flyers they'd first hired, then stolen when the money ran out. The last ship broke down halfway along the chain of caverns that ended at Interosseous. From here on a thirty-six thousand mile labyrinth of darkness lay between them and the Elbow. With no clear path to follow they would have been insane to carry on, but with the sage's map book they finally stood a chance.

He paused at a junction and glanced up at the ceiling. Still in the district called *Weeping* - giant eyes glistening with tears gazed at him. Max remembered another titanic face disintegrating in the carnage above Metacarpi and shuddered.

"He'll start crying soon."

The man's voice was so soft Max struggled hear him. The stranger looked in his mid sixties, a dapper gentleman in a tan suit and coffee-coloured bowler hat. Like Berthold he sported a goatee, though his was grey.

Max wasn't used to seeing people in these streets. When he did they were usually ragged shapes flitting from door to door or silhouettes watching him from windows. The man pointed his umbrella at the sky.

"Him, Mr Weeping up there."

"Right," said Max, wondering whether he'd stumbled across another cryptic sage or just an eccentrically dressed lunatic.

"There we go," said the stranger, opening his umbrella as the first drops thudded onto the pavement. He held it to one side, inviting Max to crouch underneath. Max started to turn away despite the rain, not interested in random camaraderie. Nothing was free in this city.

"Maximilian Ocel."

His hand went to the automatic at his back. A surreptitious glance told him they were alone, at least as far as he could tell. Around them he saw shuttered and silent houses. The downpour cascaded down, hammering on his face and shoulders. The man gave him a wide grin and gestured with his umbrella. Someone this at ease in the streets of Interosseous screamed immediate danger. He decided to brave it out. He ducked under the brim.

"It's not mere water. The moisture from the city gathers at the lowest point in the ceiling, which just happens to be the Weeping face. Perhaps our first king designed it that way," said the stranger, his voice still so low Max strained to catch the words. He gestured around him at the downpour thundering off the eaves and rolling along the centre of the streets in grubby torrents. "It's the tears, sweat and breath of everyone in this city, a storm of sobs and sighs. Quite disgusting when you think about it." He gave a theatrical shudder, pulled out a cigarette case and manoeuvred one into his mouth.

He offered another to Max who shook his head, waiting to see where this conversation was leading.

"Bearded rogues and porcelain girls," the stranger said. It was all he could do not to snatch his pistol out and point it at the old man. *Sarracinte. I'm talking to Sarracinte*, realised Max. *There's a dozen guns pointing at me now and I haven't seen one.*

Sarracinte lit his cigarette. The rain slackened.

"He's brave and loveable but unbelievably stupid. She's a rare beauty, not fit to walk these streets or journey through the Body of God. I had a bower made for her, a boudoir of such elegance, with all the books and scientific instruments a Philosopher may need. Out here she'll just sully herself. The corruption in her white heart will seep outwards, and believe me Max there is serious corruption inside that perfect whiteness." He tapped a finger against Max's chest. "Her external perfection will be tainted by exposure to all this and when that decay outside meets the evil within she'll be merely another whore."

The rain stopped. Sarracinte shook his umbrella and tucked it under his arm.

"Have a chat with Pell and Berthold. Try and persuade them to return. There's nothing better than the luxury I can offer them. Don't let them fool you into a ridiculous romance of chivalry and rescue. If you do escape me all that awaits beyond this city are shadows and monsters. Surely Chiomedes made that clear enough."

He tipped his hat.

"Tomorrow, Max. No later."

Max watched him saunter away. Perhaps he should have fled, weaving his way through the labyrinthine streets to shake off the eyes that even now tracked him from these buildings, but he knew it was useless.

He hovered for an hour on the edge of the wharf hoping to spot Sarracinte's spies. In his heart he realised it was futile. They knew where he and Abby lived, of course they did. The insouciant ease with which Pell's owner asked for her return showed he'd no fear they'd escape. It might be overconfidence. They'd met enough prematurely triumphant enemies in their travels. Most of them ended up with an expression of baffled shock on their dead faces. He hoped this was the case, another overconfident braggart used to bullying local thugs and pimps. *Brave it out, go home, pack and get out of here.*

As soon as he told Abby she dragged Berthold into the kitchen and sat him in front of the map book. Pell followed, gliding into the room as if she ran on casters. Max struggled to avoid staring at her paper skin. What had Sarracinte said? Utter corruption lay within that white body, sealed from the outside world by a pristine shell. What the hell did that mean? She just looked like a young girl to Max, but the faint radiance from her face messed with his eyes and he found it impossible to guess her age. He should have asked but it was hard striking up conversation with a living statue clearly not accustomed to small talk with scruffy adventurers.

Abby handcuffed Berthold to his chair by one hand. He shook it and gave Abby an exasperated look.

"Really?" he asked. A cocky bugger alright. Max felt he should warn him but he was curious to see how far he'd go before his next lesson from Abby.

Max pointed at the pages, remembering Chiomedes' words.

"Olecranon, the Elbow. There's a bridge from here across to the Abdomen. It may still be intact. Otherwise we'll need a flyer to cross the gap. Or risk the Ocean of Forgotten Guns which covers the singularity between the Arm and God's Abdominal Oblique."

Abby whistled and peered closer. The map showed nothing, just blank space between torso and arm, but Max could see her storybook-fuelled imagination conjuring a wilderness of wrecked battleships.

"Getting to the Elbow's the problem. There's thirty-six thousand miles of darkness between here and Olecranon. There were transit tracks once but the science is lost and Chiomedes says no-one knows if any of them still work or what uses them."

Abby turned to Berthold. The man shrugged.

"There's an old station at the top of the Glass City," said Berthold. "I know how to get there."

"Where's the Glass City?"

"This book confuses me," said Berthold.

"Would you like me to clear your head a little?" said Abby with a chilling grin. To Max's surprise Berthold gave her a smile that looked for all the world like that of a lover sharing a joke. Abby stared at him dumbstruck. That was a first. Berthold took the volume and something fell onto the table. Max picked it up. It looked like a tangle of multicoloured string. He made to throw it away but Pell reached across and held it up in both hands.

"A cat's cradle," said Abby as the Philosopher stretched it open.

"No," said the girl. "It's a map."

Max peered at the strands. Five stuck out from the main pattern like little aerials. How did they do that? He tugged on one and almost dropped it when a knot and three more threads appeared out of thin air.

"It's four-dimensional," said Pell. *That's impossible*, thought Max. Abby whistled.

"We're here," Pell said, pointing at a tangle. "I think these red filaments are roads or passageways leading from the city."

"It must be the canal system," said Max. If he was right then this showed them the way out of this pit. "The sage said the waterways stretch a thousand miles north, ending in nine oceans spanning four layers." He caught Berthold's eye. The man looked away. *Got you, that's where your Glass City is.*

"Oceans? That's ridiculous," said Abby. He knew what she meant. It was one thing to have cities, fields and caverns in the Body of God, but entire seas?

"Surely the moment God stands up they'll all pour onto our heads and we'll drown," she continued.

"Bones and forces," said Pell. She bent her face over the cat's cradle until her nose almost touched the knots. Her gaze travelled along the lines until they faded into nothingness, and then beyond. What did those hideous blind eyes see?

"I understand this," she said in a voice that sounded like dust blown across a concrete floor. "I know the way. These canals are wrapped around the bone. That's why the space they inhabit is twisted. I can unfold the path. It's one of my functions."

"Functions?" asked Max. He'd no idea what she was talking about.

Pell reached out and grasped his arm. Max marvelled at the strength of her chiseled fingers. They felt like they had more joints than was decent. He resisted the urge to pull away. Blank eyes stared into his; he saw her pure white tongue, teeth, mouth and throat as she spoke.

"God has an invisible skeleton built from the threads that stitched the old universe together. Every bone is wrapped in a force that binds the body to it, a cage of space time that holds all this wood, metal, glass and crystal fixed in its matrix. Interosseous is close to one. It runs through the Forearm three hundred miles below this city. You must have noticed how it always feels like you're standing at the bottom of a pit. That's God's radius tugging on reality. When he rises to his feet we won't even notice." Pell stamped her foot. "This will still be the floor and the oceans will keep their water far to the north."

She released Max's arm and turned back to the cat's cradle.

"My people are *Parameterised by S*," she continued. *Parameterised by what?* thought Max. Abby shook her head. She hadn't a clue either.

"We see how God's body warps space and time, and this map shows the contours."

"Can you guide us to the seas, to the Glass City?" asked Max.

"Of course," said Pell.

"The players want to leave, they're heading north as well," said Abby. That still didn't sound right. Why would a bunch of actors chance the darkness of the upper Forearm?

"What other cities are there besides your glass one?" asked Max. Berthold shrugged.

"None that I ever came across."

Max detected evasion in the man's voice.

"Who do you trade with?" he asked.

"We're self-sufficient. The city's on an island in the middle of the ocean. We grow our own food and scout for supplies. The Forearm is full of caches ready for the awakening, it's just a case of finding them." He gave an indolent wave of his hand. Despite the man's blasé manner Max almost found himself warming to the bastard. He had an air of self-deprecating bravado that piqued Max's curiosity. He'd still threatened Abby Fabrice though and that marked him as stupid as well as treacherous.

Max took Abby to one side. She looked as if she was running through a thousand scenarios in her head, none of them ending well. It worried him. Usually in a situation like this she'd be off in a shot. Max cupped her cheek in his hand. She closed her eyes as if losing herself in a second of rare happiness.

"What do you think?" he said.

"I'll talk to the actors, they're leaving anyway. They could do with protection, if I can persuade them."

"We'll have to move fast," said Max. He didn't want to stay here a moment longer but until they secured their passage out of Interosseous this house was as safe as anywhere else in the whole city. It was surrounded by space with good lines of sight, just in case Sarracinte's impatience overcame his arrogance and he decided to take Pell back sooner.

"Give me all our coins and four hours," said Abby. "Get ready to leave the instant I return."

In five minutes she'd crammed their money, half their ammunition and three play scripts into a backpack. She took his face in her hands, kissed him and slipped out of a window that looked over the lead-coloured waters of the canal. Max peered after her, hoping to catch sight as she flitted into the shadows, but he saw nothing. If he spotted her so would any hidden eyes on the other side of the wharf. He knew they were there, gathering as the air faded into night.

He uncuffed Berthold, grabbed him by the throat and pushed him into a corner. The man managed a grin despite being forced onto his tiptoes.

"We're getting you and Pell out of Interosseous," said Max. "You're leading us north to this Glass City, but the second you step out of line I will kill you. Am I clear?"

"Utterly," said Berthold in such a way that Max was obliged to gently thump the man's head against the wall for emphasis.

"I should by rights leave you here for Sarracinte's men. The only reason we're taking you with us is because you claim you know how to get to the Elbow. You'd better be telling the truth." Max saw fear flicker in the man's eyes. Good, he'd got his message across.

He gathered supplies for the journey, killed the lights and took up position by the window with a rifle in his hands. He stuffed the pistol and the automatic he'd taken from Sarracinte's thugs into his belt. The faces in the sky above Interosseous blurred into shadow. Lamps from the distant houses threw orange and red shapes across the concrete.

"You're just one man. Let me help you," said Berthold.

Max ignored him. He'd seen the way he handled a weapon. Even if Berthold didn't try to get the drop on him he'd probably end up being killed by the idiot through sheer incompetence. He wondered if Pell could shoot.

"Maximilian Ocel," the voice floated out of the darkness. Shit, he hadn't been paying attention. He risked a glance across the wharf. Nothing, just silhouettes of junk against a cracked plain.

"Max," it sounded closer, maybe from among the nearest heaps of scrap. He recognised it, the lilting tones of the man in the tower. He'd escaped the explosion and followed them here. Max strained to spot any movement amid the frames, cages, barrels and rusting sheets.

"It's him," said Pell.

"Him?" asked Max.

"Sarracinte's son," she said. Berthold swore. He looked at Max with fear in his eyes.

"He was my teacher," continued Pell. Her chalk gaze fell on Max, her statue face an unreadable mask. Max guessed the kind of lessons involved. What did Sarracinte say? *There is serious corruption inside that perfect whiteness.* The typical self-serving bullshit evil spouted when it sought to blame its victims.

"Max Ocel, give up the girl. You can keep Berthold, he's a worthless rat and he'll betray you as he betrayed us, but send back my love if you would be so kind." There was an odd timbre to the words. Where the hell was it coming from?

A half-track rolled out of the shadows a hundred yards away. It sat side-on to the house, resembling a cardboard cutout in a diorama. Max saw black windows behind armoured grills and a short turret projecting from the rear of the vehicle. He didn't like the look of that. He couldn't make out detail at this distance but he guessed it housed heavy machine guns at the very least. The car rocked back and forth on its tracks.

"One last time, Max, send Pell to me or we will come and get her and kill everyone in the house."

The announcement came from the half-track, amplified through speakers. That explained the odd echo in the words.

"Get down," said Pell. "Bullets are coming."

Something in her voice made him drop to the floor. She knelt behind him with the casual diffidence of a guest seated at a picnic. Berthold stared at the two of them.

"Berthold, you have two seconds," she said. Max reached back and swept the man's legs out from under him just as the windows burst inwards. Bullets scythed through the room at waist height, tearing apart the interior in a storm of fragments. Half a dozen rounds thumped into Abby's typewriter. It danced backwards across the table, toppled onto the floor and broke into pieces. The gunfire stopped. Berthold lay on his back with his hands over his face, gasping like a beached fish. Pell sat in the same position as before, her head tilted to one side as if listening. Max remembered a woman's voice in the tower. *Two seconds, then they lobbed the grenade. God almighty, she sees the future.*

"Pell?" Sarracinte's son called. "You can't run away. If you warned your friends and they're still alive then they realise there is no option but surrender."

Sod that, thought Max. He shuffled backwards on his bottom up to the wall between the shattered windows. He looked at Pell. She gestured, two fingers to either side of him, then mouthed *six seconds*. He counted, jumped up and shot the couple clambering through the window on his right. He turned to his left. Gunfire rang out in the room and someone outside screamed. Berthold sat on the floor holding the automatic in both hands. They still shook but his face had a grimness of purpose Max hadn't seen before.

"More bullets in four seconds," said Pell. Max grabbed their hands and dragged them through the door and onto the staircase at the back of the house. As they climbed a second volley of machine gun fire made the whole building shake. Max kicked open the window and clambered onto the roof of the first storey. It extended along the jetty to overhang the water. Once wharfmen hauled crates up from the canal, now only a rusting turntable marked the position of the vanished crane. Max ran to the edge, looking for a way down. He spotted a flash to his right and jerked his head back just in time. A slug hissed past his face. *Shit.* Two, maybe three of Sarracinte's men crept over a half-submerged barge lying parallel to the house. Max fired off a handful of rounds and ducked back out of sight. He'd been an idiot to bring them out here. They were trapped. He paced the tiles, racking his brains.

"What do we do now?" asked Berthold, his voice harsh with panic.

"Can you swim?" The man shook his head. *For God's sake, I thought you lived in an ocean.* A silhouette appeared at the window. Max fired and the attacker ducked back but when he pulled the trigger again the hammer fell on an empty cartridge. The rifle lay on the kitchen floor. He gestured to Berthold for the automatic. Berthold swallowed.

"I dropped it on the stairs, sorry."

Five figures climbed onto the roof. They were in no hurry. Realising Max was out of ammunition they let long, curved daggers drop into their hands, clearly intending to enjoy the next few moments. Berthold, whimpering in terror, scrambled on his hands and knees to the end of the roof, peered over the edge at the sluggish water and started to sob. One of the attackers chuckled. Max readied himself. He'd been up against this many before but he was out of practice and these thugs carried themselves with the insolent ease of professional murderers. He wasn't stupid. They'd have to chance the canal and hope they didn't get picked off by fire from the bank. Space under his heels told him he'd backed up to the edge. He stood on tip toes in the guttering, feeling it shift beneath his weight. Pell had read his mind and stood beside him, her arms held out so that the grey robe billowed around her. Berthold snivelled into space on her other side.

"I bet I can slice you before you drop," said a woman in the voice of a charming city hostess commenting on a trivial piece of society gossip. Her head jerked back and she coughed a fountain of blood into the night air. *What in God's name?* The two men beside her also staggered back, one clutching at his throat, gore erupting between his fingers. A fraction later gunshots barked across the river. Max glanced to his right and saw a vessel speeding towards them. A figure stood in the prow, aiming a long barrelled rifle at the remaining attackers who dropped to the tiles as bullets shrieked over their heads.

Abby pointed the boat at the jetty and opened the throttle while she picked off the men on the roof. As she came under the shadow of the eves she jumped into the back of the craft and steered it into a hard turn. To Max's astonishment Pell hooked one hand in Berthold's waistband, grabbed the scruff of his neck with the other and threw him out into space. He yelled, arms and legs pedalling as he fell with a thud into a pile of sacking amidships. Pell leaped after him, like a white angel wreathed in smoke as she dropped out of sight. Max followed, landing in the stern and nearly tumbling backwards into the water as Abby accelerated away. A few shouts echoed over the canal but a tangle of decaying piles lay between them and the sunken barge where Sarracinte's sharpshooters struggled to track their quarry. In a few moments they were between two abandoned tankers and the house and landings disappeared.

CHAPTER FOUR

"THEY'VE GOT A half-track with a heavy machine gun," said Max as he reloaded his own weapon from Abby's bag. "It's slow but they'll catch us up."

"Good," said Abby as she steered the boat under arches crusted with black fungus the texture of hair. Max thought she'd gone mad. Perhaps she hadn't heard him.

"Good?"

"The players won't take us, Vincent's being stubborn. If there's an armoured car up our arses they'll have to," said Abby. The name sounded familiar. A husband and wife team ran the travelling theatre - Vincent and what was his wife called? Thaisa, that was it.

"What's to stop the half-track blowing them out of the water?" It was a stupidly risky strategy even by her standards.

"You'll see," she favoured him with a grin, almost her old self. Max checked their companions. Berthold sat on the sacking in the middle of the boat with his head in his hands. Pell perched on the rear bench watching the canal waters seethe in their wake.

"You knew when they'd attack, in the tower and on the roof. How?" he asked. She didn't turn round. Her glowing profile cut a paper silhouette out of the gloom.

"Parameterised by S see the true Platonic clusters," she murmured.

Well that made no sense. He had so many questions for the Philosopher but now was not the time. She clearly wasn't a great conversationalist. The concerted effort he'd need to get through to her could wait for a quieter moment. She knew things were going to happen a few seconds before they did. That was enough for now - as long as she bothered to let them know.

"You'll tell us when it happens, yes?" he asked.

"Of course," she answered, still gazing at the canal behind them. Her reflection glowed on the ruffled water.

Max scanned the surrounding landscape. Abby steered the boat through a labyrinth of structures. Buildings, frames, heaps of scrap higher than a house, wrecked hulks and discarded machinery turned the disused waterways into a treacherous maze. Loops of oil crusted with rust broke apart as the prow weaved back and forth through shadowed tunnels. Max was surprised to notice no-one lived next to the water. The windows of the houses leaning over them looked dead. Once in a while he glimpsed dirty lace pressed against glass, or shadows hinting at familiar shapes in rooms beyond shattered windows, but the boat moved too fast for him to make sense of these brief images. He looked up through the gloom. Eyes screwed up in rage stared at him. They were in the district called *Furious*. Max's heart thudded in his chest. Nearby lay the tunnel leading out of the city to the maze of canals in the north. He searched for any sign of pursuit but saw nothing. The crackling roar of the boat's engine made it impossible to hear any sounds from the city. If the half-track chased them through the streets he couldn't tell.

The sides of the waterway lofted towards the ceiling which in turn curved up into the night. Ahead of the boat the entire cavern of Interosseous opened like a trumpet mouth. They sailed between two cliffs, the walls covered in houses linked by a delicate web of iron and steel staircases. He grinned. Now he understood Abby's disregard for the half-track. Even if the armoured car followed them along the top of the precipice it was too high for its weapons to traverse in their direction. At best Sarracinte's men would have to rely on small arms fire and at this distance, in this gloom, they'd be a difficult target.

The canal opened out into a square reservoir. Three squat ships sat in a line next to a wharf at the bottom of the cliff. To Max they resembled half-sunk houses punctuated by yellow and orange windows. He dared to hope they'd escaped their pursuers. Abby guided the boat between the outer vessels, flung a rope over a bollard and scrambled onto the largest craft. Max noticed that the superstructure flared into a blunt pyramid on its side. *They've got their own theatre.* Abby took Pell's hand and helped her climb out of the boat leaving Berthold to fend for himself. He hadn't moved during their escape and now he looked pale - sick with panic Max guessed. He boarded the actor's barge and stood in the shadows biting his nails.

"Let me do the talking," said Abby as Max joined her. A deck hatch opened and a woman in overalls climbed out. She'd tied her curly black hair in a scarf and oil smeared her cheeks. Max put her at about forty. She carried a spanner as big as his thigh.

"Abby? Is that you?" she asked, stepping forwards to peer at the newcomers in the orange light falling from the windows of the upper deck.

"What are you doing?" Max detected surprise mixed with frustration. "He said no."

"Thaisa, we need your help, please. We have to get out of the city, now," said Abby.

Thaisa? Max assumed the woman was an engineer. Now he realised he stood before half the management of the theatre.

"He's in one of his moods, he won't listen to me. We had this out hours ago. It's not going to happen, I'm sorry." Max studied Thaisa's face. Despite her clothes and the grime it was delicate, soft-lipped, with large eyes. He detected patient resolve behind the expression of baffled irritation. *We've got a squad of murderers and an armoured car approaching*, he thought. *If we don't get moving we'll have carnage on our hands.*

A door burst open and boots stamped onto the gantry above their heads. Max heard Thaisa curse under her breath.

"Who's there?" Max saw the hint of a beard and light reflected in a pair of spectacles.

"It's Abigail," said Thaisa, mustering as much cheery charm into her voice as possible.

"What?" bellowed the man, who Max guessed was Vincent. "Is this some kind of bloody joke?"

"It's an emergency, my love."

"Fuck that," shouted Vincent. "Get off my fucking boat."

"Please don't swear, dear," said Thaisa through an icy smile.

"No means no. Did I not make myself utterly clear this afternoon?" growled her husband. Thaisa pinched the bridge of her nose,

"Yes, of course, but…"

Something clanged off a rail in a shower of sparks and knocked a chunk of glass out of the porthole next to the actor manager.

"God's flaming balls, what's that?" he yelled.

A gunshot sounded from the cliff face. Abby grabbed Thaisa and they dropped to the ground,

"Get inside," Max shouted to Vincent, who peered into the darkness. Muzzle flashes flickered on a staircase that zig-zagged back and forth from the cliff top to the wharf. An instant later two rounds thudded into the wood above their heads. Vincent roared in fury and stormed back into the cabin.

"Abby, what have you done?" asked Thaisa in angry horror.

"They're thugs from the city, we're trying to escape," Abby said.

"You brought them here?" Abby yanked Pell's hood away from her head. Thaisa gave a cry and her hands flew to her mouth as she stared at the Philosopher.

"We need your help to get her out of this shit hole," said Abby. "You're the only chance we have."

Another crackle of gunfire. This time the bullets went wide. Thaisa still gawped at Pell, clearly struggling to comprehend what she saw. The door above banged open and Vincent reappeared with a rifle. To Max's astonishment he pointed it at Abby's head.

"Get off my fucking ship now or I will shoot you, so help me God."

Abby spat out a list of profanities and yanked Pell's robe away. The naked woman glowed in the darkness, not even bothering to cover herself. Her sheer alienness hit Max once more and he felt the hairs rising on the back of his neck. Vincent stood above them with his mouth open and the rifle loose in his hands. The gunfire stopped. Max guessed their pursuers had also spotted Pell's white form from the cliff face and didn't want to shoot her by accident.

"Get everyone below decks and start the engines," Abby shouted. "If we stay here we're dead." Thaisa nodded and pulled Pell with her, gathering up the girl's robe and using it to smother the light seeping from her body. She ran up the stairs to where her husband still stared at the Philosopher and bundled them both into the cabin. The lights flicked out.

Abby and Max sprinted along the gangway to the edge of the wharf. Max had no idea where Berthold was and didn't care. The man was a liability. If he stayed out of the way, fine, if he got shot, even better. It was he and Abby again, together, just the two of them. Elation jostled with wary fear and the nagging suspicion he was neither as fast or as powerful as he used to be.

Six thugs ran towards them across the uneven ground. Behind them another three stepped warily down a staircase. Showers of debris fell from the wall. It clearly hadn't been used for years and with any luck it might collapse, taking their attackers with it. High above them two dull yellow circles on the edge of the precipice marked out the half-track's headlights. Abby was right. The machine gun was useless at this angle. Someone stood in the hatch of the turret peering at the barges through binoculars.

One of the men took a shot at Abby but she dropped into a forward roll and the slug sped over her. Max fired twice from the hip and saw an assailant sit down with a grunt of pain. A loud crack echoed from the boats and another attacker's head burst open in a gout of blood and flesh. They had backup fire. Max hoped it wasn't Berthold. The idiot barely knew which end of a gun to hold. A blade flickered near his face and they were in the middle of the melee, back to back like old times with their attackers in a circle around them, unable to shoot for fear of hitting each other. He managed to disarm a jug-eared youth on his second lunge. He drove the knife up under the man's jaw, whipped it out, stepped back and rammed it into the side of a woman who tried to flank him. He almost tripped again and was breathing hard already. *God's cock, it never used to be this laborious.* A heel came from nowhere and slammed into his head, spinning him round. The attacker laughed in triumph just before a bullet punched a hole in his skull and he fell like a discarded puppet. Max had no idea what Abby was doing though every so often she banged into his back as if using him as a vertical trampoline. He could have sworn she whistled a tune through her teeth. A rifle rang out from the theatre ship. Someone shouted "No!" and Max found himself without any attackers. Abby's back rested against his. Her ragged panting filled his ears and her heart hammered against his spine.

Six bodies lay sprawled over the wood. The three remaining thugs ran back to the bottom of the cliff. Something was falling, flipping over banisters, rolling down broken stairs like a bundle of sacks. It came to rest hanging over the edge of a balcony, arms dangling on either side of the ragged mess that was once a man's head. As the adrenaline subsided Max turned to Abby. To his surprise she stepped back, her hands up.

"Don't touch me," she said. What in God's name was wrong with her? He heard the tremor in her voice and she looked at him with an expression of weary disgust. He stared back dumbfounded. This was Abby Fabrice for God's sake. The motors on the barges growled into life in quick succession and a wall of stinking diesel smoke rolled over the vessels' flanks and onto the wharf.

"Come on, while we've got time," he said.

She turned with a word and ran towards the boats. He followed her, worry gnawing at his mind.

They leaped aboard the theatre barge. Figures raced back and forth on the decks casting off ropes and frantically preparing the ships for departure. Max realised Vincent and Thaisa had galvanised the rest of the actors and crew into action as soon as the fight broke out. A man in baggy silk pantaloons ran towards them and Max almost shot him before realising he was an actor. He pushed past them, wide-eyed with fear, and began winching a chain out of the canal.

Max and Abby vaulted the stairs. Inside the bridge Thaisa had her hands on Vincent's shoulders, trying to force him back into a corner. Berthold marched up and down, tearing at his hair and weeping. Pell watched him stalk back and forth.

"You killed Sarracinte's son, you killed Sarracinte's son, you've murdered us all, you stupid bastard," shouted Berthold, his voice cracking on the edge of hysteria. Vincent started forward again, a powerful man with a wedge of a beard and deep-set eyes glowering in fury. His clenched fists looked like red boulders at the end of his arms. Despite his obvious strength Thaisa managed to stop him leaping across the cabin at Berthold. Max realised that for all her patrician delicacy she wielded considerable power over her husband.

Abby walked up to Berthold and slapped him hard. He slumped on a stool and sobbed into his hands. Max noticed blood soaking his left sleeve. A tear in the cloth on his upper arm showed a shallow but ugly-looking wound. A bullet or a piece of shrapnel must have clipped him.

Max peered out of the window and tried to work out how long they had. The cliffs on either side of the artificial bay funnelled together, ending at a square tunnel stretching northwards, a black hole lined with sheets of wood and iron. It looked as though the city's streets didn't extend beyond the wharf so any pursuers needed boats. Sarracinte's son had chased them on land which suggested the gang didn't have easy access to water craft. Nevertheless, even if you stripped away Berthold's obvious love of the dramatic, they were in deep shit. Max had no doubt that once he learned his son was dead Sarracinte would come after them. They had to lose themselves as quickly as possible in the maze of canals to the north. He pulled the map book out of his waistcoat and tipped the cat's cradle onto the table top.

"Pell?"

The Philosopher materialised beside him, making him jump. She picked up the tangle, stretched it between her hands and rotated the threads, her eyes almost touching the fraying knots. She looked up at Vincent.

"I know the way beyond the tunnel," she said. Max waited for further directions but instead she sat beside Berthold and teased his hands away from his face. She reached up and dabbed at his eyes with the hem of her robe. Her presence calmed him and he stopped sobbing. She examined his cut, leaning in until her nose touched his arm. *She's looking at things we can't see,* Max realised. *Things too small for our eyes.*

"I'm sorry we led those men here and put you in danger," said Abby to Vincent and Thaisa. "It was the only way we could save Pell. We have to get away from Interosseous, go north like you planned. We can protect you, but if we're quick and clever enough, they won't even find us."

"Why can't we just hand you over to those bastards?" said Vincent, glaring at Abby.

"Because you shot Sarracinte's son, you cretin," said Berthold.

"One more word out of you, one more word, and I swear to God I will tear your heart out," said Vincent.

"It's only more running, Vincent," said Thaisa in her soft voice. "We knew it would come to this at some point." To Max's surprise she took her husband's head and rested it on her chest, kissing him in the middle of his tousled hair. Vincent closed his eyes. *You're fleeing too?* he wondered. *What from?* That's why they chanced the wilderness to the north. It suddenly made sense, something chased them as well.

The barges thundered into the tunnel, the theatre ship leading the way. Max stood on the gantry outside the cabin and looked at the churning water fluorescing in the darkness. A harsh chemical stench rose in their wake, the scent of rust mixed with chlorine. He could see the second boat bulking huge in the night. A few dim lights swung back and forth. The last vessel was invisible in the gloom but he guessed it followed close behind. Despite their size they kept up a fierce pace. *These craft are designed to run,* realised Max.

He went back inside. Abby and Thaisa sat on either side of the chart table, holding tin mugs of coffee. That was a good sign. At least the situation had calmed down.

"Vincent has retired," said Thaisa with a weary smile. "You must forgive him, he has his moods. It's the price of art."

Something in her gaze intrigued Max. He saw a playfulness in those eyes at odds with her measured hauteur. From the moments he'd seen them together it was obvious she and Vincent doted on each other and she had more than enough patience to guide him through his passions.

"Berthold and Pell?" he asked.

"Locked in a cabin," said Abby, Thaisa winced. *Bugger hospitality,* thought Max. *You didn't see him with a dagger at Abby's throat.*

"This tunnel runs for two hundred miles," their host said, changing the subject. "Nothing's going to happen until morning. We might as well get some sleep."

That night he dreamed he was threading his way through the Carceral Archipelago, the two-mile high stone tower of his boyhood with its four chains anchoring it to the shore of the Forbidden Sea. He traced the familiar pathways of the Shadows, that second maze of intertwined tunnels and ducts running between the main corridors. *But it's changed*, his dream-self wondered. *It's full of light and air. Where has all the darkness gone?* He walked alone, the fortress empty. Rows of desks covered rooms the size of fields. Scraps of paper blew along abandoned galleries and walkways. Pure silence - everything clean and bright and pregnant with possibility. Elated he realised he'd found something he'd been looking for his entire life, a childhood memory that finally was as it should have been.

Somehow he came to his father's apartment at the top of the tower. To his delight he saw the old man standing by the curving windows. He wore his dark coat but his expression was relaxed and happy.

"I'm sorry I couldn't save you," said Max. "We were fooled by Odilon the Watcher. He pretended to be your closest friend but in reality he was an alien creature plotting our destruction."

Herman Ocel shrugged and grinned as if to say, *it doesn't matter*.

"You'll fix it Max, in the end you'll save us all," he said in his warm voice. *We're reconciled, we're friends at last*, Max thought. It seemed so easy.

"I've got to go to the realm of the Machine Men. The giant you imprisoned died in Metacarpi and so God's mind is incomplete."

"No it's not," said his father. "Look. Everyone is here."

He stood on the very top of the Carceral Archipelago. Titanic figures approached through the hazy morning air, three men and four women. White hair, pale faces with mournful eyes burning with what? Hatred? Regret? Revenge? The men wore black suits and crisp open-collared shirts. The hems of the women's dresses tore down the roofs and skyscrapers of Metacarpi as they stepped towards the tower. Dark mountains in the air, each as high as the Carceral Archipelago itself. To Max it seemed as if the whole Wasteland walked towards him.

"There's only seven, father, there should be eight," he said in rising panic.

"No, there's eight, look again," said the Lord of the Carceral Archipelago. A hand took his. He glanced down and saw white fingers covered in glittering insects intertwined with his own. The tower tipped and fell, carrying him screaming into Chiomedes' pit.

He woke with a start, not knowing where he was. Polished wood above his head reflected his face back at him, a smeared ghost. Max realised he lay crammed in a bunk on the theatre barge. The lamp vibrated on its chains as the motors roared below, sending flecks of light skittering across the varnished walls. The weight of the machinery above and below suffocated him. Something was missing. He reached for the narrow space beside him. Abby wasn't there. He fought the panic and stood. His legs trembled and the sweat chilled his back and stomach. Post battle shock. He checked himself - old scars, tendons knotted with stress. In this light he looked and felt like a scrawny clutch of bones and weary muscle. He dressed and padded outside, fighting the claustrophobia and the fear. He stood on a gantry in the darkness, listening to the churning water, letting the steady thunder of the engines calm his mind before he went hunting for his companion.

"Bad dreams?"

He jumped. Thaisa stood next to him with a hurricane lantern. She'd swapped her overalls for a grey gown and untied her hair. The updraft from the surging waters caught the black curls so they seethed behind her head.

"I'm looking for Abby."

Thaisa nodded towards the roof of the theatre. A silhouette fringed by lamp light sat cross-legged at the far edge, staring down the tunnel. Something in the set of those shoulders made Max hesitate. He sensed the actress studying him.

"Once we're in the canals beyond this tunnel we can hide. If we're smart I don't think Sarracinte'll find us," he said, trying to reassure her.

"What will you do with your Philosopher?" asked Thaisa.

"Return her to the Abdomen. Berthold claims he comes from a city far to the north and there's old transit tracks that might be able to take us to the Elbow," said Max.

"Claims and might?" Max saw Thaisa's mouth twitch in amusement but there was no malice in her eyes. Given that he and Abby had put the actors in mortal danger she seemed remarkably forgiving. He'd expected them to end up chained to a pipe in the bowels of the ship or floating face down in the wake of the barges. What had she said? *It's just more running.*

"You're used to this, aren't you? What are you fleeing from?" he asked. Thaisa looked sad. She rested her forearms on the rail and looked out at the night.

"I'm from Volar, in the Wrist, the daughter of one of the lords of the city. I was to marry the son of another ruler but I met Vincent and we fell in love. I eloped with his troupe and my father sent his soldiers to hunt us, kill Vincent and bring me back."

"How did you get this far?" asked Max. Three barges full of actors performing plays wouldn't exactly blend into the background.

"God is very big. It's not that hard to hide inside him. We haven't seen my father's men since we left Quadratus. His heart isn't in it. He's probably given up but Vincent's not convinced." Thaisa intrigued Max. Underneath the air of half-jokey stoicism he was beginning to detect a tired sadness, as if she felt the universe had let her down and all she could do was meet its indifference with melancholy humour.

"Yet you'll chance the northern Forearm. It's supposed to be a wilderness, a dark maze filled with creatures and danger," said Max. "If your father doesn't care anymore why don't you return south?"

"We don't have a choice now, do we?" said Thaisa, facing him as she drew her robe around herself. *No you don't, not after we dragged you into this fight.* Sorry didn't seem adequate so he said nothing.

"Besides, Vincent swears blind there are kingdoms and cities in the Upper Arm far more civilised, rich and welcoming than down this end of the limb. Two weeks in Coracobrachialis and we'll be millionaires with a chain of theatres, feted by critics and kings alike." She laughed. "We'll be out of this tunnel soon. We both should conquer our fears and go back to bed. Goodnight Max."

She went back along the gantry to the cabins. Max stared after her long after she'd gone inside. He turned back to search for Abby but she'd also vanished. He wandered the upper deck for a while, wanting to talk to her to find out why she'd abandoned their bunk to sit alone in the night. In the end he gave up and threaded his way back to the cabin. She lay fast asleep scrunched up in the blankets on her side of the narrow cot. When he eased in next to her she mumbled in her dreams and flung her arm over his chest before starting to snore again. For some reason the familiar press of her warm body and the cotton scent of her hair didn't soothe the worries from his mind and he fell into a troubled sleep, dreaming of grey gardens under a sky of burning coals.

CHAPTER FIVE

MAX AND ABBY woke just before the barges emerged from the tunnel. With no time to talk they armed themselves and took up position on the gantries running around the upper edge of the theatre. If Sarracinte's men were still tracking them they'd need to be ready. Vincent joined them with his rifle, his face a scrunched mask of brooding anger. He was clearly in no mood for conversation.

As the ships sailed out of the darkness and into the light of morning Max scanned their surroundings. They emerged at the edge of a wide lake fringed with a landscape of jumbled cuboids, prisms and pyramids. It climbed up in serried ranks towards the ceiling which Max guessed lay about ten miles above their heads. Gone were the painted faces hanging over him. This sky was a faint patchwork of metal sheets clamped together by giant cleats, a dead lid for the immense box they now traversed. He couldn't tell how big the chamber was. The distant shapes faded into the mist. After a while he realised they hadn't been followed. If pathways threaded through the surrounding blocks he saw no sign of movement and the vapour rising from the water soon hid them from the shore. He almost dared to think they'd escaped from Interosseous but experience said it was too early to judge. Even so he allowed himself to relax and look around at the fleet.

It consisted of the theatre barge he stood on, a transport for carrying scenery and props, and a boat housing the rest of the crew and performers. Strong chains tethered the craft to each other so the second and third trailed after the first like dogs on a leash. The actors stayed under hatches though he caught a glimpse of a couple of silhouettes in the wheel house at the top of the superstructure. He noted the lines of ragged washing strung between the smoke stacks. Abby pushed past him.

"Don't think those bastards followed us. I need a bath," she said, disappearing through a hatch. Max couldn't help but laugh. She still had no sense of place. Max glanced across at the bridge of their own vessel and saw Pell emerge in the company of Thaisa. The Philosopher wore a black sleeveless dress and her head and limbs cut precise holes in the landscape. She pointed into the distance, giving directions. Thaisa went back inside leaving the other woman leaning against the rail. Hoping she might be more forthcoming, Max decided to join her. Sure enough when he climbed onto the gantry she turned towards him and he saw her smile for the first time. On those cold white features it was worryingly sinister but it emboldened Max to ask her how she was. In truth he wanted to try win her confidence so he could find out if she could lead him to the Machine Men.

"Thank you for saving me," she said.

"What's *Parameterised by S*?" Max asked.

"My people."

"No, what does it mean?"

"It describes the realm in which our functions operate. All my functions are parameterised by S," she replied helpfully. *Right,* thought Max. *I haven't a clue what you're talking about.*

"And a function is?" This was going to be hard work. Pell glanced at him curiously. He noticed that white fuzz covered her scalp. Her hair was growing back, making her seem more human.

"Do you not know about Philosophers?" she asked. Max shook his head, feeling like an ignorant bumpkin. *I'm a raggedy Time Scavenger from a city in the shadow of the Thumb. We didn't even speak to our neighbouring cities, let alone people like you.*

"A billion years ago man used calculating machines to understand the universe, but they were limited. The power of the human mind is unconstrained. Our creator wanted to make entities capable of calculating the true nature of the cosmos unfettered by the limitations of cogs, wheels, energies and powers. He genetically engineered us."

The penny dropped. Max stared at Pell in astonishment.

"You're living calculating machines?"

"We're living calculations," Pell said. Max heard amusement in her voice. *I'm looking at a talking sum.* He remembered struggling with mathematics in his lessons. He baulked at even the simplest equations. Abby was better. Her grasp of numbers proved lethal when bartering. Pell seemed to read his thoughts.

"My mind carries more functions than the last calculating machine held before it died," she said. It wasn't a boast, merely a statement of fact.

"So what do you do with all these 'functions'?" asked Max. Her words hinted at knowledge beyond anything he'd dreamed of but did it equate to power or was he just talking to a woman filled with arcane wisdom of no use to anyone?

"We were journeying to the Kingdom of the Steel Queen. She has invited all Philosophers to join her in her city, promising to protect and nurture us as we work upon a great project. As man degrades in these last days we find ourselves increasingly in danger from you."

"Me?" *She means the ordinary and the stupid.* He shuddered at the contempt implicit in her words. She looked away, her expression locked into a blank mask, her voice quieter.

"Thieves kidnapped me from my people and brought me to Sarracinte. Money exchanged hands. I spent a month in a mansion beneath a laughing face. They trained me in new functions, sometimes with men, sometimes with women, sometimes with beasts or machines. More functions, more procedures, more combinations. They were delighted. They said I was the best they'd ever bought. My depravity was entirely unforced."

Max watched her, appalled. He struggled to comprehend the damage that lay behind that dispassionate voice. Questions about the Steel Queen could wait. He floundered for something to say. A hatch banged open next to them.

Berthold limped out of the cabin, a bandage round his upper arm. He stuck out his hand.

"I owe you an apology," said Berthold. "I'm a coward and I was scared. As you can tell, I'm not used to this."

Max relented. If he was honest the man had saved his life twice, though more by accident than design. He shook hands and as he did so he saw Pell turn her face towards Berthold with an expression he didn't expect. *God help us all, she's in love with the wretch.*

"What's that?" said Berthold.

A line of smoke drifted past the last boat, vanishing into the mist. Abby appeared on the deck below wearing nothing but a towel around her waist, her hair a plastered chaos over her shoulders and breasts. Max noticed Berthold's face break into a huge grin and fought the urge to punch it. Abby shouted and pointed behind them. A second thread of vapour whistled over their heads. Max watched it outrun the vessel. The fog cleared and he saw a shoreline ahead followed by a flash and the low cough of an explosion.

Sarracinte, and he's got missiles. Max grabbed Pell and Berthold and bundled them into the bridge. Thaisa stood next to the wheel with a pair of spectacles on the end of her nose, ticking off items on a roster.

"They've found us," Max yelled. Thaisa flung the glasses to one side and started flicking switches and yanking on levers. Max felt the deck buck under him as the barge's engines roared into life. Shouts erupted outside.

"Pell, where do we go?" shouted Max. He hoped to God she really did understand that mess of threads. She pointed towards the shore. Thaisa hurled herself at the wheel and the barge began to turn. Shots rang out. Max left the cabin and scanned the surrounding landscape, trying to locate the enemy. Abby ran up the stairs, her bare feet slapping on the metal. She carried another rifle in her hands. Vincent appeared. He stared at Abby standing at the rail half naked and dripping with suds.

"Good God, woman." He spotted her gun. "Where did you get that?" he squeaked.

"I stole it from your boudoir," she said. "The bastards have got a flyer."

How could he have been so stupid? He'd never seen a flyer above the cramped streets of Interosseous and so he'd assumed Sarracinte's pursuit would be by land or water. It hadn't occurred to Max that he'd come after them in a flying machine or that navigable airspace existed between the city and the maze of waterways to the north. Ships and half-tracks were one thing but the barges were hopelessly vulnerable to air attacks. Despite their speed they steered like bricks. All the enemy had to do was line up with their course, sort out the range and they'd be sunk in minutes.

There - a shadow in the mist to the south east. Max tried to make out the shape, match it to his memories of the ships he'd seen in and outside the Body of God. It looked ungainly, a clumsy thing of vanes, gas bags and turrets, and that gave him hope. He remembered the sleek fighters of the Empire of the Ear pouring out of the dreadnoughts to bathe the Carceral Archipelago in murderous fire. Thank God Sarracinte had nothing like that. No doubt he thought of himself as lord of the air with that cobbled-together vessel. With his father's ship the *Zephyr* or their own *Bricolage* they'd have laced rings around it but they were stuck on glorified floating houses with just a handful of small arms. He prayed Pell could guide them out of danger before one of Sarracinte's missiles hit lucky.

Even as he hoped a third rocket dropped away from the flyer and drew an erratic spiral in the sky. To Max's horror it turned at the last second and slammed into the side of the prop boat. The vessel lurched as a ball of fire pushed it to one side, scattering debris over the water. Vincent shouted in fury and started firing at their pursuer. Abby joined in, her shots slow and deliberate against the actor's wild fusillade. The barge faltered before pulling itself back on course. To Max's relief he saw the damage was superficial, though he noticed a body floating face down among the tattered cloth, paper and wood disappearing in its wake. He aimed where he thought the flyer's main cabin might be and fired off a few rounds. At this distance it was impossible to tell if they had any effect.

"What's that damned Philosopher doing?" shouted Vincent.

Max looked behind him. With a surge of fear he saw jagged blocks rushing towards them, polished facets of sharp ebony looming out of the fog. He threw his arm over his face and waited for the impact. The boat shuddered but the engines roared on and when he opened his eyes he found they raced along a wide channel flanked by mountainous polyhedra. Behind them the other two boats kept pace and beyond the last vessel the bulbous shape of Sarracinte's flyer roared through the mist, its outline clearer as it gained on them. Abby swore.

"She's lined us up, we're sitting ducks."

She was right. If they stayed in this channel the enemy could pick them off one by one. What in God's name was the Philosopher playing at? Max struggled against fear. *She's a traumatised girl who's spent her life dreaming numbers in trans-atmospheric space. She hasn't a clue.* Vincent looked at them, his face pale.

"What's that?"

Max listened. Above the mechanical clatter of the engines he heard a rumble growing louder by the second. He ran along the gantry at the side of the bridge and peered ahead. Sick dread puddled in his stomach. Half a mile away the water ended in a jagged line of foam. He kicked open the door. Pell stood in the centre of the room, the cat's cradle taut in her hands and her eyes closed. Thaisa grappled with the wheel. She shot Max a look of fear that tore his heart. Berthold sat on the floor, his hands over his head, rocking back and forth.

"Pell, we're heading for a waterfall," Max shouted.

"Yes," she replied, her voice cold, lacking any humanity or hint of reason. *Functions and procedures.* Max remembered Sarracinte's words. *There is serious corruption inside that perfect whiteness.* Realisation dawned. *She's committing suicide and taking us with her.*

Pell turned her porcelain face towards Max. Her gaze locked his. He searched for any hint of sanity in those blank white eyes. If it was there he didn't recognise it.

"In eight seconds turn the ship fifty degrees to the west," she said.

"We'll be over the falls," yelled Max.

"Six seconds."

They'd no time. If they reversed engines they'd back into the prop barge before they thundered over the cataract together. Max grabbed the wheel, wondering if he could jack-knife the boat to jam it against the sides of the channel. Impossible, the river was too wide. A cold white hand covered his and a soft voice whispered in his ear.

"Two seconds. Fifty degrees west."

The ship lurched forward, faltered and tipped. Someone shrieked. The cabin flipped and Max smacked against the wheel. Lamps, papers, instruments and people thudded against the far wall as the bridge windows shattered. Berthold fell through one, grabbing the frame in the last second. Max saw him dangling against a background of boiling water, staring back at him in an agony of terror.

"Now," whispered Pell in the voice Abby used when she told him she loved him in the dead of night. Max pushed himself up onto his knees and twisted the wheel, trying to focus on the numbers that flickered under the shattered glass of the dial.

Fifty degrees.

Afterwards Max realised the ship didn't move. Instead the entire universe rotated, pivoting around Pell who stood like a column of white stone in the centre of all things. The thundering waterfall rose to become a churning river as the barge slipped out of its current into a side channel. The northern wall of the cavern turned into the roof, a jagged mass of polyhedra thrusting dark peaks down towards their fleet. Behind them the other ships lurched and banged against the sides of the new canal, still bound by chains to the lead vessel.

"And again, forty-five degrees north east," said Pell. Out of the corner of his eye he spotted Berthold curled up on the gantry outside the bridge. Where was Abby? Pell's hand fell on his once more and he yanked the wheel. This time he was ready when the cosmos rotated around them but he still dropped to his knees among the shattered glass when it finally righted itself. He knew he was supposed to be falling but he hadn't a clue in which direction. Instead he stayed resolutely glued to the floor.

"That'll do," came a voice of tearing paper. "We're safe now."

Two freckled legs and a ragged towel filled his vision. Hands pulled him up and lips tasting of soap clamped themselves over his. Abby wrapped her arms around his neck and he buried his face in the damp tangle of her hair.

"I'm sorry, " whispered Abby. "I'm sorry."

Sorry? What are you sorry for?

They drifted along a winding river flanked by low hills that disappeared into the distance. Here and there vast spidery shapes thrust out of the ground. They appeared part organic, part machine and all were the colour of midnight. To Max they resembled hieroglyphs scratched across the surface of reality. The ceiling of this chamber was too high for them to see. Ragged clouds bunched under a grey, featureless sky. In the cabin they gathered around Pell.

"How did you do that?" asked Abby, her voice tight with suspicion.

"I didn't," said Pell. "I just saw the way."

She reached across and grasped Max's forearm again.

"The bone that runs through God's arm binds reality," she explained. "If you know where the lines of force fall, you can follow them." She pointed at her forefinger where it wrapped itself around him. Max looked at the white cage of her hand. He counted four joints on each finger. *Riding the forces that hold the Body of God together.* He struggled to grasp the implications of her words.

"And that's what we did?" asked Vincent, amazement and the knowledge they were still alive unlocked his face, opening it like a flattened out paper ball. Max found himself looking at weathered skin and bright eyes, the face of an actor world-weary Thaisa could easily fall in love with.

"Where are we now?" asked Abby. Pell bent down and rescued the cat's cradle from among the debris on the floor. She pointed at a knot. She might as well have pointed at the ceiling for all it told Max.

"How far till we reach the oceans?" he asked.

"Three hundred miles," said Pell.

Vincent gave a bark of disbelief. Abby and Max swapped glances as the Philosopher's words struck home.

"We just travelled seven hundred miles in as many seconds," said Max. Pell nodded.

If it was as easy as that getting to the Kingdom of the Machine Men would take days instead of months. Her explanation punctured the dream.

"With such a guide," she held up the threads, "and if the paths of man intersect the force lines it's easier to guess the route. Otherwise I'm blind."

"Guess?" asked Thaisa. Vincent's face clamped into a scowl again and he made to say something. His wife raised a finger and he closed his mouth.

"You guessed you could get us over the waterfall," Thaisa continued. "You didn't know." Abby muttered obscenities under her breath. Max grabbed the wheel to steady himself.

"What were the odds you'd guessed right?" asked Abby. Max recognised the pleasant tone in her voice. She was one step away from shooting the Philosopher there and then. Pell shrugged.

"Ten percent," she said, clearly plucking a number out of nowhere.

"God's flaming balls," yelled Vincent, stomping out of the cabin and slamming the door behind him. Max also needed air. He staggered out of the bridge and went and sat on the forward deck, trying to make sense of the landscape as it drifted by, letting the immense glyphs embedded among the distant hills fill his mind.

Twenty-four hours told Max they'd escaped Sarracinte's flyer. Perhaps the vessel overshot Pell's twist in space. With any luck the crime lord would think they'd perished in the cataract. In the brief glimpse of the void beyond Berthold's screaming face Max saw the water falling for several miles towards a jumble of titanic polyhedra. Nothing would have survived.

With the immediate danger behind them the three barges unbuttoned and the players emerged from below hatches. Max counted nineteen - ten men and nine women. Most of them kept to the third barge. He guessed they were still traumatised by the escape and the sight of the bizarre landscape drifting past. He spotted a knot of them gathered around Thaisa and Vincent, speaking in hunched and urgent tones. Vincent held his hands up, placating them. One of the women wept inconsolably. Thaisa made to comfort her but the girl pushed her away. Max remembered the body floating in the wake of the prop barge. Sadness and guilt sent him to sit alone in the shadow of a funnel on the upper deck. The last few days had returned him to a world of brutality and body counts. Standing back to back with Abby fighting off a vicious enemy felt natural, recapturing all those moments on all those worlds when they'd battled monsters and villains from the depths of time. He'd almost been happy until he saw the disgust on Abby's face as she stood on the wharf and stared down at the ring of corpses.

He heard the faint sound of a machine gun and tensed, reaching for his pistol. Hang on, that wasn't weapon fire. *Dear God, surely not*. It was another bloody typewriter. He turned to see Thaisa climbing onto the upper deck. She looked drawn, her gaze distracted, but she managed a smile when she spotted Max.

"Is that Abby?" asked Max. Thaisa listened. Her mouth twitched, a half mischievous half melancholy expression he was growing familiar with.

"She writes plays that are, shall we say, interesting. Vincent is intrigued, she may have secured your passage."

"She won't leave that thing alone, it'll drive us mad," said Max. Thaisa responded with a laugh so open and guileless that Max couldn't help but join in. He caught himself watching her profile as she gazed across the landscape, happy he'd managed to strip a little of her worry away. A warning voice tugged at his mind. *She's not for you, not in a billion years*. Even so he allowed himself the guilty luxury of a few moments lust.

"So, what's Maximilian Ocel's story?" asked Thaisa. She glanced at him with a knowing look. He'd always been too obvious. He remembered Ruth and Abby beating the hell out of each other on the deck of the *Zephyr*, though that wasn't exactly over him, even if Abby confessed her love straight after. He forced himself to turn away. Glyphs miles high joined the hills to the grey clouds.

"We're from the city of Metacarpi in the shadow of the Thumb. Abby and I were Time Scavengers. We explored the old wormholes the Black Roses made, the ones used to bring materials from the past to make the Body of God."

"You went into the ancient universe, saw stars and worlds?" asked Thaisa. He revelled in her breathless awe and nodded.

"So why in God's name are you here, inside this empty corpse?" Her fatalism shocked Max, he didn't know what to say in reply. For a second he wondered if she knew about the murder of Bassandis, that God's mind was incomplete and that at this very moment the deity was to all intents and purposes dead to them. Her gaze locked onto his but he found nothing more sinister than tired resignation.

"Since we were little children we dreamed of what was inside the Thumb, deep in God himself," said Max. "We thought there would be mighty kingdoms, beautiful and noble people - lords, warriors, men and women of learning. In the end we grew weary of ancient worlds. Because their energies are too powerful we could never stay long enough to explore their wonders, so we came to the Body of God instead."

He didn't want to tell her of the fall of Metacarpi to the renegade battleships from the Empire of the Ear, of the destruction of his old fortress home the Carceral Archipelago, how they were refugees from cruelty and betrayal and he'd been tasked to carry the news of a slain giant to the Machine Men.

"And what have you found?" asked Thaisa.

The interior of the Body of God was a place of astonishing wonder, Max conceded that. Vast structures the size of worlds filled a marionette half a million miles in length but they'd discovered no civilisations, no realms of impossible science and profound wisdom. Inside as outside mankind huddled in fractured, decaying communities, cities and towns, each the remnant of once-great nations turned fearful and inbred as the long wait for God's awakening crept by a thousand years at a time. Once in a while they stumbled across remnants of ancient power, men and women of prodigious learning hoarding fragments of a glorious past, like Chiomedes the Sage. Hints of unbelievable feats of engineering remained in the flyer tunnels that spread up through the tendons of the hand, hundreds of leagues wide and built for the passage of the intricate machines that now lay shattered on the chasm floors, and in the occasionally still-functioning transit system. They knew from their encounter with the dreadnoughts from the Empire of the Ear that powerful technology existed in kingdoms and empires elsewhere. The mere existence of Pell and the rumours about the Steel Queen gave them hope that humanity flourished, experimented and prepared for the next universe, but below the Elbow they'd seen nothing but a wilderness speckled here and there with frightened clusters of refugees living out the last days in the surreal shadows of God's body.

Thaisa saw the answer in his eyes and placed her hand on his shoulder.

"Poor Max," she said with a smile. He couldn't tell whether she was laughing at him or not. He had a sudden urge to put his hands on the back of her neck, draw her close and kiss those mocking lips but she turned and walked away, leaving him wondering at his own stupidity.

CHAPTER SIX

AFTER A FEW days the voyage slipped into a routine as the ships sailed through the chamber of the glyphs. Max discovered the boats were called *Theatre*, *Props* and *Cast*. He'd expected something more imaginative but at least it made it clear which was which. Abby did her best to ingratiate them with Vincent, Thaisa and the actors. When she wasn't bashing away at the typewriter Max often found her among a knot of performers, handing out scenes or acting her way through synopses of the dramas she composed. Once he thought he saw her stalking over the deck of *Cast* in the exaggerated stride of the gods from *The Gate of Light*. He remembered the last time he'd seen that play, desperate to talk to Odilon the Watcher about his mother. What did the old man say to him? *All I could do in the end was ease her final hours.* Max allowed himself a sour laugh. *Yes, you murdered her you alien shit.*

Abby's mad charm clearly worked. Vincent's face relaxed once more and he favoured Max with the occasional greeting. Even more unexpected was the sight of Abby roping Berthold into her rehearsals one day. She thrust a handful of pages into his hand and got him to walk up and down declaiming while she brutally dissected his performance and everyone else tittered. Pell watched from a way off, leaning against the rail with her arms folded. At this distance Max couldn't tell whether her stone white eyes were open or closed, though her head tracked Berthold's movements. Max remembered the expression he'd seen on her face just before Sarracinte's flyer attacked. There was no mistaking it. The Philosopher loved Berthold. What form love took in the mind of a living calculation God only knew. Functions and procedures - she and her kind turned everything in the universe to code, inserted into never-ending patterns of knowledge. Love, space and time, utter beauty and the wickedest perversions, it was all suspended in that cold web of her thoughts. Thank God he had Abby - red hair and freckles, vicious wit and an enormous appetite for danger and athletic sex. When she stood near Pell the contrast was so intense it made Max's head hurt.

Yet despite his admiration at Abby's efforts a nagging doubt remained. The expression on her face after they'd beaten off the thugs on the wharf in Interosseous - he'd never seen that before. Following a battle she'd often be wound up with anger and adrenaline, but this was different. It looked like weary disgust. At what? The men's deaths? She'd had no qualms in the past about dispatching enemies. It was always them or us. That night she'd vacated their bunk to sit alone on the theatre roof and gaze into the blackness. Come to think of it when had they last had sex or even slept together? Once since they'd left the city. Oddly, she'd lain under him, playing soft and helpless as he moved inside her, holding his body above as if he was a shield against the universe. She'd wept over her memories afterwards. After that she'd either been writing plays or mingling with the actors, coming to bed late or once or twice not at all, claiming she and the others had lost track of time or she'd had to finish a scene.

Berthold tripped mid stride. Everyone laughed and Abby reached to pull him up. He bumped into her and they lingered for a second, Abby giving Berthold a curious *what the fuck are you up to*? look that Max knew well. *Ridiculous*. He chuckled at his sudden jealousy. Not that snivelling fop. He glanced across at Pell. She'd pushed herself away from the rail, her hands dropped to her sides. She stared at Berthold and Abby and something in the set of her shoulders made Max stand up and call Abby over. She walked towards him, laughing.

"We need to plan the next stage of the journey, we'll be at Berthold's ocean soon," he said.

Abby nodded, her gaze far away. He fought the urge to ask her what was wrong. She stopped giggling and looked beyond the prow of *Theatre* to where the canal disappeared into the mist. He felt guilty for plucking her out of the world she loved and dropping her back into reality. She pursed her lips, clearly in the beginnings of a mood, and returned to the actors.

The following evening Thaisa, Vincent and their four guests sat round a table with a couple of bottles of wine. Earlier the ships had reached the end of the chamber and entered a tunnel that opened up into a warren of smaller caverns. Berthold told them they were close to the sea.

"The Glass City is on an island fifty miles across," explained Berthold, building images in the air with his hands. "It's clustered around half a dozen skyscrapers five miles high. They meet a second set of downward pointing towers that drop from the ceiling. At the top of these there's an old transit system that leads towards the Elbow. Some of our scientists have used it, travelled a couple of thousand miles and returned alive."

"What about rivers?" asked Vincent. "If we're to take our ships north."

"There's more canals leading out of the sea. We've got maps, at least for the first thousand miles or so."

"Monsters?" said Thaisa. Berthold paled and shook his head. Pell put her hand on his but he moved it away. *That's interesting,* thought Max.

"Not that we know of. Two thousand miles and you come to South Anconeus. It's small but a lot more welcoming than that shit hole Interosseous."

Max glanced across at Abby and to his irritation saw she was far away, her gaze dropped to her lap.

"Abby?"

She looked at him oddly for a second.

"What?"

He jerked his head towards Berthold. She apologised and pulled an *I'm listening really* face.

"But you have to stay in the Glass City for a few weeks, or longer," Berthold was saying. "The people simply *adore* theatre and we don't have any of our own."

Vincent cheered up no end, pouring everyone extra measures of wine while he chuckled over the idea of full houses.

"And I will find you a generous patron," boasted Berthold, warming to his theme. "I have such influence."

Max grew bored with the conversation. He'd got most of the information he needed. With any luck they'd be able to make the journey from this Glass City to the Elbow in reasonable time if Berthold's transit system did exist and actually worked. He looked around for Abby and to his surprise she'd gone. Thaisa caught his eye, pointed upwards and mouthed *she's on deck*. What the hell was she playing at? How much wine had she drunk? Max went to look for her.

She stood against the rail looking up at the darkness. He stepped up to her, ready to put his arm round her waist and draw her close until he could smell the scent of her hair. To his surprise she moved out of range. *What's got into you?*

"Abby?" he said. Something must have rattled her. That worried him. Abby had a hide of iron - nothing fazed her.

She ignored him, looking towards the cavern walls. He followed her gaze. Orange lamps marked a maze of walkways threading in and out of holes in the wood. Max wondered if it was a city. He noticed that most of the gantries ended in ragged fragments in mid-air. Clearly it had been home to someone or something but that was an aeon ago. The lights they saw were the last remnants, their energies fading over the long centuries. At the edge of their flickering circles he saw other beacons, dead specks scattered over the immense facade. Once he thought he glimpsed a shadow move in the corner of his eye but the lamp that threw it guttered to an end and the blackness seeped further over the face of the warren. He turned to Abby. She held the rail in both hands. She closed her eyes and took a deep breath as if girding herself for a fight. *We're all exhausted, wound tight as wire, grab a bottle and take her to bed, lose yourselves in each other's arms.*

"I don't want to do this anymore," she said. She turned her face towards him. Her gaze bored into his. Confusion chilled his heart. He saw something he'd never seen before - a desperate indifference so forced it resembled hatred.

"Do what?" he asked, dreading what was coming next.

"I'm not going with you to the Kingdom of the Machine Men. When we get to the Glass City I'm staying with the players."

There, she'd said it, given voice to those fears he'd stupidly batted away in the night, dismissed as his own naive anxiety. Of course Abby Fabrice would always be with him, always by his side, plucking him out of danger or cheerfully leading him into the thick of it. He searched her face. It looked calm but where her hands gripped the rail her knuckles showed white against the metal. A tear rolled down her cheek.

"I can't do this anymore," she said. Her voice cracked.

No, not you, not mad Abby Fabrice. I'm the coward, I'm the one who struggles, who has to push themselves off whatever god awful cliff you've found for us. This isn't real. It's some stupid joke. Har fucking har, Abby, not your best. He waited for the laugh and the playful thump. He saw nothing but desperate unhappiness.

"I can't do it, I can't love you, it's too hard," she whispered, her lips trembling and her eyes filled with tears.

He had no idea what to do. He felt more lost and alone than he'd ever done in his entire life. Abby, the last surety in his universe, had stepped away from him into the darkness. That explained her reaction to the fight with Sarracinte's men, her throwing herself into Vincent and Thaisa's theatre, even that fucking typewriter. Everything was another refusal to take part in the old familiar world of two scavengers on their adventures. He struggled to speak.

"It'll be fine, it'll be OK," was all he could manage. He might as well have uttered gibberish for all the good he knew it would do.

"No it won't," she sneered and her words cut into him. "It won't be alright. We'll go to the Machine Men and you'll die. They'll kill you because of Bassandis, or you'll perish because we can't live in their world and I'll be on my own. I'll have lost everyone and everything. I can't face it, I can't go with you and know you'll be taken away from me like Becky, the Theatre, Odilon, my home. I can't love you anymore, it hurts too much."

"I'll stay," *Don't beg Max, don't beg, even if you love her more than you've loved anyone and she looks more beautiful now than she ever did.* "I won't go to the Machine Men. I'll come with you and the players."

She was crying openly now. His own vision blurred and he struggled to master his voice. He longed to take her in his arms and comfort her but he couldn't move. It was as if she stood on the other side of transparent steel.

"The giant told you to journey to the Kingdom of the Machine Men. You may be our only hope to mend the mind of God. You have to go."

"And you won't come with me," he said. *How will I do it? How will I take even one step towards the Heart or the Head when that step carries me away from you?*

She mastered herself, a mask falling across her face, her hands unclenching. She turned into a stranger in front of his eyes, dead-eyed and indifferent. It was like watching her die.

"No."

He stumbled away, the barge rocking under his feet, threatening to tip him into the blackness that swelled around him.

"Max!" Abby called. *I don't want to talk to you, I can't talk to you whoever you are, I have to find Abby, but she's gone and I don't know where to look.* A white shape loomed in front of him, a porcelain statue that raised an arm to point at the night beyond. A ghost?

Pell screamed.

Max jerked to a halt, yanked back to reality by the Philosopher's monstrous voice just as Abby joined him. She took his arm but he shook her off with a curse. Pell made the same noise he'd heard in the shadow of the crooked tower when he'd saved her and Berthold from

Sarracinte's thugs. It started normal enough though it was absurdly loud and Max saw Abby's face go white with the shock of it. The girl's lips opened wider and wider, peeling back from teeth, revealing the hideous cavern of her throat. The shriek became an inhuman howl, skittering upwards into a furious whistle before cutting out. *She must have dislocated her jaw by now*, he thought. She still screamed, her face that of a gaping monster as she roared out her ultrasonic cry. Suddenly her mouth snapped closed and he was looking at a porcelain girl again, her expression one of mild concern.

"One second," she said.

Something hit Max from behind and he fell sprawling, his gun spinning over the deck. Abby yelled. Max glimpsed a tangle of legs matted in grey fur scuttling over the boards. A volley roared out, one bullet hissed just above his head. It smashed a lantern and burning oil splashed onto the wood, blue fire racing towards him. He managed to roll back and scramble to his feet as it licked around his boots. Another creature blundered past him, long limbed with a bobbing head the shape of a bread loaf. He caught a glimpse of eyes the colour of pitch and yellowed dog teeth bared in a grimace. Beyond the bridge more shadows swarmed across the planks. He spotted two briefly silhouetted against the glowing square of a hatch. They dropped into the corridor below. Glass shattered, followed by more screams. A rifle thundered and Max heard Berthold's voice, shrill and hysterical.

"Kill it kill it kill it."

He looked round for Abby and Pell. They'd retreated into the bridge, Abby covering the door with her gun while Pell stood behind her as mute and dispassionate as ever. *Here we go again*, Max thought but the memory of Abby's words stabbed at his heart even as he retrieved his revolver and jumped down the ladder to the main deck. *This time it's different, this time you're on your own.*

The instant he landed something slammed him into the wall, a bony arm covered in coarse fur pressing across his chest. Teeth as long as his hand snapped at his face while claws bit into his wrist. He fired and the creature leaped away with a squeal. It sped up the ladder into the night, leaving drops of viscous blood on the rungs. More movement to his left. He almost shot an actress who ran towards him in a blood-stained nightdress, mad terror in her eyes. Max saw the gashes in the cotton and the blood running down one leg in rivulets. He grabbed her and ripped the cloth apart. Two shallow cuts on her hip, nothing serious but they looked like bite or claw marks.

"Stay with me," he yelled in her face, hoping to get past the mindless panic. She nodded, pointing at the next door in mute fear. He padded forwards. It sounded as if someone was demolishing the room. Max risked a glance inside, ready to shoot whatever monster pulled the cabin to pieces. He froze, trying to understand what he saw.

Another actor sat slumped in the corner, blood running from a gash on his scalp. He looked alive, his head nodded back and forth as he struggled against unconsciousness. The creatures who attacked him hunched over an open chest. One held a sack while the other stuffed clothes, shoes and anything else it could lay its hands on into the bag.

Good God, they're robbing the place, thought Max even as he caught his first proper view of the monsters swarming the ship. They were human, after a fashion. Short barrelled torsos hung in the centre of arms and legs like dead branches tipped with black talons. Their heads were blocks of muscle and bone. Eyes the colour and size of plums sat above slitted nostrils and a mouth hinged at the back of the neck. Lank hair trailed from their bodies. Despite the obvious relish with which they scrabbled at the clothes they were naked.

He aimed. Catching sight of his movement they froze and turned their hideous gazes on him. Something in their expressions made him hesitate. They leaped for him and he staggered back to crash against the far wall. A claw planted itself in the centre of his chest but the creature just used him as a springboard to leap past the screaming actress towards the ladder. The monsters vanished up into the night.

A shot rang out. Max followed the sound to Thaisa's cabin. Berthold was pushing himself back against a corner as if he was trying to force his way through it. Thaisa stood in the centre in her nightgown, a short carbine in her hands. Max noticed she pointed the barrel at the floor. Her expression was a mixture of disgust and… was that pity? At the other end of the room Vincent trained a derringer on one of the creatures. It lay propped against the bulkhead, one claw reaching out to the actor, the other clamped over its side. Blood the colour and texture of tar welled up in glossy sacs between its fingers.

"Kill it, kill it," yelled Berthold. "She knows where each one is, if it lives it will bring her to us." Sweat stood out on his chalk white face. He could have been Pell's brother if it weren't for his staring eyes and matted hair. Max saw three long rents in his shirt, more claw marks from their attackers.

"Vincent?" said Thaisa. "It's wounded, it's asking for help."

"Kill it," shrieked Berthold.

"Who will come?" asked Max. Berthold turned towards him, insanity in his gaze.

"They're just actors, they have no idea. Kill it or she will come."

He hadn't a clue what the man was raving about. All he could see was an injured creature begging for mercy. Vincent pointed his gun at the monster's face but his hand wavered.

"Wait," said Max. Those creatures possessed teeth and claws capable of gutting a man in seconds but he'd only seen shallow scratches on the others. These things were thieves, they weren't interested in slaughter.

The beast lunged forward, struggling to stand.

"Vincent no!" cried Thaisa.

The gun cracked and in weary dismay Max saw the monster's head snap back as the bullet punched a hole in its skull. The actor manager stared at his smoking pistol. Berthold pushed himself out of the corner.

"We have to get it off the boat. She knows where they are, even in death. Its body will call her to us."

Exhaustion came crashing over Max. He didn't give two fucks for whatever nonsense Berthold was blathering but he went along. Berthold wouldn't go near the corpse so Max grabbed the feet and Vincent the head. They felt like lumps of dry wood coated in greasy fur. A musty smell rose from the body - old leather mixed with ammonia. They manhandled it onto the deck and swung it over the side. The creature disappeared into the black waters with a glutinous splash. Max instinctively looked for Abby but she wasn't there. Hopelessness swept over him again and he didn't notice Pell next to him until she spoke.

"They aren't monsters," she said. "They're people, changed by the long darkness. Who knows what functions they've discovered?" She went back below deck.

Max stood watch for while longer, trying to concentrate, searching for more creatures. Berthold yelled about a 'she', suggesting something worse lurked out there, but nothing emerged from the shadows. The conniving shit had clearly known about their attackers all along and said nothing. In the mood he was in Max was prepared to cheerfully pistol-whip the rest of the bastard's secrets out of him so they'd be prepared for any more ambushes. He went in search of the others.

Thaisa and Vincent checked the other boats. The raiders had focussed on the last ship but caused only superficial damage. Apart from one man with an ugly bite to his shoulder after he went for a creature with a knife, injuries were confined to scratches and bruises. A crowd of the monsters swarmed through the corridors of *Cast* at high speed, grabbing clothes and supplies and stuffing them into sacks before disappearing into the tunnels. Max reckoned they were scavengers. If Pell was right and they once were human thousands of years in the abandoned caverns of God's body had made them monstrous. He shuddered at the thought. Was that the eventual fate of all of them? It would take God aeons just to get to his feet and journey to the God Door. *After centuries nestled in the hollows and cavities of the titan, feeding from ancient caches, cultivating food in vats and oceans of chemicals, what will remain of humanity when the time comes for him to scatter us across new worlds? What will we have become?* Now he understood Chiomedes' anguish. *Too late, far too late. It's hopeless.*

Max returned to the cabin where Pell tended Berthold's injuries. The beast had sliced the man's back before Vincent shot it. The rents in the cloth looked as clinical as scissor cuts but the gouges underneath were shallow. *It could have ripped your spine out.* Pell sewed up the wound, her nose touching Berthold's skin. He glimpsed a shimmering line between her hand and the torn flesh.

"Steel wire," whispered Thaisa. "She used her nails to split it." Max looked at her and saw his own disbelief mirrored in her dark eyes. *Philosophers have nails strong enough to shred steel?* Pell wiped the blood away from Berthold's cut. The repaired skin looked unblemished. Keeping a wary eye on the Philosopher's hands Max sat opposite Berthold. He looked sick, still in the grip of panic.

"What were those things?" asked Max.

"Abhumans. There's a legion of them out there in the night. We've been at war with them for over fifteen years." *War?* Max could have cheerfully shot the bastard there and then.

"War? You've led us to a war?"

"It's not a war like that," said Berthold, seeing murder in Max's eyes. "They raid, we keep them back. Abhumans envy the Glass City for its wonders. They steal food, clothes, tools, the things they can't create themselves. Once we get out to sea we'll be fine, they hate the ocean."

You lying toad, there's more to this.

"Who is 'she'?" *And why does the mere mention of her make you almost piss yourself?*

"They are ruled by a demon. We call her the Brittle Hag." Max heard Abby snort behind him. He hadn't notice her come in. It should have made him happy, secure. Now all he wanted to do was flee the room and find a hole to crawl into. Waves of sadness crashed over him at the sound of her voice, forcing himself to concentrate on Berthold instead. He fought the urge to punch the gurning idiot's face into a bloody mess, vent all his desolation on this simpering cretin. Berthold sensed the change in Max's mood. He looked even more frightened but this time it wasn't the monsters causing him to shake.

"She wields power, horrible power," Berthold continued.

"What power?" asked Max.

"She drives men mad," said Berthold. "She drives us all mad. Some kind of psychic weapon. She gets inside our heads."

Ice blossomed in Max's stomach. It took what left of his courage to ask the next question.

"How big is this Brittle Hag?"

"Same height as a man, more or less," Berthold said, puzzled.

"What if he can talk to them like you?" asked Abby. Max almost turned round and told her to fuck off but he stopped himself. At this point in time his conversation with Berthold overrode everything. If the fop was one of the few able to speak with giants he'd see them as humans.

"Has anyone else encountered this Brittle Hag?"

Berthold nodded.

"And she's never bigger than a man?" said Max, dreading the answer.

Berthold nodded again, clearly believing Max had cracked.

Max dropped his head into his hands. For one second he feared he'd found another giant, insane and despairing, tunnelled deep into the body of God like a maggot, but it was clear that whatever this thing was it had no relation to mind of the deity. A hand lighted on his shoulder. Thinking it was Abby's he made to push it away. Thaisa stood next to him, her touch gentle, calming.

"How long till we reach this ocean of yours?" she asked Berthold.

"We'll arrive tomorrow morning," said Pell without looking up from her sewing.

"Vincent, Abby and I will take a barge each and stand watch," said Max. "If you have any other weapons give them to whoever's prepared to fight. We'll just have to hope those things don't come back."

He stood up to leave. At the door Abby whispered to him.

"We must talk. I know you're hurt but please don't do anything stupid."

He forced himself to look at her. *Your eyes are so green, no-one else has eyes like that.*

He pushed past without a word.

CHAPTER SEVEN

MAX STAYED ON *Theatre*. To his relief Abby took *Cast* so the bulk of *Props* floated between them, sparing him glimpses of his old partner standing guard over the actors. The framework of stairs and walkways petered out and the cavern narrowed until they were sailing along a tunnel. The boats picked up speed. Max doubted the Abhumans planned on returning but he kept scanning the walls as they rushed past, anything to take his mind off Abby. Their conversation on deck lay like a black cloud in his thoughts and he hovered at its edge, terrified to step inside and relive the anguish of rejection.

The air lightened, the choppy water beneath the prow turning into a sheet of seething reflections. The walls rushed away and Max gazed out across an immense sea. He turned to look behind him. A cliff of uneven blocks reared up into the sky, disappearing into grey-green mist far above his head. On either side the shore vanished in the haze. Even Max, who'd seen beings two miles high striding through the ruins of a burning city, caught his breath at the sheer size of the ocean.

Pell helped Thaisa with the navigation. They emerged from the bridge to stand with Max, the Philosopher pointing into the fog while Thaisa swept the distance with a telescope. Max looked at the surging waters, the space before and above them, and the fast-receding wall to their rear. Pell gave a cry and clamped her hands over her face. Max and Thaisa exchanged puzzled glances as the girl peeped out between white fingers before snapping them shut again with another sob. By now he was used to her weird behaviour but this unnerved him.

"There's a hole, up there," she said. For the first time she sounded genuinely scared. Max looked at the cliff face. There were lots of holes - rusted gaps peppering the metal and cavities where slats or beams had decayed and fallen into the sea.

"And?" asked Max.

"There, it's horrible," whimpered the Philosopher. "I can't look at it." A gantry ran along the wall a mile up. Max spotted a jumble of shapes, barely discernible against the precipice. With a twist of shock he recognised it as a person, standing perfectly still, watching the boats as they sailed over the waves.

Thaisa bumped a pair of binoculars against his hand. He took them and focussed on the figure.

"A statue?" said Thaisa as she looked through her own telescope. Possibly. Max had come across iron twisted into human shapes before, crafted by sculptors of varying degrees of ability. This wasn't one of the most inspired - a roughly soldered bundle of metal shards gathered into the rough approximation of a woman in a dress and broad-brimmed hat. What in God's name was that doing there? A bizarre mascot, perhaps, left by an ancient civilisation to ward off evil and protect travellers.

He swept his gaze over the surrounding wall. No holes. Stupid girl imagining things.

"It's just a sculpture," said Max, exasperated by Pell's fear. In his current mood he didn't have the patience to listen to her cryptic eccentricities.

"There is a hole in the universe," said the Philosopher, spitting each word out from behind her hands. "There is a hole in the universe and there is a monster sitting in the centre of it watching us and she's filled with anger."

Max's stomach clenched in fear. Thaisa muttered a curse and looked through her telescope again. Before Max could bring the binoculars to bear she gave a cry, staggered and dropped it. A lens fell out onto the deck.

"It moved then vanished," she said in a small voice.

"Moved?" Max searched the walkway. He saw nothing other than endless planking and iron sheets. Pell summoned up the courage to peep through her hands again.

"The hole's gone." Her dead-eyed gaze flickered across the wall. "The universe is whole once more," she added with a smile.

Max swore. Had they seen Berthold's Brittle Hag? If so she hardly seemed intent on calling down destruction on the fleet and they were out of range of any ordinary weapon by now. Nothing else materialised - no energy beam, missiles or flying machines. By rights he should have warned the other boats but he was shattered. He searched the wall for another fifteen minutes, keeping vigilant out of grim duty. In the end he left Pell and Thaisa to it and climbed back below decks, desperate for the amnesia a few hours rest might bring.

Max couldn't sleep. He sat in a chair and stared at the empty bunk unable to summon up the energy to feel anything. Abby's rejection had hollowed him out. He'd become a shell. Thoughts and images trundled through his head but none of them made sense. They weren't his. They belonged to someone else. He knew what was happening. He'd seen his father do it so many times. As a child he'd hated Herman Ocel, not understanding what he'd done to be punished with his parent's stony indifference day in day out. As an adult he'd come to realise how the Lord of the Carceral Archipelago ached from the loss of his love, Max's mother. In the end he'd learned the true extent of that tragedy. His father's closest confidant, Odilon the Watcher, murdered his mother to prevent her revealing the nature of the giant Bassandis and in the very end Odilon killed Herman Ocel too. In the lonely chambers of his mind he replayed the scene in Bassandis's prison. *'You did what you thought was best, you weren't to know'*, said Odilon. *He pulled out a long knife and stabbed you through the heart. Your old friend. But he wasn't your friend was he? He was a Black Rose, an alien from the outer night. They all turn away, they all betray you. Even Abby Fabrice. Shut yourself down, be your father's son. Stone duty. Leave these wretched players, climb the towers of the Glass City and find your way to the Kingdom of the Machine Men.*

Sleep came and he woke half a day later to find the room filled with grey light. For a second he wondered where Abby was before the memories came crashing back into his head. He dressed and washed, feeling the hard bones of his face beneath the stubble. He didn't look at himself in the mirror - he was scared of what he might discover. Instead he went on deck to search for Thaisa. She stood on top of the theatre, watching the blunt prow of the barge part the sea. On all sides water and sky disappeared into a uniform haze. Max couldn't make out any sign of the ceiling, the walls of this immense cavern, or the Glass City itself.

Thaisa turned and he noticed the concern on her face.

"As soon as we reach the city I'm leaving," he said. Was that regret in her eyes? If so it flashed out of sight in a moment. "If you have any supplies it'll help, just a bag and some food, ammunition if there's any spare. I don't plan to hang around."

"Of course," she said. "If that's what you want." He was glad she knew better than to try and persuade him otherwise. He sensed people on the boat watching him. Perhaps his old partner was among them but he was damned if he was going to turn round. *Bide your time until we arrive.* There was no point in talking to Abby. He understood her well enough and had seen all he needed to know in her expression just before the Brittle Hag's Abhumans attacked.

"Berthold says we're nearly there," said Thaisa. "I'll get you what I can."

She left him alone, staring out across the sea, searching for any sign of the Glass City. He sat down on the edge of the roof and closed his eyes, letting the sharp air and distant hiss of the parting waters fill his mind.

"Max?"

He looked up. With a flash of anger he saw Berthold standing beside him, wearing an expression of solicitous concern. He toyed with the idea of telling him where to go but relented. If Berthold was going to show him how to reach the Elbow then he needed to put aside his irritation at the man's incompetence and mannered self-regard. It would just be the three of them taking Pell back to her people. God, he'd have to teach the idiot how to fight properly. To be fair he had some courage. How else had he managed to rescue Pell from Sarracinte? But Max wasn't looking forward to spending the next however many months in his company.

"I don't want to waste time in the Glass City," he said. "I want to move on as soon as we get there. One day to gather supplies then we climb those towers of yours."

"Right," said Berthold. He didn't sound convinced. Max looked at him sharply. He was in no mood to tolerate stupid games. Berthold peered into the mist.

"We're here. They've come to meet us," he said. To Max's surprise he appeared frightened, as though he'd decided he didn't want to be on this boat sailing across this sea at all. Max followed his gaze. Three shadows broke through the vapour half a mile ahead, ironclads shaped like inverted baking trays. Squat funnels belched greasy soot into the air.

"Keep your weapons down and let me do the talking," called Berthold to the people standing behind them. "It's fine, it's fine," he added in an urgent whisper to Max who stood up, flexing his hands and calculating the tactical permutations of what might unfold. "They're ships from the Glass City, trust me." *Trust you*? On a better day Max would have laughed out loud.

Max studied the approaching ironclads. Two of them took up position on either side of *Theatre* as it slowed to a stop. The third lay athwart their prow, a hard-angled ungainly vessel with a single turret sticking out of the centre of the deck. To his surprise no guns projected from its ports. Up close the boats looked tatty - streaks of rust and oil marked the seams between the armour cladding.

A sailor threw a long plank between the ships and before anyone could stop him Berthold ran over to the ironclad, his arms stuck out for balance as if he pretended to fly. A knot of people gathered around him on the other vessel. Their dark uniforms blended into the ship's hull making it hard for Max to see details, but he could have sworn one of the women saluted. That relaxed him a little. Berthold, for all his dilettante posturing, held authority among these newcomers.

Berthold came skipping back as Vincent and Thaisa joined them. Max caught sight of Abby standing next to the bridge, her head bowed and her arms folded, her gaze lancing between the ships. He took the surge of misery in his heart and kneaded it to a point of crystal anger.

"The fleet will escort us to the Glass City. We'll be there by nightfall," said Berthold. Max detected a new confidence bordering on arrogance in his voice.

"I told them of our encounter with the Abhumans, so they are understandably jumpy. The inhabitants of the Glass City can be eccentric."

"Really?" said Max. Berthold ignored him.

"I understand them. Let me do the talking. Forgive me if the things I say are exaggerated or odd. I only do so for effect and to increase our natural advantages."

Vincent nodded and threw a questioning glance at Thaisa who turned a warm smile on Berthold.

"Thank you for bringing us here." He bowed.

Max had had enough. All he cared about was getting to the city so he could return to his journey. He left them to their discussions on protocol and returned to the edge of the theatre roof. He looked ahead, searching for any sign of the approaching islands in the haze.

"Max?"

Abby stood beside him. He refused to look at her.

"We need to talk about what we do when we get to the Glass City," she said.

"We know what we're doing, what's to discuss?" *I go north, you look after your actors.*

She tried to force him to meet her gaze. *Isn't this hard enough?* Nevertheless he looked into her face - tired and miserable, her freckles grey, shadows round her eyes.

Lack of sleep always made her jumpy, never a good sign.

"Did you get a look at those boats? They didn't seem right, or the crew," she insisted, ignoring his comment. He cast his mind back to Berthold talking with a handful of men and women. He couldn't think of anything out of the ordinary apart from the impression of general tattiness.

"They looked beaten, cowed," she continued.

"They're at war, according to Berthold, what do you expect?" asked Max, tearing his gaze away.

"Just be careful," said Abby with a sudden burst of irritation. "Don't do something stupid to make some kind of fucking point."

Max turned and looked her full in the face to let her understand the depth of the wound she'd inflicted. With sour pleasure he saw her eyes fill with tears. She stepped back, uncertain. He nodded towards the actors.

"Take care of your friends, they need protecting, that's your job now," he said. She opened her mouth, thought better of it and left him alone.

He looked ahead. Shapes coalesced in the distance, a jagged bundle rising out of the sea, clustering at the base of thin shadows that soared into the lowering clouds. The ironclads ahead began to slow, the thrum of their own engines under his boots subsided. He glanced around. The actors gathered on the roofs of the barges, most of them clustered amid the funnels of *Cast*, talking and pointing as they approached the end of their journey.

As the shapes clarified in the mist Max realised why it was called the Glass City. It began with a network of wooden platforms and jetties spread across the waves ahead. Beyond those rose mountains of glass blocks, all various sizes but none smaller than a house, threaded with more landings and scaffolding connected by rope ladders and bridges. They were a dirty green, as if someone had frozen chunks of sea water and piled them into hills and precipices. He couldn't see inside any of the opaque slabs but he caught sight of a few blurred shadows and, once or twice, movement. *People live in those things.*

The flotilla sailed along a wide channel flanked on either side by cliffs of glass. Up close Max realised that the colour of the walls ranged from a faint algae stain to a deep turquoise. It was as if they drifted underwater, flaws and bubbles trapped in the glass increasing the illusion of being submerged. Above all he didn't sense he'd arrived at a thriving metropolis. This was more like the storehouse of a giant alchemist, a student of the filthy secrets of the old universe keeping his dead specimens in a city built of translucent boxes. Twilight fell. Lamplight appeared behind some of the glass while other blocks stayed dark. Max made out pools of liquid in one or two, speckled with shapes he didn't want to study too closely. He suspected Abby was right. All was not well in the Glass City.

At last they came to a landing that blocked the channel. A crowd of people gathered on the boardwalks carrying torches and lanterns, peering out at the approaching ships. Beyond them Max saw the towers in the centre of the island. They reminded him of the buildings south of the Brick River in Metacarpi, though the old skyscrapers of his home city were children's toys in comparison to these shafts of grey concrete and metal. He noticed a ramp leading up from the glass houses to a square entrance cut in the base of the central column. Above it thousands of windows rose into the night. *Not one light*, he thought. *It's abandoned. Why?*

Berthold stood next to him, adjusting his cuffs and smoothing back his curled hair with his palms. He had a jaunty air that Max hadn't seen before.

"Full houses and a powerful patron?" asked Max, not bothering to hide his contempt.

"Max," said Berthold. "Don't judge and don't assume. Brave and clever as you are, you're not fighting the scum of Interosseous now." He gave Max a wink and a matey slap on the shoulder. His earlier fear had transformed into a confident anticipation that bordered on the hysterical. *What the hell's going on?*

The ships bumped up against a jetty. The smoke from the ironclads bunched above their hulls before sliding over the armour to puddle in a greasy cloud on the water. Berthold walked up the gangplank, waving for the others to join him. Max followed. Behind him came Abby and Pell then Vincent and Thaisa. The Philosopher wore a robe with the hood pulled over her face. He wondered whether that was on Berthold's advice. The girl stood out like a beacon wherever she went. It was probably a good idea not to draw too much attention to her just yet. The crowd parted to form a circle. Berthold murmured something to a couple of men who carried shotguns. Max took the opportunity to scan the inhabitants of the city.

The first thing that struck him was the weariness in their eyes. They watched the newcomers with a dull, unsmiling curiosity. Heavy suits shiny at the elbows and knees mingled with black and grey dresses falling over unpolished boots and sandals. *Is this it?* thought Max, searching for more prosperous-looking citizens. He reckoned a couple of hundred were gathered on wooden tiers rising up to the glass blocks fronting the harbour. He looked at the faces gazing back at him. They all wore the same tinge of sad apathy.

"It's a prison," said Abby at his shoulder. Despite his anger at her he conceded she had a point. He'd seen similar expressions before in the cells at the bottom of the Carceral Archipelago when his father took him to see the price of dissent and rebellion. Even the dozen or so guards and sailors from the ironclad wore the same scowls of fear and furtive tiredness. Berthold addressed the crowd, waving his arms and striding back and forth. Max caught his words for the first time.

"And the Brittle Hag herself, monstrous, with talons extended, rose out of the mound of bodies that littered the rear of the deck and came towards me, howling and shrieking in her bestial tongue."

What in God's name was the idiot boasting about now?

"I tumbled, the sword slipping from my fingers," he flung his arm over his eyes. "What was I to do? Fear paralysed me."

All faces were on Berthold and Max was astounded to see mute worship in the citizens' eyes as he carried on with his surreal lies.

"As I fell in terror my hand lighted upon the handle of a shotgun, I whipped it up and fired into the witch's hideous face. The blast knocked her off the deck and she plunged into the turbid waters of the canal."

A gasp rippled through the crowd, followed by a ragged smattering of applause. Berthold held out his hands to quieten his audience.

"Alas, good friends, the Brittle Hag is considerably weakened, but will not have been so easily overthrown. We must remain ever vigilant even though the war is within measurable sight of its end."

Despite himself Max swapped glances with Abby whose face mirrored his own confusion. Behind them someone clapped slowly. He turned to see one of the women from the theatre applauding, a sarcastic grin plastered over her face. Thaisa shot her a warning look. The actress responded with a shrug and a dismissive gesture towards Berthold.

Berthold gave a self-deprecating laugh and faced the players. He shook his head as if he too acknowledged that it was all a bit of a joke, yet Max noted looks of real hatred and anger among the crowd, directed at the girl who'd interrupted Berthold's speech. He realised this could get ugly.

"Honoured guests," said Berthold, spreading his arms wide. "I welcome you to the Glass City, Kingdom of Theuderic, Lord of the Machine Men."

It was Max's turn to glare at Berthold in astonishment.

"What did you just say?" he said, trying to keep his voice even. Berthold looked back at him with an expression of calm command, defying Max to challenge him.

"This is the Kingdom of Theuderic, Lord of the Machine Men," he repeated. He wore the smile of a parent on the verge of losing patience with a stupid child. Behind him Max saw a few of the crowd nod.

"That's insane," growled Max. Berthold's grin froze. *Play along with me, please*, his eyes said. *For your sake*.

"Max," warned Abby.

"This is the Kingdom of Theuderic, Lord of the Machine Men," repeated one of the soldiers, an officer if the crumpled cap on his head was anything to go by. "And the noble Berthold is his prince."

Max snapped. He marched up to Berthold and shoved him backwards. The man staggered into the crowd who caught him before he fell.

"You piece of shit. What idiot games are you playing and what hole have you dragged us to?" said Max. Fury and anguish swept over him. Fuck stone duty, fuck Berthold, Abby, the lot of them. He wanted to tear the universe asunder and piss on the fragments. He reached behind him for the gun stuffed into his waistband. The crowd was shouting now, surging back and forth, pointing at him in rage. Berthold raised his arms again to placate them and as he moved his hands it looked as if he conducted wave upon wave of grey, angry faces. Max thought he heard Abby's voice yelling his name. He started for Berthold again but something smacked into the back of his head. He dropped to his knees, the ground gave way, and he fell through the endless spaces of God's body.

CHAPTER EIGHT

MAX LAY FROZEN in green ice. It rose in walls around him and sealed off the sky with dirty swirls peppered with bubbles. He lifted his hand to touch it and pain lanced through his arm. Swearing he tried to sit up. His hair stuck to the floor and when he reached behind to feel his scalp his fingers came away bloody. He struggled upright again, if only to check how badly he was injured.

"I stopped them. They are incredibly loyal to their prince."

Berthold sat on a stool at the end of the room, elbows on knees, chin resting on his hands.

"Five minutes in the Glass City and we have two subversives chucked into prison," he shook his head. "Ridiculous. All I asked is that you let me say the things that needed to be said."

Max pulled himself into a sitting position, trying to ignore the pain from the beating he'd received after he passed out. *Two subversives* - that could only mean one thing.

"What have you done with Abby?"

"Abby?" Berthold laughed. "Abby's fine. She's with the players at the moment planning their performance. You thought I meant Abby," Berthold shook his head. "That woman's chaos incarnate, I agree." Max recognised the lust in Berthold's eyes. *She'd have you for breakfast*. This Prince of the Glass City was truly mad if he believed Abby Fabrice would fall for that louche smile.

"Abby's fine, don't worry about her, she'll be looked after. No, I meant that sarky little cow, what's her name? Tafaline." He clapped his hands slowly in imitation of the actress. "She's three blocks below us, curled up and wailing. I told them to be gentle, though."

Berthold winked. *Keep going*, thought Max. *Everything you say, every sneer and every boast, I will make you pay for it*. He'd been stupid letting himself give way to misery and anger. *Not again, Father. Be patient a while longer, I will be as flint-hearted as the old Tyrant in the Tower. That'll bring me through this.*

"So that nonsense about this being the Kingdom of Theuderic, Lord of the Machine Men?" he asked. A bizarre fantasy concocted to sway the gullible minds of the inhabitants of the Glass City. Berthold's answer took him by surprise,

"Oh no, Theuderic rules over us. He is our king," he looked serious.

"The Machine Men live in the Heart and Head. King Theuderic dwells in the Skull of God. This is nowhere, it's halfway up the left Forearm," said Max.

"No," answered Berthold, his voice a little louder. "Theuderic Lord of the Machine Men is here, in the Glass City. He rules us and guides our hand against the Brittle Hag with his wisdom and council. This is his kingdom."

Max wasn't going to argue. He didn't have the energy and he guessed there'd be a beating, or worse, at the end of it. He lay on the glass. The cool surface soothed his pain.

"Now what?" he said to the ceiling.

"I'm not a bad man, I'm just weak." The admission took Max aback. He'd pegged Berthold as an arrogant liar, boasting his way to power over an ignorant audience. Was this another one of his clumsy strategies? But he detected something else in the man's voice, a note of confession that made him sit up again despite the pain. Berthold looked at the floor, his voice stumbling as he spoke half to himself.

"You're brave and strong, a great fighter. I'm not, I'm a, what was it? 'A worthless wastrel' - that's what my brother and father called me. But I ended up here in control of this city, governing in the name of his lordship." He jerked his thumb behind him towards the central tower. *So that's where this false Theuderic lives.*

"I need help, you've seen my city. We're struggling. As long as we stay here we're alright but the second we step onto the shores of the ocean the Abhumans are all over us. So we're trapped. We get food out of the tanks that remain," Berthold rapped the glass with his knuckles. Max remembered the blocks he'd passed when they arrived, half filled with liquid and twitching shapes. He wasn't looking forward to his first meal.

"I need warriors and learning - an understanding of how to fight so we can defeat the Brittle Hag, and science to repair the wonders this city once housed and create new ones to help us find ways to feed the populace. Max, Abby and Pell," he looked up at Max. "Theatre's good too, culture for this grim shit hole."

So that was it.

"You never had any intention of taking Pell back to her people. There's no transit system at the top of those towers, is there?" said Max. He almost admired the man. True, the liar dragged them here with his false promises but they'd been fools to follow. In truth he was more angry with his own blindness than with Berthold.

115

"Oh there is," said Berthold. "It's up there, and it works. Max," he leant forward. "I'll do you a deal. Help me defeat the Brittle Hag and I'll take you to the transit system."

"And Pell?" He almost asked about Abby too before he remembered she wasn't going with him. Berthold looked sheepish.

"She's got to remain I'm afraid, at least for a while. We can learn how to fight from you but we'd never understand her wisdom in a thousand years. I need to persuade her to stay and help us."

Max didn't believe half the story. It sounded a vain delusion. Berthold the noble saviour of the city didn't gel with the opportunistic dandy in front of him gloating over a violated actress. What was the alternative? Part of him wanted to surrender to the grinding loneliness and rejection that swilled through his exhausted mind. He fantasised about staying in this glass coffin - it had a grim emptiness that echoed the Abby-shaped hole in his life. He remembered his father standing at the top of the Carceral Archipelago, the Tyrant of the Tower implacable in his isolation. *Stone masked duty, no self pity.* He'd go along with Berthold for the time being. If the man wanted him to help defeat the Abhumans he might even get a weapon in his hand and a chance at the towers leading up to the old transit station. At least he could look forward to shooting the smarmy bugger. One thing still nagged him.

"Theuderic Lord of the Machine Men lives in the central skyscraper," he said watching Berthold's expression for any *fooled-you* tell. To his surprise a second of desperate unhappiness flickered in the other man's eyes. He hid it well but there was no mistaking. *There's tragedy behind this*, thought Max.

"Yes, he does. He's our king, and he loves plays. He's asked the players to perform for him. When they do, if you've been a good, co-operative Max, you'll get a chance to meet him. Abby told me she'd do anything to get you out of here."

She probably didn't mean it quite the way you hope, thought Max, lying back on the glass floor.

"So I'm free."

"No, not yet," said Berthold. "We have to play the game. You insulted the Prince of the Glass City in front of his people. I can't let it lie. You'll be re-educated and if you study hard, you'll win your release."

Glass scraped on glass and Max lay alone in his translucent box. Eventually he struggled to his feet. A woman in a vaguely military-looking tunic, baggy trousers and shapeless boots brought a bucket of water and a cloth. She put it at the end of the room and left without a word. Max caught a glimpse of dead eyes staring out of a face lined with tiredness, the same hunched, beaten posture he'd seen in the inhabitants on the quay. He cleaned himself up - thankfully he had nothing more than a handful of ugly cuts and bruises. He searched his prison. The door was a hinged glass block impossible to move. He mopped a clear patch on the wall and tried to see outside. He couldn't make sense of the jumbled shapes beyond. Once or twice he glimpsed blurs flickering in the green depths and guessed they were people. He thought of hammering on the glass but it looked more than two foot thick and he doubted he'd be heard.

Another night came and went. Max brooded, forcing himself to wait, trying not to think of Abby, a near impossible task in a room the same colour as her eyes. How could he not have realised, seen it coming? He'd stupidly thought they'd carry on as before when charging cheerfully towards death was just part of the job. In those days they measured life in the distance between wormholes. He guessed Abby knew she could always haul him out at the last minute by the scruff of his neck. He replayed a dozen examples in his head but the memories hurt too much. This time there'd be no last minute. The second he met the Machine Men his fate was sealed. He might live, he might die and neither of them had any power over the outcome. That's why Abby cast him aside. It was the last thing in her control.

Four guards with rusting shotguns came for him. They took him outside and he realised he was in a prison complex on an artificial peninsula stretching south from the island. The towers cut dull-edged shadows out of the pewter-coloured sky. He followed his captors along trenches of glass that angled down into the centre of a jumbled mountain of blocks at the end of the spit. He found himself in a hall filled with wooden stools. A couple of dozen men and women sat near a table covered in a cloth. Max guessed they were fellow inmates. He searched for Tafaline but didn't see her.

None of the prisoners looked up or acknowledged his presence as the guards pushed him onto a seat. They waited for what felt like hours, the soldiers pacing up and down the edge of the room, watching Max and the others. Once they seized an old man and dragged him from the hall, holding him up against the outside of the glass wall for all to see as they beat him in turn. When they finally let him slide down his head left a dark smear. No-one inside spoke. Max saw nothing in the dull gazes around him - no fear, compassion or anger. After they hauled the body out of sight everyone turned back to stare at the floor. Max's nails dug into his palms as he fought the urge for cruel revenge. He wanted to kill them all but he had to keep control, stay alive and get out of this place. Vengeance would wait.

At long last, as evening fell, two men came into the room and set spluttering kerosene lamps at the four corners of the table. They whisked the cloth away to reveal a relief map covered in black and green blocks.

"Gather round, gather round," said one, waving his hands impatiently. The people shuffled up to the display. Max joined them. The guards forming a ring around the group. He counted twelve incompetent-looking thugs, slovenly dressed with ill-kept weapons and expressions of truculent brutality. If those shotguns worked he could disarm a couple and kill most before they overpowered him but it'd be a futile gesture. He doubted he'd get out of this penal colony alive if he made a break for it. He turned his attention to the diorama. The man launched into a lecture while his companion poked blocks around the map with a stick.

"Following his glorious triumph in the Lost Sands, Prince Berthold pushed the Abhumans back towards the Cerium Mountains here and here." He was a self-satisfied, round-faced boor. Max knew his type. He'd bumped up against them often enough in the Carceral Archipelago. The tale he told was a fantastically absurd narrative of battles and campaigns in which, time after time, Berthold and Theuderic, King of the Machine Men, led thousands of brave troops to victory after victory against the monstrous hordes of the Brittle Hag. After each rhetorical flourish the audience dutifully applauded. Max joined in after noticing the guards staring at him when he failed to show his enthusiasm first time. He tried to make sense of the map. There was the Glass City in the middle of a papier-mâché sea, but the realms bordering the ocean came straight from a child's story book. He saw forests and mountains, swamps and deserts as if the model-maker had set out to include every conceivable variety of terrain. Berthold defeated

the monsters in jungles and ruined cities while Theuderic guided divisions across rolling plains, winning titanic
conflicts in which millions of the enemy perished.

The absurd pantomime dragged on for hours. At the
end the guards gave the prisoners a hunk of bread and a
pitcher of water each and led them back to their glass
cells. The next day the whole ritual was repeated. Max
endured endless farcical narratives while the two men
shoved wooden blocks around the table. On the third
day one woman fell asleep. The following morning her
body swung from the outer wall.

Max knew what was happening. He'd seen his father do the same. Isolate the dissidents, disorientate them
with monotony and re-educate through the incessant re-
petition of lies piled upon lies, each more ludicrous than
the last until the final desperate self-abasement rested on
an unshakeable mountain of compacted madness. By the
seventh day Max realised how seductive it could be.
Week in, week out, trudging the same paths with the
same faces, eating the same food and listening to the
same nonsense induced a hopeless surrender. Frantically
trying to make sense of the endless absurdity the weary
mind perceived it as the only reality left. But Max's bitterness over Abby's rejection planted a sour kernel in his
heart that he drew on for strength. He swore he'd get
out of this place and take Pell back to her people so
they'd lead him to the Machine Men. He could endure
this charade for the time being.

On the morning of the ninth day he woke to find
Berthold sitting on the stool at the end of the room.

"How's the re-education going?"

"I've been hearing all about your victories," said
Max. Berthold laughed.

"Just propaganda. Keeps the people focussed on
what's important." Max wouldn't have dignified any of

his lessons with the title of propaganda but he let it rest. He saw smug bravado in Berthold's eyes.

"Your time here is over," he said. "I pleaded eloquently on your behalf and Theuderic, Lord of the Machine Men, agrees to release you into my charge."

"Wonderful," said Max. Berthold gave a short *watch it, I could leave you here* laugh. He leaned closer.

"Help me, please. I'm trying to keep this place from falling apart. That's why we have all this," he gestured around him. "It's not forever, it won't always be cruelty and rules."

There it was again, that flash of bitter sadness in Berthold's eyes. He didn't act the tyrant, iron willed and implacable in his belief in the system he used to beat the people down. Max tried to make sense of the conversation. He guessed Berthold wanted to take him into his confidence, use him to accomplish a mysterious plot he'd fabricated. Why, what was he after? Max doubted it involved the betterment of the citizens of the Glass City.

"I want to get you out of here and put you in front of Theuderic himself, you and Pell, so he can see for himself what wisdom you bring to his kingdom, a Philosopher and a warrior, but I have to do it in stages. Your unhelpful episode when we arrived has marked you out," he poked Max in the chest. Max resisted the urge to break his arm. Instead he forced an expression of interest onto his face.

"Abby pleaded most delightfully for your release. There's to be a play for King Theuderic's entertainment and you are needed for a most important role. That will give me the chance to present you."

Max almost laughed. The man was as transparent as the prison walls. He wanted Abby, of course he did. *Good luck with that, you poor bastard.* He heard her voice now, playing the sweet ingénue. *No Max, no play, but if you could weave your charm and influence, oh so handsome Berthold, and get him out of jail, then who knows what might happen?*

"Wonderful," he said, the picture of grateful relief.

Berthold clapped his hands.

"It'll be a long road, but we will be triumphant in the end, you and I, Pell and Abby." He sounded like that idiot in the re-education room, playing out stories from a bizarre fantasy world where Berthold and Theuderic led their armies time after time to endless victory.

They released Max, and Berthold took him back to the main island across a glass causeway made treacherous by ocean spray. After abjuring him to behave himself the prince walked back up towards the towers, leaving him in the company of a couple of guards. Max guessed he went to visit his so-called king. The player's ships floated next to each other along a sheltered wharf. His companions leaned on their shotguns and watched as he boarded *Theatre*. He didn't find anyone in the bridge so he made his way below deck.

He found the actors and Abby in the auditorium, rehearsing a scene. The instant they spotted him Thaisa, Vincent and Abby came thundering up the aisle, Thaisa trying to keep between him and her beloved who had murder in his eyes. Abby looked sick with a mixture of anguish and relief. At the last second Thaisa turned to Vincent and put her hand on his chest. It seemed to calm him down as he stopped in his tracks and gave her a *I won't snap his wretched neck just yet* nod.

"Where's Tafaline?" he growled over Thaisa's shoulder.

"Still in prison," said Max.

"Is she alright?" asked Thaisa. Max glanced at Abby. She recognised the look in his eyes and paled. Vincent also read the message, shouted in rage and kicked a chair so hard its back shattered.

"Why are you free and not her?" said Thaisa, struggling to master her own feelings. Max told them Berthold's tale, his claim that he'd brought them here to help the Glass City, Max as a warrior and Pell as... where was Pell?

"Berthold took her with him to meet King Theuderic," said Abby. "We haven't seen her since."

Max swore. Berthold was smart enough to know her value, why else had he rescued her? She must be in the tower.

"He says he needs our experience of fighting and Pell's science to make this a better place," said Max. Abby spat on the carpet in disgust.

"I tell you, sir, as soon as we've done this play we're leaving," said Vincent. "Have you seen the shit hole you brought us to? Both of you? It's a glass dungeon, nothing more." He turned to Thaisa. "Now Taffy's raped because of these two. We should have thrown them into the canal."

"Enough," she said. Max saw fury glittering in her eyes. Vincent had the sense to clamp his mouth shut. Thaisa rounded on Max. All melancholy wit had fled and her face was a cold mask of distaste. "You can atone for this fucking mess by getting Taffy back and helping us escape."

Abby nodded. She looked truly wretched. Thaisa shot them both a crushing look and led her husband away, whispering into his ear. Max turned to his old partner. *Stone duty.* He sensed muted relief in her eyes that he still lived, the echoes of what once lay between them, but she was damned if she was going to let it show. So be it.

"What are the options?" he asked.

"We're performing a play for this fake Theuderic," she said. "Up in the tower. It'll give us a chance to find Pell. What about Tafaline?"

He told her about the prison and Berthold's gloating over the brutalised actress. He hadn't seen her in the lecture rooms and didn't even know if she still lived. She pursed her lips, watching the players lurch through a rehearsal.

"You spring Pell and take her up the tower. That should distract them long enough for me to find Tafaline and get this lot away from the city. These ships can out-run those ironclads. They're piles of crap, badly maintained, and I didn't see any guns on them."

Silence fell. *What do you want me to say?* thought Max. It was a plan, crazy and ill-designed enough to succeed, knowing Abby, but it put a seal on their breakup.

"OK," Max said. Muscles bunched in Abby's jaw. She pushed a script at him. *The Gate of Light. God almighty, a fairy story for kids and Odilon's favourite.*

"You're Salabanco, the total idiot of a servant."

He watched her stalk out of the theatre, her head slumped and hands in pockets.

Over the next few days Max struggled to learn his part. To his surprise Vincent and Thaisa had never heard of the play and the script was Abby's version, typed from memory. The original called for giant puppets, acrobatics and firework-powered spaceships. While Max languished in prison the Glass City guards had plundered the three ships, stealing provisions, clothes, props, even wigs and grease paint, leaving the second boat a wrecked mess. Ever resourceful, Abby claimed she'd re-invented the performance for a Theatre of Light, whatever that was, so all they needed were lamps and a reliance on the audience's imagination. Max had seen the results of Berthold and Theuderic's story-telling in the re-education room of the penal colony. This whole settlement rested on fantasy.

The rehearsals were grim, miserable affairs. Despair and anger seeped into the boat, cold and dark like the rancid sea water slapping against the hull. Tempers frayed and scenes degenerated into shouting and tears. Max sensed the hatred directed at he and Abby. He locked himself down, turning inwards and trying to re-erect his father's stone walls inside his head so he could focus on his goal - find Pell, climb the tower, journey to the Elbow and from there over to the Abdomen where he hoped he'd persuade the Philosophers to help him contact the real Machine Men. Every day it got easier. At night he stole away from the others and spent hours exercising - practising shadow combat and going over the rudimentary tactics he knew for narrow corridors and confined spaces. He'd let himself go in Interosseous and needed to get back in shape for what might come in the long trek up those towers. It also kept his mind free of bitter memories. Abby had the good sense to stay out of his way.

When the atmosphere in the theatre descended into a chaos of desperate tantrums too hard to bear, he climbed on deck and looked across the city to the buildings in the centre of the island. Clouds hung forever around their upper floors. He reckoned the most he'd seen was a mile of iron and rotting concrete. Beyond that, so Berthold claimed, rose another four miles of towers and above that five miles of their downward-pointing twins. Once, despite his better judgement, he took Thaisa's binoculars and studied the skyscrapers from inside the bridge, turning the lamps off in the hope he wouldn't be seen. Nothing but acres of crumbling wall and blank glass reflecting the churning sky, though he thought he spotted a mask at one of the windows, a brief glimpse of something that looked like rents torn in cloth to make crude eyes and a mouth. When he looked again it had vanished. Probably a trick of the light or his own nightmares stumbling through the clutter of his weary mind.

Even so he left the cabin hoping that whatever it was hadn't seen him. A shadow flitted across the deck of *Props*. With only he and Abby to look after them the actors had abandoned the second boat. She kept watch on *Cast* while he spent the nights alone in *Theatre*. Clearly another guard in search of plunder. Max's hatred and resentment at the arrogant brutality of Berthold's regime welled up. Keeping out of the light he ran over the roof of *Theatre* and vaulted onto the next ship, ready to snap the neck of whoever fancied his chances, bugger the consequences. He padded up to the bridge and pressed himself back into the shadows, waiting for the intruder to return.

A dish shattered on the planks and a blade flashed in the darkness. He ducked and the point slammed into the wood above his head. He grabbed his attacker's arm, yanked their hand free of the hilt and pushed them to the deck, his fist ready to pound their face into a pulp.

"Max."

Thaisa stared up at him, her expression creased in pain. He let her go and she staggered back, massaging her wrist.

"I could have killed you," he said, appalled.

For a second he saw the desperation in her eyes. Her gaze flicked to the hatch leading into the bowels of the ship.

"What's down there?" He wasn't going to waste time playing games. Thaisa stood up and moved between him and the entrance, her expression a hard mask.

"Our daughter."

Max stared at her thunderstruck. His first thought was that she lied, but why? She faced him down with such command that he found himself believing her.

"She's a child, we've kept her out of sight since we arrived at Interosseous," she continued. "I was taking her food."

He had no reply. With the easy confidence between them destroyed by the brutality of the last couple of weeks what could he say? If Thaisa and Vincent had a daughter she'd been well hidden from their guests, but that wasn't surprising. After all what were he, Abby and Berthold but two thugs and a liar? He stepped back.

"I trust you to keep this secret," said Thaisa, kneeling to pick up the shards of the bowl she'd dropped while trying to stab him. "Even from Vincent. He thinks her safe. If he realised you knew it would cause him yet more sorrow."

Max nodded. Thaisa's expression softened and he caught a brief glimpse of the amused resignation of old.

"We'll get you out of here, I promise, and Tafaline," he said.

"Thank you." said Thaisa. She looked about to say something but stopped. Sadly Max watched anger close her face again. She gestured for him to lead the way and together they returned to Theatre, parting without a word when they reached the entrance to the auditorium.

CHAPTER NINE

THREE DAYS LATER one of the actresses ran into the theatre claiming she'd spotted Tafaline escorted up to the tower by guards. They bombarded her with questions. She'd only seen her briefly and at a distance, limping head down between the soldiers, her hands bound in front of her, but she was convinced it was her friend. Max swapped glances with Abby whose eyes shone with renewed purpose. He doubted it meant good news for the prisoner but it made their plans easier. With Pell and Tafaline in one place they wouldn't have to waste time rescuing her from the penal colony. Shortly afterwards Berthold's men appeared and told the actors to get ready to perform the play before King Theuderic. After they left Max and Abby asked the actor-managers to prepare the boats as best they could without arousing suspicion. He hadn't spoken to Thaisa since the night she tried to stab him, keeping her secret locked in his mind. He saw the gratitude in her face, mingled with an expectation that discomfited him. In truth they'd no idea what awaited them in the skyscrapers or how they'd find Pell and Tafaline, let alone rescue them.

At midnight guards took them from the barges through the Glass City. Flaming torches lined both sides of the main path leading to the central building. Max and Abby walked in front. It wasn't ideal. He still didn't want her near him, but they were the only two in the troupe who stood a chance of defending the players if things got ugly.

"Where is everyone?" asked Abby. No-one else approached the towers and to Max the city looked no different. He saw a jumbled landscape of glass blocks lit by a few flickering lamps. *Perhaps they're already inside*, he wondered. They always had a full house for *The Gate of Light* in Metacarpi. He doubted it.

His misgivings increased when they arrived at the central building. A hundred-yard high passageway cut a hole in the concrete. Lumps of broken ceiling littered the floor. When he looked up he could just make out ragged holes in the roof revealing the decayed iron frame. *This is the palace of King Theuderic?*

"Twenty-seven guards," said Abby at his side. "If we had two shotguns apiece it'd be easy to blast our way free." Did she realise every time she spoke that way it felt like old times and so twisted the blade she'd planted in his heart even deeper? It was all he could do to stop himself rounding on her and telling her to fuck off.

"Don't do anything stupid," he managed to say. The tone of his voice shut her up but he knew her thoughts ran on the same tracks as his - they approached a trap and they'd have to fight their way out. He glanced at the actors, seeing wary surprise turn to anxiety tinged with terror. Thaisa shot him a look of baffled fear as one of the actresses started to cry.

"Ladies and Gentlemen, welcome," rang out Berthold's voice. The passage opened into a hall that lofted up three floors. Stairs dropped from unlit levels above to the ripped carpet at their feet. In the gloom Max made out scratched steel walls and doorways. If anything the dwelling of King Theuderic looked filthier and more ramshackle than the city. The place reeked of surreal evil. Was this Berthold's idea of a joke? The prince stood at the foot of the stairs surrounded by an armed squad. Max tensed. He heard Abby swearing quietly.

"If you would be so kind as to follow me, I will take you to the hall where you will perform for the King himself," Berthold bowed.

"Where's Tafaline?" said Vincent, looking round.

Berthold gave Max a *doesn't he ever shut up?* look.

"In good time. Impress King Theuderic and you will see her again tonight. You have my word."

Max waited for someone to state the obvious about Berthold's word but luckily the others were too cowed by the derelict scene around them to comment. Vincent opened his mouth but Thaisa elbowed him sharply before he dug himself deeper into trouble. Berthold and the guards led them up the stairs to the first floor. At the end of an unlit corridor more torches flanked a pair of wooden doors. They glistened red with fresh paint. Berthold paused.

"I've worked very hard to turn this into a theatre. I hope you appreciate my efforts. I should point out before we enter that King Theuderic is a little, shall we say, particular."

Here we go, thought Max. *Surprise surprise it's a big joke. There's a firing squad on the other side and you're all going to die.*

He stepped closer to Berthold, planning on using him as a shield when the bullets started flying, noticed sweat on the man's face and hesitated. *The prince is as frightened as the players. What scares him so much?*

"I would advise that you don't make eye contact. It's a little foible of his, charmingly eccentric but quite important. Perform the play to best of your ability and I know he will be delighted, utterly delighted, and you will receive rewards and more commissions than you have ever dreamed of."

Bugger commissions. After tonight these poor bastards are out of here. Nothing Berthold offered would induce them to stay. The prince opened the doors and invited them to enter. The second Vincent crossed the threshold he gave a shout of anger and rounded on their host.

"What is the meaning of this? Where is the audience?" His fists bunched into rocks despite the glares of the guards around them. Max realised the reason for his fury. *This is a joke, right?* At one end of a long hall he saw a rough stage of planks, canvas and boxes. The rest of the immense room was empty save for the debris and dirt littering the floor and a single metal seat in the middle. To Max's surprise it rose twice the height of an ordinary chair. Deep scratches marked the arms and back, as if someone had been using it to blunt an axe. Dirty carpet spread to the walls, torn in places and rucked up in others. A couple of the panels had fallen away to show the rusted shadows of the skyscraper's main fabric. Light came from torches and lanterns set around the edge of the auditorium.

"You will play to King Theuderic tonight," said Berthold, a warning note in his voice as he stepped back among the guards. "He is your audience. I suggest you get ready, you have an hour before the performance begins."

The soldiers moved to the edge of the room and extinguished the lamps until only the ones at the front of the makeshift stage remained lit, their smoky light obscuring the rest of the hall. Max peered into the darkness. He could just make out the steel chair in the centre. When Berthold first mentioned his King Theuderic Max assumed he either didn't exist or was another charlatan who'd given himself such a ridiculously grandiose title.

Perhaps he was a mad man who honestly believed he was Theuderic, Lord of the Machine Men, wearing a pan on his head and wrapping his limbs in foil to fool no-one but himself and his indulgent minions. Looking at that throne Max started to feel an unaccountable dread. He still refused to believe that the monarch of the Machine Men, architect of God's mind, was going to watch their pantomime from that seat but he wasn't sure he wanted to find out who or what their lone spectator really was.

After a few muttered words Vincent and Thaisa gathered the players together and gave them a whispered pep talk. Max was surprised to see the actors busy themselves ready for the performance. He didn't know what to make of their sudden focus. Either they'd acted in places just as disturbing or they simply didn't register the danger that clawed at Max's mind and soaked the small of his back in sweat. Abby sidled up to him.

"Some of those loose panels open onto crawlspaces. When the play is over, I reckon you and I use them to get into the rest of the building."

"Any idea where Pell and Tafaline might be?" asked Max. Abby shook her head. Their plan sounded increasingly stupid and without affection to buffer his irritation Max walked away fuming. *There's five miles of tower above us, over two thousand floors, she could be anywhere.* He'd go with Abby, of course he would, if only to stop her getting herself killed.

With ten minutes left Vincent helped the actors playing the family to gather round the little puddle of light that, in Abby's new theatre of the imagination, represented their hearth. Max, as Salabanco the foolish but faithful servant, got into position and struck his pose. Out of the corner of his eye he saw a room filled with shadows fringed with smoking lights. The universe fell silent save for the distant creaks and grumbles of an ancient building under siege from the ocean winds.

Berthold appeared on the other side of the makeshift footlights, his arms out at the sides, palms upwards - a priest making an offering to his own deity. Max saw his face. *He's scared, no, he's completely terrified.* Max's own stomach sank into his feet. He didn't know if the others realised. No, they were head down, getting themselves into character no doubt. Berthold turned. Somewhere in the depths of the building a gong sounded - a thunderous clash of metal muted by the distance into a single, thudding heartbeat as if the tower itself had woken up. Berthold dropped to one knee.

"Bow down, avert your eyes before the glorious majesty of Theuderic, Lord of the Machine Men and King of the Glass City," he shouted in a voice cracking on the edge of hysteria.

At first Max thought someone switched on an engine that spectacularly misfired and started to come apart even as its gears and pistons shuddered into life. A clattering came from the stairs outside, metal upon metal screeching and hammering as something either descended, or more likely, fell down the staircase. The door to the hall banged open, bringing with it a wind that stank of steel, brass, old leather and a sharp chemical stench that nipped at the back of Max's throat. On the stage behind him he detected a whimper. The mechanical cacophony separated out into footsteps. *Whatever it is, it walks on legs, though God knows how many,* thought Max, fighting terror.

The newcomer stopped and in the moments of silence that followed Max heard breathing, a wheezy, laboured bellows of a sound that reminded him of someone sobbing in pain and exertion after a race. Steps again, this time closer. A bunch of shapes slammed into the planks on the edge of the stage and Max found himself looking at a fist bigger than his own head. Four fingers and a thumb tipped with claws like curved knives gouged splinters out of the boards. Now he knew what caused those deep scratches in the chair. Canvas wrapped round the hand in a rough imitation of skin, bound to the articulated joints with wire. It was a clumsy and futile attempt to give a semblance of humanity to that monstrous limb. The sharp edges underneath had ripped the cloth and it hung in tatters from the machine skeleton. One finger tapped the wood. *It's thinking.* He wanted to look up, but judging by Berthold's posture anyone with any sense right now kept their eyes fixed on the floor.

The ragged claws vanished and the stomping din of machinery moved back into the centre of the room. A sound like a truckload of old pans emptied into a skip rang through the darkness.

"Begin the play."

Max jumped. It was the voice of a giant broken clock, deep and resonant, believably human but filtered through a storm of cogs, chains, spindles, weights, cylinders, pistons and polluted diesel. *The command of King Theuderic, Lord of the Machine Men.* Of course it wasn't. This bore as much relation to a real Machine Man as a child with a wooden sword did to a General from the Empire of the Ear, but what in the name of God was it? Vincent, playing the narrator and sounding slightly strangled by nerves, thundered out the opening speech behind Max and the play began.

Max did the best he could, given the circumstances. As his role largely consisted of pulling faces, tittering and falling over he could ad-lib his way through the times when fear blotted the script from his mind. The other players struggled, forgetting lines and entrances, especially when the story called for them to peer out into the auditorium, pretending to search the empty universe for the light of the door to the new cosmos. He glimpsed their expressions afterwards as they exchanged panicked, tearful glances. *What in God's name is sitting in that chair?* He felt particularly sorry for the actor playing the mad King of Men in his yellow tattered robes. What if this monstrous Theuderic recognised himself in that capering tyrant? The consequences didn't bear thinking about. Judging by the actor's impressive delivery he'd decided to go all out, realising if he was to die for his impudence he might as well turn in the performance of his career.

As he navigated the stage Max tried to catch glimpses of the room. It was impossible. The smoky lamps created an orange wall obscuring the void beyond the footlights. Once, after a comic fall, he lay on his side and peered between two hissing storm lanterns. He could just make out the chair and it looked as if someone sat in it. The back sprouted a jagged oval that might have been a head as big as his own torso, but then an actor jabbed him with a cardboard spear and on cue he jumped up and ran around the platform in circles flapping his hands and whimpering, barely needing to act. He didn't get another chance to see Theuderic. Vincent spoke the final words of the play and before the players could take a bow the hammering din of metal retreating up the stairs outside told Max their audience had departed.

Berthold came to the front of the stage. He looked drained. Sweat ran down his grey face as he managed a weak smile. Max saw utter relief in the man's eyes.

"King Theuderic was enchanted by your play. It was a delight to the senses that lifted him out of the dreary day-to-day grind of lordship and transported him to a universe of wonder. He sends you his undying admiration and thanks."

"It didn't say anything," said Vincent.

Berthold winced at the word *it*. Thaisa elbowed Vincent so hard he glared at her and rubbed his side. She gave Berthold a sweet smile.

"Thank you, we are honoured."

Max suspected the fact they still lived meant that Theuderic had enjoyed the performance. Berthold clapped his hands and beckoned the guards to help the actors gather the few props they'd brought. Several of the players huddled in knots, whispering, crying and comforting each other. Thaisa caught Max's eye and nodded. She started to argue with Berthold and his men, buying them time. Abby sidled up to Max and pointed towards a stack of broken tables in the corner of the room. *Here we go, our last adventure together. After this I climb the tower and you return to your new theatre.* Whatever had led to this and whatever happened next, he'd make sure whoever they encountered, monstrous or human, remembered Max Ocel and Abby Fabrice for the remainder of their sorry lives.

They moved into the shadows at the back of the stage. Abby scampered along the wall to a loose panel, lifted it up and ducked inside. Max saw a narrow corridor running between the walls. At the end they emerged into a wide passageway snaking through the tower. Broken doors and archways on either side opened onto spaces and halls untouched for years. Dust lay on the floor and drifted through the pale light slanting from the few illumination panels still working. A silence pervaded the landscape, made dreadful by the stark contrast between the hush they padded through now and the cacophony of Theuderic's arrival at the play. Max longed to ask Abby what she thought the creature really was but she was locked in stalking mode, running ahead in loping strides, her gaze sweeping their surroundings for clues or foes. It hurt to watch her so he concentrated on covering his own lines of sight.

They found another set of stairs in an alcove - crumbling stone covered in dust. Max knew they needed to get a sense of the geography of the upper floors. He hoped that the random scattering of halls they'd seen so far gave way to order in the higher levels. They hunted for signs of habitation, anything that might lead them to the imprisoned women. On the next four landings Abby scouted a few yards down the corridors before returning, shaking her head. Max grew exasperated. It wouldn't take long for Berthold to notice their absence.

She stopped and he almost collided with her. They stood on an unlit landing, just inside the entrance to a red-walled corridor stretching away on either side. The floor was pitted concrete dotted here and there with cracks and holes exposing the rusted frame beneath. Abby pointed halfway down the passageway to where the light from a narrow lantern fell across the plaster. From this angle Max could make out a network of marks covering the surface. What was Abby doing now? She paced up to the wall and stared at the pattern. Her hand went up to her mouth. *Nothing fazes Abby*, thought Max. *What is she looking at?* His heart thundered against his ribs.

It must have been gouged a hundred times in letters ranging from two foot high to barely an inch. Max realised the claws that carved chunks out of a solid metal chair could write with an intelligent dexterity he'd only seen in the finest calligraphy. *Pain* - the word repeated again and again - *pain pain pain pain pain*. In many places new iterations overlaid old scratches. Abby shot him a look. *What is this creature?* Was it a threat - sadistic graffiti for the walls of a dungeon or a tyrant's castle, or a plea for help?

"They're here somewhere," whispered Abby. "This is his lair."

He wished she didn't sound so excited. They crept through the inner sanctum of a mechanical beast twice the size of a man and ruler of a kingdom founded on fear and oppression. The continuation of that single word in a floor to ceiling mural of gouges, scratches and finely etched lines did nothing to lighten Max's mood. *You really have excelled yourself this time Abby. If we meet this thing we are royally fucked.* Every cell in Max's body tugged him back down the passage, pleading with him to run to the relative safety of the barges. They'd be missed by now, the guards searching for them, no doubt under Berthold's command. *I can't return,* he thought. *If the transit station is at the top of these towers I have to go further in, further up.* And he'd have to do it without Abby, God help him. He spotted her peering round the corner. She waved and he forced himself to follow. The passageway jack-knifed towards the centre of the skyscraper. A few yards in he found the first of hundreds of tiny lanterns ranged at the bottom of the walls, leading to a doorway half way along the corridor. Abby approached it, keeping as close to the shadows as possible. Max trailed after her, trying not to read the word that yelled at him from both sides - *pain pain pain pain.*

It opened onto a low ceilinged hall decorated to look like a forest. Max saw fading wallpaper covered in grotesque paintings of flowers interwoven with strange beasts and organic machines flowing into each other in a storm of amorphous beauty. The murals stretched up to the roof where they turned into three-dimensional plaster sculptures. Snakes, branches, tentacles, cables, hair, fronds, weeds and blossoms whirled over the ceiling in a confusion of lines that made him think of Pell's cat's cradle.

The explosion of exotic imagery in the middle of a wilderness of concrete decay took Max's breath away. He felt Abby's hand grab his forearm as she forgot herself in the wonder of the moment and he didn't care. Under that writhing ceiling the room was filled with sculptures, strange machines, delicately wrought chairs, vases as tall as a man, impossibly fine carvings and a thousand other artefacts, each one a unique piece of stunning art.

Once Max and Abby had spent their days climbing down wormholes drilled into the singularity upon which God lay. They stole rare treasures from deep time, from ages when the skies of ancient worlds still blazed with stars. They sold them to the rich sybarites and lotus eaters of Metacarpi. Sometimes they came across exquisite works of art they longed to keep for themselves and for a while hoarded one or two. Max remembered a coiled serpent arm band Abby wore for six months, the musical instruments she could never master. But in the end they got rid of them, not merely for greed but because a seductive aura radiated from those billion-year old treasures, engendering desires and obsessions. They curled up in his mind, insinuating a thread of cruel passion that weighed him down and tugged his thoughts in directions he didn't want to go. He rarely regretted selling his booty and was even less surprised to hear of the murders and betrayals amongst those who took it off his hands.

Looking at this hoard of alien wonders he sensed the old siren call. To possess even one of these treasures - that chair carved from blue crystal as fine as hair, the jewel-studded shield humming quietly to itself, the book as large as a man dripping glowing water onto the floor beneath its stand - would threaten his sanity.

"It's a storehouse. Whoever built this place planned to take treasures from the old universe into the new. They must have been Time Scavengers like us," said Abby.

He doubted Berthold and the creature Theuderic were responsible for this collection. He guessed they found it long after the original inhabitants abandoned the tower. Max looked at the floor. A wide path wound between the artefacts and it bore the unmistakeable scars of Theuderic's claws. *This is his inner sanctum. He lives among this stolen treasure - a demon of old protecting his hoard.* He traced the route to a heap of tapestries bulking up in the half light. *Odd.* Compared to the meticulous placing of the other treasures, each in its own space with its own lamp to pick out its beauty, the weavings appeared to be laundry tossed aside. On one he could just make out a line of girls' faces stitched in an alien thread that glowed with a colour he didn't recognise.

The mound of tapestries shifted. Max felt as if someone whipped the bones out of his legs. Abby's grip on his arm became a sharp-nailed vice. The voice, that voice, rolled across the room.

"Berthold, is that you?"

And then the noise followed, the mind-splitting sound of an immense clock being pounded into fragments by a demented steam hammer and the fake Theuderic rose to his feet barely yards from where they stood.

CHAPTER TEN

THEY ALMOST MADE it. Theuderic stood with his back to them. Max saw the silhouette of a massive torso twisted out of machinery standing on two splayed ape-legs, each a cluster of pistons. The creature hadn't seen them and his movements looked confused, tired, as if he'd just woken. They turned and Abby brushed against the vase.

It rose shoulder height from the floor - a tulip head of rare crystal teased out so fine the edges faded into nothing like dissipating mist. She clipped it with her nail and it rang, the faint ting growing to become a peal of music so exquisite Max felt his mouth drop open and tears spring to his eyes. An instant later Theuderic turned round and the machine racket of his stamping feet drowned out the vase. Abby yanked Max away and they ran for their lives down the red-walled corridor.

"BERTHOLD!" bellowed the creature behind them.

They took the stairs three at a time. The cacophony pursuing them made it impossible to tell whether they'd escaped or not. The whole staircase shuddered and a hail of concrete fragments and dust showered over them as they stumbled across the next landing. *He's trying to squeeze through the doors.* Another pounding collision told him the monster had failed. Maybe they still had a chance.

They didn't. At least a dozen guards waited for them at the bottom of the stairs, shotguns and a couple of rifles aimed at their heads. Abby ducked to the left but more of the enemy emerged from the doorways on all sides. Max cursed. They'd been so stupid to enter the tower unarmed. Even if they'd carried guns they'd have stood no chance against the ring of thirty men and women staring at them in loathing and disbelief. Above them the constant iron-foundry cacophony of Theuderic's passage echoed through the building, punctuated by incessant broken-clock yells for Berthold. Max saw fear twitching in the soldiers' faces. He realised it only needed one false move for the pair of them to get shot.

Berthold stepped into the circle. He glared at the intruders with an expression of fury and grim purpose that took Max by surprise.

"Ten of you, take her to my rooms and keep her quiet," he snapped. "I said ten of you, you morons," he added when four ended up groaning on the floor clutching balls, jaws and stomachs. Abby shot Max a look of desperate appeal. He shook his head. He guessed Berthold wanted her out of the way when Theuderic arrived and that was probably no bad thing. Tears spilled from her eyes as they grabbed her arms. *She thinks this is the moment she sees me die.* They dragged her away wriggling and kicking, before they had a chance to say goodbye. Berthold stepped up to Max and slapped him across the face, a feeble blow but the mere fact he'd done it astonished Max.

"You've ruined everything. I had it all planned, Pell, the players, Abby, you. It would have worked." He turned to the guards. "Bring him to the theatre."

They manhandled Max back to the hall and forced him to his knees between the steel chair and the stage.

"If anything happens to Abby…" Max started to say. A rifle butt smacked into the back of his head and the universe lit up with pain. Berthold yanked his face up by the hair.

"Not a word," he stuck a trembling finger in front of his eyes. "Not a word if you want any of us to get through this."

Was Berthold trying to save him? Why? He'd assumed he was a sacrifice to Theuderic's rage but clearly the Prince of the Glass City had other plans. Half an hour passed and the searing pain in the back of his head faded to a dull ache. Berthold grew impatient, pacing back and forth in front of the stage, muttering to himself. *The creature hasn't gone to Berthold's rooms, has he?* Max thought. *Gone to get Abby?*

"Down, all down," yelled Berthold as something kicked open the doors behind them and came roaring into the room like a runaway tram. It stomped past Max, the fury of its passage kicking up clouds of dust, fragments of stone and shreds of faded carpet. Theuderic stepped up onto the stage. It groaned and splintered under his weight.

"You think everything and everyone you own is safe from me," bellowed the voice.

Max looked up and uncontrollable terror swept over him in waves. He cried out and started forward but half a dozen guards brought him to his knees, bending his arms back to force his head down. He strained to look at the monster, catching a brief impression of warped cages of metal wrapped over iron limbs as thick as his own body, of a hideous face of shining copper, glass and tattered canvas. It was his first full glimpse of the demon that called itself Theuderic, Lord of the Machine Men, but he didn't care. His gaze locked on the woman who struggled in Theuderic's claw, her back towards him and her insane cloud of red hair shimmering in the lamplight as he held her up by the neck. Her legs kicked frantically as the huge fingers choked out her life. Max raved and twisted. Beside him Berthold shouted for Theuderic to stop.

The creature cocked his head as if considering what to do next. In three swift movements he disembowelled his captive with his other claw. A torrent of blood and entrails splattered across the stage where, a few hours ago, Max and Abby had re-enacted a children's pantomime. The monster lifted his victim even higher and flung her onto the steaming mess.

In that instant Max went insane. He roared out all his madness, hatred and sorrow in one desperate, hopeless shriek. He barely registered Theuderic stumbling down on one knee, his bloody claws clutching his head, or the guards nearest to him throwing up, one falling in a heap as he spasmed his way through a fit. Max wanted to die there and then, to roll up this worthless universe and all its empty, evil history into a shroud to cover him as he fell into nothingness. But death didn't come, only a horrible silence lasting for aeons in which he realised he had to look at Abby one last time. It was the hardest thing he'd ever done but he opened his eyes. She faced him, curled up on her side, her stomach a ruined mess. Her open, dead eyes stared into his. By her feet the red hair, now soaked in blood, lay in a soggy bundle. Despite himself Max gave an exhausted laugh of sheer relief that would haunt him with guilt for years. Tafaline the actress. In his malevolence Theuderic had taken a wig stolen from the actors and stuck it on her head to mock him. No, not him. He remembered the anxiety on Berthold's face when he'd sent Abby away. *He's taunting Berthold, he knows he wants her.*

"That was unnecessary," muttered Berthold as he stared down at the carpet. Theuderic lowered his claws and looked around in confusion. He clambered to his feet and turned his attention to Max and the prince.

"No, very necessary, Berthold." Max detected pain in the creature's voice. Theuderic spoke with the impatience of the suffering. He remembered the murals above, carved from that single word.

"This man who stole into my room, and his woman, tell me again why they should live," said Theuderic. Iron feet slammed into the floor in front of Max. A claw the size of an axe blade touched him under the chin, forcing him to look up. He found himself staring into a filthy sheet of canvas fringed with copper wire and punctured by holes. A light glittered on the other side - the reflection of an eye perhaps. He remembered the face he'd glimpsed at the tower window through Thaisa's binoculars. Now it was as big as a cabinet, reeking of chemicals and filled with a cold, petulant rage.

"He will kill the Brittle Hag for us. He is a great fighter, I've watched him slaughter hundreds with ease. He is brave, cunning and clever and he knows the strategy and the tactics to rid ourselves of that monster and her Abhumans once and for all," said Berthold with careful fury. The claw retreated. Max felt blood trickling down his neck.

"Will he, indeed? And how do you intend to make him do this?" asked Theuderic, clambering back onto the platform. One foot kicked Tafaline's body aside like a heap of bloody rags. Anger left a burning taste in Max's mouth.

"His woman. He will do as we tell him and defeat the Brittle Hag as long as we keep her safe," said Berthold.

Theuderic laughed, a bizarre sound that made Max think of half a dozen misfiring generators.

"Is that so?" he yelled. Max could have sworn he detected almost-human sarcasm in the creature's voice. "Well Berthold, I have a better idea. This man and you will go into the realm of the Brittle Hag together and you will defeat her and bring me her head."

Berthold jumped to his feet and strode towards the stage. Max couldn't believe his eyes. Everyone else cowered in terror but not the Prince of the Glass City. He stood before Theuderic, fists clenched at his sides,

"This isn't what we agreed, it isn't how it's supposed to be," he said. The creature stamped to the edge of the stage, splashing blood onto the floor around Berthold. Max saw the man spasm in fear even as he held his ground.

"I brought this man and the Philosopher here to aid the city, to help you create the greatest kingdom in God's Forearm."

Copper and steel fists slammed into the platform, shattering the planks and sending splinters arcing through the air,

"I don't need your help!" Theuderic bellowed. His shoulders sagged, his monstrous head slumping onto the canvas skin carelessly woven through the cage that held the churning engine of his body. When he spoke Max sensed the pain again, stronger this time, his words tinged with a weary desperation. *What in God's name are you, what did you used to be?*

"I'm tired of waiting, tired of your lies. You and this man will journey to the kingdom of the Brittle Hag and bring me her head, or I will do this to all your precious women, here and on those boats." He gestured with a bloody claw at the corpse. He stepped from the stage and limped through the hall. Max heard his feet crash on the stairs.

They stepped out of the tower into the dawn. Rain trailed across the glass blocks. Max stared at the universe anew. He'd thought Abby dead. For a few seconds she'd been torn from him, forever wiped away by a monster seeking to prove a point. A moment later she was back, alive, insane, a pain in the arse, all defiant eyes and gobby attitude. Now you see her now you don't, as simple as that. She could be snatched from him like a toy grabbed out of a child's hands. *That's how she sees me. Machine men will yank me out of her life as that monster took her from me the second I fell for his charade.* When she'd split up with him on the barge he'd felt so helpless and alone but that was nothing compared to the instant of utterly empty devastation when he believed her gone forever.

Anger swept over him again. He watched Berthold striding ahead. His jaunty lope had an edge of hysteria to it and his hands flexed spasmodically. Grinding fury welled up in Max's stomach. The guards stumbled along on either side, tiredness and wooden despair stamped on their faces. Berthold stopped and everyone else halted. Max walked towards him, wondering how far he'd get before the others realised what he was planning and clubbed him to the floor. Half of him desperately wanted to find out what in God's name that monster was, half of him burned with the urge to snap the other man's neck.

"That wasn't meant to happen," said Berthold, his voice choked with tears. "He wasn't supposed to do that."

He ripped a helpless woman apart with his claws and scattered her entrails over the stage. What did Berthold expect? Did he think he had a hold over that thing?

Theuderic was clearly insane, ruling this city through terror. Max faltered. Killing Berthold would achieve nothing and at the moment the man was his only link to Abby and Pell.

"If anything happens…" he said.

"It won't," said Berthold, a little too desperately for Max's liking. Without thinking the man glanced up at the tower and Max followed his gaze to where the rain-clouds encircled the building.

"He won't go above the fiftieth floor," said Berthold. So now Max knew Abby and Pell were in the upper reaches of the skyscraper. The prince looked around him. The guards waited as water from gutters above cascaded onto the concrete and flung whorls of spray from the roofs beyond. He stepped up to Max.

"The only way to save them is to attack the Brittle Hag. Any victory will assuage his anger, give us the time we need," he whispered. *Time for what? Time to escape?* "You've got to help me Max, please."

The self-deluded idiot thought he had a pact with that insane creature. *All those plans of turning this place into a thriving city are just desperate fantasies you've carved out of your dreams. Your soul's in hock to that demon in the tower.* Berthold was bound to the King of the Glass City in some way but he wasn't merely the being's slave, otherwise why return to this shit hole? Why didn't he stay in Interosseous or take Pell south to more civilised realms? Why did he come back to this island with a Philosopher, mercenaries and a bunch of actors? He saw more than terror in Berthold's face, a sadness lurked behind the man's eyes, clutching him to this wretched island as surely as the claws of Theuderic himself.

"We go to the shores of the ocean, hide ourselves," said Berthold, keeping his voice low so only Max caught his words. "Kill a couple of the Abhumans and bring their heads back. That'll placate him."

"What's to stop him slaughtering anyone else while we're away?" asked Max. He wanted to ask what the creature really was but doubted he'd get any sense while they stood in earshot of the guards.

"He won't," said Berthold. "He's made his point."

This is madness, thought Max. But surrounded by an armed escort what choice did he have? He'd have to battle the agonising fear for Abby and wait until he could get his hands on a weapon and back into the tower. Fighting now would achieve nothing but an ugly, futile death. He figured Berthold was the key. If he understood the bizarre relationship between him and Theuderic it might give him the advantage he needed. He mastered himself with difficulty. Berthold told the guards to bring him to the docks. The rain had stopped by the time they'd descended to a wharf encompassed by twenty-block high barriers of glass. The containers in the lower half were part-filled with a black liquid that left crusted stains on the inside of the walls.

Berthold and the leader of the squad argued while the others watched. Max guessed they were deciding who'd accompany them to the realm of the Brittle Hag. It turned into a struggle between fear of the Abhumans and Theuderic's retribution. At one point the commander drew a pistol and shot a soldier in the face. She toppled into the water and sank out of sight. Even that didn't clinch the argument and in the end Berthold returned with only eight soldiers in tow. Max saw traces of defiant bravery in the eyes of some, resigned horror in most. Their weapons had seen better days and he doubted some of the guns could fire. Berthold attempted a commanding smile but God knew who it was for. Max realised the full truth. *That monster's condemned us to death in a fit of pique. Right now he thinks no more of you than he does of these wretches.* He remembered the map in the meeting room and the pompous soldier pushing his blocks and statues over the toy landscape, talking of attacks and counterattacks, supply lines and matèriel. This was the reality of the Glass City's forces - a handful of desperate, ill-armed thugs, a dandy and himself.

"Ok," said Max. "Let's do it." He'd help Berthold slaughter a couple of those grey-furred creatures if it would put a weapon in his hand and get him back to the city. They boarded a boat at the end of a jetty, coaxed the engine to life and headed for the open sea. The glass blocks gave way to tumbled mounds of empty containers then heaps of wood, broken glass and iron. The guards sat on the benches, cold faces devoid of any emotion, infected with the same resignation he'd seen in everyone save Berthold and Theuderic himself. How had they come to this? Isolation, subsistence living in a monotonous world, a hideous enemy prowling its borders and an unending stream of outrageous lies building fiction upon fiction. He suspected they acquiesced because they'd lost hope of any other choice. They'd march to their own executions. Did they believe they were part of a glorious attack on the Brittle Hag or underneath it all did they realise the truth?

Max sat opposite Berthold. The man's hands were jammed between his knees to keep them from shaking. He stared at his boots.

"Who is that creature in the tower?" asked Max. Far away from the city and out of hearing of the others he hoped to try and tease some truth out of Prince Berthold.

"He is Theuderic, Lord of the Machine Men," came the answer.

"No he's not, what is he?"

Berthold continued to stare at the floor. He seemed to be struggling with himself. Max waited. If he used force the guards would stop him and he'd need this fool's co-operation to rescue Abby. Berthold shook his head.

The Glass City receded in the mist. The ocean surged and ebbed, waves slapping against the sides of the boat, casting spray into the faces of the men and women who sat in lines on either side of the vessel. *Forget Theuderic, if you can't destroy him, get past him - up the tower beyond the fiftieth floor. But first you have to return alive.*

"Tell me about the Brittle Hag."

Berthold looked up.

"It's a rival Machine Man. It wants to control the Glass City, defeat Theuderic so its filthy creatures can enjoy his treasures and bounty," said Berthold as if the answer was self-evident. It sounded like a response from a child's book of propaganda.

"No it's not," said Max, fighting to keep his temper. "There are no Machine Men out here. Whatever these beings are they have nothing to do with the real Theuderic and his court in the Head of God. Pell said she spotted a hole in the universe where the Brittle Hag stood."

Berthold looked as if Max had slapped him.

"You saw the Brittle Hag, what did she look like?" His answer stunned Max. *You said you'd seen her when I asked if she was a giant.*

"How many battles against the Brittle Hag have you taken part in?" he asked. Berthold said nothing.

"How many battles have there been?" he persisted. Berthold's eyes said it all. Max almost laughed out loud. Of course, he'd been blind not to realise from the beginning when Berthold gave that absurd speech about personally defeating the Brittle Hag or during the preposterous lectures in the re-education room.

"God almighty," said Max. "There's no war is there? All that bullshit in the city, all those meetings and maps and strategies - it's in your heads. You hide on your island and tell each other fairy stories to frighten yourselves into obedience."

"I am Prince Berthold," said the man loudly so the others could hear. "I am charged with taking the war to the kingdom of the Brittle Hag."

"Oh fuck off." The man was ridiculous. Max stared beyond the prow of the boat at the endless sea, alternately running plans through his head and trying to make sense of this realm. He remembered how his own father had imprisoned the giant Bassandis, thinking him a weapon he could bend to his will in defence of the city. Was this the same? Had the inhabitants of the Glass City and the Abhumans formed pacts with Theuderic and the Brittle Hag because they were powerful creatures who could protect them in the hostile labyrinth of the Forearm? If so Berthold's guardian monster was out of control and as much a threat to his own people as to their enemies, real or imaginary. Beside him Berthold had lapsed back into his self-absorbed misery.

"Ok," said Max at last. "I'll help you get a couple of Abhuman heads to Theuderic if you take me, Abby and Pell to the transit station."

Berthold looked at him with a mix of hope and gratitude. He nodded.

Night fell. Max managed to snatch a few hours of sleep before a shout woke him from uncertain dreams. The air ahead looked darker. In an hour it resolved itself into the wall of the cavern. Max couldn't see any landing point. Waves hammered against glistening sheets of metal and tumbled reefs of rubble and machinery at the base of the cliff. The boats turned to follow the line of the shore. At last the precipice gave way to a beach leading towards a range of distant hills. They drove into the shallows and Max climbed out. To his surprise the sand was made of millions of minuscule machine components. He reached down and lifted up a palm full of cogs, screws, scraps of steel and iron, beads, chains and finely tooled springs, none larger than his little finger nail. He stared at his hand in wonder. What ancient machines cast their remnants here? How long did it take the ocean to build this strand from the guts of countless dead engines? He looked around, wondering if they were the first humans ever to tread this ground. Most likely, if the so-called war with the Brittle Hag was nothing but a lie.

CHAPTER ELEVEN

AS SOON AS the squad disembarked two set off at a slow run. Berthold swore and picked up a rusty carbine. The gun cracked and one of the deserters sprawled over the metal sand. She crawled after her companion on hands and knees but he didn't even break stride as he left her wounded on the dunes. After a few yards she gave a hopeless cry and collapsed. She didn't move again. Berthold aimed at the other deserter but Max grabbed the barrel.

"You're wasting bullets. Let him go. If he's fleeing now, he'd be no use in a battle." He confronted the others. "Any more?" Most flinched and averted their gaze, a couple glowered in sullen defiance, hefting long knives in their fists. "You're with us," Max told them. "The rest stay behind and keep together."

That was the extent of his strategy. Max realised Berthold genuinely believed he was an expert at fighting but his understanding of combat stemmed from years of rough and ready experience at one-to-one. He had half a dozen tricks up his sleeve, most of them gleaned from Abby, and a rudimentary grasp of tactics. Everything else came from shrieking panic whose guiding principle was to stab, shoot or clout the bastard as hard as he could in the initial attack so it wouldn't rise again.

They trudged over the strand. After three hours it changed to paper-coloured scrub stretching over endless rolling hills. He couldn't see any other vegetation or sign of a settlement. They could be anywhere, dumped on a shore surrounded by hundreds of miles of monochrome nothing. He tried to coax information from Berthold. How did the Abhumans fight? Did they hunt in packs? Did they have any weapons besides those sooty talons? Evasive mutterings showed the man hadn't a clue. Max suspected that the Abhuman Vincent shot on the boat was the first Berthold had ever encountered and all his histrionic terror originated in picture books and stories. He noticed the sky getting darker as the cavern roof angled down to meet them. The landscape turned into a vast slot, the curving terrain below mirrored by the jumbled angles and blocks hanging in the vault above. It felt as if he entered a trap about to slam shut.

They crested a ridge and Max found himself looking at a stone road winding through a steep valley. Far below pale figures manhandled a cart over its uneven surface, the larger of the pair pulling the shafts while the other pushed the solid wooden wheels. There was no mistaking those spindly limbs and rectangular skulls - Abhumans. Max dropped into the grass. Berthold and the men stared at him until he hissed for them to hide. Against the skyline they'd be spotted. After the guards shuffled onto their bellies Max focussed his attention on the scene below, cursing the idiots he'd been lumbered with. The Abhumans had displayed intelligence when they raided the barges. Here was more proof they weren't merely scavenging beasts. Was he watching draft animals or slaves? He doubted it. As they pulled and heaved the load of white tubers over the cobbles it dawned on Max that he was in the presence of a pair of farmers. *They're taking their crops home*, he thought. *This isn't a monstrous horde prowling the edge of civilisation. Pell was right. They're just more people surviving in the darkness.* He remembered the one Vincent killed pleading for help. Guilt soured his stomach. He'd promised to return with severed heads for that monster in the Glass City, killing innocents to humour a tyrant's whim. There had to be another way. He wasn't going to spill more blood to satiate the petulant wishes of a malfunctioning clock.

Gunfire rang out from bushes beside him. *What in God's name?* The lead Abhuman keeled over as the second ran to its aid on all fours. A louder volley burst around Max. He jumped to his feet and shouted for the soldiers to stop firing. Had they no idea what they were doing? God knew how many more of those things lurked in this shadowed world. Most ceased, though a fat bearded lieutenant got off a final round before Max kicked the weapon out of his grip and punched him in the face. *Ill-disciplined cretins.* Berthold cried out. Max watched the remaining Abhuman race into the distance at a frightening speed. He tracked it in his sights but the bolt struck an empty cartridge. The fugitive disappeared over a distant crest. Every other bullet had missed, peppering the wagon with holes. Max reckoned they had minutes at best. He snatched a knife from a soldier and pelted down the slope. One would have to do, if they managed to leave alive.

The Abhuman lay tangled in its harness, the lower abdomen a tarry mess. At least he wouldn't have to put it out of its misery. To his surprise Berthold stood next to him, staring at the body with an expression of terrified disgust. Everyone else had vanished, craven bastards racing back to the boats no doubt. Max went about his grisly business. Cutting through the mass of compacted bone, sinew and muscle proved exhausting, pitiful labour. In the end he thrust the dripping trophy at Berthold who looked ready to throw up.

"There's your prize," he said. "We need to get away before the whole tribe appears."

He stooped to retrieve the blade. Something wet and furry hit him and he fell, tangling with the stiffening corpse of the dead creature. He struggled upright, wiping sticky gore out of his eyes to see Berthold sprinting up the hill, the head dangling from his hand like a bag of groceries. The treacherous shit had clubbed him with it. He became aware of a hissing roar. A grey wave filled with black claws boiled along the gully towards him.

Max woke with a splitting headache inside an iron cube. He remembered Berthold cresting the rise, arms and legs pumping like a pantomime villain as he raced back towards the boat. If Max ever got his hands on the bastard's throat he'd wring his perfumed neck. He imagined the prince waving the head in front of Theuderic, claiming his rights over Pell and Abby. *Good luck with that, you deluded moron.*

The Abhumans had swarmed him and he'd passed out, suffocated in a boiling maelstrom of reeking fur. At least they hadn't slaughtered him in revenge. They clearly had another punishment in mind within this cold, empty cell. He looked at his surroundings. The only light came from a square panel in the floor. Despite the brightness a grainy darkness seethed at the periphery of his vision. It reminded him of the walls of Ragaleis's house in the Wasteland north of Metacarpi. It leached the radiance from the air so that only a fitful dome of illumination remained in the middle of the room.

Something was wrong, seriously wrong. Terror clawed at Max's mind. He felt as if he sat on thin paper suspended over chaos. He scrabbled at the ground, battling his fear. His nails skittered over rusted plates, ancient and unyielding. The floor tilted, sloping towards the far corner. This was it, the sentence for murder in this unholy, iron world. Max jammed his palms and feet against the metal to stop himself sliding into whatever pit opened in the blackness. *But I'm not falling*, he realised, even though the surface under him tipped at an impossible angle. By rights he should have tumbled down the slope but his body stayed fixed as if he sprawled on a level plane.

The corner bellied out as though reality floated around a transparent sphere. In the centre he saw a shadow gliding towards him, approaching from a direction that didn't exist. It brought with it a hideous wind from regions man had never seen and was never meant to see. He shut his eyes and whimpered, begging for a quick death.

He sensed a presence in the room, the sound of its breathing. No, that wasn't it - it was as if the universe flexed and contracted around another, impossible mind, inhaling and exhaling space and time in the same way he dragged air into his own lungs in short, desperate pants. After an age he summoned up the courage to open his eyes.

His first impression was of a figure standing on the periphery of the light. He recognised the sculpture he'd spotted on the gantry when they arrived at the ocean - the Brittle Hag, leader of the Abhumans. Pell saw a hole in the universe that terrified even her, and it was in the corner of this room. Max sat on the edge facing a monstrous gatekeeper the hidden corners of creation had spat into the realms of humanity. *We killed Abhumans, your children*. What hope remained for him now? He waited for death, unable to tear his eyes away from the jumble of curved shards forming the creature's body.

The Brittle Hag moved, or rather reality clicked through a series of still tableaux, each showing the monster a step nearer to the middle of the room. Max heard a sound like shattering bones, *crack crack crack*, as each image superseded the last. The final one showed the creature in the centre of the glowing panel. She'd dragged the distortion sphere with her and Max sat on a floor that tilted at almost ninety degrees. A line of twisted metal pointed to the space next to his left side. Was it an arm? Did this thing even have limbs? He thought he could see thinner shreds of darkness that could have been fingers. Something thrust talons into his mind, wrenching open a hole in his consciousness. Max shrieked, hammering at his skull with his fists as inhuman ideas ricocheted through his brain. Five of them coalesced into approximations of human words.

"Who is that beside you?"

It was agony. Thoughts never designed for human minds crammed into his head. The phrase repeated itself. As he curled up on that absurdly tilted floor, begging the universe to slaughter him there and then, he sensed them morphing into gentler forms.

"Who is that beside you?"

They had a timbre now, slow and ancient, the voice Time itself might use. He still waited for death but it didn't come, just the same question repeated, and each time the pain was less as if his wounded mind reformed around the alien thoughts like a body enfolding bullets embedded too deep for a surgeon to extract.

"Who is that beside you?"

Max opened his eyes and sat up. Whatever this thing was it hadn't killed him yet and it spoke to him. That gave him hope. He wrenched his eyes away and looked to his left. Nothing, only grainy darkness filling the corners of the room. He summoned up his courage.

"There's no one there."

"Someone walks next to you," came the reply. Max didn't know what to say. When he looked at the Brittle Hag her shape formed and reformed like an image on water. Sometimes parts of her vanished into the shadows, other times new limbs and structures loomed around her as if the figure he saw was merely part of a vaster creature hidden somewhere beyond the light, and each time it shifted position it revealed more of its monstrous form.

"What does it look like?" asked Max.

"He has white hair."

He sat, unable to move, for what felt like hours. The Brittle Hag hadn't killed him but he wasn't sure whether this was worse. What in God's name did she see? He'd no doubt it was Bassandis she pointed at - what else fitted the description? Max wanted to look to his left but dread kept his gaze fixed on the tangled mess of shadows. He closed his eyes and listened to his mind. Nothing. He tried to remember the warm room the giant Ragaleis had built from his thoughts - the carpet by the fire where he and his mother taught the pale stranger what it was to be human. He found the memories but they were as indistinct and abstract as his other recollections. They had none of the sharp reality of the hallucinations the giants created. He summoned up the courage to look to his side. Nothing, just grainy shadows falling across iron.

"Bassandis?"

Despite the size of the room his voice carried an echo that suggested vaster spaces beyond the light. Silence. The last time he'd met a giant was on the journey from the ruins of Metacarpi to the Thumb. He and Abby rested for a night and in the morning the house built by Ragaleis from his childhood memories stood in front of their ship. Inside Bassandis lay dead, in the human form only Max could see, and Ragaleis talked of flinging himself into the darkness beyond the singularity, made wretched and betrayed by ignorant men and treacherous aliens. But he spotted something in Max's eyes that gave him hope. He'd let Max go, telling him to travel to the Kingdom of the Machine Men. Max wanted to forget the encounter. Filled with remorse and a crushing sense of failure, standing by the corpse of the giant he'd failed to protect, he'd tried to ignore Ragaleis's expression as the giant looked beyond his eyes. Since coming to the Body of God Max sometimes searched his thoughts for any hints of what the being saw but all he ever found were his own battered dreams and recollections. In the end he'd assumed that Ragaleis had taken comfort in Max's simple humanity - the stupid duty and fake bravado he'd call on to carry him through the immensity of the deity in his mad attempt at restitution, hoping that the Machine Men wouldn't kill him the second they clapped eyes on his sorry carcass and that somehow they'd be able to repair the destruction to the Mind caused by the Empire of the Ear and Odilon.

But it wasn't just a spark of nobility the giant spotted, was it? The hope he was free of the psychic net woven by the titans of God's mind was false. Why would the Brittle Hag claim Bassandis stood beside him? Who else could it be? But why could she see the phantom and not Max? Was the giant really there, hovering on the interstice between this universe and where, for God's sake? Pell could comprehend further dimensions but she'd never spoken of their inhabitants. Max clasped his hands to his head, fighting waves of panic. He sat on the edge of the Brittle Hag's distortion sphere, clinging to a slope leading down into seething chaos but unable to fall, tormented by glimpses and suggestions of realities he both yearned to see and desperately wanted to avoid. The terror came coupled with a loneliness he hadn't felt in years - the isolation of a little boy standing in the darkness of the Carceral Archipelago surrounded by stone, space and indifference.

"Bassandis?" The question dropped into his mind like jagged metal.

"There's a man beside me, with white hair?" said Max. He tensed, waiting for his thoughts to be violated once again by alien words.

"Who is he?"

If he was going to die so be it. He chanced all.

"It's the ghost of a giant," said Max. "One of the eight spirits made by the Machine Men to form the Mind of God. Traitors from the Empire of the Ear killed him, with the help of a Black Rose."

Silence. Hours, minutes or years, he couldn't tell. On the edge of this unholy void space and time no longer held meaning.

"It's the end," said the Brittle Hag at last. "The end of hope, you stupid creatures, you humans."

"And what are you?" said Max, curiosity at her words eclipsing his terror.

"We came from the furthest stars, cursed in our vanity, ignorance and self-hatred. We perceived ourselves and all around us as enemies to be crushed in a scramble for the mastery of worlds. I hated my own kin, as did we all. One tyrant, one empire - that was our creed, to be alone, each lord of a domain that spanned galaxies. In the end I was triumphant, but only after my race had perished in bitter loneliness. I am the last of my kind, and the cause of its destruction."

God almighty, I'm talking to another bloody alien.

"You have no god to take you through the door to the next universe?" he asked.

165

"Why would we need them? We were gods ourselves."

Her words astonished him. What was it like to be the only one left? To realise in the instant of triumph that you were utterly alone, the final thread in an unravelled weave spanning billions of years? Wonder overwhelmed him. He forgot the tangled monstrosity before him, the constant terrifying sensation of falling into a pit beneath creation itself, even the ghost of Bassandis this entity saw beside him.

"If you became gods, you can pass through into the next universe," said Max. "Why linger here?

"We built our empire from envy and hate. The insane passion to outdo each other drove us to perform wonders. We strode between the galaxies, fashioned realms in unseen dimensions and what did it achieve? I am all that is left and in me behold my victory. If I travel to a new reality what purpose will it serve? How would I redeem the blind stupidity of the dead?"

The penny dropped. *You're not here to hitch a ride, are you?* thought Max, overcome with awe.

"You care for the Abhumans, that's your atonement," he said.

"I have a chance to prove to this ancient cosmos that we too were of value and not just creatures filled with hatred. I shepherd my children so they can walk beneath young suns."

Max stared in mute admiration. Everything made sense. This creature rescued the Abhumans as a defiant gesture of goodness set against millennia of self-obsessed malice. The contrast with Theuderic couldn't have been more extreme.

"I discovered them when they were dying," said the Brittle Hag as if reading his thoughts. "Deep in your god. I brought them food, taught them how to be people again. I protect them from the deluded beast on the island who seeks to exert his petty dominion over me. I shall continue to nurture them until your deity steps through the gate but now you tell me all my efforts come to naught."

Max didn't want to say it. He realised that uttering the words was tantamount to pronouncing his own death sentence but what choice did he have? He guessed Theuderic was little more than an insane monster ruling through terror and brutality. The Brittle Hag was something else altogether - an alien whose very existence warped reality, hinting at unheard-of powers. He didn't doubt she could wipe out the Glass City in a moment, that she knew it and yet chose to do nothing. Did pity stay her hand? Could she be an ally? He had no option but to risk the truth.

"What you see is part of the slain giant's spirit. If I journey to the Machine Men maybe they can use it to make Bassandis whole again."

"I help you. My vessel is yours."

Before he could move the Brittle Hag's night black hand clamped over his. Unimaginable pain coursed through his arm as if his body turned inside out, cell by cell. Max shrieked and tried to pull away. He would have hacked through his wrist if he'd had a knife in this alien nightmare, but he was pinned by the creature's grasp. He glanced down and watched flesh peel from bones. The cells, nerves and blood vessels spread into an immense landscape through which the Brittle Hag's shadowed frame threaded like stitches in a demonic quilt. Max pleaded and sobbed until the agony subsided. With a sudden jerk he snapped free. Instead of human fingers the alien's talons sprouted from his sleeve. He beat the shapes against the iron ground, trying to break them from his limb. Sparks flew into his eyes, blinding him. He collapsed back against the edges of the pit, clawing at his face with nails transformed into shards of metal.

He woke in a stone bed. Lamplight slanted through a window across coarse sheets. The chamber looked like a play house with toy furniture cobbled together in imitation of the grownups. He forced himself to look at his hands. Both ordinary, both Max's. He must have hallucinated about the jagged shreds spiralling out of his forearm. He examined his palm. Normal. When he pinched it he felt bone under the skin. Max got up and propped himself against the rough wall, waiting for the concrete to warp in an unholy direction. It stayed level. He spotted jars on a table and took an unsteady step towards them. He unscrewed a lid - red paste criss-crossed with gouges. It smelt familiar. He touched it. *Grease paint. They stole it while piling the contents of that actor's bureau into their sack. This is an Abhuman's home. They live as we do.* With sick guilt he recalled decapitating the corpse tangled in the traces of the cart.

Escape was not a problem. One kick would shatter the casement fastening. Either the Brittle Hag knew he wouldn't get far or she counted on his awakened curiosity to keep him from fleeing. She was right. He had to know what she'd seen beside him in whatever dimension she peered into. He struggled to breathe, his mouth was dry and his heart thundered in the silence. Could it be that Bassandis really sat in his skull, in the same way that Ragaleis once used him as a scrying glass to view the realms of man? But that was impossible, Bassandis was no more. The last time he'd found him alive was in the midst of the battle for Metacarpi. In a dark and monstrous dreamscape, Bassandis had begged Max to save him even as he died from the horrendous wounds inflicted by the missiles and guns of the *Beatrice*. Did some-

thing pass from Bassandis to him? Was that what remained, a fragment of the giant's mind lodged in his
own? Was it enough to recreate the giant? If so, what
would happen to him?

Outside he saw a road flanked by single-floor
cottages, all identical and each in a square garden lit by a
dim light on the end of a pole rising out of the middle of
the plot. No lights shone, though he noticed drawn curtains in a few of the dwellings. It reminded him of chil-
drens' toys - a town of simple wooden blocks worn
down by years of constant use. The Abhuman city. He
summoned up the courage to go into the next room.

CHAPTER TWELVE

AN ABHUMAN STOOD by a pot-bellied iron stove, one arm pointing towards him with claws splayed out. In its other hand it held a knife. They could handle weapons. He tensed, calculating his escape route, but a second creature waited next to the door. A face like a grey furred loaf stared at him with eyes the size of billiard balls. *God almighty, it's wearing makeup*, thought Max, spotting two clumsy circles of red on what he guessed were the creature's cheeks. Its jaw hinged down to show curving teeth. *The future of humanity might depend on you, you cretin, and look where you are now.* They probably meant to eat him. He glanced at the table in the middle of the room. Three plates piled with white slices. *Must be those tubers they harvested.* He became aware of a clicking sound and realised the Abhumans' fingers flickered incessantly. They'd be licking their lips next. He made to leap for the window but before he could move the creatures swopped glances, sat down and looked at him. *What in God's name?* The penny dropped. *They're inviting me to dine with them.*

It was the strangest meal Max had ever eaten. To all intents and purposes it was an awkward dinner similar to the many he'd suffered as a child, different only in that he shared it with a pair of nightmares pretending to be human. He gamely struggled with the food. It tasted of cardboard soaked in formaldehyde. *They live their lives as people, sleeping in beds and eating from plates in cottages. They aren't monsters, that's what they want to show me. The Abhumans are us, the same as those wretches in the Glass City, but they have the Brittle Hag to watch over them and she cares, unlike mad Theuderic.*

When he'd finished the Abhuman with painted cheeks grabbed his arm. Max tried to pull away but the creature proved too strong. Instead of fighting him it waited patiently until he stopped battling against the grip. It coaxed him to his feet and led him out into the street. Unable to break its hold Max had no choice but to allow it to guide him between the houses. It turned a corner and he saw a crowd ahead. *I'm to be sacrificed.* Sudden fear made him dig his heels in and grapple with the claw around his forearm. He aimed a blow at the creature's face but it snatched his wrist in its other hand and stood there immobile and disinterested, like an adult waiting out a tantrum. In the end Max gave up. Even if he escaped he was in the middle of the city and he'd never get out. *The Brittle Hag said she'd help you,* a voice in his mind told him. He wished it was more reassuring faced with hundreds, if not thousands of the Abhumans.

He noticed a path opening as they moved back on either side. A few wore clothes hand-stitched from rags or canvas or refashioned from human garments they'd found or stolen. Max wondered how many dressed themselves in the costumes pilfered from *Props.* He spotted a few children squatting next to their parents like grey spiders missing half their legs. His heart thundered in his chest. He was alone, surrounded by creatures he'd come to kill, whose guardian was the last in a race of aliens who'd wiped each other out through envy and hatred. Max looked around, expecting to see the Brittle

Hag. He saw nothing but black eyes filled with... Was that awe? *They know what's in my head, she's told them I carry the fragment of Bassandis the giant.*

To his surprise his escort led him to the edge of town, leaving its fellows to climb to the top of a ridge. It paused, searching for a route, and Max took the opportunity to glance behind him. In astonishment he realised the Abhuman city was an enormous mathematical figure built from peaked blocks, a set of concentric circles sliced by six precise roads radiating out from the centre. Every cottage sat in an identical square lit by a lamppost. Max marvelled at the contrast between the island and this place. Instead of a chaotic jumble of filthy glass and rain-soaked detritus this had all the pristine elegance of a circuit diagram etched on lead.

They walked over an undulating plain covered in pale scrub and shrouded in mist. The cavern ceiling lifted upwards and Max realised they approached the ocean once more. Their path took them into steep-sided valleys and over hills as precise as sine waves. It felt like another hallucination, two cyphers - one human, one monstrous - intertwined scribbles across a page in a mathematician's exercise book. *We are the last men,* he thought. *The two of us are walking through God's body in the hope I can save us. Above and below lies the entire sum of human existence, the trillions upon trillions who lived before and all those ghost eyes from deep time are on me.*

They came to the shore and Max spotted a shining bowl the size of a large bath at the water's edge. The Abhuman coaxed Max into the dish like a mother about to wash a toddler. It looked at its palm before poking at the buttons running round the inside of the rim, occasionally checking its hand again. Max glimpsed writing on the leathery skin. *It can read. It wrote the instructions down so it wouldn't forget them. My ship is yours, that's what the*

Hag said, this must be it. A huge flying machine of impossible metals twisted into grotesque, inhuman shapes would be more suited to the alien but this had enough of its own minimalist weirdness to discomfit him. The Abhuman finished and pushed the vessel down to the waves. The instant it touched the water it leaped forward, almost sending its passenger overboard, and sped across the ocean at a heart-stopping rate. In seconds the lonely silhouette of the Abhuman vanished into the mist.

The dish raced across the ocean, barely skimming the waves, but Max still had a day by himself in a white and green emptiness to mull over the Brittle Hag's revelation. A storm blew up around him but the rain bounced off an invisible hemisphere projecting up from the rim, sliding down the air in dirty runnels. In this cage of water, lit by random shards of lighting, Max searched for Bassandis in his head. Every memory he conjured up was nothing more than the usual muddy recollections of a human mind - a pale, nervous man playing with wooden animals, a rotting giant chained to a throne in the prison citadel beyond the Forbidden Sea, the titan battling the dreadnoughts with foul wind-born acids and deadly psychic attacks. His heart hammered at his ribs as he relived the fear and trauma of each but none had the sharpness of a second intelligence intruding into his own. In the end he gave up and turned his thoughts to crafting a plan to get him inside the skyscraper so he could rescue Abby and Pell and make his way up the tower to Berthold's transit station. Every so often he glanced at his right hand, expecting to see talons of alien metal but finding only the familiar scarred fingers of Max Ocel.

Eventually the dish brought him within sight of the island. As soon as he could make out its towers as shadows in the mist it changed course and sailed round the perimeter. Max reckoned an alien intelligence rested in the metal surrounding him, keeping enough distance so they stayed concealed in the fog. He guessed he was a mile away. Max could tell by the movement of the bowl no currents lurked beneath the waves and so, when he was north of the skyscrapers, he slipped over the side and swam towards the shore. He glanced behind to see his ship, job done, speeding in the direction of the Abhuman city.

This end of the settlement was less populated. The blocks tumbling in heaps into the sea looked empty. Years of contact with the ocean turned many of them into mere lumps coated in algae, salt and filth. The long dead contents of others stained the inside of the glass a venomous black. He avoided the spits of wood and iron where they clustered, aiming instead for a more orderly set of walls rearing vast and translucent out of the shore ahead.

Max climbed out of the surf, hoisted himself up a rotting post and scampered along an abandoned jetty. He slipped beneath the shadow of a walkway slung between two stacks. It formed a long tunnel running towards the towers. He followed it, hoping he'd end up close enough to creep up to the walls themselves without being spotted. To his surprise he emerged on a platform cluttered with broken crates and furniture, an old refuse tip for the skyscrapers. Peering between mounds of shattered boxes he felt his heart lurch. Below him, nested in an artificial bay surrounded by iron tidal barriers, sat the three barges, *Cast*, *Props* and *Theatre*. Lights shone in the windows and he noticed shadows drifting back and forth. The rest of the performers still lived - that was some consolation. He remembered the despairing shrieks of Tafaline as Theuderic disembowelled her and his desire for revenge came upon him so suddenly it took his breath away, not least because of his shameful relief when he realised it wasn't Abby lying dead on the stage.

He spotted a movement on the roof of *Theatre* and almost called out. Thaisa walked towards the forward edge, her sleeping robe pulled tight around her. In the lamp light he could just make out her hair falling about her shoulders, the oval of her face pale against the darkness. She folded her arms and gazed at the distant sea. He knew she was desperate to escape, that she feared for Vincent and the others. Did she fear for him as well or was it hate that tainted her thoughts of Max Ocel, anger that he and Abby had brought them to this miserable prison? He wanted to call out to her, to reassure her in some way. No, he wasn't that stupid. He allowed himself one last look at the actress standing silhouetted against the barge's navigation lights, turned away and crept up to the towers.

Max wasn't going to risk the main entrance, it was too well guarded, so he made his way to the back of the central tower. He didn't find any other doors but a decaying chaos of concrete, metal plates and broken tiles stretched up to the first windows twenty yards above his head. It looked an easy climb and once he started he'd be almost invisible against the bulk of the skyscraper. The cloud bank hid the fiftieth floor, the upper limit of Theuderic's kingdom according to Berthold. He hoped it was true. If the creature found him in the levels below he'd stand no chance. He doubted he'd be able to climb that far but if he could enter the building as high as possible maybe he could get to Abby and Pell without being detected.

In the beginning he made rapid progress, reaching the first row of windows in a couple of minutes. Filthy lace curtains hung on the inside of the glass, hiding the interior. Max remembered Theuderic's face staring out at the city from the other side of the tower. A moment of fear made him press against the wall. If he put his ear to the steel plates would he hear the lumbering steps of the monster stalking through the corridors? He fought the temptation - he was scared enough. A wind rose from the ocean. In the dawn light he saw streamers of mist grow out of the sea fog like the ghosts of slender flowers. Sweat made his palms slick and his shoulders ached. He pushed himself onwards.

From the tenth floor a harsh wind tugged at his back. Each new handhold dug into his fingers and his legs trembled with tiredness. He'd barely started but now the fear of falling drove him to hunt for a way into the skyscraper. There, four floors up. A shattered frame rocked back and forth in the updraft next to the slimy remnants of a curtain plastered to the outer wall. He summoned up his strength and hauled himself towards it.

By the time he reached the opening a screaming gale poured over him. With a final burst of effort he pulled himself into the building, not caring who or what waited inside. He glanced around in a haze of exhaustion. Empty. Good. He rested for a while, eyes closed, on a carpet that smelled of mould, in the silence of the deserted room. Now came the hard part, ascending from the fourteenth floor to the fiftieth without getting eviscerated. He toyed with the idea of going back outside to complete the climb but an ocean-born storm threw bitter rain through the window. Too risky. At least in here he could hide, find shadows to scuttle through, if he kept his wits about him.

He opened his eyes and sat up. Grey wallpaper peeled away from damp plaster. A single painting rested at an angle in the centre of one wall - the only piece of furniture in the room. It showed a house on a hill but the muddy colours obscured the detail. Mould spread like ink over the bottom edge of the picture.

The entrance stood ajar so he peered into the corridor. A passageway stretched the length of the building. A window at the far end cast watery light along the floorboards. He listened, hearing only the rain on the glass and the constant percussion from his own heart. Theuderic made a colossal racket wherever he went so the silence relaxed him a little. He chose the direction with the fewest open doors, walking as softly as he could, keeping against the wall. At last he came to the staircase. It shrank to a point over his head. He started to climb.

He rose through the silent building. On the forty-fifth floor he felt confident enough to pause and glance into a few rooms near the landing - all empty, all decayed. Most contained sagging or broken beds and filthy washbasins. Some resembled offices with shattered telephones and overturned desks, some laboratories with cabinets and fume cupboards filled with indistinct shapes that could have been equipment or specimens. He realised the skyscraper was a city in itself. No doubt other floors held the ruins of shops, restaurants, theatres and halls long abandoned or, more likely, never opened.

Max climbed four flights and heard voices coming towards him from a corridor, accompanied by the unmistakeable sound of Theuderic's claws on the floorboards. He'd be exposed on the stairwell but an unlocked door to his right suggested cover. He slipped into a room stacked high with chairs and accidentally knocked against one, almost dislodging it. He stared in mute terror as it rocked back and forth. It stopped. He breathed again and moved into the shadows next to the entrance, praying the monster and his prince would find no reason to follow him here.

The voices grew louder, Theuderic's broken gearbox rumble overlaid with whining from Berthold. He strained to catch the words.

"She can help him but only temporarily. We have to move on. Her people can cure him, and you, but we have to make the journey," the man said, his voice desperate, exasperated. *He must mean Pell*, thought Max. *Cure who? Theuderic?* He remembered the scratches covering the wall of his lair, that incessant word, *pain.*

"I want more plays," said Theuderic. "They help me forget. Command the players to perform again."

"You killed one of the actors," said Berthold, his voice rising. "You banished their leading man to the realm of the Brittle Hag." It was the same tone he'd used when he confronted the monster over the death of Tafaline, petulant but defiant, hardly the voice of a cowering minion.

"I banished you too."

"And what will he say to that?" That caught Max's attention. *He?*

"You made me do it," came the answer, filled with the truculent resentment of a child. "You say you will help me but it's all lies, false hopes and stupid dreams. Why should I trust you?"

Max struggled to make sense of their words. Theuderic and Berthold were bound to each other in a relationship he didn't understand. He wasn't even sure who was the master and who the slave anymore. If Berthold had power over the creature, and its tyranny was just a charade, did that mean that Berthold was the true lord of the Glass City? Yet Theuderic had forced him into that pathetic attempt on the kingdom of the Brittle

Hag and Berthold was clearly terrified of him. Who was the third, unseen member of this mad triumvirate?

"The Philosopher will take us to her people and they will cure you both. You can be as you were," tried Berthold again. Max detected a note of panic in his voice as if he realised he was losing control of the argument.

"Why should I? I am lord of this realm, and when the Brittle Hag is dead I will rule all of the Forearm," the voice became malevolent, cunning. "I should kill your women after all. That would put an end to the stupid lies you bring to me."

Max realised Theuderic meant Abby and Pell. They were close by, he guessed that. What was to stop the monster slaughtering them? He couldn't prevent it, he had no weapon to use against a twelve-foot-high man of metal and wire.

"Get out of my way," said Theuderic.

"No," Berthold's voice held firm. Max had to admire his bravery in the face of such a creature.

"Get out of my way or I will kill you too."

"And what will Father say to that?" came Berthold's voice, a mix of steel and tears.

Father? It was all he could do not to cry out in astonishment. *Theuderic and Berthold are brothers? So that thing was once human?*

"He cares not. He's dead to me - and you know he's dead to you if you look into your heart, Berthold. When did you last speak to him?"

Silence, not even the sound of claws on wood. Max frantically tried to stitch a plan out of the fragments in his mind. He guessed a standoff played out on the stairs outside. Should he help Berthold stop his demon sibling getting to Abby and Pell?

"I want new plays. You can keep your women in your nest, but bring me new plays," said the monster.

Max heard the thunder of his descent, the clanking and teeth-gritting shriek of his talons fading as he returned to the lower levels. A thunderous stillness settled on the tower. Max edged his way to the door and risked a peek into the landing. Berthold sat on the stairs, his face in his hands. His shoulders shook and Max realised he was sobbing with genuine misery. Questions and wild speculation raced through Max's mind. He'd have it out with the bastard now, bugger the consequences. Before he could move Berthold stood up, wiped eyes with his sleeve and climbed upwards. He decided to let the man lead him to Abby and Pell.

Berthold's unhappy self-absorption made it easy for Max to track him by staying two flights below and keeping against the wall. After half a dozen floors his quarry disappeared down a corridor. Max gasped as he topped the stairs to find himself in a passageway lined with hanging carpets. Lamps cast a muted glow across polished wood. For a second he thought he was back in the warm room of his childhood. Scents of pipe smoke and wine, coal fires and perfume wrapped him in their familiar musty embrace. *Berthold's nest. He's built himself a fantasy retreat to soften the tragedy filling his life.*

He had to admire the effort though the monster downstairs had better taste. Instead of the delicate and mysterious artefacts humming and glowing in their own patches of light this resembled the cluttered parlour of a petit-bourgeois dilettante desperate to show off his wealth. He suspected he was looking at Theuderic's cast-offs - unimaginative tapestries of landscapes next to nude sculptures bordering on the burlesque, ornate cases filled with heavy crystal glasses and decanters. The books, on the other hand, took his breath away. Thousands of them sat on polished bookcases on either side of the corridor. Shelves stretched into the gloom beyond the entrance to the man's apartments. He could have sworn he saw more piles of volumes in the distance, spilling out of crates to form untidy pyramids. *How did he manage to get this lot up fifty floors?* Max's mind boggled. The self-indulgent opulence here and the exotic treasures in the creature's forest room below stood in stark contrast to the squalor of the Glass City.

The sound of clinking glass came from an entrance ahead. A quick glance revealed a short corridor with doors on either side. To his left Max could just see a long wooden table set with silver and, beyond that, thick curtains bordering a picture window. Berthold crossed the hall in front of him. Max froze but the man sailed by oblivious. He disappeared through an archway on the right. In a few moments Max heard drawers opening and shutting. Berthold started humming. He sounded like a child singing away his fear. Max crept into the first room.

They sat opposite each other at a long table set for dinner - mannequins dressed in silk gowns. Abby's dress was blue, Pell's black in stark contrast to her own stone white skin. In the second after the incoherent rage flashed across his mind Max realised both women were drugged. Their heads slumped forward. Abby's mouth hung open as if she'd spotted something shocking on the table top. He could try and snap her out of it but he'd no idea what opiates Berthold had poured into her. It must have been a hefty dose for her to end up as comatose as this. Berthold was coming back. He picked up a steak knife and slipped behind the curtain. A quick jab punched a peephole in the cloth.

Berthold returned in elegant striped trousers and Max's lizard skin waistcoat, the scales moving and shimmering in the light. He held a glass of wine in his hand, not the first judging by the unfocussed look in his eyes.

Max guessed he'd comforted himself by knocking back a couple while changing. Berthold walked up to Abby and lifted her chin with his hand. He kissed her on the cheek, let her face fall forward again and slipped his hand inside her dress, feeling her breast as he took another sip from the glass. Max glanced at Pell. She was a statue in a mausoleum.

"King and Queen," slurred Berthold expansively, still pinching Abby's nipple. "And Pell will be my consort. I've seen how she looks at me with those white eyes, so fond and doting. Am I not the luckiest man in the universe?" He withdrew his hand and raised his drink to the ceiling as if toasting the upper floors.

"Am I a fool to play this game?" he continued, warming to his theme. Max waited. He had every intention of sticking this knife into the idiot's heart but he wanted the whole story first.

"Am I a fool to think I'm a ruler on an equal footing with Theuderic? Playing out lies, lies upon lies. I should have been the honest idiot, like Max," he spat the name at Abby and Max heard all his venomous resentment channeled into that single syllable. "He was loved because he deserved to be loved, not because he lied his way into affection like handsome Berthold reduced to pouring drugs down your throat on the off chance you'll open your pretty cunt for me tonight. Shame he's dead, ripped apart by the Brittle Hag and her beast men. I wanted to be his friend. He was so brave and clever."

To Max's surprise Abby stirred, her hand clawing towards a knife on the table as she fought against the narcotics in her blood. Before she reached it Berthold took her fingers and kissed them. *She must have enough in her to stun God himself if she lets him carry on like that,* thought Max. Berthold rambled away, soliloquising

about being a hero too, killing the Brittle Hag, even
Theuderic, and escaping from the Glass City.

"Perhaps we will go to the kingdom of the Steel
Queen after all and see this wonderful project of hers.
You will still be my queen," he bowed to Abby before
turning to Pell. "And you will be my whore who can en-
tertain us both with all those blissful perversions they
taught you in Sarracinte's brothel."

Enough of this garbage. Max threw the curtain aside,
vaulted over the table and pushed Berthold against the
wall, the knife at his throat. Berthold stared at him more
in bafflement than rage, struggling to comprehend what
he saw.

"Greetings from the Brittle Hag," said Max. That got
a response. Berthold went pale and his knees buckled.
Max stepped back as fear took over the other man and
his bladder let go. He took Berthold's hair in his hand
and forced his face towards the women.

"What's wrong them? Drugs?" Berthold nodded.
Max slapped him hard. Berthold fell over the table,
sending plates and cutlery scattering across the room. As
the man tumbled onto the floor on the other side Max
strode round and hauled him up by the scruff of the
neck.

"How long before they come round?"

"Half a day," mumbled Berthold through swollen
lips. Max drew back his fist in frustrated anger.

"I have an antidote," yelped the man in desperation.
The alcoholic bravado had fled leaving nothing but fear
and humiliation.

While Berthold administered it Max searched the
room. He found a pair of revolvers in a case. Good. One
each for he and Abby. His old companion started to
come round, shaking her head and banging her palm
against her temple as if trying to shake water out of her

ears after a swim. She turned her gaze on Berthold. Before she could launch herself at him Max pushed her back into the seat. She stared at him in confusion. Her face flashed a crazy grin that tore his heart.

"Max!" Then she remembered and he saw sorrow and regret in that gaze before the green eyes became a stranger's. He pointed at Berthold who sat cowering on the floor, waiting for his doom to fall.

"We need him alive. If you want to do something useful sort out Pell."

CHAPTER THIRTEEN

MAX HUNKERED DOWN opposite Berthold. He smelled piss and fear above the scent of elegant aftershave.

"I will ask you one more time. Who's Theuderic and who is 'Father'?"

Berthold's shoulders sagged in utter defeat.

"Theuderic is my brother," he said, his voice filled with a bitter sadness that even now woke remnants of pity in Max.

"Go on."

"He was born with a disease that left him in constant pain, dying from the moment he drew breath, slowly and in increasing agony. Our father is, was, an alchemist who journeyed to the realm of the Machine Men to ask if they could cure my brother by making him one of them. He returned two years later, half mad, refusing to speak of what he'd seen but bringing with him pieces of machinery, fluids and energies inside cylinders of living metal, swearing he had the cure. Father wanted to save him but in reality had no idea what he was doing and any science he'd learned in his travels was far beyond his grasp. In the end he staved off the sickness but trapped Theuderic in the body of a monster. We tried to comfort my brother by telling him he'd become a Machine Man as noble and powerful as the real Theuderic.

It was a kindly lie at first but as he grew to understand the truth it became a bitter jest that feeds his anger."

"So where's Father?" said Max.

"Above us, higher up, kept alive by more machines," said Berthold.

It all made sense. Theuderic's kingdom was nothing more than a sad fantasy concocted by the two brothers as compensation for the torment the half-monster endured. Max remembered the scratches on the lower wall. *Pain*. It wasn't a threat, it was a plea to the universe for mercy. *Mercy*? He thought of Tafaline and her abject, hideous death. He pressed the knife against Berthold's neck.

"If you're lying…"

"Why should I lie anymore?' said Berthold, his voice drained of all will. "Look at me." Sitting on the floor, bruised and soaked in his own piss he looked truly pathetic.

"I rescued Pell because I believed she'd save my father and brother, or at least help me get them to her people where they'd both be cured."

Very noble, but how much is true? His story didn't chime with the sight of him fondling Abby's tit while boasting about Pell's capacity for perversion.

"So why the Glass City. Why all the oppression, the fake war and the prisons?"

"The Forearm is a wilderness where the scum and the exiles fleeing Interosseous and the other cities crawl away to die. We found this ancient city and tried to set up a haven, a new kingdom, to keep them alive. The cruelty, the guards, the Brittle Hag - temporary lies to frighten the lost into staying here."

Max glanced around. In the face of such indulgent luxury, while the people of the Glass City lived in cracked tanks and ate things nurtured on slime and sea water, Berthold's explanation sounded nothing more than self-serving bullshit.

"Take us to your father," ordered Max. He nodded towards Pell. "You want her to cure him and your brother, let's go." He poked Berthold in the chest with the gun for emphasis.

Max allowed the man to change, making sure to reclaim his old waistcoat. It tightened around his torso and the sensation of the scales moving comforted him like the embrace of an old friend. Abby staggered back and forth by the window. He could see she was trying to speed up the effects of the antidote. Pell sat upright with her hands flat on the table. Her white eyes tracked Abby and Max guessed this was a sign she was also regaining control. After an hour he decided they'd waited too long. Abby clambered unsteadily into her old clothes, even managing to thread her pins through her hair so they stuck out at crazy angles.

After raiding the rooms for supplies, Max handed one gun to Abby and gestured at Berthold with the other. Their prisoner led them back to the stairs and they began to climb. Max made sure Abby brought up the rear. From the expression on her face whenever she looked at Berthold she clearly remembered his hand on her breast. Max feared she'd have no compunction about shoving him down the stairwell at the first opportunity. Pell walked in front of her and Max noticed her cheeks glistening. *My God, she's crying. She heard his stupid boasts and realises he doesn't love her.* He dreaded to think what a scorned Philosopher might do. That was all he needed, two wronged women to watch.

With each new landing the interior of the tower grew darker. Visible signs of rot appeared on the walls, patches of black mould that buckled the wood, plaster and metal into cancerous mounds. On one level water seeped from beneath every door to puddle on the sagging floor. Max swore he heard muttering from somewhere in the gloom beyond but Berthold hurried onwards without pausing. *Other things live in this building.* Max and Abby exchanged glances. She didn't meet his gaze for long. In the moments when he'd rescued her it'd been like old times, until her grin faded and a stranger looked out of her eyes, trying so hard not to care. Half of him had hoped they'd fling themselves into each other's arms after thinking the other dead, solving nothing and renewing the heartache. Instead they battled with their own feelings in a state of mutual truculence - Max cursing her, himself and the universe as he clumped up the stairs.

At last they came to a floor without corridors. Night fell once more and a space opened out, filled with darkness. Max thought he could make out a distant line of windows, midnight set in black, but it was hard to tell. He held his own hand up and saw mist hanging in the air like soot.

"Look down." Berthold's voice came from somewhere ahead.

Max glanced at his feet. A single thread of light curled away into the gloom. He followed it. Other strands joined the first. They pulsed with a weak energy. He looked up and gasped. Berthold stood outlined against a glowing cloud. Shining threads covered the floor and hung from the ceiling, converging on whatever rested in the centre of this building-wide cavern. Max felt the hairs on the back of his neck rise. He realised he was in the presence of technology far beyond his experience, even on the distant worlds in the old wormholes. *Machine-Man science,* he thought. Brought out of the seething maelstrom of God's heart by Berthold's father.

Pell walked past him. The fine threads thickened as he followed her until he found himself surrounded by cables, every one disappearing into that glowing shape ahead. He spotted Berthold hovering on the edge of the light. His hands writhed over each other and his expression betrayed a strange mixture of longing, hopelessness and fear. Max shielded his eyes, trying to understand what lay at the centre of the hall. Somewhere in that tangle of radiant branches was the man who'd created Theuderic, but he couldn't make anything out, just an insane net of conduits and fibres. It reminded him of the cat's cradle map. Pell turned and pressed her nose against the nearest wire. *Seeing things invisible to us.* She jerked her head back, as if startled, before stepping towards the mass. *We can't go any further. Whatever's in there is covered in these tubes.* He looked at Berthold. This was beyond madness. If his father lived in the middle of whatever this thing was he wasn't going anywhere soon. If anyone could fix him it had to be here.

"When did you last speak to your father?" Max asked. Berthold looked desperately sad.

"Three months ago, when he was still visible. It's too tangled now," he said.

"It's growing?" said Max in disbelief. Pell looked at him.

"This is his father. He has become this," she said. Berthold started to cry.

"How do you know?" said Abby. Her voice had lost its drugged slur.

In answer Pell turned sideways and as she did so flattened into a two-dimensional silhouette so thin that edge-on she disappeared. Abby swore long and violently, Berthold cried out in horror and Max recoiled despite himself. He stepped to one side to see where the girl had gone. There, a paper cutout, sliding through the web. *She can move into other dimensions*. Pell vanished into the soft light. *Now what*? He turned to Abby but before he could speak the Philosopher stood in front of him again. He jumped. *God's cock, woman*. To his relief she'd become three-dimensional once more. Pell looked up at him with those terrible white eyes. With her whole body glowing in the darkness and surrounded by a forest of shimmering cables she looked like an etiolated spider.

"He's no more," she said in her paper voice. "Whatever remained of him is in here now," she lifted up a cable. Max considered Berthold to be a devious, manipulative little shit with a ridiculously over-exaggerated idea of his own charm, but he still felt sympathy for a man faced with the death of his father. He remembered his own cluttered feelings when Herman Ocel died at the hands of Odilon the Watcher and turned to tell Berthold he was sorry.

"He's escaped," shouted Abby.

Max ran to the stairwell. He heard footsteps clattering down the levels. *He's gone to fetch Theuderic*. How many times had he resisted the temptation to shoot the craven bastard? Stupid honour and pity. He tried to aim but Berthold kept out of sight. Max banged his hands in frustration on the bannister before turning to the others.

"We have to keep going. We must get to the transit station before they catch us."

Pell stood with her hands on the rail, looking into the void. A white tear glistened in the dim light, falling after Berthold. *For God's sake*, thought Max. *If he was ever interested in you it was only for the gymnastics*.

"We have to go, now," he said. He pushed the girl towards the stairs. She stumbled ahead of him, mechanically climbing to the next level. Max didn't know how long they had. He guessed Theuderic had no real reason to stay below the fiftieth floor, it was just a grudging compact between two brothers. He'd no doubt that, goaded by Berthold, the monster would hunt them to the roof of the cavern.

Up and up they climbed through endless stairwells filled with shadows and decay. Many of the corridors looked half-finished - materials and tools littered tattered plastic sheets, hammers and saws rusted into stains on the floor. Max noticed disturbing signs of life - semi-fossilised bones scattered across faded carpets, drapes tacked to ceilings to create makeshift walls. A cluster of figures staring down at them over a railing gave them a serious scare. They wasted an hour trying to find an alternate route before realising their audience was nothing more than a line of human-sized statues built out of scrap, with broken taps for hands and heads made from immense valves. Artistry, madness or a fake army to frighten away intruders? Max had no idea.

On the next level he spotted daylight through a hole in the wall left by an ancient explosion. The storm still hurled rain into the building and clouds churned in the sky above and below. He guessed that at this height a constant tempest raged through the weather systems of the cavern.

They kept going but at last exhaustion and hunger forced them to rest. Max shared out the bizarre delicacies from Berthold's pantry. Pell shook her head and gave him the food back, stopping only to drink rain water puddling on a steel desk. Abby wolfed hers down, pulling faces as she read the label on a tin of rancid pate. Max wished they still had some pomegranate seeds but they'd finished their stash months ago.

Every so often they paused and listened. At this height the skyscraper swayed and shifted, its fabric murmuring and sighing as it flexed. Other sounds drifted up from below and echoed overhead - objects falling, windows breaking as glass finally fell from crumbling frames, water running and dripping from leaks in the partitions and between floors. Sometimes Max swore he heard living creatures - whispering from the black corners of an unlit hall, doors slamming, gentle laughter drifting from beneath a closed door where faint red light flickered across the passage floor. In this ancient tower the sanest, most domestic murmurings seized him with fear. Indeed, they were the worst because such pleasant noises were the last thing he expected to hear in this monstrous building. Above it all he strained to make out the sound of any pursuit - the remorseless clatter of Theuderic stalking the passageways. He detected nothing amid the susurration welling up from below.

After two more levels everything changed. Gone were the regular corridors, rooms and stairs. Every ascent led to a nightmare labyrinth of random spaces, as if the architect had given up, filled the rest of the tower with junk and told whatever inhabited the upper floors to get on with it. Sometimes they found themselves edging their way single-file along unlit passageways curving in and around themselves like burrows. At other times they came across wide open areas devoid of walls or furnishings. In the face of such fragility Max marvelled at how the five-mile skyscraper stayed upright.

Eventually the stairwell ended and from then on they had to search every floor for the route upwards. Often the only exit was via a rickety ladder, or a rusting net of cables or pipes. Once or twice they found themselves standing under a hole in the ceiling so they had to pile whatever debris they could find high enough to reach the gap over their heads. At first Max had reckoned it would take a few days to get to the down towers. Now he wasn't so sure. Each ascent became a tedious grind and they still walked in fear of the shapes they glimpsed at the end of passageways and under guttering lights, or the muffled whisperings that grew more loathsome the higher they went.

They climbed for another day before resting again. Max chose a floor that looked relatively normal - eight immense windowed rooms surrounding a landing covered in steel plates. They camped in a corner sheltered by stacks of transparent lead dusted with white oxide from the rain blowing through a broken window. Max tossed Abby a jar of stuff in aspic from Berthold's fridge while Pell stuck her hand outside to gather raindrops. Max toyed with the idea of talking to his old partner but she folded her arms on her knees and buried her face without saying a word. Snoring filtered out around the edges of her ragged hair. He sat against the wall and watched the Philosopher licking the last drops of water from her palm.

"You can see the future," he said. She looked up at him and smiled. Even after many days in her presence that horrible empty grin terrified him. Her body glowed with cold light.

"Just seconds."

"Every second counts." Her enigmatic reluctance to communicate anything in a helpful way got on his nerves. He didn't know if it was a deliberate affectation or whether all Philosophers talked liked this

"And going flat like a sheet of paper?"

She shrugged as if to say *what's to tell* and turning two dimensional was as commonplace as catching rain-water to lap out of her palm. He knew one thing would get a reaction.

"I met the Brittle Hag. The alien you saw on the wall when we arrived at the ocean."

He shouldn't have told her with her hand halfway through the window. She jumped and snatched it back, slicing her thumb on the glass. Beads of white blood spattered on the floor. Pell frowned and sucked at the wound, looking intently at Max.

"She stood in a distortion sphere," he continued, trying not to stare. "When I was close it felt as if the ground sloped into a pit."

Pell shuddered.

"She's punched a hole in the universe. Where she stands, the universe ceases to be," said Pell. Her lips glistened with her own blood.

"She's an alien, the last of her race. They fought amongst themselves until only she remained," he explained. "She came to the Forearm to care for the Abhumans as atonement for her people's cruelty. She plans to care for them until God walks into the new universe."

Why did the Brittle Hag frighten Pell so much? White eyes drilled into his. He spotted terror in her face. It made her look as alien as the very creature she feared.

"She's opened a hole in creation," she repeated. "Where she stands everything I understand is whisked away into nothing. I cannot read this anymore," she waved her hand at the room, the windows and the churning clouds. "She makes it meaningless."

Was that it? Did the Brittle Hag render all those complex functions and calculations in Pell's mind useless? *That's why you hate her. She turns you into one of us - men and women who just see chaos in the universe.*

Pell cocked her head as if listening. Max joined her. In a second he was on his feet, kicking Abby.

"Wassup?"

"Theuderic."

Above the hiss of the rain and the myriad creaks and whispers of the tower he detected the sound of clashing metal, like trains colliding in a distant valley. They still had time. Some of the gaps they'd crawled through were barely large enough for humans let alone a twelve-foot-high creature of iron and canvas. The topography of the skyscraper was on their side.

"How far to the top?" asked Abby.

"Maybe a hundred and fifty floors to go," said Max, doing the sums in his head. If they speeded up and met no major obstacles they could be on the roof in half a day. Would the monster follow them into the down tower? He'd assumed there was a way of crossing between the skyscrapers but now he wasn't so sure. Still, if they had to fight Theuderic he'd rather it was in an open space instead of among all this treacherous clutter.

The stairs took them three more floors and no further. A ramp led up to the next level and at the top they found themselves in a warren of boxes lit by clouds of flickering lights that buzzed away when they approached. Up close Max saw tiny machines in the shape of heads, each no bigger than a pea. They looked like so many Pells, white eyed and cold faced. He could have sworn their mouths moved and they spoke to him and each other in words too faint to hear. He paused to listen, and detected the distant clatter of clawed feet passing over concrete and rusted iron far below. *They're getting closer.*

Abby batted away the floating lights as they sprinted from room to room, looking for the access point to the floor above. Nothing. Max grew desperate. There had to be stairs or a ladder somewhere, or even just a hole in the ceiling, but in the honeycomb of shimmering steel and tiny faces it was impossible to gauge direction. He suspected they ran in circles. He looked to Pell. Perhaps her trans-dimensional sight would find the way out, but he saw only another blank white face in a cloud of alien indifference.

Abby called him from the next room. He found her leaning out of a window into the mist. A rusted set of stairs clung to the wall a couple of yards below. It rose to their right, disappearing round the corner of the building. He remembered the collapsing gantry on the outside of the Carceral Archipelago when he'd sneaked into his father's apartment just before Odilon attacked him. How could they tell if this was strong enough to bear their weight?

Abby thumped onto the gangway below him. *What in God's name is she up to?* He looked for clouds of dust where the steps touched the concrete, the tell-tale signs of bolts pulling free.

"It's fine, look," Abby said, jumping up and down on the spot. The stairs creaked. She pulled a face and waited.

"No, we're good."

Not for the first time Max mentally called her every name he could think of as he lowered himself down. Hadn't their recent brush with death taught her anything? The infuriating woman complained about losing him and then almost pitched herself four miles into the ocean. He banished her to the corner where an iron brace clamped the stairs to the fabric of the tower, until he knew the gantry was solid. Pell came after him, moving so swiftly she looked like milk pouring over concrete. Max couldn't believe their good fortune. Theuderic would never get through the window. He'd have to break down the wall - and even if he did he'd collapse the walkway with his weight. If these stairs carried on to the roof they'd be poised to climb to the next tower while the monster still floundered through the interior. He wondered if Berthold was with him, egging him on.

He hoped so. Their arguing would slow them and with any luck Theuderic might finally snap his brother's neck.

They ran ever upwards through a churning mist laced with rain that tasted of concrete dust. It lashed against the windows on their right, blurring the interior and preventing Max from seeing what lay on the other side. Once in a while he glimpsed lights deep inside the building, even the suggestion of movement. Later they passed ragged gaps revealing cavernous interiors studded with arches or honeycombs of rooms. Some looked disturbingly normal with rusting bedsteads set against striped wallpaper. Most were odd-angled spaces filled with machinery and detritus hinting at rituals and experiments long forgotten. Once in a while Max saw energy weapon splashes on the walls - swathes of soot and warped metal. If only they had those guns. He doubted the revolver he carried was much use against Theuderic. He saw a hall coated in dried blood. Hooks and chains hung from the ceiling. Chiomedes' despairing words rose into his mind. *What are we becoming, what have we become?* Abby took the lead, with Pell a paper wraith floating between them.

Two floors up he turned a corner and almost collided with the Philosopher. She studied her distorted reflection in a window, reaching out to touch it with one many-jointed finger as she cocked her head from side to side. Had she never seen herself? If so it'd be a shock, but there was a time and a place.

"What are you doing? We can't dawdle admiring ourselves." he said. The image vanished and he jumped back, nearly falling over the rail. Pell turned towards him.

"There are people in there, lonely and hungry. This tower is filled with pain and loss."

Ye Gods, thought Max, pushing her roughly ahead of him while simultaneously shoving his heart into its proper place. He wasn't going to waste his time persuading the weird bugger to move, he just wanted to get away from whatever creature she'd been nose to nose with and separated from by nothing more than filthy glass. He had a sudden vision of the building beside him filled with writhing ghosts, like maggots in a rotting corpse. The only consolation was that Theuderic and his brother had that to look forward to. Good luck to them. He avoided looking into any more windows, keeping his eyes on Pell's glowing head.

At last they came to the roof of the skyscraper, a wilderness of crumpled plates and boxes undulating into the fog. Max looked up and gasped, fighting the urge to hurl himself flat. A few hundred yards above them the down tower cut a square out of the sky, its surface a mirror image of the surrounding landscape save for gaps where centuries of decay had dislodged panels and sent them crashing onto the roof below.

"Half way," he said, allowing himself a grin. He didn't spot any stairs or ladders but a multitude of cables and pipes bridged the gap between the buildings. None looked strong enough to bear the weight of the creature that hunted them. A tough climb but not impossible. Get to the next tower and they'd escape Theuderic.

He looked at Abby. Their eyes met and he saw nothing but anguish in her gaze. Sadness flooded through him. He knew what she was going to say. The first time she'd forced herself into a cruel indifference, surrounding her thoughts with walls of carefully engineered logic and self-delusion. Now it was different. He sensed she still loved him desperately yet determined to cast him aside once more. A thousand arguments sprang into his own wounded mind - how did she plan on getting back to the actors, past that machine monster? It'd be impossible, stupid, suicidal. *For God's sake, what do you expect? This is Abby Fabrice.* She opened her mouth and he prepared himself to tell her not to bother, he knew the sentence and didn't want to hear it. *You are your father's son. Forget her. Stone duty.*

"Max..." she began.

A hundred yards away the roof plates erupted in a fountain of debris and Theuderic clambered out of the hole like a wasp crawling out of its nest.

CHAPTER FOURTEEN

BEFORE ANYONE COULD react Theuderic wrenched a copper sheet out of the ground and threw it at them. Max dived, feeling the wind ruffle his hair as it skimmed above him, missing Abby and Pell by inches. He watched the spinning wreckage disappear into the void.

"Theuderic, no," yelled Berthold as he climbed out of the hole, his elegant clothes torn and a haunted look on his face. Oil or blood stains covered both of them. More of Theuderic's fake skin had pulled free of his upper torso. God, was that a dent? What caused that? He propped himself on his fists. Max dared to hope the King of the Glass City was either too ill or exhausted by the journey to fight. He searched for the nearest cable. There, in half a dozen strides, a chain swinging from far above. Pell would have to go first so he and Abby could tackle their pursuer.

"Listen to me," Berthold said, hand on an iron-threaded arm as thick as his own body. "We can join them. Pell will take us to her people and they'll cure you." What was he talking about? Even if Theuderic could climb the gap Max was never going to let him anywhere near Pell or Abby. He was mad, wracked by pain and boiling with a furious resentment directed at everything, but mainly Berthold. He'd gut any of them on a whim to spite his brother. But Berthold's plaintive argument bought them time. Max nodded to Abby and they crept towards the links. Two more steps and they'd be there. He tried to catch Pell's eye but she was a rigid statue, staring at Berthold.

"Theuderic please, we mustn't kill them. They'll make you a human once more."

"I don't want to be human again." Max heard the cracked bellows of whatever passed for lungs in that warped chest, laced with the constant grating sound of clashing gears and chains.

"We can be brothers together, like we once were, before father made you into this."

Max sensed honest sorrow in Berthold's words. Was that his ultimate plan - to ask the Philosophers to restore this mutated engine crouching under the weight of its agony? Was this the real Berthold and the treacherous fop, the lecher groping a stupefied Abby, the liar and the boastful fool all an act? He glanced at Abby. She stared at their pursuers, clearly struggling with the same questions.

"Come on dear Theuderic, a little further. They'll help." Theuderic stood up and bellowed. "NO. I AM LORD OF THE MACHINE MEN. I AM KING OF THE GLASS CITY!"

He hoisted Berthold aloft by the throat and hurled him twenty yards. The man smacked into a heap of boxes. Pell shrieked and ran after him, her inhuman voice rising once more as her jaw hung down to her breasts, turning her into a white demon. Theuderic clutched his head as Pell went ultrasonic. *He hears her*, thought Max. *This is our chance*. He aimed for the tattered eyeholes in the canvas. The bullet tore through the cloth but struck metal on the other side. Theuderic roared and batted at the air. Max fired again. Abby joined him but though the impact of the bullets forced the creature to retreat they left no visible damage. Pell ceased scream-ing and leaned over Berthold. He lifted unsteady fingers to his neck. The bastard still lived.

Theuderic charged at them in a remorseless caco-phony. It sounded as if the skyscrapers themselves were falling. This was what the suicides who jumped in front of the trams of Metacarpi saw in their last moments. Max leaped out of the way. Claws crumpled the steel sheets sending waves rippling through the surface. Abby retreated, fetching up against a stack of cylinders. Theuderic halted at the edge and faced her, ready to at-tack. Max scrabbled around for anything he could use as a weapon. He picked up a metal rod. Rust flaked in his palm but it felt heavy enough. All he had to do was dis-tract the creature before it attacked his partner.

Something glided past him, a vertical scratch in the sky. He paused, thrown by its essential wrongness. An-other heartbeat and the paper image of Pell drifted over the roof tiles. She became three-dimensional again, a fra-gile doll no higher than Theuderic's waist. He spotted her and swivelled in their direction. Max paced after the Philosopher, hefting his makeshift mace, hoping to get one blow in while she distracted the monster. A hard swing to the crook of his knee might bring him down. Pell morphed into a cutout and vanished two paces later. That pinched line again as if the two halves of real-ity had slipped out of alignment. Max noticed Abby cli-mbing up the pile of scrap.

"Leave me alone," said Theuderic. Flat Pell reap-peared and Max realised what was happening. *Three-di-mensional, two-dimensional, one-dimensional, she's flipping through space.* Normal Pell again, glowing in the mist from the lowering sky. *One-dimensional, two-dimensional, three-dimensional.* It was a clever trick and it scared Theuderic but for how long? Pell exploded into a cloud of angles and shapes. Max saw every part of her, inside and out, unfolded across whirling vortices that slid through his mind in rapid succession like panels in a rotating stereoscope. A shattered clock howl thundered between the two towers. *Four-dimensional.* He collapsed to his knees just as a black shape ran past to launch itself at Theuderic. As Pell transformed into an alabaster woman once more Berthold hit Theuderic in the side with both feet. His brother staggered and the plate under him flipped up, canting over the gulf. He struggled to regain his balance but lost his grip, gave a despairing cry, and disappeared. Berthold followed but Pell, balancing on tiptoes on the parapet, grabbed his ankle, yanking him to safety with incredible strength. Far below a broken machine collided with the tower. The floor trembled briefly beneath Max then all was silent.

Berthold crawled to the edge of the roof and looked into the clouds that swallowed his brother.

"I did it, I'm free, at last." He sat back on his haunches and wept, tears mingling with the blood running from his nose. Pell knelt beside him and gathered his head in her arms, stroking his hair and whispering strange words of comfort. Max limped over to where Abby clung to a chain twelve feet up, her knees next to her ears. She stared down at him wide-eyed as the enormity of Theuderic's death sank in. She unfolded herself and slid back down.

"He's gone?"

Max listened - nothing but the hiss of rain as it sheeted across the roof.

"He's gone."

Berthold struggled to his feet, supported by the Philosopher. Max pondered the man's words, *free at last.* Was that nonsense about curing Theuderic another ruse? Max's head ached. Berthold's plots upon plots exhausted him along with the carnage they scattered in their wake. He was rapidly coming to the conclusion that the idiot just made stuff up on the spur of the moment, ducking and weaving towards each catastrophic opportunity as it arose. He'd be glad to get rid of the dangerous fool. Yet whatever he thought of the man's inept scheming and unctuous bonhomie he'd saved them from an ugly, brutal death, killing his own brother in the process.

"Thank you," said Max to both of them. Berthold grinned painfully, the right side of his face a mass of bruises.

"Onward and upward," he said.

"No." Max shook his head. Nothing in God's body was going to persuade Max to take him any further. "You need to go back and sort out that mess you and your brother made. I'll take Pell with me to her people."

"I'm not going without him," said Pell. Max couldn't believe his ears. *He doesn't love you, didn't you hear him in his boudoir? Abby's the queen to be, you're just his bizarre fuck doll*. He struggled to keep his thoughts to himself. At this rate he'd be doing the rest of the trip on his own. He shook his head in exasperation and looked up at the bulk of the down tower looming through the clouds.

"You need me," added Berthold.

"No I don't," said Max. Of course with Abby the journey was possible but he didn't know what her next move was and he didn't want to. For a few moments he was happy to pretend this was just the beginning of yet another adventure. *What did she say before we stepped into the Thumb? 'This is why we're here'.* Bitterness made him reckless. He walked towards an angled pipe that rose to the building above. Rings every few feet would give him the handholds he needed. Abby called after him but he ignored her.

"It's worse up there," Berthold shouted after him. "I know the route and I've stashed supplies and weapons. Without me you'll never make it to the transit station."

"Why do you want to leave?" said Abby. "Your brother's dead and you're King of the Glass City."

Berthold looked at her as if she was the biggest idiot in God's body. He was clearly asking to be thumped.

"Why would I go back to that shit hole to lord it over a bunch of fucking peasants, bullying them with propaganda because they're too stupid to look after themselves? Father's experiments failed - the city, Theuderic, me - and now he's dead." His self-pity disgusted Max. He'd seen those so-called peasants brutalised. They were stupid because their wills were crushed by a lethal combination of tedious, endless lies and cruelty. He was so tempted to climb that pipe and leave the lot of them behind but he might still hold the future of humanity in his head and he couldn't afford to take risks. He needed Pell with him at the very least.

"You're in charge of him," he told the girl. "He will do everything you say the instant you command it without complaint or question. If I get one iota of grief I will shoot him in the head. Do you both understand?"

Berthold opened his mouth. Max whipped out his gun, jammed the barrel between the man's eyes and cocked the hammer. In his mind he dared the idiot to come up with one more smart arse comment or ingratiating plea.

"We understand perfectly Max. Put the weapon away," said Pell, resting her fingers on his. Her paper voice had a new lilt to it, a sense of determination laced with a hint of disturbingly inhuman pleasure. She kissed Berthold on the cheek with her chalk white lips.

Max turned to Abby.

"You're going back to your players," he said, saving her the agony of rejecting him again.

"They've gone," said Berthold.

"What?" said Abby in a voice that prompted Max to step between them.

"When I went for Theuderic they'd sailed north."

"How did they escape?" Max remembered the barges in that iron bay, Thaisa pacing the deck, the wind catching at her long black curls. But the guards disarmed the players when they arrived. They had no weapons - how did they manage to get away?

He put his hands on Abby's shoulders ready for the storm. She shook him off, shot him a look of hatred and anger that cut his heart, stalked away and sat on an overturned pipe with her back towards them.

"They unleashed an Abhuman," continued Berthold. "It must have hidden on one of the barges after we were attacked. I guess they found it and let it go in the city. In the chaos and panic they disappeared, boats and all."

"An Abhuman?" Max couldn't help but grin at the memory of Thaisa picking up the fragments of a shattered bowl from the deck of *Props. Daughter my arse.* Clever, beautiful Thaisa with those weary eyes and permanent half-smile at the universe's cruel absurdities. She probably found the creature cowering in an unlit corner, left behind after the raid. She confided in no-one, not even Vincent, hiding it until the time came to unleash the Glass City's worst nightmare. He hoped the beast managed to escape.

"If you come with us to the Elbow you can get to South Anconeus," he told the back of Abby's head. "Rejoin them there."

She ignored him. He watched her for a few moments more but knew better than to push his luck.

"Pell, it's time to go."

They climbed the pipe, Max leading the way with Berthold just behind him and Pell bringing up the rear. Every so often he glanced down, not trusting the man below. He caught Pell smiling a couple of times and the sight disturbed him. In reality he was looking to see if Abby followed. She still sat on the roof staring at the clouds that bellied and seethed across the sky. *She's not coming*, he realised. He had an uncontrollable urge to return, grab her, slap her, beg her, do anything to keep her but he knew it would be hopeless. He struggled on, forcing a path through the relentless waves of misery crashing over him.

At long last they reached a platform slung under the down tower. A rusting set of stairs led to a hallway with a shattered floor criss-crossed by iron beams. Hopscotching across half a dozen took them to a corridor slanting up into the gloom. Max crushed all his feelings into a diamond point in his heart, turning himself into a stone automaton. He glanced at his companions and something in his eyes caused even Pell to look away.

"I stowed a cache of food and weapons two floors above us," said Berthold.

"We'll rest there," said Max.

Total darkness filled the surrounding space. The ground underfoot had a greasy, organic feel that made him want to run across its surface, desperate to minimise contact between his boots and the spongy tiles. For once he was thankful for Pell's faint radiance as she drifted at his side. He guessed they had turned a corner because a rectangle of dirty light appeared ahead, opening on to a tiled passageway barely wide enough for them to walk in single file. They crept between rows of doors bolted shut with immense padlocks long decayed into lumps of verdigris. Max began to understand why this tower spooked Berthold more than the one below. It was as chaotic, but carried with it a hint of madness, as though the walls themselves shrieked out their own insanity just below human hearing. Did this building have its own psychic defences, circuitry behind these cracked and stained panels broadcasting fear into their minds? It seemed like an age before Berthold pointed at another flight of steps leading to the next level. At the top more shadows enshrouded them but the itching dread faded and a feeling more akin to normality returned.

Berthold stayed true to his word. On the other side of a pair of zinc doors lay a room full of crates filled with tins of food and spare clothing. He lifted out a bottle of red wine and a tin of truffles. The dandy had a surreal notion of what constituted an explorer's rations but at least he'd made the effort. Max reached into the nearest box and his fingers touched a leather pouch. He opened it and to his delight saw tiny red beads - pomegranate seeds. Did Berthold know what he had here? He doubted it, otherwise he wouldn't have left them at the bottom of a crate. Berthold and Pell piled blankets out of another chest, making simple beds on the floor, their backs towards him. He slipped the bag into the pocket of his waistcoat. It tightened as if recognising what he'd found. If only Abby were here. Wave one of these under her nose and she'd do whatever he asked, or at least make some reluctant attempt at obedience. He shook her from his mind.

"Here." Berthold handed him a shotgun and a couple of boxes of shells. He had a revolver in his own hands. He snapped it open and checked the cylinder.

"Give it to Max," said Pell. Berthold looked at her with a grin, thinking she was joking. She clearly wasn't. The smile faded.

"So I'm to be unarmed?" he asked.

"You have me," said Pell with a sweet, adoring look that, on her face, appeared toe-curlingly horrible. Berthold paled and passed the gun to Max. Good, at least now they were better armed, though he knew he'd have to rely on Berthold's shaky aim at some point between here and the transit station.

Max dumped a heap of clothes by the door and fell into an uneasy doze. Once he woke to hear scuffling at the far end of the room and Berthold's frightened whimpering. He saw Pell, naked once more, glowing in the darkness as she squatted over the makeshift bed, her multi-jointed fingers wriggling and snapping like cave worms. She lowered herself, whispering incessantly, and Berthold gave a muffled yelp. *More functions, more procedures*, thought Max. *Serves you right you poor bastard.*

He fell asleep again but this time he dreamed. He walked through a garden under a lowering sky lit by occasional flashes of red light. At first he thought it was lightning but soon realised the tops of the clouds burned with a dull crimson roar. It felt like he stood underneath a fire, looking up at the embers from below. A vague memory tugged at his mind. Had he been here before? A boundary wall of pale bricks and charcoal mortar encompassed a lawn. *This is a cheap set. The players have flats like this stacked ten deep on the Props barge*. It was tempting to go up to one and poke holes in it with his finger but he noticed someone sitting at a wrought iron table. He had long white hair and wore an ill-fitting black suit. He didn't notice Max - he was busy moving objects back and forth across the filigreed metal surface. Max approached. Slender fingers took cutout wooden animals from a pile and put them carefully in slots carved in a painting of a farm. A horse, a dog, a duck and a sheep.

"Bassandis," said Max. Dream sorrow and joy passed through him in swift succession.

"Hello Max," said the giant. The titan placed the last animal in its hole and leaned back, smiling at a job well done.

"'When I play with Max and sometimes chide him, it speaks of patience and loving kindness'," Bassandis quoted his mother's words. Max laughed in happy recognition.

"We were teaching you what it means to be human," said Max. "When you return to the Head and join with your brothers and sisters to make the mind of God you'll understand the beings you have to save."

Bassandis looked at Max, eyes narrowed as if trying to find something in his face. *If he's only a fragment of the giant how much does he remember? Perhaps he's not even that. Perhaps the Brittle Hag didn't see him after all, and he's nothing more than my own guilt.*

"What happened to me, Max?" he asked. *You can't lie. He's in your head, whether or not he's just your own brain playing tricks.*

"My father didn't know you were part of God's mind. He imprisoned you. His friend Odilon was a Black Rose in disguise. He plotted to kill you because he doesn't want God to wake and carry humanity into the next universe. The Empire of the Ear invaded the city. Odilon persuaded him to use you as a weapon against their dreadnoughts. There was a battle in Metacarpi. We managed to stop the attack but it was too late. Even your brother, the giant Ragaleis, came to rescue you - but you died in the streets."

In his dream memory he saw the decaying titan howling in wretched fury and terror as he tried to defend himself against the murderous fire of the Beatrice's cannon, sinking to his knees as his body disintegrated. He looked at Bassandis, his face a pale symmetrical mask with soft eyes. Next to him Pell's head would have resembled an ugly lump of concrete.

"And yet I'm here," said the giant.

"I think a part of your mind survived in me," said Max. "In the last seconds before you died I saw you in the room where we used to play. I tried to help you. I took your hands in mine and in that instant I guess a fragment of your being entered here." He tapped his dream temple.

"Is this my dream or yours, Max?" Max gave an involuntary shudder as he realised the implications. *I don't recognise any of this.* He looked at the roiling clouds above, the grey walls and the hills looming beyond. *If this is what a giant's dreams look like, God help us all.*

"I was angry, wasn't I? Filled with hate and fury, long years of madness taking their toll," continued Bassandis.

Max remembered the titan's cry, that faint shriek that drove men mad, sent them falling to the floor to writhe in their own piss and vomit. *Wait a second.*

"Yes," said Max. "It happened again didn't it, recently?" Bassandis seemed to think for a few seconds.

"Did it?" He looked unsure, struggling with his memories.

In the moment Tafaline's guts splattered onto the stage and Max thought she was Abby he'd gone mad, howling in anguish and desolation. He saw Theuderic staggering, down on one knee, clamping his hands to his ears. Guards collapsed, foaming at the mouth. *My God. You are real, of course you're real, and you are in my head. When I screamed you added your voice to mine and turned it into a psychic attack. Could I do it again*? he wondered with a giddy mix of elation and fear. In Metacarpi Bassandis's cry had sent thousands to the edge of insanity and crippled dreadnoughts. Max had made a few soldiers throw up and a monster lose his balance. His power was weak, the last resort of utter despair, but at the very least it proved that part of Bassandis still lived within him and that meant hope lingered for humanity. He placed his hands on the wrought iron table. The contrast between the titan's slender, delicate fingers and his own made him feel lumpish and half-formed.

"What happens now?" asked the giant.

"Wake up, you stupid bastard."

Someone gently thumped his head repeatedly against the floor. He opened his eyes. Red hair, freckles, an expression like an ill-tempered toddler and that ridiculous emerald gaze. Without thinking he yanked Abby's head down and kissed her. She managed to swear copiously even as he ground his lips against hers and she pummelled half-heartedly at his chest with her fists. Realising what he was doing he pushed her off and she sprawled back on her bottom, flustered and blushing.

"It must have been a nightmare," she said to Pell and Berthold who stood behind him. Berthold managed a weak grin. He looked like he'd had his own night of horrors. Pell just cocked her head to one side and gave Max a knowing look that made him shudder. Abby wiped her mouth with the back of her hand and checked it for blood.

"Only as far as the Elbow," she said. "After that I'm off after the actors."

"Whatever you say," said Max getting unsteadily to his feet. Whether the dream was just a phantasm or something else there was no denying the effect of his cry when Tafaline died. He must have a fragment of Bassandis in his head - what other explanation could there be? More than ever he had to journey to the Machine Men. Up till now he'd no idea what would happen when he confronted the architects of God's thoughts. He'd tell them what had happened, apologise and no doubt get killed for his pains. But if he carried the seed of a new giant inside his skull it changed everything and Max Ocel, like it or not, might be the last hope for humanity and their deity.

CHAPTER FIFTEEN

THEY LOADED THEMSELVES up with supplies and ammunition and continued to climb through the tower. Despite his suspicion of Berthold, Max realised the man knew the way through territory far more treacherous than before. In these unlit spaces forms lumbered and scuttled beyond what meagre lamplight remained after thousands of years of disuse, or reared in brief silhouette against broken windows in empty halls. The muttering and faint laughter, when it did come, was inhuman. On more than one occasion Berthold hissed for them to get down and hide. They crammed into corners or behind shattered structures while shapes crossed corridors ahead of them or multi-limbed shadows with lolling heads ascended the stairs they would have to tread when Berthold finally claimed the coast was clear. But sightings were rare and most of the time, from what Max could see, they paused for nothing. As they crept from each unseen encounter to the next Max wondered how much was real and how much an act put on for their benefit to prove how vital the disgraced prince was to their quest. Once they hid for nearly two hours from something completely invisible. But Berthold sweated, wept and prayed while Pell peered through a gap with an expression of fascinated loathing. At the end of the first day he delivered his pièce de résistance, removing a couple of panels from a wall to reveal a lift shaft rising up into the darkness.

"It works," he said before yanking a few times on an iron handle, his grin crystallising as the seconds ticked by. Max saw Abby gearing herself up for a sarcastic broadside but just as she opened her mouth they heard the grinding sound of distant gears and the oil-slicked cables on the back wall curled upwards. A squat lift made of navy-coloured metal clattered to a halt. Berthold opened the doors. *It's got gun ports*, thought Max. That didn't bode well.

"What's the alternative?" he asked.

"We sent thirty-eight looking for a route to the top," said Berthold. "Three came back. They killed themselves within twenty-four hours. One disembowelled herself and ate her own innards."

"Nice," said Abby.

Max remembered the expedition to the realm of the Brittle Hag and the dead soldier sinking into the water. He doubted any of the men and women sent into this tower volunteered. Berthold read his thoughts and for once had the decency to look ashamed. Abby shrugged, stepped into the lift and took up position next to a gun slit. The rest followed and Berthold slid the doors shut.

"It'll take us to within a hundred floors of the transit station, hold on," said Berthold. Max steadied himself but the rapid ascent still made his knees buckle and the thundering clatter reminded him of Theuderic charging across the roof. Perhaps once the lift had risen smoothly but centuries of neglect turned the trip into a nightmare confusion of abrupt stops, grating ascents and, once, a fifteen second drop that had them floating in mid air, Pell drifting between them like a white angel. Thankfully the mechanism managed a gentle halt otherwise they'd have ended up with shattered bones.

They stopped and Abby made to open the door. Berthold shouted in panic and hurled himself between her and the entrance. Max glimpsed shadows falling across the forward gun slits but the cables yanked them up again before he had a chance to see what lay outside. The third time they halted something thudded into the side and Max heard claws scrabbling at the hinges. Abby peered out, went pale and started shooting. The cabin shook again, the impacts increasing. Max detected a hideous chittering and then they were aloft again but instead of rising through the narrow confines of the shaft they seemed to be swinging free, oscillating like a pendulum. The lift jerked and shuddered. Max tried to look through the slit beside him, fighting the nausea as they whirled back and forth. They appeared to be in a vast arena lined with glowing foil. Shapes leaped at them, arms high and talons bared as the creatures fought to drag the cage back down. He fired at the attackers until the cramped box stank of cordite. For a moment the mechanism slowed as if a weight hung from it but the remorseless winch above triumphed in the end. Surrounded by a chorus of sibilant howls the lift shot up once more, banging against the sides as they funnelled back into a pipe.

The ride smoothed out and flickering lights replaced smokey darkness beyond the embrasures. At last they slowed to a halt. Berthold opened the door. Max gasped and Abby swore. Gone were the twisted corridors littered with the decay of aeons, the stench of ancient chemicals, blood and sweat, the mutterings and evil, crumbling echoes of the tower's slow dissolution. A round corridor of gleaming plastic framed with steel arches curved up into the distance. Max stepped out of the cage and gazed in wonder. The harsh light made it hard to calculate distances but he reckoned the ceiling was a good hundred yards above their heads.

"We're safe, I think," said Berthold. Max noticed Pell walk over to the wall and brush it with her finger tips.

"This is a Philosopher design." She closed her eyes and her other hand flicked back and forth as if she listened to music only she could hear. She suddenly gave a tinkling laugh that made Berthold jump. "Quotient Orbifold."

"Bless you," replied Abby and stalked off down the corridor.

The transit station reminded Max of Odilon's tower. Its intricate weave of rare metals, crystal and plastics spoke of science, alchemy and powers long forgotten. Three stations radiated out from a central chamber built from a cube four miles on each side. Holes covered the southern wall in a hexagonal pattern that made Max think of an insect's nest, the illusion compounded by the oily rust dribbling from most of the tunnel mouths. He couldn't see any trains and the dust and rubble on the platforms suggested nothing had run from this terminus for decades, if not centuries. Berthold's boast of Glass City pioneers riding the lines north for thousands of leagues looked like another lie, but instead of the inevitable shifty embarrassment and attempts to bluff his way out of his own mendacity he led them through the hall until they arrived at the grid. The holes became caves fifty metres in diameter. Max noticed chains dangling from the lips of a few. He smelt a headache mixture of bismuth, diesel and sharp iron and sensed a humming so low he felt the vibrations in his bones. He turned to Pell, expecting her to disappear into more weird dimensions, but she just stood next to one of the metal tracks, hands plaited at her waist with what might have been a smile lingering on her lips. Since Max made Berthold her ward she'd relaxed, losing some of her clinical indifference to the universe around her. Max guessed Berthold had paid the price for Pell's lightened mood in the deep of the night.

Berthold picked up a chain protruding from one of the cleaner looking holes.

"I'd stand back if I were you."

He gave it a gentle tug and the engine of an immense train slid out of the tunnel onto the gutter next to them. They jogged back to avoid being crushed by the house-sized block of angular metal. The humming rose to an audible pitch. A second articulated unit appeared - another cluster of dark tubes, angles, sensor pods and windows barely larger than Max's hand, set high up and circled with rivets. Max counted twenty carriages before he turned to Berthold.

"How long is this thing?"

Berthold shrugged.

"Fifty miles, maybe more."

Max's mind struggled to grasp the concept. For him a mass transit system meant trams rattling over the Brick River of Metacarpi - draughty boxes of wood, iron and cracked glass with barely room for a dozen people. This shining articulated monstrosity could transport nations and judging by the size of the wall the terminus had once held thousands. Max had seen stations before. When he and Abby arrived at the Wrist they'd found empty chambers littered with wreckage, even the rusting hulks of cars, flyers and trains, but nothing compared with this. Berthold stuck his hand out. Max winced, expecting the machine behemoth to rip off the man's arm. Instead it came to an instant stop. He craned his head to look at the curving hull.

"How do you know we can ride this, let alone that it'll take us to the Elbow?" Abby asked.

"I've ridden it," said Berthold. Max looked at his face. There it was again, that flash of tragic seriousness undermining all the deceit and jokey banter.

"You said your 'scientists' mapped the tracks to the north, but that was a lie." said Max.

"Only me." Berthold wouldn't meet his gaze. He tugged at the hull and steps sprang out, leading up to a hatch.

"I ran away," he said to the wall. "I ran away from Theuderic and Father. I wanted to escape, to be free of all that cruelty and oppression."

"Which you engineered," said Abby. She had a point, thought Max, but then they knew the man was a scheming, amoral shit. Yet he recognised something of himself in Berthold's answer. *Running away from Father, running away from tyranny.*

"Why didn't you keep going?" asked Max, surprised at the gentleness in his own voice. Berthold shrugged.

"Duty, stupid duty. My father was sick, my brother was sick. Who else would care for them? So I came back, and went to Interosseous instead. I heard a local whore master had stolen a Philosopher, a rare creature of insane appetites and incomprehensible knowledge." Max noticed Pell's face harden. "I thought she would cure them both, or get her people to fix them."

He put one foot on the bottom rung.

"I should have kept running," Berthold said and climbed up to the hatch.

Grey panels covered in winking lights surrounded full length chairs padded with a fabric that enfolded Max in a weightless embrace. The control room at the front of the carriage gave way to racks of bunks stacked on opposite sides of a corridor. Max reckoned it was designed for a couple of families. If the creators of these machines intended them to carry populations deep into

God's body it was no surprise they stretched for miles. Berthold sat on a couch with an expectant look on his face as if he waited for a ticket inspector to turn up. Pell drifted through the interior, peering into random corners with her microscopic gaze, bringing her face so close to the wall it looked like she was having a massive sulk. Abby climbed inside and shut the hatch.

"How do we get this thing to move?" asked Max. Berthold pulled a supercilious face and waved at a porthole. Walls raced past at an unfathomable speed yet Max felt no sensation of movement.

"Impressive, no?" said Berthold as if he'd built the machine himself. Far behind them came a thunderous sound of collapsing metal and the cabin lurched. Berthold's eyes went wide with fear.

"That never happened before," he said. They waited but heard nothing more. Max guessed the passage of the train had triggered a collapse in some ancient structure. He didn't need reminding of the risk they took. If Berthold had lied about taking this route any one of a thousand disasters could await them ahead, but the Prince of the Glass City had fallen asleep in his chair so perhaps that part of his story was true.

Max made one last security sweep of the carriages fore and aft. Most of the interiors mirrored their own - control panels, chairs and bunks swathed in the same grey foam silence, the only sense of movement coming from the flickering windows. Thick doors with portholes separated the cars. Two units ahead of them a cargo of metal blocks lay scattered over the interior of an empty hold. Three jammed against the bulkhead prevented him going any further. He got a greater shock peering through the window into the ninth car rearward. The shapes sitting chained together on steel benches were long dead but that didn't stop him sealing every hatch between them and their own cabin and dreading the dreams he knew would come that night. Berthold still slept and Pell rested cross-legged in a corner staring at her hands lying palm-up in her lap. Abby lounged in one of the chairs at the front with her feet on a control panel, looking pensive. Max steeled himself and sat opposite.

"Thanks for helping us through the tower," he said.

"Didn't have much choice, did I?" She still refused to meet his gaze. That made it easier to talk to her, along with the stony anger he channelled from the memory of his father

"You'll find your players again." Max hoped Berthold hadn't lied when he claimed the actors escaped. He described the death of Tafaline and his meeting with the Brittle Hag. He toyed with keeping the news about Bassandis from her but in the end told her that as well. In the silence that followed he saw the tears in her eyes as she gazed at him, clearly hunting for the giant. She wiped her nose with the back of her hand and stared at the toes of her boots.

"That's it then. The Machine Men open your head, pull out Bassandis and all is put to rights."

"It means there's hope again," said Max, searching for something that might give her comfort despite his resolve to stay distant.

"Hope? Hope for who?"

"For everyone alive and their children and their children's children," he said. Her fake indifference irritated him.

She snorted and closed her eyes. Max guessed she was feigning sleep to avoid talking to him any more. He left her to it and a few minutes later saw her head lolling and her mouth open as real exhaustion took over.

Max suspected they were travelling faster than a fly-er but even he was shocked when three days later the track emerged onto a shelf that ran over the surface of the Forearm, descending across the skin to the gulf sep-arating the limb from God's hip. If he stood on a control panel and peered out of the porthole he could just see the wall to their right curving ahead as it bulked to-wards the immensity of the Elbow. Half of him dreaded the conclusion of their journey - it brought him close to his goal too quickly, but part of him thrilled at the thought of crossing to the Abdomen. Abby hopped up and down on a table further along the car, trying to get a glimpse of the singularity far below the mist filling the void to their left. Max knew what she was searching for, the Ocean of Forgotten Guns.

"Pell said she crossed it when they captured her, maybe it's further south," he said to Abby as she descen-ded, disappointment on her face. She glanced up at the arm-ward portholes in surprise and Max followed her gaze. The flickering noticeably slowed as they watched and in a few moments the train stopped.

They'd banished Berthold and Pell into the next car-riage at the start of the journey. The girl had no grasp of privacy and cheerfully subjected her newly discovered thrall to a range of bizarre sexual experimentation whenever and wherever the fancy struck her. The first time she'd yanked his trousers down they'd been too stunned to intervene and in the end Max told the blush-ing Abby to close her mouth and stop staring. After that he'd exiled the other couple, ignoring the desperate plea for rescue he'd seen in Berthold's eyes as Pell took his hand and led him away. They returned as Abby opened the hatch, Pell gliding into the room as if she ran on casters, with a subdued Berthold limping behind.

They clambered out of the train into a domed hallway open at one end. Outside Max saw a plain stretching into the distance. It came to an abrupt stop on the south side and he noticed mist drifting up from the gulf beyond. They walked through the arch and Max looked up to see a purple sky fading to black. A frisson of wonder shook him. *We're below the atmosphere.*

"It's the Olecranon Bridge," said Abby.

This isn't a bridge, thought Max. *This is a world.* Two hundred miles wide and twelve thousand long, it stretched from the side of the Elbow to God's hip. At this distance the Body of God was a thickening in the haze ahead and more blackness upon blackness in the starless sky. Max realised they'd arrived but faced an impossible task. How would they get across? If they crossed it on foot it would take, what? Five years? Ten? The pomegranate seeds nestled in Max's waistcoat pocket but he reckoned the bag held half a year's worth at most. He peered into the distance. Was that a city in the distance, spires rising above the fog, or just wishful thinking? Cities might mean supplies, inhabitants even. He glanced at Berthold who shook his head. Joking aside the man looked ill. Dark circles ringed his eyes and he seemed on the verge of tears. *His father's dead and he killed his brother*. He ought to tell Pell to go easy.

"I didn't get out of the train, I was scared that if I did I'd never return," said Berthold.

Abby called. She stood at the edge of the bridge waving to him. He wondered what she'd spotted to make her so agitated. When he approached she pointed into the mist.

"There, Max, do you see?" Happy Abby again, like the old days, filled with wonder and breathless excitement. Max looked over the rail. The bridge supports fell away, slender stalks of metal that looked barely strong enough to support their own weight let alone the billions of tons of the Olecranon Bridge. Mist flowed and ebbed, ragged holes appearing here and there as rogue winds from the shadows under the Arm tugged the clouds apart. The floor of the universe shimmered through the gaps. *It's another ocean*, thought Max.

"What am I looking at?" he said. Abby gave an exasperated laugh.

"Can't you see it, you dozy bastard? Look!"

"Where?"

"There."

The fog pulled back from a jagged lozenge covered in polygons and tubes. A little further off two more arrow-shaped objects rose from the sea followed by another emerging from beneath a bank of clouds. This had a dome with four cylinders rising from its upper surface to angle over the water. Max tried to figure out the distances and whistled under his breath. If his maths was right those barrels were the length and width of the Carceral Archipelago.

"It's the Ocean of Forgotten Guns," said Abby. "They fought the battle here, millennia ago - a hundred thousand ships from Olecranon, a hundred thousand ships from the Upper Thigh. They all died and only their navies remain. We found it Max, another wonder, it's here."

He turned to look at her. She smiled up into his face like a happy child on her birthday, despite the sadness and the pain in her eyes. *Hell of a finale*, thought Max. He shook out half the bag of pomegranate seeds into her palm. She stared at the fruit.

"Have these," he said, fighting to keep his voice even. "It's a long way to South Anconeus."

Abby didn't say a word. Max couldn't tear his gaze away from the top of her head, buried somewhere under

that crazy thicket of red hair with its two pins, one innocent, one deadly. She took his hand and poured the
seeds back into them.

"You'll need them," he said. "There's no guarantee
you'll find supplies."

"No," answered Abby. Exasperation welled up inside and he was about to launch into a tirade on the
fickleness of self-absorbed redheads but she looked up
and he caught his breath.

"Of course I'm coming with you, you moron," she
said. "I'm not traipsing off with a bunch of actors."

"I don't want you with me. You'll watch me die," he
said. She flinched, searching his eyes, shocked by his
cruelty.

"Maybe. How many times have we watched each
other almost die? We're still here."

Max recalled Tafaline's empty eyes, the red wig sitting in the puddle of her guts. He took a deep breath. *This
time it's different. Not even mad Abby Fabrice can save me
from the Machine Men if they decide to turn my head inside
out.*

"Come if you must. But we can't go back to how we
were, it will never be the same." It was the hardest thing
he'd said and he saw the misery flash in her eyes.

The sound of collapsing metal echoed from the archway. Berthold appeared at his elbow, looking nervous.

"This place is unstable. Part of the station just caved
in. We should keep going."

Max looked back at the Elbow. Rubble clattered to
the floor beyond the shadow of the train and he heard
more of the structure falling apart at the rear of the hall.
For a second his heart lurched, remembering Theuderic
and the sound of his claws gouging furrows in the walls
and floors of the Glass City. Gaps and caverns pocked
the surface of the Forearm where ancient structures had

tumbled into the sea. *He's right, it's coming apart.* He turned to go but a movement caught his eye far to the south. Something sped over the skin, a disc barely larger than a pin head. He watched it grow, realising too late that it was heading straight towards them.

CHAPTER SIXTEEN

"RUN," MAX YELLED but they had nowhere to hide and the hall was too far. Instinctively he and Abby scattered - she raced for the parapet while he drew his own gun and scampered sideways, his gaze locked on the object, trying to work out its trajectory. In the corner of his eye he glimpsed Pell and Berthold crouching together. Idiots. They were sitting ducks. A revolver wavered in the man's grasp. The thieving bastard must have stolen Max's spare when he slept and Pell had given him a respite from her experimentation.

The shape coasted between him and the terminus, swooping towards him in a lazy arc. Max saw a flat disc, a coin grown big enough for a giant's pocket. It re-minded him of the cube flown by Odilon when he chased them across the Forbidden Sea - a brutal lump of stained metal. Was this another Black Rose intent on destroying him and the giant he carried in his mind? He heard Abby shouting at him to get out of its path but something made him pause. He spotted a slot in the edge facing him but no sign of any weapons. What stared at him from that dark interior?

It halted fifty yards away and a ramp dropped from the underside with a loud clang, chipping lumps out of the stone. A grey figure loped out of the shadows. Max holstered his weapon.

"Good God, they have flyers?" said Abby, excitement in her voice as she joined him. Max gestured for the others to wait while he approached. A sharp crack echoed to his rear and the Abhuman collapsed. Max shouted in fury and sprinted forwards. Scuffling noises told him Abby was disarming that cretin Berthold. He knelt next to the creature. It fumbled at its neck to stem the blood dribbling between its talons, its billiard ball eyes pleading. Max called for Pell to come and heal the beast but she ignored him. The curtain eyelids closed and the claws dropped away. Filled with a sour rage Max stalked back to his companions. Berthold hovered behind Pell who waited, a glowing wall between them.

"It was an Abhuman," said Berthold as if that excused all. Max dodged past Pell and hit him. Berthold staggered and fell. In an instant the Philosopher pushed Max backwards, white fingers pressing against his chest like six cold spikes.

"Cease, if you ever want to meet the Machine Men." Max forced himself to calm down. The Brittle Hag might be on board and she'd just witnessed the murder of a being she'd sworn to protect. He needed his attention on the flyer not on the bloody-nosed fool moaning on his knees. Pell looked over his shoulder but he saw none of the desperate dread she'd displayed on the barge.

"Can you detect the Brittle Hag?" he asked.

"No."

"What if she's hiding?"

Pell flipped two-dimensional before collapsing into a vertical fracture in reality. A second later she returned.

"The universe is untainted here, though that thing extends into the fourth dimension."

Why was it here, and without its owner? *My vessel is yours*, she said when she turned my hand inside out. He thought she meant the bowl that carried him over the waves to the Glass City. *She meant this, the craft she used to come to the Body of God, it's a bloody spaceship*. If it really was for him they could go above the air to the trans-atmospheric wastes of the Torso. Was the Abhuman merely a valet handing over the keys? *One way to check*. Abby accompanied him and they climbed the slope, guns at the ready. Max didn't care whether Pell and Berthold followed. Right now he'd cheerfully abandon them to cross on foot.

The inside appeared as basic as the exterior. Corridors curved in both directions, flanked by crudely built cells with riveted walls. Max listened. The soft hiss of the wind filtered up through the hatch, barely touching the silence. They padded along a passageway, keeping to the curve of the disc's perimeter. Once or twice Max lost his bearings as they stumbled across halls and crawlspaces that, if he calculated right, extruded beyond the limits of the hull. Eventually they reached the command centre, marked by the rectangular window he'd seen from the outside and a rod stuck in a gimbal set in a shelf underneath. Max found no trace of the Brittle Hag or the Abhumans, nothing to disturb the emptiness of this chaotic warren. He cursed Berthold's panicky brutality and swore to lock him and that porcelain harridan in a cabin if he could find one with a door. *The sooner she fucks the idiot into four-dimensional oblivion the better*. He sent Abby to fetch them. He still didn't trust himself after Berthold's performance with the revolver.

In a couple of minutes they worked out how to operate the spaceship. Grasping the stick caused the vessel to accelerate, moving it determined direction. To Max's relief artificial gravity kept them glued to the deck and a collision detection system stopped them smearing themselves over the concrete as Abby struggled to manage the controls. She backed into the Forearm, the floor juddering as debris crashed over them. Max guessed the upset from their exchange by the rail was to blame so he took the control from her, pointed them at the Torso and tightened his grip, feeling the surge of acceleration beneath his feet. It was disturbingly easy. The craft responded to his movements with a grace that belied its appearance. He glanced at his hand. Definitely Max Ocel's - square knuckles, scars and tendons. He recalled the iron shards sticking out of his sleeve. *Only a dream.*

The surface below became a blur. Clustered spires whipped by as they flew over cities, but Max had no desire to hang around. He still couldn't make out God's waist through the mist despite it towering above them for over fifty thousand miles. He remembered Metacarpi and the impossible immensity of the Thumb, a mottled barrier cutting the sky in half. God's midriff was nine times higher. It defied all thought.

They left the atmosphere as dusk turned the surrounding landscape the colour of lead. A handful of lights sprang into life on the Olecranon Bridge - more kingdoms perhaps. To his surprise a few glimmered on the sea, winking through the gaps in the cloud. If they came from the abandoned ships he doubted any of them were lit by humans. Were they the last beacons of intelligent machines fantasising of a never-ending war? Abby stood on tiptoe, craning to look at the ocean, her shirt riding up to show her slender, muscled back and the s-shaped scar on her spine from a power-lash she'd failed to duck on a desert planet all those years ago. Max seethed. He really wished she'd gone in search of her actors.

"What's the plan?" asked Abby, climbing down. To be honest he'd winged it since they'd left the train at Olecranon. Getting away from the Glass City and to the Elbow consumed all his thoughts, that and dealing with the bouts of anger and longing that plagued him whenever he caught a glimpse of Abby. Journey to the Abdomen, hand Pell over to her people and persuade them to help him contact the Machine Men. But how? Pell had mentioned the Steel Queen. All the Philosophers were answering her summons to take part in some great project. The thought of going near her kingdom made him uneasy. On the *Beatrice* he'd heard the rumour she was in league with the traitor Hathus, but what was the alternative? Flying back and forth over five hundred million square miles of stomach in the hope of finding a Philosopher's caravan?

"You haven't got one, great," said Abby. She slumped on the floor, spread a handkerchief over her lap and stripped her revolver, pointedly ignoring him. He toyed with a ratty answer but kept his peace in the end. Even irritated banter hurt too much.

Berthold sat in a rusty corner of the room with his face buried in his knees, hiding from everyone, but especially Pell. She knelt beside him occasionally running a finger along his forearm or twisting a lock of his hair, making him twitch and shudder as if a deadly snake threaded itself through his limbs. Max called her over.

"Tell me about the Steel Queen."

The girl shrugged.

"I don't know much. She's told everyone her city is the last fortress of science and learning. I heard rumours of fantastic discoveries in ancient philosophy, whole new parameters and functions to explore, that's why we were going there."

"What discoveries?" asked Abby. Max noted the suspicion in her voice. Pell shrugged, "All the groups are heading to the Steel Queen's Kingdom - Parameterised, Transitional, Unfolded, Integrated..."

"And what's that supposed to mean?" interrupted Abby.

"Every function and procedure known to us is being assembled, it must be an immense project."

So our best chance of getting you back to your people is to head there.

"Does the Steel Queen talk to the Machine Men?" he asked.

"Her kingdom is famous and many creatures come and go," the Philosopher answered. Max looked over her shoulder at Berthold. The man shuffled on his bottom, trying to get comfortable enough to sleep while avoiding looking at Pell.

"He didn't mean those things, about you being his whore," Max said. "He's lost his father and his brother. He might be a treacherous little shit but go easy on him." Perhaps he remembered his own father's death and felt sorry for the idiot. "He loved his father and his brother too I think, and just wanted to cure them."

"I don't care," answered Pell, looking out of the window. "He's mine now, you said so. If he doesn't behave you'll shoot him between the eyes." She uttered a quiet papery laugh that made the hairs on Max's neck stand up. Abby's expression was a treat. She shook her head and went back to cleaning her gun while Pell floated over to her prisoner.

Max guessed they were travelling at a phenomenal speed, judging by the blur in the pale disc of light cast by the vessel. Eventually the fifty-four-thousand-mile cliff of the Abdominal Oblique would flatten into the Rectus Abdominis to the west. They took it in turns to keep watch. Max ordered Pell and Berthold to stay in the cabin, and Pell to restrain herself for just one night to give the poor bastard a rest. He steered the ship north for a few moments to alleviate the tedium, turning it in a long curving arc across the insane patchwork of God's skin. With a shock he realised it was daytime again. Far below the atmosphere glowed once more, a shimmering river of blue air flecked with clouds, stretching into the darkness, flanked by shadows. To the right lay the Bicep. To the left the wall of the Abdomen stretched towards Costae Fluitantes. He tried to make out the contours, to see some semblance of humanity in the titanic forms that reared on either side, but all he sensed were immense landscapes and world-sized shapes rising black on black. They were thousands of miles up now but he still saw no indication they were close to the curve of the stomach. After a few hours Pell joined him.

"We're levelling off," she said. Max couldn't detect anything.

"Are there any of your bones or forces here?" he asked, hoping she could find another kink in space to slip them a few thousand miles nearer the Kingdom of the Steel Queen. She shrugged. If there were she didn't know or wasn't going to tell him. He looked at the others. Abby stared back, exhaustion in her eyes. Berthold rested a listless head on his hands and Max felt shattered. They'd all need proper food and sleep. The Brittle Hag had given him a spaceship but it was a shell filled with an empty maze, like the lacunae of a dead skull.

When Pell confirmed they were horizontal Max landed on a cliff high above a plain stretching to the west. He hoped he might spot something he could use as a landmark. In the gulf he saw chains of tiny stars, vast seas of amber, yellow and a sinister, corrupt blue that oozed out of numberless pits. In the distance mists formed iridescent barriers and by their glow he could make out a range of peaks as jagged as a dog's teeth. He swore he spotted flickers of movement in the shining vapour, things striding back and forth, an immense face that briefly swam into view like a sea monster approaching a porthole, but he didn't know if they were really there or merely hallucinations from his tired mind.

"Makes the Wilderness look like a garden," said Abby.

She had a point. Max found himself longing for red deserts, plastic mountains and rusting engines bigger than a city. By contrast this was a mathematician's nightmare cobbled together from the primordial components of the universe - angles, surfaces, polygons, shattered fractals and tenuous curves arching across shimmering nodes. A perfect landscape for Philosophers. *This is what the inside of Pell's brain looks like.*

He tried to grab some sleep but woke a couple of hours later to find Abby at the doorway, pistol in her hand. Pell and Berthold stood by the window. The man looked terrified.

"Pell heard something," said Abby. Max struggled to his feet.

"Heard something?"

"There's another creature on board," said Pell. "It weeps."

An Abhuman maybe, mourning for the one Berthold shot.

"I walked through the interior to try and understand its forms," continued the girl. "They drift near to the boundaries of our realm."

Max remembered the crawlspaces spiralling past the limits of the hull.

"The sound came from there. It's crying and hammering on the walls. It wants to escape but it's trapped in a place beyond the ones I perceive."

Pell lifted her hands to her throat. They trembled. It was the second time Max had seen her genuinely scared.

"Can you show us where?"

Pell shook her head.

"The passageways and rooms change, haven't you noticed? It might be further off by now, it might be closer."

Max seethed. *That's all we need, alien demons stalking the ship.* But what choice did they have? The ship was their only way to reach the Kingdom of the Steel Queen. He could locate a route into the Epidermis where they could breathe again but they'd be thousands of leagues from their destination, faced with months, if not years scrambling through the labyrinth of the Abdomen.

"We'll have to stay in this room," said Abby, reading his thoughts.

"Guard the door, and let's hope whatever it is stays locked up, or if it gets out doesn't decide to vent its misery on us."

Max eased the disc over the edge of the escarpment. It dropped a dozen miles before he levelled off to coast over the jumbled clutter of blocks, broken frames and heaps of debris, weaving in and out of radiant fog. Abby sat cross-legged on the threshold, her revolver on her knee, staring along the passageway. Max toyed with the notion of arming Berthold but suspected the first thing he'd do was shoot Pell. Giving the Philosopher any weapon of any kind was out of the question. He gripped the control tighter and the terrain merged into a hectic blur in the vessel's ghost light.

He nearly missed it. They'd been travelling for a day and tiredness turned everything outside into a monotonous smear. The mountain reared up to the left and vanished in a blink, but something about it had him slow the spaceship.

"What is it?" asked Abby. They'd detected nothing stirring in the craft. Perhaps the hidden prisoner still scrabbled at the walls of its cell. He knew he shouldn't linger but the shapes at the top of the peak made him steer them around in a sharp turn.

"It's a castle," said Abby, her voice filled with awe.

Max guided them up the slopes. Ahead the citadel clinging to the summit resembled a hunched demon waiting to fling itself into the night. It appeared for all the world like the gabled mansions north of the Brick River in his old home town Metacarpi, but impossibly large and covered in a chaos of roofs, arches, buttresses, slender windows and filigreed stairways encased in glass galleries threading in and out of the main towers. A mile below sets of winking green lights led to an arched entrance in the southern flank. Pell materialised between Max and Abby, making them both jump.

"Behold," she said, pointing to the highest tower. A white toroid rotated in the darkness, throwing pale bands over the crags and ravines. "It's our beacon. This is a haven for my people, a way station where we rest, refuel and take on supplies."

The deck lurched and Max almost lost his balance, despite the gravity. In the depths of the vessel he heard a crash - a heavy body thudding into a bulkhead or something tearing through a hatch. It sounded close by. He tossed Abby his gun and she pointed both down the corridor, ready to blast whatever fancied its chances. Batting his fear away Max aimed for the opening. Land, get off this unholy lump of iron, pray the being Pell sensed would miss them in the corridors and the dwellers in the house - if it was occupied - wouldn't see them as invaders. They drifted into the tunnel following the guidance beacons. It bored deep into the skin, the passage curving to the right before ending in a featureless chrome wall. Max let the Brittle Hag's craft settle on the floor. As he did so two figures climbed down from a gantry opposite.

"They're not suited," said Abby. "We're back in the atmosphere."

"Are you sure?" Max asked. As far as he could see they'd crossed no perceptible barrier, but he noticed dust kicked up in the tunnel by their landing drifting lazily back and forth in eddies of air. That sealed it. They jogged along the passageway ringing the vessel's interior, ignoring the corridors that span beyond its walls. Pell led Berthold by the hand. He hadn't spoken since they boarded the ship. Max guessed that the terror at riding the Brittle Hag's vessel, combined with whatever Pell put him through on a nightly basis, drove him deep inside himself. That suited Max fine. The scheming bastard could stay there.

Nothing attacked. The corridors were empty. They edged down the ramp into the cavernous hangar and Max turned to face the figures standing in front of the ship, revolver clasped in both hands but pointing at the floor. Abby did the same. The old routines clicked through his mind, leaving trails of regret.

They were the tallest, skinniest women he'd even seen. They stood at least ten foot high and their bodies, heads and limbs looked as if they'd been stretched to accommodate their height. Their ebony dresses and waist-length black hair compounded the effect. Sharp bladed noses jutted out between slanted almond eyes. To Max they resembled a nightmare vision of demonic scissors, all slender blades, ornate spikes and an overall air of menacing lethality. They carried rifles as long as they were tall, studded with discs along their barrels and flaring into glowing trumpets at the end. Any advantage Max may have had disappeared in the stupefaction that claimed him as he gawped at the newcomers. They were beautiful, in an insanely etiolated way - the disturbing sculptures of a mad artist. They stared back. One pointed a finger at Pell.

"Who the fuck are you, and what's she doing here?" Despite the spluttering outrage she had the voice of an opera singer, low and resonant. The other woman chipped in.

"Your lot's not due here for another two days."

"We're bringing her to her people. We rescued her from a brothel in Interosseous," said Max. The women looked into each other's eyes. *Twins*, realised Max. Their faces snapped back towards him.

"Is this true?"

Max opened his mouth.

"I'm not asking you, I'm asking the white one," said the woman on the right. Abby swore and shifted her stance. *For God's sake Abby, they're carrying ray guns.* He got ready to jump on her before she started a fight. The other woman pointed at Abby.

"Don't even think about it."

Max heard Abby mutter something under her breath but mercifully no-one caught the words.

Her companion looked at Pell who nodded back. The tall woman walked forwards, her steps measured and stately. She peered at Max, eyes narrowed. Her mouth dropped open, showing white pointed teeth like a shark's, and she gave him a curious look. *She's seen Bassandis.* Max felt his legs go weak.

"We have some very interesting guests here, Som," she said over her shoulder. She looked at the ship.

"And that's a funny looking pile of junk. Lucky you got it in here before it completely fell to bits."

Suspicion replaced fear.

"What do you mean?" asked Max.

"We spotted you from the window," said the woman called Som. "A lump dropped off the back and landed on the mountain slope. Hope it wasn't important."

Max remembered the sudden lurch and the sound of clashing metal. Was the Brittle Hag's vessel surrendering itself to aeons of decay?

"This is Som and I'm Ioam. We're sisters, just in case you were too stupid to realise."

Ioam reached out and touched the ship. Before anyone could react the ramp clanged up into the hull, the machine lofted into the air, rotated and sped back along the tunnel. Max watched it go in helpless amazement. Perhaps it believed its task complete and winged its way back to the Brittle Hag.

"Ah." said Ioam. "Sorry. Looks like you'll have to stay."

"That was carrying us to the Kingdom of the Steel Queen," said Abby with barely concealed fury. "What are we supposed to do now?"

"A bunch of Philosophers arrive the day after tomorrow, on their way to Umbilicus. Hitch a ride with them," said Som with maddening insouciance. "You're three weeks away by caravan."

Three weeks? Elation jostled with fear in Max's heart. He'd no idea the alien craft had brought them so close. The two sisters climbed back up the stairs. Halfway up they stopped and looked down at Max and his group. He remembered how they'd blundered into the Glass City. Could this be yet another trap?

"What do we do, Max?" asked Abby.

"Come or stay, it's up to you," said Som. She pointed behind them. "The exit is that way but you'll need to hold your breath if you're thinking of walking to the Umbilicus."

"It's safe here," murmured Pell. "They have our beacon over their house."

Safe for who? he wondered but with the Brittle Hag's spaceship gone what choice did they have?

CHAPTER SEVENTEEN

THEY ENTERED A colonnaded hall with a roof so high it was lost in the gloom. Perfumed censers swung on chains, casting scented light over a polished wooden floor. In the distance Max thought he saw staircases leading up into the rest of the citadel. Dust drifted in the smoky glow. Som and Ioam turned to face them, looking like two trees in winter.

"Right, who is whose mate?"

Pell snatched at Berthold's hand. He didn't even bother to pull away. Max glimpsed a disturbing bleakness in his eyes. At first he'd thought it poetic justice to give him over to Pell, a spur of the moment joke, but now he wasn't so sure.

"That's settled then," finished Som. He hadn't been paying attention but Abby gave him a curious look that didn't bode well.

As they trailed behind the twins Max dared to hope they'd found a brief haven at last. How long had they been running? Ever since he'd rescued Pell and Berthold the days blurred into an endless litany of fear, rage and desperate survival. Half of him expected more monsters to leap out of doorways or burst through those delicately tinted windows, or for the sisters to turn on them, ray-guns blazing, to begin yet another battle. But all he saw was an ancient mansion as tall and crazy as its two inhabitants, suffused with an overwhelming sense of silent hospitality. Without thinking he stuffed his revolver into his belt. Abby did the same.

They climbed up through the house. On either side spread vaulted corridors furnished in rich woods and silks, tapestries depicting landscapes and figures, some from the Great Task, others showing vistas of forgotten worlds. They spotted no other sign of life as they passed colonnades, rooms, halls and alcoves. It was a realm ordered, clean and precise through which Som and Ioam glided with obvious pride. Max summoned up the courage to walk alongside them. Ioam glanced down at him from the corner of her eye and her mouth twitched in amusement.

"We have servants," she said. "You may notice them but they are, how shall I put this? Exceptionally discreet."

"They scared the shit out of the last visitors," added Som, unfurling her hand to coax Max and Abby into a room. *Damn*, thought Max, understanding Abby's embarrassed glance earlier. An enormous double bed stood opposite a fire of blue coals. Curtains opened on a bathroom as big as a field.

"You will be summoned for dinner," said Som and closed the door behind her.

"OK," said Max, trying not to sound too angry. "You have the bed, I'll sleep on the rug." But Abby disappeared into the other room and he heard her whistling her way around the facilities. In the end neither of them had time to bathe. Ioam returned to lead them to a crystal dome protruding from the side of the house. Pell and Berthold sat at a black lacquer table. Beyond them Som looked down on the eternal night landscape. It lay miles below, spattered with shimmering lights and fringed in the distance by a lambent purple glow. They took their places and Max noticed a seventh set for dinner.

The twins exchanged glances.

"Our sister, Nem. She is a bit, what's the word...?" Som twiddled her finger next to her temple.

"Unpredictable?" said Ioam.

"Deranged," said Som. She gave a sniff that said it all.

Max stared at a bowl of soup that appeared in front of him from nowhere. He caught a shadow flicker across the periphery of his vision but when he looked the rest of the room was empty.

"Fucking hell," said Abby, jumping in her seat and banging her knees on the underside of the table. She too had a dish before her and a napkin draped over her lap. Max became aware of constant seething motion in the corner of his eye though whenever he turned his head he saw only the six diners. An invisible hand stuffed a serviette into his collar. Opposite him Berthold's face was as white as Pell's and he glanced around with terrified eyes. *He's going to crack*, thought Max.

"Servants," explained Som, nipping lumps out of a piece of bread with her shark teeth.

"Nem does research," Ioam carried on, oblivious to the panicky discomfort of their guests. "She has probably stumbled across ancient lore best left hidden, and may well have gone insane as a result, but we keep her place for dinner. She'll roll up eventually in a decade or three. She's done this before. How's the soup?"

Max tried to get used to being served by fleeting shadows but found it impossible to concentrate on either the food or the conversation. By the end of the meal he felt a nervous wreck. Abby survived by lowering her face to within two inches of her dinner and jamming every scrap into her mouth like a frenzied mechanical digger. Halfway through the main course Berthold burst into tears, shaking with helpless sobs. Som poured him a large glass of a wine so dark it looked as if she'd scooped it from the night. He gulped it down but started weeping again when a shadow dabbed drops from his moustache with a cloth. Pell just stared into space and sipped water, far away in her own mind. Som and Ioam continued to chatter, oblivious to their visitors' distress. They gave up trying to make polite conversation and talked between themselves - about the house and the chambers below in the hollowed-out mountain where they kept supplies for the passing Philosopher caravans. At last Som got up and clicked her fingers at Max's companions.

"Time to rest. Come along. Let's give you a respite from these irksome shadows."

Ioam leaned sideways to Max.

"Maximilian, a word, if you'd be so kind."

Max found himself in the library of Abby's dreams. Compared to this, Odilon's collection in his tower looked as impressive as a half-empty shelf. Book stacks rose in ascending tiers in an immense bowl-shaped hall, rising so high they faded into the distant gloom. Spidery ladders and stairways led to walkways along the upper racks. Whereas the Black Rose's archive was a jumbled chaos of overstuffed cabinets and heaps of discarded books and scrolls, here he saw nothing but care and precision in hundreds of thousands of spines whirling away from him in a vortex of coloured leather. Ioam gestured around her with pride.

"Stories. Millions of tales of every kind collected since the very beginning of the Great Task, to be read, absorbed and pondered. Everything that makes us what we are transformed into the words of poets and writers - deep wisdom like stones of jet lying at the bottom of silent oceans, light thoughts like the clouds that skitter across the interface between the atmosphere and the dead universe." Max stood beside her, his head barely reaching the woman's shoulder. He looked about him in awe. If Abby ever found this place he'd never get her out.

Ioam led him to a table with two chairs and they sat. She leaned forward. For a terrifying moment he thought she was going to kiss him. The sharp V of her mouth curved in a smile, revealing those hideous teeth. He noticed, with a shock, that her eyes were the same colour as Ruth an Vircana's - violet flecked with mica. Was there a link between these two bizarre women and the Empire of the Ear? Were these sisters in their baroque fortress all that remained of another vast kingdom sprawling through the darkness shrouding God's skin? Max couldn't think of any other explanation. They'd seen no signs of civilisation within a thousand miles of the citadel.

Ioam peered into his eyes.

"You've got a giant inside your head."

Max struggled to control himself. He'd guessed she'd seen the echoes of the titan in his mind but to hear her state the blunt fact was still a shock. He suddenly felt very exposed.

"How do you know?"

"I can talk to giants, like you," Ioam said. "Which one is it?"

"Bassandis." Ioam looked impressed. She tapped his brow with a bony finger as long as his forearm.

"Hello, delighted to meet you," she said to someone beyond Max's eyes. She refocussed on her guest.

"He's looking through your eyes but I guess he's nearby? Please invite him here. I'd love to read to a giant again," she gestured to the books stretching up into the haze. "Sorameistre was my childhood friend, so beautiful and pale. I used to tell her stories, hence this lot."

Sorameistre. He had the vision of a white haired woman with liquid grey eyes, holding his own hands in hers as she leaned forwards to give him a farewell kiss. *She went west.*

"Eighty years we were together. Then one day she just upped and left. I watched her from my window, banging on the glass and crying for her to return - a giant striding across the Stomach of God, heading north towards Sternum. She couldn't hear me. Didn't even look back. That must have been, what? Two centuries ago."

Two centuries ago? Despite her hair-raising appearance Max had guessed Ioam to be little more than thirty.

"I collect my books in the hope she'll return. The Philosophers bring them to me as payment for our services. I'd love to read to her again, one day."

Ioam fell silent, her eyes glistening. She blinked and favoured Max with a melancholy smile. It looked capable of flaying his face in seconds. Max swallowed. *She's the first one you've met who can also speak with the spirits of God's mind, she has to be an ally.*

"Bassandis is dead."

Ioam gave a short laugh but her gaze filled with cold danger.

"What do you mean 'dead'?" she asked, lips drawn back over razor teeth.

He told his story. The smile faded and Ioam's expression became an inhuman cluster of blades and edges. When he'd finished she stood up and walked away. A shadow flickered at the edge of his vision and she held a wine glass with a stem as long as her arm. She lifted it with both hands and drank the contents in two gulps. Her eyes rolled up in her head and she shuddered. The goblet shattered on the floor. More flutterings and the fragments vanished.

"Who else knows about this?" she asked.

"Just Abby."

"Your woman? Good, keep it that way."

He almost said it. *Not any more.* Ioam must have caught something in his expression.

"You'll need all the friends you can get." She returned to her seat. "So why are you here, Max Ocel? Why are you two creeping across God's stomach in the company of a Philosopher and her idiot pet?"

"I must contact the Machine Men. The fragment of Bassandis in my brain might be the only chance we have. I'm hoping that they can use it to rebuild the giant. I want the Philosophers to help me communicate with the architects of God's mind."

Ioam steepled her fingers and tapped a chin as sharp as a knife.

"The Machine Men are retreating into the Heart and the Head. I haven't seen one in decades. They must be readying themselves for God's awakening though now it may never happen."

Max fought against despair. Wasn't there anybody in this poxy universe who could offer him one single word of hope?

"What about the Steel Queen?" he asked. Ioam looked troubled.

"She's up to something, Her Majesty Leontine XXIII. We've had four caravans of Philosophers pass through here in as many months. Usually we see one a year. They're converging on the Umbilicus. They won't say why, cryptic lot, but they're taking part in some great project. God knows what. I'm hoping it's just more arcane madness like her upstairs," she pointed at the distant ceiling. Max guessed she referred to the mad sister

251

Nem. "But on a grander scale. Thousands of those white buggers with their functions and their numbers and their strange dimensions all congregated in one place doesn't bode well for the rest of us." Max thought of Pell bursting open into the fourth dimension on the roof of the tower, Theuderic's wail of desperate fear as he plummeted into the clouds. Disturbed by the recollection he pushed the images from his mind.

"There may well be an ambassador from the Machine Men lingering in that big steel ball of hers, one of the remaining few before they all vanish into whatever unholy furnace they've built in his Heart or the ruins of the Mind." Ioam looked at Max again, shifting her head from side to side as if searching for Bassandis once more.

"And what will happen to Max Ocel when you meet the Machine Men?" she asked. Max shrugged. What could he say? Perhaps they'd simply poke a cable in his ear and pipe the titan out into a new body. It seemed unlikely.

"You ought to go to the Steel Queen and search for a Machine Man there. I'll talk to Virasoro. He's head of the caravan that's arriving in a couple of days. He should be happy to take you, especially after you rescued the girl."

Ioam clicked her fingers, shadows rippled and a volume appeared in her hand, bound in blue leather.

"Your woman likes books, I can tell. Give her this. He's one of my favourite poets, though he writes of little else than the silent, forgotten places in God's body. It might help ease her pain when you're dead."

"Lovely," said Max, taking the book between finger and thumb.

He returned to the room to find a mountain of white towels in front of the fire with Abby's head sticking out of the top. She stared into the blue flames, her gaze a million miles distant. Max didn't have the energy to talk to her so he went into the bathroom, trudged his way to the tub and spent half an hour soaking away the grime and pain, emptying his mind of thoughts by counting the number of people in the panoramic image of the building of God's foot painted across the opposite wall. To his irritation shadows whisked his clothes out of sight while he bathed, replacing them with a coarse robe that puddled on the floor around his feet. Back in the room Abby still watched the flames.

"What did she say?" she asked without turning round.

"Ioam saw Bassandis in my head. She can talk to giants. She'll get us on a caravan to the Steel Queen's kingdom. There may be an ambassador from the Machine Men in her court." He walked over to the fire. "Come on, budge. I'm tired and you're having the bed."

Abby didn't reply. Max girded himself. He didn't have the patience or the energy to play games now. He handed over the book from Ioam's library.

"You can read this."

Abby flicked through a few pages. He saw the wonder in her gaze. She stood up. Apart from a towel knotted around her waist she was naked - high breasts, stomach ridged with muscle, scars, freckles - as familiar as his own face. He recognised her expression.

"Please," he said. "Don't make this harder than it already is."

But God she was still so beautiful. Crazy hair, jade eyes, a too-sharp chin and that bee sting mouth, longing tinged with desperation. She moved towards him and he tried to step back but couldn't. He searched for the stones in his heart but they turned to vapour in his hands.

"I want to begin again," she said. So did he, more than anything. She reached up and kissed him lightly on the lips, on the neck. He felt her tug at the belt of his robe and the sudden scrape of her teeth as she took his penis in her mouth.

"No, for God's sake," he snapped, pushing her away. She stood up, hurt in her eyes, and let the towel drop. Anger and lust hammered at each other in Max's head as he saw those muscled thighs, broad hips, the red hair between her legs. Abby often grumbled about her freckles, saying she looked as if she'd been caught in an explosion in a brick factory, but in the blue light they made her skin scintillate. He knew what should happen next. They'd fuck like crazy for an hour, surrendering every part of themselves to each other as they batted back and forth across the floor before collapsing in an exhausted, sticky heap.

"I love you," said Abby.

"I'm going to die, one way or another. You left me because you didn't want to be there when it happens," said Max, struggling to keep his voice even. He forced himself to turn away. "And you were right. There's no happy ending to this, for us. We can screw each other's brains out and pretend everything is wonderful again but all it'll do is prolong the agony."

He re-belted his robe. He could still sense the echo of her lips on his body.

"Better to end it now."

"And what? That's it?" said Abby, her own voice rising. "We carry on to the Heart or the Head and I'm what, just backup? A spare pair of hands? Another gun? And you get killed and it's all over? In six months from now? A year? If you have to die can't we love each other for these last months so that when you've been ripped apart or turned into a fucking giant or whatever I still have the memory of something other than merely carrying out your orders and picking off the bastards you're too dozy to spot?"

In his heart he knew she was right. It had to be all or nothing. He looked at her again. He longed to lift her in his arms, to fall into those eyes once more, to come inside her and feel her spasm as she came. The memory of every touch, every kiss and every exhausting fuck flooded through his mind. But he also remembered the utter desolation when she cast him aside on the players' ship. What was to stop her doing the same again in a month, two months from now?

"I can't trust you," he said. Even outlined against the blue firelight he saw her face pale. He took a deep breath and faced her. How else would he get her to realise what she asked was impossible?

"I don't love you any more."

She went for him with murder in her eyes. He jerked back just in time as she kicked out, her foot skimming past his face. She'd have broken his nose. She pivoted and kicked again. He jumped onto the bed, rolled off the side and crouched into a defensive position. He'd never fought Abby but he'd seen what she was capable of and saw the same hard fury on her face. It broke his heart.

"Stop it, for God's sake.' She swung at him, left-right-left, with the measured brutality of a pugilist. He managed to block her arms but God it hurt. He barged into her with his shoulder and she went staggering back to thump into the wall next to the fire. The blow snapped her out of her rage for a second and she looked like a distraught child betrayed by those she loved most. Tears poured down her face. She picked up a poker and threw it at him. It rebounded off the door to land on the bedcovers. They started to smoke. Darkness rippled across his vision and the red-tipped bar vanished. He heard a splash and hiss from the distant bath.

Abby fumbled in her pack and pulled out her re-volver. She pointed it at Max, holding it in both hands, weeping in desperation.

"Abby, put the gun away." She cocked the hammer. Her lips framed a word but before she could pull the trigger her wrist yanked out sideways and the pistol vanished. Shadows flickered back and forth between them as her other arm disappeared behind her. She strained and kicked, screaming abuse as she writhed in the grip of the invisible servants.

"Don't hurt her," yelled Max to the air.

"I hate you," she shrieked at him. "I hate you, you fucking cunt. Go and die! Go and die alone in the dark-ness you fucking bastard."

Max staggered into the corridor and the door closed behind him. He turned to re-enter, terrified the shadows might harm her. He heard crying, the uncontrolled sob-bing of the utterly desolate. No sound of a struggle, no cries of pain, just the lonely weeping of the woman he knew he still loved more than anything in this wretched empty universe. He lifted his hand to turn the handle, but let it fall to his side.

"Please look after her," he said to the house.

He walked along the corridor not caring where he ended up. What had he done? Broken Abby's heart, des-troyed her world? Didn't she do the same to him on the barge? Was he looking for revenge or did he do it to be kind, to make her hate him so that if and when the Ma-chine Men killed him it wouldn't matter? He stopped in a vaulted hall. Statues carved from molybdenum stared down at him, angular inhuman sentinels with shadowed brows and clenched fists. *Giants, gods, demons, witches and hags. The universe is full of monsters waiting for the last darkness and I thread my life between their legs, clinging to scraps of comfort. The comfort's gone. I left it sobbing its*

misery out in the bedroom. Nothing remains but stone duty.
He looked up at the figures, expecting to find Herman
Ocel in his billowing coat looking at him with stern indifference. *He's not here. He burned away on a pyre by the Forbidden Sea.* Max looked at his hands. They were shaking.

"I need a drink,"

It appeared in his hand, thick amber liquid. He remembered the effect the wine had on Ioam and hesitated. *Fuck it.* He drained it in one gulp. Fire burst
throughout his body and he staggered, dropping the
glass. It vanished, whisked away before it hit the floor.
The roar of the alcohol, if that's what it was, faded and
he felt a wave of lassitude spread across his mind. His
thoughts reassembled, clearer and less anguished but
still tainted with the realisation he'd lost Abby forever.

The left wall of the corridor ahead was transparent
and as he approached he saw the plain below. He
stepped up to a window and gazed at the jumbled darkness of God's skin, picked out here and there by patches
of light - diffuse radiance from hidden sources and
sharp-edged blocks of colour like windows into the Abdomen. He noticed his own reflection stamped on the
terrain. *I'm a giant*, he thought. *Wandering over the Stomach of God searching for humanity. Ragaleis, Bassandis,
Sorameistre. There were another five.* He struggled to remember their names but neither he, or Bassandis, could
recall them.

"They're out there."

Max jumped. *God almighty.* Berthold sat on the window ledge a few feet away staring out into the eternal
night. Right now he was the last person Max wanted to
see.

"Shouldn't Pell be turning you inside out somewhere?" he said. He wondered how Berthold escaped.

He made to turn away but something in the man's expression stopped him.

"Who's out there?"

"Father, Theuderic, Tafaline, others," said Berthold. "Sarracinte's thugs. Do you remember the woman I shot on the edge of the ocean? She's there too."

The back of his neck felt cold, as if one of Ioam's shadows was trailing invisible fingers across his skin. Max looked down the slopes of the mountain. Nothing, just clumps of blackness punctuated by lights.

"What do they want?" he asked.

"To make things right again," said Berthold. "Theuderic is their leader. He's king once more. They gather and wait for me to join them."

"Berthold, Theuderic is dead," said Max. "He was mad and sick. He fell from a tower five miles high. You saw him."

Berthold shook his head.

"I hear him. He strides through the night, walks around the mountain and his ragged claws scrape across God's skin. He wants to get in, out of the cold. He tried to talk to me through the window but there's no air out there and I couldn't hear the words."

Despite himself Max stepped back from the glass.

"Berthold, listen to me. The Philosophers will take us to the Steel Queen's kingdom. Once we're there you can leave, get away from Pell, get away from all of this. Start a new life, return to the society of men."

Berthold shook his head with a sad smile.

"I can't return, she's taken me too far."

Max gave up. He had his own demons to wrestle. He left Berthold looking for the ghost of his brother and wandered back through the corridors, wondering where he could sleep. A door swung open and he looked inside to see his clothes neatly folded next to a bed and another blue fire smoking in a grate.

"Thank you," he said to the house, crawled under the sheets and fell asleep.

CHAPTER EIGHTEEN

NEITHER ABBY NOR Berthold appeared the next morning. Ioam met him on the way to breakfast and handed him the blue book, its covers singed.

"She threw it in the fire after you left. My servants are swift and rescued it. They will care for her."

"Thank you," said Max. She looked at him with her purple eyes, V-mouth pursed.

"You'll have enemies enough without pushing the ones you love away," she said. Unused to such advice from an ten-foot-tall woman with a shark mouth Max was too stunned to respond.

After eating another shadow-haunted meal he took Pell to one side.

"Berthold's sick, he needs help, either from your people or in the Steel Queen's kingdom," he said. Pell stared back at him with her blank eyes. Max struggled to control his temper.

"I saved your life. I'm asking a favour. Leave him alone now, he's suffered enough."

White eyebrows arched under ragged newly-grown hair the colour of chalk.

"Suffered? But I love him," she glanced away. "And he loves me."

"No he doesn't," said Max without thinking. "He wanted to use you as his whore, that's all, get you to perform those functions and procedures they taught you in Sarracinte's brothel. If you do care for him, leave him be, Pell, please."

He shouldn't have spoken in that way, he knew. He'd seen the adoration in her eyes whenever she looked at Berthold. Maybe she did love him and sought to cleave him to her through the perverse rituals she'd invented for them in the night but he feared for the man's sanity. Whatever he'd done in the Glass City he didn't deserve the dark madness that the Philosopher girl now cultivated in his mind. Pell smiled her horrible white smile.

"You're wrong, Max, oh so wrong." She walked away.

Max gave up. Abby, Berthold and Pell, he was sick of them all. He thought he'd found a temporary haven in the house of the sisters, surrounded by elegance and beauty, pampered by the flitting shadows, but he'd fooled no-one but himself. It was time get on his way, ride the Philosopher's caravan to the Kingdom of the Steel Queen and find his Machine Man.

Max spent the day wandering the mansion, avoiding anywhere where he might bump into the others. He sat in the library for hours, leafing through books, unable to concentrate. Everywhere he looked he saw the hatred on Abby's face as she screamed at him to go and die in the darkness. It replayed itself time and time again. After a lonely dinner in his room he drank too much of the amber wine and fell asleep in a chair in front of the fire. After midnight he awoke to find himself in bed. He stifled a cry of horror at the tall figure leaning over the table, folding his clothes, black hair hanging like curtains suspended from silhouetted branches. Som or Ioam? She smoothed his waistcoat into a precise square and stood up. She approached and leant over him. He saw matted locks and a crazed glint in those inhuman eyes. Realisation paralysed him. *Nem, the mad one.* She picked up his hand between finger and thumb, sharp pincers of bone. She studied it, turning it this way and that, a half smile on that demon mouth.

"Lucky boy."

She placed it back on the coverlet and stroked his forehead, her fingers hot sticks plucked from a fire. Unable to meet her gaze he closed his eyes and waited for the end. Moments passed, he heard a click and when he dared to look again the room was empty. He spent two hours sitting bolt upright, wondering how she'd entered his room and whether she was coming back. He looked at the hand the Brittle Hag had seized. It seemed ordinary - no twisted shards, only a red welt on the back and palm from Nem's nails. At last sleep claimed him once more.

Max woke to the sound of trumpets echoing through the house, high and bright clarion peals from the lower floors. He dressed and made his way to the hall they'd first entered. Som and Ioam stood in the middle of a crowd of white statues that moved and talked as the two sisters bent over them like farmers trying to herd geese. Max couldn't help but stare. He felt his heart banging at the inside of his rib cage and sweat prickle the small of his back. Pell bothered him enough and she was just one young girl. He stood in the presence of at least thirty of the enigmatic ghosts, though they appeared more human than Pell. God, one of them was even laughing, sharing a joke with Som who smiled back and clapped her hands in delight at a witticism. The Philosophers fell silent and looked towards Max. He wondered why they stared with such concerned surprise but then Pell glided past to join them. The newcomers gathered round her, stroking her hair and touching her hands like physicians fussing over a delicate patient.

"So she's back with her people."

Max jumped and swore. Abby stood beside him, staring at the Philosophers and chewing the inside of her cheek. He didn't know what to say. He looked at her face but it was a hard mask of indifference. Her eyes looked puffy and red and she'd pulled her hair into a stone tight bun with the hairpins sticking out like swords plunged into a corpse. He knew better than to speak, despite his relief at seeing her again. She refused to look at him.

"If you won't say anything I will." She walked towards the crowd. *God, now what's she going to do?* he thought and hurried after her.

"We rescued her from Interosseous, where she'd been imprisoned in a brothel, and brought her to you," said Abby. The Philosophers looked at her and Max could have sworn he saw hatred flash in Pell's eyes. A craggy faced man approached them, the others moving back to let him pass through.

"I'm Virasoro, the Guide of *Transition to R*," he turned to Pell. "Is this true?" Pell looked at the floor. *The bitch isn't going to lie is she?* thought Max. He could swear she toyed with the idea. In the end she nodded. To his relief Max saw gratitude on several faces. Virasoro put his hand on his chest and gave a short bow.

"We heard misfortune struck *Parameterised by S* but didn't know any of them were taken into captivity. You have our thanks."

Som clapped her hands and invited everyone to a meal once they'd rested and refreshed themselves. The Philosophers broke into groups and drifted out of the hall. Either they knew where to go, or shadows guided them. Max looked round for Pell but she'd vanished.

Abby climbed the stairs in the distance, her shoulders hunched and her eyes on her boots. Good deed done. He'd rescued the girl and given her back to her people. It was the gift that promised so much - curing Theuderic and Berthold's father, bringing Max closer to the Machine Men. In reality what had it achieved? Dread fell upon him. He had no idea what lay ahead.

Dinner was yet another ordeal. He and Abby sat at opposite corners of the table, Pell among her people, with Som and Ioam topping and tailing the diners like two giant black brackets. Berthold was nowhere to be seen. Max had no idea what to say to the statues who ate on either side of him so after a few smiles and pleasantries he concentrated on his meal. Abby did the same, mechanically shovelling it into her face with an expression of subdued fury. She didn't once look his way and Max wasn't going to speak to her. If he did she'd probably try to gut him with that knife she used to hack at her food. He wished one of them had stayed away and he fled the room when it was over and Som had finished her short speech welcoming the travellers and offering them the run of the lower floors.

He didn't get far. Ioam caught up with him and asked him to accompany her to the library once more. He found himself in the company of the gaunt sister, Virasoro and another Philosopher - a round-faced woman with large eyes and short hair. She seemed more at ease than the others, tucking long legs under her bottom as she perched on the chair. She gave Max a smile of friendly curiosity and introduced herself as Chiral. Virasoro, in contrast, reminded Max of the officious bastards he'd sometimes dealt with in the Carceral Archipelago.

"Explain again how you rescued Pell," said the leader of the Philosophers. Max felt himself bristle, it sounded too much like a command, but he told the story anyway.

"Pell claims she comes from *Parameterised by S*," said Virasoro when he'd finished. He tapped his fingers on the arm of the chair, swapping glances with Chiral. Ioam caught Max's eye and shrugged.

"Do you know anything about Philosophers?" asked Virasoro. Judging by his tone of voice Max expected him to add *you cretin* but he didn't.

"You're living calculating machines with a load of functions and procedures in your head. Different groups have different ones. Pell's are all to do with *Parameterised by S*, whatever that means, and I guess yours are to do with *Transition to thingy*," he said.

"*R*," said Chiral.

Virasoro winced. Chiral gave a wry smile that intrigued him. She appeared to enjoy her leader's irritation. Underneath it all, however, Max detected unease in both of them.

"What is it?" asked Ioam, giving voice to his unspoken question.

"From what I can tell so far, Pell's functions do not belong to *Parameterised by S*," said Virasoro.

"Oh dear," said Max. He hadn't a clue what the man was talking about. "So she's making it up."

"Philosophers don't lie," said Chiral. "We simply can't. We're living calculations. We are mathematical truth, it's impossible for us to utter anything else." Max found it hard to believe the woman despite the fact he found himself liking her. The artless sympathy in her voice and looks stood in stark contrast to Virasoro's supercilious arrogance.

"So what does this mean? She's deluded?" said Max. The conclusion hardly surprised him.

"*Parameterised by S* disappeared several months ago. We've lost touch with them and don't know where they are. If they were attacked and Pell abducted it would make sense. But Pell's functions are different. She's not from *Parameterised by S*, even if she travelled with them."

"Where's she from then?" asked Ioam.

"I have no idea," said Virasoro. "I don't recognise any of the functions or procedures she's revealed so far. Whatever group she belongs or belonged to is not known to us." That didn't seem such a big deal to Max but he could see it bothered the two Philosophers.

"And you know all the Philosophers on God's body?" asked Max trying not to sound sarcastic.

"We thought we did, until we met Pell," said Chiral.

"We will have to investigate further," said Virasoro with an air of finality. "I'm sure there's a simple answer." Max realised the man was embarrassed. *He's airing the Philosophers' dirty laundry in public and he doesn't like it.*

"I have a favour to ask," said Ioam.

"Go on," said Virasoro.

"As a reward to Max and his friends for returning Pell to you, and in return for our hospitality, I ask you to take Max to the Kingdom of the Steel Queen."

Clearly put on the spot the Guide of the Philosophers shot Max a glance of distaste. *What do you think I'm going to do? Molest your daughters and piss in the sink?* thought Max. He held his tongue. Ioam steepled her fingers and fixed Virasoro with a gaze that would have discomfited the foulest demon. He glanced at Chiral who turned to Max and gave him a friendly grin.

"You can ride in my caravan. We have spare berths," she said.

"Thank you," said Ioam, pointedly smiling at the woman while ignoring Virasoro's tetchy sigh.

"Yes, thank you," added Max with genuine relief. Virasoro gave Chiral a *you made it you lie in it* look and rose to leave.

"We will depart tomorrow at noon," he said. "I apologise for our brief stay but our journey is of great importance and we can't tarry."

He nodded curtly to Max and left the room. Chiral followed, leaving Ioam and Max sitting opposite each other in the vastness of her library.

"Pompous arse," said the sister to no-one in particular. "Pell's rattled them, wonder what that's all about?"

Max didn't care. He was glad to get rid of the girl and her sinister, cryptic utterances. If he could extricate Berthold from her clutches then it'd salve his conscience but as for Pell - the Philosophers could deal with her now.

"Nem came to my room last night," he said. Ioam cocked her head to one side and gave him a nonplussed frown.

"What did she do?" Max could see her mind clicking through half a dozen assumptions he'd rather not hear.

"Put me to bed, folded my clothes and told me I was a lucky boy because of this," he held up his hand. Ioam took it in her own. It looked as if his fingers lay in the embrace of an immense spider. Her curving nails reminded him of the Abhuman's black talons.

"Odd. Wonder what she was ranting about." She marked the disappointment in his eyes. "Can't help you. I've no idea what goes through her head." She gave him a frightful grin. "You got what you wanted. I'm sorry you've had to sacrifice so much to get here. Good luck Maximilian Ocel and if you meet Sorameistre tell her Little Ioam would love to read to her one last time before God wakes up."

On the morning of their departure Max found Chiral in the tunnel, directing a chain of Philosophers who passed supplies up a ramp from the storerooms in the caverns. The caravan consisted of six angular vehicles punctured by windows of thick orange glass, fretted with aerials and scanners and sitting on fifteen-foot high rubber wheels. "You and your woman are with me in *Three*," she said pointing at the car. It was as big as a house.

"She's not my woman," said Max without thinking. "Sorry," he added at Chiral's raised eyebrow. He looked around for Abby, Berthold and Pell but couldn't see them in the busy crowd.

"What about Pell?"

"She'll ride in *Four* with her man."

Max remembered the haunted look in Berthold's eyes as he talked of his dead brother.

"Berthold should come with us. He's not well. His relationship with the girl is placing him under a lot of stress. I'm worried he's going to crack."

"He said he wanted to stay with her." That surprised Max. All he'd ever seen in the man's face were desperate pleas for rescue, until the other night. Chiral studied Max. It was like being scrutinised by a glowing statue. Despite her open friendliness he still found her proximity disturbing.

"Pell argued with Virasoro, saying she doesn't want you or your friend on the caravan. Do you know why that might be?"

The ungrateful shit, thought Max. He couldn't guess what reason she'd concocted in the self-absorbed labyrinth of her mind. Pure whim, or maybe he and Abby had reached the limits of their usefulness now they'd returned her to her people. He said he'd no idea. Chiral watched him for a second. He fought the urge to point out that just because Philosophers never lied it didn't mean that everyone else did, but he let it drop.

"I vouched for you," said Chiral. "Though why I should have to do so is a mystery. Virasoro's suspicious of anyone who's not a Philosopher and too quick to judge others. You clearly came through great danger to get her here. Taking you to the Steel Queen is the least we can do." She rested her hand on his shoulder. "Thank you, Max." He found himself wondering how she'd appear coloured in. Impossible to tell and he thought it would cheapen her, make her less beautiful, like daubing paint on a real statue.

"Choose a berth and stow your gear," said Chiral. "We'll be leaving in an hour."

He climbed up a ladder into the vehicle. The inside reminded him of the Olecranon train, all clean lines and surfaces interspersed by furniture swathed in pale foam and a myriad of consoles and readouts spreading their muted tints throughout the interior. The cabins lay to the rear of the house-sized machine. Edging along a corridor he glimpsed Abby sitting on a bunk cleaning her pistol's barrel with a spiky brush. She glanced up and spotted him. He caught a glimpse of the angry stranger in her eyes before she closed the door on him with the toe of her boot. Sadness rolled through his mind but he shook it off and tossed his bag onto a narrow cot in the room furthest from hers.

At noon the hatches slammed shut and the electric motors of the car span up. Max made his way through the vehicle to the bridge. He passed several of the crew and they favoured him with a nod and the occasional smile. After journeying with Pell he'd come to associate a porcelain face with disturbing faraway stares and cryptic smirking. He noticed none of that here, just a mixture of serious efficiency and friendly curiosity.

Three weeks among these people no longer seemed such a daunting idea and to be honest he was glad to be rid of the girl.

Chiral stood in front of the curving window wearing a long grey hooded gown and holding onto a ceiling rail to steady herself as the vehicles lurched and jostled into line, heading back along the tunnel to the outer slopes of the mountain. On either side more Philosophers sat at consoles, turning wheels and operating a myriad of switches. Abby wasn't there. That surprised him. Her berth didn't have a porthole and he thought she'd want to watch as they rolled out of the cavern mouth and across the Skin of God. He almost decided to persuade her to join them so she could see the jumbled wilderness of the Abdomen sweeping away from the sisters' castle, but thought better of it.

The vehicles picked up speed, racing over the uneven ground. Max caught glimpses of the wheels jouncing up and down to alarming heights through the portholes on both sides of the cabin, though inside he felt nothing more than a faint vibration through the soles of his feet. Max realised they were approaching flyer velocities, jagged shapes whipping past on either side at a terrifying rate. He started to appreciate the sophistication of the machinery surrounding him and the calm focus on the faces of the drivers either side of Chiral. He sat on a spare seat and watched with undisguised awe at the landscapes opening up before them. Chiral glanced over her shoulder and grinned at his expression, and for once the sight of a pure white tongue, teeth and throat didn't make him shudder.

For several days they travelled through valleys lit by glowing mist that cascaded down fifty-mile high cliffs to pool in the shadows. Beacons and lights drifted ahead, winking in and out of existence, always far to the north of the lead vehicle. More than once Max swore he spotted shapes striding around the edges of pits, faces glimpsed in huge windows set into mountains. Once the caravan paused and the six cars doused their lamps. Chiral beckoned Max to the control centre and pointed across the narrow defile at a window hundreds of yards wide set in the face of the escarpment. The silhouette of a winged man vaster than any human stood against the blood coloured glow, one hand resting on the pommel of a sword that stood point-down at his side. Max realised he had two heads. He turned to look at Chiral and saw with surprise that her cheek almost touched his. She rested her fingers on his shoulder and nodded up at the monster with an expression of fear mixed with hungry excitement. After what seemed an age the figure folded its wings and strode into the depths of the Skin. The red light flicked off and the message came over the radio to proceed. Max and Chiral stood up, still closer than Max found comfortable, and the Philosopher looked into his eyes with a curious, searching gaze. A sudden thought struck him. *She wants you.* He pushed it from his mind. It was the last thing he needed.

Nevertheless a couple of days later, when the journey had settled into a routine, Chiral invited him to dine with her in her cabin. He'd stayed out of her way since they spotted the demon in the valley but he couldn't refuse this time. He resolved to keep her at a distance, wondering if she'd planned anything other than just a meal and conversation. When he arrived he spotted a third place set at the table and relaxed.

"I invited Abby but she refused. I don't think she's set foot outside her room since we started," said Chiral. She poured a couple of glasses of wine and pushed one over to Max. He stared into the liquid glumly, wishing for all the world he could bring Abby back to the universe again, rescue her from whatever miserable pit she squatted in. Impossible. He'd put her in there in the first place.

"She's avoiding me," he said. "We were lovers, then we broke up in the sisters' house." Chiral watched him over the rim of her glass with stone white eyes, her expression unreadable. "I split up with her. Now she hates me. It might be better if she rode another vehicle."

"She'll have to stay here," said Chiral. "We can't swop you around mid-transit. You'll have to find a way to live together for the next two weeks, though if she stays cooped up in her berth it won't be much of a problem." She rested her chin on her hands and gave Max a smile. Once he would have thought it ghastly but as the wine took hold he found himself growing used to such glow-in-the-dark beauty.

"Tell me about Max Ocel."

He told her all he could without mentioning the giants or his search for the Machine Men. He remembered Ioam's warning to keep the real nature of his quest to himself. Chiral listened intently and at the end of his narrative reached across the table to touch his hand. *Here we go*. He stared at her fingers. They felt so cold against his. The captain must have misread his expression as she held them up and wiggled them, laughing.

"Six on each hand - four joints. Always frightens you lot. They call us 'snake fingers'. What else? Diamond nails, microscopic vision, nictitating membrane," something flickered sideways across her eyes. "And I have two tongues." She laughed again as Max stared at her mouth. "But you can't see the other one." The penny dropped. *God almighty*. That explained Berthold's haunted expression.

"We're made, Max, we're artificial. When our creator engineered our genetic code he threw in a load of other attributes as well. He must have had a wicked sense of humour."

"That explains Pell's screaming and that horrible thing she does with her jaw," said Max. Chiral stopped laughing.

"What do you mean?"

"She has a weird scream. It goes ultrasonic and when it happens her mouth distends," he held his hand at chest level. "It looks like she's dislocated her jaw." He tailed off at Chiral's expression.

"That's not normal, is it?" he said. She shook her head and frowned.

"You've seen her do this?"

Max described the three times he'd heard the girl's banshee shriek - Interosseous, before the Abhuman raid and on the roof of the Glass City skyscraper.

"I should talk to Virasoro," she said.

"Is it a problem?" He saw the worry in her face.

"I hope not. We still don't know where she comes from. She might have attributes we don't. Once we get out of these mountains I'll discuss it with the others." She relaxed, stretched and poured more wine.

"Thank you for your company, Max. It gets tedious among the oh-so-serious savants of *Transition to R*. It's a luxury just to talk of something other than functions and procedures." She stood up and walked to a round picture window set in the wall. Max joined her and they sipped their drinks in silence. Gaps opened up in the cavern walls and beyond he caught glimpses of a wide plain scattered with huge discs like coins dropped in mud.

"We're getting near to the flying cities. It's a sight to behold," said Chiral. She stood so close her thigh pressed against him and threaded her arm through the crook of his elbow. He looked down at the marble sheen of her hair. *God almighty*, he thought. *Abby's in the same vehicle. If she got wind of this we'd all be dead*. He couldn't think of anything more stupid than bedding the captain of a Philosopher's car. Weren't there laws and regulations about this kind of thing or were these inhuman statues beyond such crude notions as discipline and self control? Before he could respond Chiral turned, put her hand on his cheek and reached up to kiss him lightly on the lips. It felt as if they'd been dabbed with snow.

"I've enjoyed this," she said with a smile. "As soon as we reach the cities I'll send for you so you can see them."

Inside his head Max's mind collapsed into a puddle of relief. Gently dismissed he left Chiral and made his way back to his cabin, thanking all the powers in the universe when he saw Abby's door closed.

CHAPTER NINETEEN

AT LAST THEY exited the labyrinth of canyons and rolled down a gentle slope to the north. After that evening Chiral left him to his own devices, to wander the corridors or sit at windows and watch the crags and gullies drift by. He suspected she toyed with him, but who knew what went on in that chalk brain of hers. He worried about Abby, resolutely sulking behind a locked door, until Chiral told him she came out when he slept and spent the hours sitting by the portholes in the control room. On the sixth day Chiral called him to the bridge. He arrived as they descended onto the lowlands. The structures Max glimpsed from Chiral's cabin resolved themselves into abandoned flying cities, angled into God's body or lying in fragments over the hills and valleys of the Skin. Max gazed entranced at the empty remnants of forgotten civilisations.

"Why are they here?" he asked.

"Who knows?" said Chiral. "At best guess they're over eight hundred thousand years old, from the very beginning of the Great Task."

Max struggled to comprehend the majesty and raw power of those shattered machines, coated with whole continents of delicate architecture and stretching as far as the eye could see. "Some sages claim they created the Epidermis itself, carrying materials from the singularity to build all this," she gestured at the jumbled chaos. "Once it was complete they simply faded away, ancient empires bereft of purpose wandering through Trans-A space until they exhausted their energies and fell from the sky. Their atmosphere plants ceased functioning and the inhabitants fled into the Abdomen or perished with their homes."

The scene reminded Max of the world he'd found with Abby and Ruth where floating kingdoms battled in an infinity of air. He spotted streets and houses, citadels and fortresses, even a park that sloped upwards beside them as they crept past a crumpled edge. In the afternoon Abby emerged from her cell and sat with her chin on her knees, staring in mute awe at the landscape. She didn't acknowledge his existence let alone utter a word in his presence.

The next morning Max woke to find the caravan in a semi-circle on a ridge above the wreckage of a fallen island. He couldn't see any more beyond and in the distance he thought he could detect a faint silver glow. Fresh anticipation gripped him. Chiral had explained that once they'd passed the wrecks they'd be a mere two days from the shore of the Umbilical Ocean. So why the delay? Looking out of the opposite window he caught sight of a transparent tube between the fourth car and their own. Chiral appeared and threaded her arm through his. He'd grown used to her casual intimacy but still didn't know what to make of it. This time worry creased her alabaster beauty.

"Virasoro is here with Pell and her mate. I told him what you said about her screaming and he needs to speak with you."

"Why is it so important?" asked Max, not relishing another conversation with the arrogant leader of *Transition to R*. Chiral glanced around and moved closer.

"The girl troubles me. Virasoro has learned other things about her but he won't share them with me yet. He says he wants to see with his own eyes."

He thinks I'm making it up. He was in half a mind to tell Virasoro where to go but he didn't want to disappoint Chiral. Whatever Pell turned out to be was of little interest to him now, but it was clear the Philosophers were sufficiently excited by it to halt the convoy. Virasoro met them in Chiral's berth.

"Chiral told me you heard Pell give an ultrasonic scream, three times," he said.

Fine thanks, and how are you? Max nodded. "Has she shown any other procedures or functions that struck you as strange?" Max burst out laughing, he couldn't help it. Anger flashed in Virasoro's eyes.

"Come on," said Max. "You're all strange to me. How am I supposed to recognise what's normal and what isn't? She screams like a demon. She sees into the future. She's visited untold perversions on that poor bugger Berthold. She claims she can navigate the lines of force that hold God together and she goes flat like paper. She went one-dimensional and four-dimensional, I think. God's cock, I haven't a clue. It was all very impressive."

He tailed off at Chiral's expression - visibly upset, hands bunched at her throat.

"What is it?" he asked.

"She sees into the future?" said Chiral. It seemed the hardest question she'd ever asked.

"Don't you all?" asked Max. He felt the temperature drop. He saw the answer in their expressions.

"Go flat? Navigate the lines of force?" Chiral shook her head.

"Weird sex?" he finished. Virasoro gave an irritated sigh.

"So every one of those tricks that Pell does are unique to her, that's what you're saying?" said Max.

"We believe Pell is a special case," said Chiral. Max agreed there.

"I have a theory," she continued.

"Chiral…" warned Virasoro.

"He has a right to know," answered Chiral, glaring at the Guide. "He lived with her for weeks, he rescued her and he brought her to us."

"I forbid it."

Chiral rounded on the Guide. Stunned fury was twice as intimidating on a face the colour of bone china.

"You *forbid* it?" she asked as if he'd just broken the most grotesque taboo imaginable. Virasoro's self-righteous mask slipped for a second and he looked uncertain.

"In the name of Queen Leontine XXIII, I forbid it. In exceptional circumstances I can call on the mandate given to all Guides in her name. I now invoke those circumstances." The situation had escalated way beyond Max's comprehension. He realised he was caught up in a political incident with ramifications far outside the walls of the caravan. Chiral pointed at the door behind him.

"You invoke the Queen's mandate? Over *that* girl?" Chiral's voice cracked with furious disbelief. She glared at Virasoro.

"What's going on, what are you hiding from me?"

Virasoro turned on Max.

"You are dismissed."

Max ignored him. This was getting interesting. Why was Pell suddenly so important, and to the Steel Queen?

"Max!" screamed Abby from the depths of the vehicle. The whole car lurched sideways and the three of them crashed into the wall. Max heard the pattering of rocks and shrapnel across the hull above his head, followed by two muffled explosions. Shouts and screams echoed through the corridor. He bundled Chiral to the floor, shielding her with his body, waiting for the shrieking wind as the vessel's atmosphere emptied into space. After a few seconds he realised with a surge of relief they hadn't been breached. Red and green emergency lights scampered over the walls like frenzied insects. He raced for the bridge, Chiral beside him. Abby met him in the corridor, desperate alarm on her face.

"Theuderic, it's Theuderic," she said. It sounded as if she couldn't believe what she was saying. *You haven't gone mad as well have you? Locked up in that cabin nursing your misery?*

"He attacked *Four*. He was trying to get in but he triggered an explosion. I saw him run towards the city."

This was beyond insane.

"Theuderic's dead, he fell off the tower, remember?" said Max. Whatever she'd seen must have got mixed up in her grief-addled brain. She sounded like Berthold rambling about ghosts gathering in the shadows below Ioam's citadel. *Surely not. He didn't really see his dead brother, did he?* Abby gave him a look of contemptuous fury.

"I saw what I saw. It was Theuderic. He followed us." she said.

"There's no air out there and the temperature is minus 180. Nothing could survive," he explained, trying to ignore his growing fear.

"Nothing human but he's not human is he?"

None of this made sense. How did the monster trail them all the way from the Glass City?

"Do you remember when the train left the terminus we thought it'd snagged on something, then again when we arrived at the Olecranon bridge," said Abby. Max recalled the debris tumbling across the hall floor. He'd assumed it was just decay. *He got aboard the Brittle Hag's ship and Pell heard him crying. Som and Ioam watched him drop onto the mountainside before we entered the tunnel. He attached himself to one of the caravans, but how could he survive with no air and in those temperatures? Abby's right. God, he's part machine. He can live out there.*

The linking corridor lay in fragments between the cars. Theuderic, if it was he, had almost wrenched the airlock door of *Four* from its hinges. Max felt his palms chill when he saw the bright gouges around the edge of the outer portal. He remembered the marks of Theuderic's claws in the Glass City skyscraper. He glimpsed a body crumpled against the inner bulkhead. Having failed to get in that way it looked as if the creature had tried to broach the engine room. One wheel had collapsed and black smoke poured out of a shattered porthole, drifting across the jagged landscape. In their own vehicle Philosophers crowded round instrument panels while clipped, fearful orders hissed back and forth over the radio.

"Three dead, five wounded and a hull breach but they've sealed it. Engine's crippled," came the report.

"Where's Virasoro?" shouted Chiral. "He should be here." She shot Max a worried glance. "I bet he's fussing over that girl." Pell could wait. Max's main concern was the return of Theuderic.

"Do you have weapons?" he asked. Chiral shook her head. Abby gave a bark of disbelief.

"You're unarmed?" she said, exasperated contempt written over her face.

"We don't need weapons," announced Virasoro as he strode onto the bridge. "People fear and respect us. No-one dares attack our caravans."

Max didn't bother pointing to the proof of the man's delusion sitting on the Skin of God venting smoke and

sparks into the night. Chiral shot the Guide a questioning look, clearly expecting leadership.

"She is safe. I have made sure," he answered. Chiral's expression said it all. She wasn't interested in his
new found obsession with the girl, she just wanted to
ensure the protection of everyone else.

"What do we do?" asked Abby. She still avoided
looking at him and her voice sounded dead. A plan
formed in Max's head.

"Get Berthold here."

Having his visions in the sisters' castle confirmed
elicited nothing more than a slow nod from Berthold. He
came alone. That surprised Max, normally Pell drifted
after him like his inverted shadow, but he suspected Virasoro had her locked up somewhere given the importance he attached to the girl. Max explained about
Theuderic to Chiral and Virasoro, who listened wide-
eyed.

"Theuderic couldn't have survived that drop," he
said. "He must have caught onto the tower on his way
down. He's dogged us here and chosen now to attack
us."

"He's after you," said Abby to Berthold. "That's
why he went for *Four*." Berthold stared into the middle
distance, apparently not hearing her. It didn't sound
right to Max. Theuderic was strong enough to break into
a car. Why did he stop? Was he injured? Weakened?

"Forget the lies and the bullshit," he said to Berthold. "If he's after you we're the only ones with a
chance of stopping him."

"What does he want?" asked Chiral.

"He wants you to make him better," said Berthold.

"Bollocks," said Abby. "He's an insane monster and
a tyrant who kills without a thought. We heard him,
Max, on the skyscraper remember? Berthold offered to

bring him to the Philosophers so they could turn him into a man again and what did he say?"

"I don't want to be human," answered Max. He recalled Tafaline, gutted in seconds by those claws.

"If the creature is sick and we have the art we have a duty to cure him," announced Virasoro. Chiral nodded.

"Very noble," said Abby. "But if you look outside this white fairyland of yours you'll realise we're sitting targets for a deranged monster with the power of a fucking enormous can opener. We have a handful of kinetic weapons and - as far as I can see - only two people who know how to use them, me and him," she pointed at Max. "So bugger compassion. I say we find the thing and kill it before it does the same to us."

The Philosophers looked at her aghast. Max conceded she had a point but their expressions told him it'd be a hard sell. Virasoro in particular regarded Abby as if he'd found her smeared to the sole of his boot.

"Can you talk to him?" Chiral asked Berthold. He looked at her with a puzzled, far away gaze as if he'd just woken up and noticed where he was.

"I can try," he said.

"We have environment suits," said Virasoro. "If you find him perhaps you can persuade him to come to us so we can cure of him of his pain and madness."

The whole idea was preposterous. Three dead and five wounded and they appeared more concerned for the well-being of Theuderic, but Max knew there was no point waiting for the next attack. They had to take the conflict to the monster. If Berthold could reason with his insane brother then fine, if not they stood a better chance of destroying him out there than sitting in these cylinders watching him pull the doors off their hinges and scissor open the hulls. Berthold was another worry. For someone who'd acted as if he'd gone mad in the castle he was being far too reasonable and considered for Max's liking.

"Berthold and I will go after him. Abby, you stay here and guard the cars in case he tries to return." He waited for the argument, her insistence that she lead the attack or at least come along to guard his back. She just shrugged and even though the plan was his he couldn't help feeling hurt by her indifference.

Chiral wanted to send a couple of Philosophers with them but Max said no. He'd have enough on his hands keeping an eye on Berthold without having to nanny well-meaning ascetics. They put on environment suits made of rubber and canvas with helmets the size and shape of wastepaper baskets sheathed in pale yellow glass. Chiral helped Max into his suit, giving him another enigmatic kiss and telling him to take care as she closed the seals. He looked at her through the tinted visor as she backed away, trying to fathom her expression.

The three of them climbed out of the car. Abby took up position amid a heap of twisted metal plates so she had a clear sweep of the landscape leading up to the semi-circle of vehicles. The crew of *Four* managed to stop the smoke and reseal the hull breach but Virasoro forbade them from going outside to carry out any more repairs while Theuderic still roamed at large. Max carried a revolver and a shotgun. Abby had the two remaining pistols. Berthold didn't ask for a weapon and Max had no intention of arming him. Perhaps he was being cruel by leaving the man defenceless but he'd endured enough of his lies, treachery and, now, madness to have any qualms. He'd have to fend for himself. Besides Max remembered emptying his gun into the monster's face on the roof of the skyscraper with no discernible effect. He prayed that his fall, the journey and the harsh environment on God's stomach had weakened the creature sufficiently to allow him to be defeated. Either that or their survival really would depend on Mad Berthold's power to persuade his brother.

Abby claimed she'd seen Theuderic run towards the crashed city. Crew members from *Four* corroborated her story, describing a figure of metal and cloth staggering over the landscape at an impossible speed. The flying metropolis lay in a valley beyond the narrow plateau they'd been traversing when the creature struck. Max stood on the lip of the escarpment and looked at the immense disc. Time had snapped it in two like a twenty-mile-wide biscuit and the halves shelved away from a ridge of shattered buildings and twisted wreckage. Max spotted a path angling down the cliff and caught the gleam of recently scarred iron and broken wood. Theuderic fled in this direction, no doubt searching for refuge in the dead streets. Why do that? Surely he realised the Philosophers were no match for his vicious, bladed strength? Did he know that Berthold would come after him. Would he talk or was he seeking to lure his brother out to enact hideous revenge upon him? Max contacted Berthold by suit radio.

"We'll go down. I want to get him out in the open so you can have a chance to speak to him. He'll see us coming and might try and ambush us. Stay close to me. The second you step out of line or fail to do exactly what I say I will put a bullet through your helmet and watch you suffocate. Do you understand?"

"Yes Max," said Berthold, a little too easily for Max's liking. He sent the man ahead. He wasn't going to let the scheming fop out of his sight no matter how contrite he seemed.

They descended into the valley, following Theuderic's trail by torchlight. The creature made no effort to conceal his passage and the path was littered with shreds of freshly gouged wood and iron. The closest edge of the city had driven into the Skin of God, but the ages had collapsed the breach making it an easy task to find their way onto the angled streets.

Max felt like he was entering the ghost of Metacarpi. He stood on the pavement and stared along a boulevard flanked by lamp posts and ornate facades studded with mullioned windows. Some still held glass and Max wondered what lay beyond. Steep roofs cut shapes out of the ever-present purple glow surrounding the valley. This looked like a residential area and he imagined quiet bedrooms and parlours, their carpets and curtains heavy with the passing aeons. He guessed that once a dome of brightly lit air had encased these streets and noble men and women met in these cafes, ate in these elegant restaurants and slept in those abandoned rooms, seeking respite from the inconceivable task of crafting God's skin out of a million substances common and rare dragged from deep time. He thought of his own city - tenements, mansions and town houses in the shadow of the Carceral Archipelago, trams and cars rumbling over the Brick River, shrieking jazz in low-roofed cellars, flickering torches captured in absinthe the colour of Abby's eyes. Loss and longing caught him unawares and he faltered in his stride. *Get a grip. Father is dead, the Carceral Archipelago is rubble in the sea and you've a monster to hunt.*

They climbed up the gentle incline, heading towards the centre of the city where the broken ridge marked the boundary between the two halves. Berthold moved to the other side of the road, peering along alleyways as if looking for his brother. Max kept his eyes on the cobbles, watching for the cracked stones, the chips that would show him the monster had come this way. After half a mile the trail turned down a cul-de-sac, ending at the entrance to what looked like a stadium. A steel gate lay twisted across the approach. Bright scratches shone in the light of Max's lamp.

"You first," said Max. No answer. He turned to find himself alone. *Fuck fuck fuck*. How could he be so stupid? He'd thought the mere fact Berthold was unarmed and near to the monstrous brother he'd tried to kill would have persuaded him to stay close by. Max was his only chance of survival. He called on the radio again but heard nothing but static. He tried to raise Abby and the caravan but either he was out of range or there was too much collapsed metal between him and the others and interference killed the signal. Where was Berthold? Running back to the Philosophers if he had half a brain. Max would have to face Theuderic by himself but he'd save one bullet for that moron if he survived. He caught a movement in the distance and turned to see rubble clattering down a collapsed section of the amphitheatre's outer wall. *That way*. He cocked the shotgun, made sure the pistol was tucked inside his suit's belt and padded across concrete to the debris slope. He scrambled over the stones, trying to keep into the shadows, and looked into the stadium.

The tiered seats rose in concentric rings from a raised stage to an arched wall that towered far above him. He made out a slumped shape in the centre of the podium. At this distance he stood a better chance with his pistol so he swapped it for his shotgun and gripping it in two hands drew a bead on the shadowed form and cat-stepped his way down the stairs between the rows of seats. The cluster of shadows resolved itself into a stone seat. He saw a tangle of metal and canvas, the jagged lump of a head resting on a machine chest. Theuderic. Now what? The figure didn't move. Had the creature seen him? Was it dead or dying? How to communicate with it and, in the absence of Berthold, what would he say? He'd learned enough about the monster and his ly-ing brother on their island. Kill it and have done.

Theuderic remained still. Max reached the bottom of the steps. He could keep sight of the King of the Glass City if he stayed back against the first row of seats but the ground here was uneven and part of the auditorium had collapsed, exposing jagged girders and clusters of twisted steel plates. He tried to keep one eye on the path and one on the monster but found himself stumbling over the cluttered floor. Still the figure didn't move. This wasn't right. He stopped and shone his torch through the gloom. Metal bars, a couple of old sacks, a dented oil drum.

Shit. He turned to run but it was too late. Theuderic rose from among the chairs behind him. The figure on the stage was nothing but a dummy, a mannequin cobbled together by the beast from scraps and frag-ments. Max fired and Theuderic staggered, waving at the sky with his scythe-nailed hand. Even as he aimed again Max realised the monster had lost his other arm and cables hung from a shoulder rimed with black ice. Theuderic stumbled and fell to his knees. *He's dying,* thought Max and something made him hold his fire. That was a mistake. The creature scooped up a handful of twisted metal and hurled it towards him. Max flung himself sideways but cannoned into a wall of rubble that crashed on top of him. A shattered chair bounced off his chest, sending him sprawling onto his back. He felt a bone snap in his leg and yelled out as agonising pain lanced through his thigh. He tried to sit up. A knot of tortured beams lay across him, pinning him to the floor. *Wait, shoot when he's on you, you still have a chance.* But his hands were empty and no matter how frantically he scrabbled at the ground, whimpering at the agony, he couldn't reach his guns.

CHAPTER TWENTY

THEUDERIC REARED OVER him. For the first time Max saw the effect of the creature's long journey. Half his chest was staved in. Frozen fluids matted the torn canvas and his mask flapped away from the hideous machine skull. He took a step and fell to his knees, crawling closer across the rubble. Max prayed he'd collapse and die but a claw clutched at his body as the monster hauled itself over him. Theuderic grasped Max's helmet like a child clutching an apple. *He only has to tighten his grip.* Instead the creature lowered its face until it rested against the glass. Max had been this close once before and seen a glimmer of light that might have been a human eye. Now he saw nothing but blackness beyond the ragged holes. With a shock he detected words filtering through the helmet. *He's talking to me. He's pressed his face to mine so the sound carries.*

"I'm sorry. I wanted to be perfect. He made me as I am and I tried to be what he wanted but it hurts so much and I'm so tired. Don't listen to Berthold's lies. He always lies. Make the white ones help me. Make them stop the pain. I want to be a man again."

Max stared into the monster's face, his mind racing.

"Please help me," said Theuderic.

"Get these beams off me, I'm pinned. Take me to the caravan and I'll get the Philosophers to help you."

"Swear it." The glass creaked as Theuderic's fist tightened.

"I swear," said Max, fighting the panic.

Theuderic sat up and looked at the girders lying across Max. He reached to pull them away. His head snapped back and he slumped sideways. Max saw Berthold standing behind him, swinging a three foot length of filthy steel. Theuderic lifted his arm to defend himself but overbalanced and fell. Berthold drove the end of the pole into the creature's face with all his strength.

"Berthold, no!" yelled Max. The bar fell again and again. The creature tried to bat his brother away but his monstrous energy had long deserted him. Max heard sobbing over the radio, the desolate crying of a child, and realised it came from Berthold. Something yellow and grey stained the end of the bludgeon. Theuderic's arm stopped moving but still the man hammered at the fallen body. A shattered voice gasped through the static.

"Die you monster. Why won't you die?"

In the end Berthold dropped the bar, knelt, gathered up his brother's remains and hugged the immense crumpled remnants of his torso in a desperate embrace as he cried his heart out.

Berthold stopped weeping, released the body of Theuderic and clambered to his feet. Max tried again to free himself but the bars across his legs refused to budge. Jagged pain lanced through his left thigh and he cried out. A break, but his suit wasn't breached. They had time. He tried calling the caravan but something still blocked the signal. If Berthold climbed to the top of the cliff he could summon help from the others. The man walked towards him. Max gestured for him to try and lift the girders.

"I think my leg's broken," he gasped. It was going to be a bastard of a trip back to the Philosophers unless they rigged up a stretcher.

Berthold put his hands on his hips and looked beyond Max at the path they'd descended. A chill settled on Max's heart. *What's he playing at?*

"King once more," said Berthold. He didn't sound like a man who'd slain his brother. The breezy cheerfulness in his voice did nothing to calm Max. "And I think this time it's definite, don't you?"

He sat on a pile of masonry next to Max. Max saw his face through the visor. His eyes looked far away.

"She is beautiful," said Berthold. What in God's name was he talking about? Max had no idea how much air he had left but the growing pain in his leg told him they had to move fast.

"Berthold, get the others. I don't think you can shift this beam by yourself."

Berthold looked at the bars and shook his head, but still he sat and mused at the night landscape around them. *He wants me to die*, realised Max. He struggled and cried out again as agony slammed through his limbs.

"You parted company but you're still an obstacle, a constant reminder of a love that used to be. After you die defeating Theuderic she'll mourn for a while, the loss re-awakening regrets and memories long enough to re-kindle hopeless affection, but then that will fade too."

Abby, the lunatic's talking about Abby.

"I fell in love with her when she almost broke my nose in Interosseous. That mad red hair, those fuck-me eyes and that mouth. Oh Max, that mouth, so sweet. What is it like to feel those lips enfold you? What have I endured waiting for the moment when I break her to my will, when she whimpers my name in the dead of night?"

Max would have laughed himself insensible if he hadn't been pinned to the Skin of God with a dwindling oxygen supply. He realised the man was a deluded fantasist but this was taking it to inhuman extremes. *You're talking about Abby Fabrice.* She was a stunning woman, true, but she was also, in her own words, a scrawny, flat-chested, freckled scarecrow with a death wish and a colossal attitude, which was why Max still adored her. Whatever image of her Berthold held in his heart bore no relation to anyone he knew. Was the man genuine, had he really fallen for her or was this just another mercurial hallucination plucked out of his deranged imagination?

"What about Pell?" he found himself asking. The woman loved Berthold and was dangerous and mad enough to worry the Philosophers themselves. If Berthold went after Abby what would the girl do?

"Very funny, Max. That little monster tried to take me into her insane world, capture me with her twisted cruelties and foul perversions, each more evil than the last. Pain and ecstasy, both so extreme they ceased to have any meaning, just more slurry from her black heart. The leader of the Philosophers has seen her for what she is, I can tell. He will tear out the darkness from her heart, shatter those white limbs, rip out those monstrous eyes, slice her open from alabaster throat to demon-tongued cunt and scour out the filth. I am free of her, of Theuderic, of you. Now there is only King Berthold and Queen Abby. We will return and be rulers of the Glass City."

Max swore in desperation. The man was mad and filled with a messianic resentment, all channeled towards him. His only hope was in getting a message to the caravan, but how? He couldn't move, his leg was broken and he lay pinned under a girder.

"King Berthold, please, help me," he said, knowing full well it was useless. The man stood up and stepped over the rubble. Max's sight blurred and he found himself gasping for breath. He called out for Abby but no reply came. Berthold brought his boot down on Max's helmet. Max yelled in agony as he instinctively jerked away, yanking on his trapped leg. Berthold stamped again and this time Max saw cracks in the yellow glass. He tried to fend off Berthold but the man kicked his arms out of the way. Darkness seeped into the edges of his vision. He cried out again for Abby. The foot slammed into his visor once more and the fracture starred across the landscape. He thought he heard whistling as the air escaped. He begged Berthold to stop but his attacker reared above him like a giant. Max screamed defiance, calling on the fragment of Bassandis in his mind to help him, to fight back at Berthold with his psychic powers. Berthold faltered for a second and Max felt a brief surge of desperate hope, but the iron-cleated sole lifted again and he knew it was over.

Berthold's foot halted in mid-air. A smattering of red dust trickled over Max's damaged helmet. He heard screaming from somewhere. He tried to focus but the crazed pattern on his visor made it hard to see. Was that a barb projecting through Berthold's stomach like a huge fish hook? The man scrabbled at the point, his gloves shredded by the knife edge. He was jerked into the sky with a despairing wail and hurled into the darkness over the city on the end of a chain. A platform stood way above Max, poised on four shining legs. Figures peered down. Another cable whipped downwards, something slapped across his vision with a thud and he went blind. The weight on his leg vanished. He howled at the sudden agony as his body shifted. He couldn't breath. They'd catch him on their hooks, flipping and wriggling as his blood crystallised in the vacuum. A vast hand pinned his arms to his side and he passed out.

Max woke in a white room to find Chiral watching him. A second woman in an unfamiliar environment suit waited next to her, helmet off to reveal short dark hair and blue eyes. Her tanned skin stood in sharp contrast to the Philosopher's porcelain face and hands. She looked like a sculptor presenting her first work to the public.

"Welcome back," said Chiral. Relief glistened in her white eyes but she kept wincing as if she had a headache. Max felt a dull throbbing in his leg but when he touched his thigh the skin was smooth. He moved it tentatively.

"I fixed your injury," said Chiral. Max assumed it was broken, in at least one place.

"I stitched the cells back together." The Philosopher's mouth twitched in amusement at his expression. He remembered Pell mending Berthold's cut with invisible steel wire, eyes millimetres away from his skin as she plied her inhuman craft.

"Berthold and his brother?"

"Dead," said the human woman. "We killed the man who tried to murder you. The other creature had already perished." She spoke with the clipped precision of the military. Her accent had an unusual lilt to it. "I'm Captain Helena Namsone from the Steel City. We were patrolling the Fallen Realms when we found the three of you."

"Thank you for saving my life," said Max. Captain Namsone gave him a self-deprecating *it was nothing* smile. Max remembered Berthold shrieking and wriggling on a fish hook as big as his arm and shuddered.

"We'll escort you to the shore. It's less than a day," Namsone said to Chiral. "We've notified the city and a ferry is on its way." She nodded once more to Max and left the room. Chiral sat on the end of the bed and pressed her finger to her temple.

"What's the matter?" asked Max.

"Pell. She started screaming when she found out Berthold was dead," said Chiral. Max saw pain and worry in her face. Without thinking he took her other hand. He listened.

"I can't hear anything."

"I can," said Chiral. "She went ultrasonic. It's beyond your range but not ours. That was two days ago."

She's been screaming for two days? Max fought the sudden urge to flee, to take his chances in the endless night of God's abdomen rather than stay knowing the monstrous howling of that blank-eyed girl filled the air around him.

"Virasoro isolated her but it doesn't block out the noise. We asked her to stop but I don't think she can control it."

"What is she, Chiral? Why does she bother you so much?"

Chiral traced the line of his fingers with her own. He could see she was struggling with herself, summoning up the courage to speak.

"She's a weapon," she put his hand back on the covers and looked into his face. "Pell is a weapon."

Max gawped at her.

"Philosophers don't have weapons, don't use weapons. You're all pacifists dedicated to the nobility of higher truth," said Max. The idea appalled him. Knowing these ghosts possessed knowledge far beyond anyone else was bad enough but realising that science could be weaponised sounded like the death knell for humanity.

"In ancient times there were rumours of a dark group in the hidden places of God's spine, so secret and reclusive they didn't even have a name - or at least one known to the rest of us. They took it upon themselves to aggregate those functions and procedures that could, in times of need, be turned against others."

"You're talking about a clandestine cell of warrior Philosophers," said Max. Chiral nodded.

"Warriors, trans-dimensional assassins, murderers, weapon makers - their knowledge came from the black, distorted fringes of our art. They placed no restraints upon themselves, searching through realms forbidden to everyone else."

"What happened to them?" asked Max.

"They were erased," Max could guess what that meant. "Destroyed before they became too powerful and inhuman to be controlled."

"But Pell is here."

"Yes, Pell is here," Chiral sighed, winced and rubbed her forehead. "And I hope for all our sakes she is the only one left."

"What will you do with her?" asked Max. He knew what the answer ought to be but it was hard imagining this woman giving the order.

"She should be erased," said Chiral in a matter of fact voice that sent a chill through Max. "But Virasoro says no, he says she's too important."

It was clear Chiral found her leader's decision incomprehensible.

"Why is she so important?"

Chiral froze and cocked her head. Her eyes went wide and to Max's surprise a happy grin broke out across her chalk face.

"She's stopped screaming. Thank God for that." She stood up, leant across and kissed Max on the forehead.

"I've said too much. Keep this conversation locked in that pink head of yours and try to get some rest."

Max had one more question.

"Abby?"

Chiral shrugged.

"Fine. She clearly can't wait to leave this caravan though." Chiral noticed his expression and shot him a look of affectionate pity.

"She didn't visit you when you were unconscious if that's what you're asking. Let her go, Max."

Let her go. Max allowed himself a couple of seconds of sadness before cramming thoughts of Abby into the back of his skull and starting to formulate his plans for the coming days.

The Steel Queen's patrol rode howdahs - metal platforms that strode across God's skin on articulated legs fifteen yards high. Their clawed feet kicked aside fragments of metal and wood as they marched either side of the caravan. Half a day found Max able to limp his way along the corridor to the control room where Chiral and her crew guided the vehicle towards a silver mist filling the northern sky. Abby sat cross-legged on a seat by the window. She glanced at him but said nothing, turning to gaze at the passing landscape. Max looked forward to the time when they'd no longer be crammed together in this vessel. It was big enough to hide from each other but still small enough for their closeness to abrade raw wounds. To his relief Virasoro returned Pell to *Four* after they'd repaired the damage to the car. Chiral's explanation disturbed him, though the fact the girl was an ancient weapon seemed to explain a lot. He put it from his mind. Let the Philosophers sort out their own. His priority was finding out if there was a Machine Man in the Steel Queen's city and, if so, how to contact it.

They came to shores of the Umbilical Ocean where slow, writhing waves broke over a beach of shattered wood, metal and glass. With every surge and withdrawal millions of droplets raced hither and thither over the shore like silver insects. Beyond, to the north, the ocean dipped and billowed. Max wondered how it moved with no air to blow across its surface. Perhaps, far below, quakes and stresses in the floor of the Navel fuelled the titanic eddies of liquid metal as it swirled around a basin six thousand miles wide. A shining vapour hung over the seascape, fogging the distance but imparting to the whole scene an unearthly glow that picked out the edges of the cliffs, mountains, hills and escarpments on the edge of the bay. *I'm standing next to God's belly button*, thought Max with a wry smile. Whatever the first creators of God had in their head when they decided to craft one the result was as magnificent as it was terrifying.

The platforms guided them along a mile wide jetty. Out of the mist came a ship as big as a mountain - a catamaran with broad wings ending in two hulls sheathed in banded white and yellow metal. From its central superstructure yawned a mouth filled with blue lights. In the cavern's interior tiny figures strode back and forth in glass cubes suspended from the ceiling and projecting from the sides. A single fin rose from its spine and on both sides Max saw painted the stylised image of a woman's hand holding up a mirrored ball to a star. So that was the sigil of Leontine XXIII, the Steel Queen - all science, hope and metal.

As it approached the jetty the ship lowered ramps and the caravans rolled into the hold. After a few moments Max heard the radio announce the hatch was sealed and the atmosphere stabilised. For the first time in weeks he stepped out of the caravan without an environment suit, hardly daring to believe that at last he might be within reach of the Machine Men. Years of experience warned him against relaxing his guard, no matter how welcoming these new strangers, but two of his latest enemies lay dead on the shattered Skin of God and neither Abby nor Pell were anywhere to be seen.

On the invitation of the ship's captain the Philosophers dispersed throughout the ship as it backed away from the jetty and turned to head north. Within minutes it hissed over the billows at phenomenal speed. Max stowed his rucksack in an empty cabin and went to explore the catamaran. Its long corridors of polished wood and steel reminded him of the interior of the *Beatrice*, but it lacked the persistent sense of calculating cruelty that suffused the dreadnought and the looks and words of the invaders from the Empire of the Ear. This clearly wasn't a war ship.

He found himself next to a picture window on one of the upper decks, looking beyond the front of their vessel. The mist made it hard to see. Shimmering waves faded to grey and then to the eternal blackness of the universe. He knew the Umbilical Ocean stretched six thousand miles from side to side but he'd no idea how big the Kingdom of the Steel Queen was or how long the journey would last. Did she and her people really live inside a giant metal sphere bobbing along these mirror-bright eddies? How would that work? He recalled stories Abby shared with him from her childhood and he'd imagined them living in spaceships like big shiny balls with jets on either side, noble scientists and warriors in brightly coloured space suits peering out of yellow portholes as they steered their super-powered craft through narrow defiles and over cataracts of mercury. Maybe it was even as big as the Carceral Archipelago. Not exactly a kingdom but he'd grown used to the deluded exaggerations of royalty.

"Can you see it?" asked Chiral, appearing at his side like a ghost. In the dim, warm light of the cabin she glowed with the same radiance as the mist outside.

"Where?" asked Max.

She threaded her arm through his and nodded northwards.

"There."

He peered into the distance and spotted a disc so pale it was almost lost against the seething vapour. *Is that it*? he thought with disappointment. He could just make out its top three quarters rising above the waves. If he'd held his hand up he could have blotted it out with his thumb.

"Didn't take long," he said. Chiral gave him a curious look.

"We're still six hours away," she said with barely concealed amusement. That wasn't right. It was hard to tell but he guessed they were travelling at several hundred miles an hour.

"Max," said Chiral, holding him close so her body pressed against his side. "The Kingdom of the Steel Queen is a metal sphere a thousand leagues in diameter. It's a whole world."

Max looked into her blank white eyes for the tell that showed she toyed with him. It wasn't there. His mind reeled.

"The Steel Queen's realm is one of the last places to find real hope for the future of humanity," said Chiral. She sounded deadly serious. Max admired her phosphorescent reflection in the window as she spoke.

"She's gathering all knowledge and science to her - what fragments remain that haven't been destroyed in the ennui-fuelled wars that tear God's body apart at the moment of His awakening. Leontine will do anything to keep us from guttering out in the last darkness, anything to make sure that our descendants walk in the light of new suns." She fell silent and Max noticed worry in her face.

"Is this the great project she's summoned you for?" Chiral glanced at him and he could have sworn he glimpsed anger. She relaxed and shrugged, drawing his arm tighter.

"Wait and see Max, wait and see," she brightened and smiled up into his face. Confusion fell over him. *I dumped Abby, I'm going to die and now I'm falling for a statue woman with terrifying anatomy that glows in the dark.* It was unreal, a strange story from Ioam's ancient library. He fought the urge to kiss Chiral. She must have sensed the struggle in his head because she broke into a knowing grin and he felt himself blush.

"What will Max Ocel do when he arrives at the Kingdom of the Steel Queen?" she asked.

"I need your help again," said Max. "I think there's a Machine Man in there," he nodded towards the disc. Despite their speed it wasn't growing any larger. "If there's an ambassador at the court of Leontine XXIII I need to make contact with it."

Chiral looked at him in disbelief.

"A Machine Man? Why do you want to talk to a Machine Man?" she asked, searching his eyes for clues.

"I can't tell you," he said.

"I guess we both have secrets then. There may be one in her court. I'll see what I can do."

"Thank you Chiral," said Max with heartfelt gratitude. She grinned again.

"It'll cost you though."

Oh fuck, thought Max, remembering Berthold whimpering in the darkness.

Over the next few hours the disc grew steadily in size until it filled a third of the sky. What started as a flat grey cipher reformed into a sphere floating on the mercury ocean. Three quarters of its bulk projected through the mist into the empty night. Bands of light circled it, looping back and forth in no discernible pattern. Max looked for windows or portholes in the surface. He spotted a few shadowed holes but nothing to suggest what lay within. When he and Abby descended the wormholes into the distant past and stepped out onto the surface of ancient worlds they'd seen moons drifting above, though they'd never had the time to stop and wonder at the beauty of those long-dead nights. As the surface of the Steel Queen's kingdom flattened out to form a vertical landscape towering above the vessel and stretching into the distance on either side he realised this artefact was as big as one of those satellites. He finally understood what Chiral meant when she said it was an entire world.

As the ship approached an entrance irised open in the surface of the sphere and they coasted into a long tunnel. Max watched in childlike wonder as the valve behind closed once more and the mercury drained from the vault, leaving the catamaran resting on a ceramic plain that stretched to the misty distance where window-speckled walls arched up to the roof overhead. He knew Abby would want to watch this as well. He guessed she'd be standing at another porthole, seeing her childhood dreams take life. He thought of her hopping from one foot to the other with excitement like the Abby of old and grew angry at himself for indulging in the sad memory.

Even so he looked for her when he rejoined the caravan but didn't spot her in the milling crowd of Philosophers and ground staff. He clambered back on board *Three* and joined Chiral in the command centre. She noticed him searching around for his old companion.

"She grabbed a lift on *One*. I twisted its Captain's arm to let her go."

Another gate lifted in front of them and they rolled along a narrow corridor. Light spilled from an archway ahead, turning the milled steel of the road into a blazing line of white fire. Max shielded his eyes.

"Welcome to the Kingdom of the Steel Queen," said Chiral.

CHAPTER TWENTY-ONE

THEY EMERGED AT the bottom of an immense bowl curving up on all sides, patch-worked with pale greens and blues, fading into white mist in the distance. Max struggled to determine scale, trying to absorb the knowledge that they were riding across the inside of a sphere over a thousand miles in diameter. They'd entered a quarter of the way up so he expected them to dip down into the part submerged in the mercury sea, but instead they rolled along a level grey-stoned road.

"Artificial gravity," he said to Chiral.

"Of course, otherwise we'd puddle at the bottom." she answered. He ignored her grin, it made him feel too much of a peasant. At least now he understood what those green and blue markings were - fields, rivers and lakes. The beauty of this world took his breath away. He'd only ever seen places like this in books or in brief glimpses when he and Abby visited planets from an age when the universe still glowed with light. They could never stay for more than a few minutes, their atoms dissolving in the intense energies of those eras. Later times posed less of a threat. Max walked the surfaces of dying worlds beneath the last clusters of blood-red stars and freezing cinders for days before he noticed his soul evaporating through his skin. The landscape of his own time was a wilderness of red dirt, purple sky and the patchwork contours of God's body built from the cast-offs, jumble and wreckage of the ages. It was nothing compared to this and he drank in the sight.

Once the euphoria faded he realised that the interior of the Steel Queen's kingdom consisted of towns and cities linked by a triangular lattice of roads. They left the squat building complex that served the entrance and joined a highway stretching away into the mist. Max spotted other vehicles, teardrop silver, passing them on the boulevard or drifting through the sky above the meadows. After a few hours the road angled towards a dark barrier rising out of the terrain ahead. It rose for a mile into the sky. Max's gaze followed it as it swept up the interior of the sphere. He could just make out a second wall on the other side, running in parallel with the first to form a corridor filled with shadows. He wondered what it was, defences maybe - but against who? Was it part of the mechanism keeping the sphere afloat in the mercury ocean? It looked dead, functionless. Their route ran alongside for another hour before angling back across the landscape. All the time it seemed as if they travelled along the bottom of the sphere while it rotated about them. By now they could have been upside down for all Max knew.

At last they diverted down a short road that ended in a gate set in translucent calcite walls. It slid to one side and the Philosopher's caravan entered a compound dominated by a multi-storey building fashioned like a jumbled stack of giant dominoes made of white stone and curving sheets of transparent steel. It looked precarious to Max but he spotted people in the windows above, walking back and forth or looking at the newcomers, oblivious to the impending collapse.

The second the caravans rolled to a stop two men appeared at the top of the steps, one tall and laconic, dressed in a crisp suit and smoking a cigarette, the other in a tunic and baggy trousers who hopped up and down and waved at each of the cars in turn. Unable to contain his excitement he bundled down the stairs and waddled towards the Philosophers. Max spotted Abby standing next to *One*. She gazed up into the sky and the curving interior of the sphere, her mouth open. *Still revelling in wonders.* A twinge of admiration and sadness distracted Max. She glanced his way. He half expected her to point and say *God's cock, look at that*! but she stared right through him.

"Well you're not a Philosopher, are you?" said a breathless voice at his side and pudgy but surprisingly strong hands sandwiched his fingers.

"Max, this is Count Xix our patron," said Chiral, emphasising the last two words with meaningful glance. "Count Xix, Maximilian Ocel. He saved our lives." Virasoro stood on the other side of the tousle-haired man who looked up at Max. The Guide glared at him over Count Xix's head.

"Really?" asked Count Xix, investing the word with half a dozen extra syllables. He shook Max's hand even harder. "Peril and adventure. Peril and adventure. The Queen loves it. You will come to her court with us and regale her with your tales." Max couldn't believe his ears. If ever there was a chance he'd meet a Machine Man this was it. He had the presence of mind to remember Abby.

"And her - she helped as well." Count Xix charged across the courtyard towards Abby in a determined flurry. For a horrible moment Max thought she'd assume he was attacking her and shoot him. Instead she threw a panicked look at Max over Count Xix's shoulder as the man yanked her hand up and down. Max saw her blush and smile as she heard his effusive praise, finally understanding what was happening.

"Athangild. I'm Count Xix's partner and overseer of his estate and businesses." Count Xix's companion put his hand out and favoured Max with a wry smile. "Forgive him. He runs on utter enthusiasm and total excitement in equal measure."

"Athy, Athy, Athy," cried Count Xix as he scampered back towards them. "She's coming too. She can, can't she? The Queen won't mind, will she?" Athangild closed his eyes, clearly wading through some labyrinthine protocol in his head. He sighed and nodded.

"I'm sure we can sort something out."

Count Xix and Athangild led them up the stairs into the mansion. Clusters of servants moved to intercept them and lead them to their rooms. With a shock Max saw that Virasoro had Pell in tow. She walked behind him with swift steps, her face down and her hands clasped in front of her, a chastened pupil following her teacher. *You screamed for forty-eight hours*, thought Max. She didn't look like a weapon but after Chiral's explanation the image of the porcelain girl, looking so fragile and light-footed amid these ceramic and chrome walls, disturbed him.

He got another shock to find himself sharing a two bedroom suite with Chiral. She burst out laughing at his expression, took his arm in hers and led him to the window. They looked over long gardens littered with delicate sculptures intertwining the branches of black trees.

"You need an ally, Max," she explained. "If you are close to me then you are close to Count Xix, close to the Queen and therefore close to your Machine Man. Also, I can protect you."

"From what?" asked Max. He realised it sounded like a challenge and regretted it. The Philosopher looked up at him with a half smile.

"You're not safe. Guns, fists and clever tactics won't work in the Queen's kingdom. You're no-one here - an entertainment for the evening perhaps, nothing more. Once everyone's grown bored with your adventures and Virasoro drops a few words in someone's ear that'll be that. You'll be no closer to your Machine Man than if you were still stuck in Interosseous. Everyone needs a patron here. Virasoro has Count Xix, I have Athangild - which is even better because he has Count Xix like this." She wiggled a four-jointed little finger.

"Athangild?" asked Max. He'd pegged Chiral as a wandering ascetic journeying across the remoteness of God's skin under an empty sky, lost in a world of incomprehensible mathematics. She looked at him archly.

"An old friend, from way back," she said, shutting down that thread of the conversation. She reached up and ruffled his hair. Max fought the urge to flinch.

"And you have me. Stay close and I will help you navigate this," she nodded at the landscape. "So you can have your meeting and then run as far away from here as possible."

It sounded like patronising bullshit to Max and he was disappointed to hear it from Chiral. He disentangled himself and faced her.

"Why would I want to escape the sphere?" he asked. "What's going on?"

Chiral shook her head, her face dropping into the statue mask he'd seen on Pell and Virasoro. Was he looking at fear?

"Chiral, why are you here? What is this project?"

"Just higher truth, functions and procedures," Chiral smiled, though Max thought he saw anxiety linger in her white eyes. "Ancient Philosophy so abstruse it's turned into meaningless art. The Queen fancies herself as the last patron of noble science. She's showing off, nothing more."

Max wasn't convinced but he let it drop. He had more important matters to attend to and if Chiral could aid him, as she claimed, it would be pig-headed to object.

"Thank you for your support," he said. "If you're looking after my interests, who'll help Abby?"

"Somehow I think she needs less help than you," said Chiral drily. Max conceded she had a point.

Once again he found himself at a banquet thrown in honour of the Philosophers, though this time the servants were reassuringly visible. He learned that *Transition to R* were the last group taking part in the Queen's project to journey to the sphere. Another eight were already lodged in the great houses scattered across the inside of Leontine's kingdom. Count Xix evidently felt he could finally stand tall among his peers and celebrated with magnificent ostentation, mingling strange food, dark wines and a sequence of terrifying performances amid the trees and sculptures of the garden involving liquid fire, sex acrobats and house-sized floating bubbles filled with drugged vapours that burst over the diners, showering them with intoxicating incense. More than once Max saw Athangild with his head in his hands while Xix pointed, cheered and applauded. Virasoro and the captains of the caravan sat on either side of the two hosts with Abby and Max at opposite ends. Chiral perched beside Max, her cold thigh pressed against his leg no matter how many times he shifted in his seat.

At the end of the meal the guests wandered through the garden, watching more vignettes, singers and mini plays scattered amid the night landscape. In this world, as in the Body of God, the air brightened and dimmed with the passing of the hours and at midnight it cast a deep indigo over Max, the servants and the Philosophers who drifted across the lawn like sapphire mannequins. The performances grew calmer, the music lost its frantic rhythms and only the occasional explosion revealed writhing bodies balanced on poles or swinging between spider thin branches.

"Max Ocel?"

Max turned to see Athangild standing in the shadows by a dry fountain, his face marked out by the guttering ember of his cigarette. He bowed and complimented the man on the evening. Athangild gave a snort.

"His idea, not mine. I just handle the expense and the emotional damage." He ground the stub out with his foot.

"You want to make contact with the ambassador from the Machine Men."

Max froze, remembering Chiral's comments before dinner. He'd bristled at her advice but now wished she was with him. He felt vulnerable, as if Bassandis stood beside him for all the universe to see. But she claimed Athangild was an old friend. Did that make him Max's ally?

"He will be at the court of the Queen tomorrow," continued Athangild. "His name is Anselm. May I ask why you want to speak with him?"

"It's private business," said Max, scanning the grove around them, working out the tactics just in case. The idea was stupid. In this realm violence would be as unexpected as it was subtle. Nevertheless old habits died hard. The other man watched him in the darkness. Max wondered if he found his obvious suspicion amusing.

"I understand, but you should be aware that the relationship between the Steel Queen and the Machine

Men hasn't always been easy. Leontine is obsessed with science and learning." Athangild stepped closer, glancing around as he did so. "Obsessed almost to the point of sickness. She thinks the Machine Men are wrong to keep knowledge from us. Their wisdom could be used to our benefit and they should surrender it to their original masters. Unsurprisingly the Machine Men disagree, claiming they work with forces so powerful ordinary mortals can't wield them, not without it leading to utter disaster."

"You've spoken with them?" asked Max.

"I used to be an intermediary between the court and the Machine Men but the Queen said my loyalties were, how shall I say this, divided and thenceforth decided to deal with them direct. But I know how they think and as a favour to Captain Chiral I am happy to offer my services as a go-between once you have established contact, if you so wish it."

That's me warned. He thanked Athangild though he had no intention of taking him up on his kindness if he could help it. The last thing he wanted to do was reveal the real nature of his journey - he hadn't forgotten that the Queen's name was linked with the treachery of Hathus. The man must have detected something in his voice.

"Max, be circumspect in your dealings with Anselm. Although he is the ambassador to the court of the Steel Queen there are those who believe his presence to be unhelpful. I suggest that as soon as you have made contact you continue whatever discussion you might have far away from the Steel Sphere."

Shrieking burst out from a nearby copse and Max heard the excited tones of Count Xix. A gout of orange and green flames rolled into the sky.

"That's my cue," said Athangild. "Someone needs an early bed if they're to be presentable to Her Majesty." He nodded his goodnight and went to extricate his partner from the last of the revels. Max watched him go. Chiral trusted him but that meant nothing to Max. A day in the Kingdom of the Steel Queen showed Max that this realm ran on the old familiar drugs of intrigue and manipulation. He'd have to watch his step. Maybe the man was right. Once he'd made contact with Anselm he'd be better off far away from the Umbilicus, but for him the only road out of here led into the Heart or Mind of God.

"Hello Max."

Abby stood next to him in a short black sleeveless dress belted at the waist and ankle boots of soft grey leather, with a glass in one hand and unfocussed eyes. She'd stuffed her hair into a bun spiked with those vicious hairpins of hers. She looked stunning and, by God, she had a smile on her face.

"Friends?" she asked.

"Stupid question," answered Max, trying to keep the choke out of his voice. She showed him her palm.

"I've still got the scar from that fucking poker, look."

"Your aim was shit," said Max.

"We're here at last," said Abby, ignoring the jibe. "Tomorrow we go to the court. I get to meet the Steel Queen and you find your Machine Man. I wonder if the story books will turn out to be true?"

"I hope so," said Max. He couldn't think of what else to say.

"Stars, look, like the next universe," said Abby, pointing upwards. Max glanced into the night. Through the indigo mist he saw bright points and fuzzy smudges in a ring around them. They tailed off towards the top of the sky. *Cities and vehicles, towns and homes*, he thought. What would it be like to live as an ordinary man, pottering out his days in and around one of those glowing clouds? He felt a kiss on his cheek.

"Goodnight Max," said Abby and she was gone, leaving him alone under fake heavens.

Later he returned to the suite to find Chiral sitting by the window with her hands on her lap and her eyes closed. Concentration creased her face and he guessed she was navigating the insane complexities of her mind, picking through those billions of functions and procedures stored in her skull. He poured himself a drink and watched her. He should have gone to bed but her ceramic beauty fascinated him. The alcohol and the lingering effects of a bubble-born narcotic probably had something to do with it but he no longer found her chalk white phosphorescence disturbing.

Chiral cried out, jerking back in the chair so that she almost fell, arms floundering for balance. Max saw fear in her eyes. She mouthed a name, *Pell*.

"What is it?" he asked, moving towards her. She stared wildly around, spotted him and swiftly mastered herself.

"Nothing, a nightmare, nothing," she said. *You weren't dreaming, you were thinking. What did you find in that mind of yours?* Max wanted to challenge her but before he could react she wrapped her arms round his neck and buried her head in his shoulder. Her heart hammered through her chest. He put his hand on the small of her back, the cold ridges of the muscles hard against his fingers. They softened as he stroked her spine. Her hair smelt of lemons. She took a couple of deep breaths, lifted her face and kissed him. He returned the kiss. Her lips and throat were metal cool but soft. Max picked her up and carried her into the bedroom, tearing off her long dress so he could cup her breasts and run his hands across her legs and buttocks. Chiral copied him, undressing him with impressive skill before pulling him onto the bed. He looked down at her, a delicate white ink sketch against the night sheets. She gave a sly grin.

"Ready?"

He felt something wrap itself around his penis. *Fucking God almighty*. He almost panicked and jerked away, remembering the look of haggard terror in Berthold's eyes every morning. Chiral's many jointed fingers were bands of iron encircling his biceps, holding him down.

"Relax," she said. Whatever it was gave a gentle tug, guiding him into her. Cool, like water. Was this what Pell did to Berthold? If it was the idiot didn't know he was born.

Max woke to see Chiral dressing by the window, her white body surrounded by the flaring drapes that whispered across the floor in the morning breeze. Once he'd got over the initial shock they'd fucked for what seemed like hours. His groin still buzzed in the after glow. But at last they'd fallen asleep at a mad hour and for the first time Max allowed himself a few moments of relaxed happiness. He was about to meet a Machine Man, he and Abby were reconciled and he was under the wing of a powerful Philosopher with the bonus of insane sex. Chiral had to ask him to wipe that grin off his face as he pulled his clothes back on.

They breakfasted together, Max picking his way through his store of small talk to cover the mixture of tentative lust and embarrassment that lay between them. Chiral was distracted. He could tell that whatever vision she'd had of Pell the night before still haunted her. More and more he realised that the girl impacted on the Philosopher's journey to the Steel Queen's kingdom and this project of hers. He guessed Virasoro had decided she had a role to play while Chiral just wanted the weaponised creature dead. No matter how much he tried to forget Pell and concentrate on his own quest he couldn't shake the puzzle from his mind. He daren't compromise his own position in this world by getting involved in a feud between Philosophers, but he sensed real danger. The cryptic refugee from Interosseous was a nexus for powers and plots he feared had implications far beyond the walls of this titanic ball.

In the afternoon servants came to prepare Max and Chiral for the reception at the Steel Queen's court and as the light began to fade once more Virasoro, the captains of the caravan, Count Xix, Athangild, Max and Abby climbed into three flyers - glass cylinders with lace metal wings crackling with electricity. Chiral must have worked more magic because they found themselves in the same vessel as their hosts, much to Virasoro's disgust. They floated up into the white sky, Abby and Max gazing in wonder as the curved bowl of the sphere rolled under them. After a while he noticed Count Xix studying a piece of paper, alternately reading it then pressing it to his chest, closing his eyes and mouthing words. Athangild leaned across. "He's written a poem for the Queen. He composes sonnets to her and she tears them apart in front of everyone. It's an amusing game they've been playing for years now."

Looking at Count Xix's terrified eyes as he struggled to memorise the lines Max guessed the amusement was largely on one side. Even so Count Xix caught Athangild's eyes and grinned like a happy child.

"She will adore it. This is it, Athy, this is the poem."

"Of course it is, Count Xix," said Athangild, his love for the man plain in his eyes.

"Max," called Abby from further down the craft. She pointed through the glass. He looked out and noticed a row of bonfires curving over the shadowed fields. He glanced up and further along a second line angled to intercept the first, then another burst into flame beyond that, all three converging on a glittering mass in the mist ahead. With a shock he realised he was looking at the palace of Leontine XXIII, an immense diamond of jewelled metal rising out of the side of the world, defying the sphere's own gravity field. They circled the upper structure, Count Xix clearly wanting to put on a show for his guests, and Max laughed in sheer wonder. Gardens, rooms, villas, houses, fountains and statues all clung to the delicate tiers that formed the main complex. To his surprise he saw no artificial light, just thousands upon thousands of fires, torches and flambeaux threading in and out of arches, corridors and halls. He guessed this was specially for the revels this evening, an amusing conceit on behalf of the Queen to turn her back on the science she loved and recreate a primitive age from the abyss of deep time. After one more circuit the ships landed in a courtyard projecting from a facet of the citadel and they stepped out to be greeted by servants running towards them with coloured lanterns and trays of food and wine.

CHAPTER TWENTY-TWO

THE SERVANTS USHERED them into a vaulted hall filled with guests and courtiers who parted as they made their entrance. A herald called out to the assembled throng and Count Xix ploughed on at the head of their group, holding his head high and reserving a couple of haughty glares for a handful of men and women watching him from between chrome pillars. Max noticed more Philosophers among them and realised these must be rival lords. He searched the crowd, looking for anyone or anything that might signify the presence of the ambassador from the Machine Men. What would it look like? An incredible statue of metal? A delicate piece of living jewellery woven into the shape of an insect? A squat engine on tracks or wheels? Perhaps it was a tidier version of Theuderic. He spotted nothing in the throng, just people - some wearing fantastic costumes, others simple outfits. Hoods covered a few heads, elsewhere exquisite headdresses rose above the crowds. He saw bald skulls painted and unpainted but all human. Count Xix stopped and his entourage gathered around him. He bowed to a knot of figures standing beneath a twisted arch built from fragments of pig iron.

"Your Majesty," he said in tones of deep and reverent awe. "May I humbly present my honoured guests, the Philosophers *Transition to R.*"

Max had expected an all-powerful monarch, aged and imperious, sitting on a steel throne to dispense favours and justice with icy impartiality. Instead he found himself standing on the opposite side of a circle to a woman who looked barely out of her twenties. At first he thought she must be the scatty daughter of a Lord who'd wandered into the Queen's proximity by accident and he continued to search for someone more regal looking. Then the truth dawned on him. This was she, the mysterious sorceress-queen of Abby's story books.

Leontine XXIII wore a suit of shimmering steel wool with a simple circlet sporting a polished disc in the middle of her forehead. Her hair was sharp cut into midnight blue layers. The woman's expression suggested wide-eyed awe and her gaze flickered back and forth between the others with a mercurial giddiness that made him wonder whether she was drunk or just foolish. He looked at the faces of the crowd gathering around her and realised, to his astonishment, that most of the men, and a significant number of the women, were head over heels in love with her. Clearly they saw something he didn't. It was hard to believe that not only was this giggling debutante the most powerful person in the entire sphere but she was also leader and patron of a project of such significance that it had enticed Philosophers from all over the body of God to make the journey to the Umbilicus.

The Queen opened her arms and gave a cry of delight.

"Friends, friends, at last we are all here. We are complete. Welcome to the kingdom of Leontine XXIII."

Everyone bowed, including Max. Leontine waved her hands at them as if to say *don't be silly*, then fixed her gaze on Count Xix.

"Well?"

Count Xix turned crimson.

"Now?" he asked in panic, looking at the crowds gathering around them.

"When else?"

Max caught Athangild's eye. The overseer gave him a grin and a wink. Count Xix gasped like a beached fish for a few seconds, realised there was no escape and launched into his poem. Max was no judge but halfway through the Queen rested her chin on one hand and peered at Count Xix through her fingers. He struggled on regardless, finishing to a polite smattering of applause. He awaited his judgement. Leontine shook her head and looked round the crowd.

"Anyone else?" she asked in a voice that suggested even a dirty limerick from a footman would be a vast improvement. Count Xix looked so crestfallen Max couldn't help but feel sorry for the man. Leontine's gaze locked on him and eyes the colour of honey bored into his. He sensed a real power behind that look and hurriedly revised his opinion of her.

"You?"

Shit, he didn't know any verse.

"I've got a poem," said Abby. She stood next to Chiral who raised an eyebrow at Max. *Fuck, Abby, no!* He panicked, trying to catch her eye and hurling psychic pleas at her to shut up. God only knew what would come out of her mouth in the guise of poetry. Perhaps he could leap across the distance, knock her out and haul her off before anyone realised. It was too late.

"Go on," said the Steel Queen. Max closed his eyes and waited for the universe to end.

"And I recall when as a child
I felt your hand take mine
To lift me up from squalid wood and iron

To guide me over nickel floors, past cobalt walls
To point through crystal at an empty sky
And fill my head with dreams.
But most of all you taught me how to hate
The loving lies that said I'd found a home
In your cruel dark-feathered heart."

The silence lasted for centuries. Max opened his eyes and heard a murmur run through the assembled throng - polite approval, a chuckle, a few wry glances. No expressions of utter horror or deep offence. The Queen looked at the ceiling, as if running the words through her mind once more. Count Xix stood next to Athangild, head down, his humiliation complete as his partner whispered reassurances in his ear about next time.

"Not bad. What is it you do exactly?" asked Leontine.

"I write plays," said Abby. *When you're not stealing things or shooting people*, thought Max, finally able to reassemble his shattered nerves.

"We need new plays, the old ones bore me stupid," mused Leontine. She leaned towards an official. "Is Peshon here tonight? Go and fetch him and tell him to talk to…" she looked across the crowd at Abby who blushed.

"Abigail Fabrice," she said.

"Abigail Fabrice," continued the Queen. "She might be able to inject life into the old fart."

The servant melted into the crowd which sensed the entertainment was over and started to relax. Max took the opportunity to grab Abby by the elbow and manhandle her over to the wall.

"What the fuck was all that about?"

"Good, wasn't it?" said Abby, clearly delighted at the thought of having a chance to interfere with the local theatres.

"Are you completely out of your fucking mind? Where in the Body of God did you get that poem from?"

Abby looked at him as if he was being particularly stupid.

"It's mine. It's from a play I started writing in Interosseous, about Odilon."

Max felt as if his jaw had just hit the floor.

"You're writing a play about Odilon?" he said, aghast. She was mad, completely mad. Rejecting him had pushed her over the edge into the realm of the hopelessly insane. She looked back at him with that infuriating expression of innocence he recognised from old.

"Why wouldn't I?"

Max opened his mouth to give her several hundred extremely good reasons.

"Max?" Athangild was at his elbow. Still unable to comprehend what had just happened he turned to Count Xix's partner.

"Someone wants to meet you."

Max saw the look in his eyes and all thoughts of poetry vanished from his mind. Athangild led Max away from the crowds to a quiet corner of the hall. A slender woman in a tight-fitting navy blue suit stood ramrod straight, cradling a glass of wine in her hands. With her bald head and pointed chin and nose she looked for all the world like a bird perched in the shadows. She watched them approach out of the corner of her eye.

"Max, this is Persephone, servant of Anselm the Machine Man," said Athangild. Max looked at the woman in fascination. She appeared human to him although he noticed her pupils were barred like cell windows and she never blinked.

"Your master isn't here tonight?" asked Max, half disappointed, half relieved at not having to face the creature yet.

"No," Persephone sipped her wine. Athangild shot Max a look that said *politics* and melted back into the crowd leaving him alone with the woman. She continued to stare ahead, only occasionally glancing at him. He guessed that working for the architects of God's mind would put a strain on anyone. She'd buried hers under a precise and mannered reserve. *Now what do I say?* Having journeyed all this way small talk seemed pointless but he hesitated to cut to the chase. He'd imagined announcing his mission to a shining automaton of steel, crystal and glass in a hall filled with gleaming machinery, arc lightning and writhing vapours. Instead he found himself struggling with an embarrassed silence in front of someone who resembled a mime artist's nightmare. In the end her mouth twitched into a smile.

"You wish to speak with Anselm the Machine Man," she said. "Concerning?"

Max decided to gamble all. He no longer had the patience to handle a prolonged diplomatic back and forth with all its attendant euphemisms, half-guessed protocol and tedious evasion.

"I come from the City of Metacarpi in the shadow of the Left Thumb."

If she recognised the town or knew anything of what transpired there she didn't show it. Max soldiered on.

"I bring a message from Ragaleis." That should do it.

Persephone took another sip of wine, cradling the base of the glass in her hand. The moments ticked by. Max wondered if she'd misheard or chose to ignore him. He was about to speak again when she nodded.

"Anselm the Machine Man agrees to meet with you. Tomorrow. We will send a flyer to Count Xix's mansion. You will come alone."

Realisation dawned.

"You're in contact with him now?" he said. Persephone allowed herself a smile. She held out a delicate hand. Max shook it - dry and hot like the palm of a fever victim.

"Until tomorrow, Max," she said. She turned and drifted into the crowd. Max watched her spidery form flicker in and out of the gaps between the revellers until she'd vanished. *Too easy*. Max grabbed a glass of wine and hid in the corner of the hall, brooding as he drank. Had he just walked open-eyed into a trap, blurting out his mission to one of the Queen's spies? But what had he said? The name of a giant. What did that signify? He pushed his doubts to the back of his mind. Athangild's warnings had made him paranoid. If someone wanted him dead they could have killed him at any point between the flying cities and here.

He took another drink, allowed himself to relax and wandered through the crowds. Few people appeared interested in him and he was happy to stay in the background. The Philosophers were the focus of attention among the revellers after the Queen herself and Abby hadn't done so badly following her impromptu performance. He spotted her re-enacting a scene he recognised from *The Gate of Light* before a gaunt man with a bristle cut who studied her intently with his chin on his fist. Max guessed it was Peshon the Old Fart.

Count Xix had recovered from his humiliation with impressive speed and was clearly back in favour with Leontine whose shrieking laughter at his latest jokes became so loud that an embarrassed clerk was driven to whisper in her ear and receive a box round the ears for his pains.

The night wore on. Max went hunting for Chiral but didn't find her. Virasoro had also vanished. He ended up cornered by a pale youth with copper coloured eyes who claimed to be a Sonian Poet, whatever that meant. He insisted on repeating Abby's poem word for word and then asking Max to comment on each line, offering his own increasingly bizarre interpretations when he found Max's wanting. In the end Max left him in the company of two women painted like the halves of a broken vase. Around midnight he climbed into one of Count Xix's flyers with a handful of Philosophers. On returning to the mansion he made his way to the suite. Raised voices inside stopped him at the door.

"You cannot insert any of her functions into the process," Chiral's voice sounded furious. "It doesn't matter whether you think she can break the impasse. You have no idea what you're doing. She's a weapon, Virasoro, we have no clue of the extent of the poison in her mind. Every single number in that head is compromised."

"It's not for you to decide, Chiral," Virasoro's voice carried the testy impatience of an arrogant man convinced he faced nothing more than irrational hysteria. He was asking to be punched.

"Put it to a vote. The others will agree with me," said Chiral.

"Very well, I'll take her with us to the palace tomorrow and present her to the other Guides. Then we'll vote."

"Virasoro, please, you have no idea what you're doing. She is one of *them*, she should be erased." Chiral sounded desperate.

"We don't erase people any more Chiral, those days are long gone." Virasoro's voice carried the finality of someone who'd decided they'd already won the argument.

"You're losing focus, Chiral," he continued, his voice coming closer to the door. "You're distracted by that man. We need every Philosopher to concentrate on the task in hand. It's too important to fail."

Max scampered backwards down the corridor half a dozen steps so when the arrogant bastard emerged it appeared as if he'd just staggered off the landing. Virasoro shot Max a glance of impatient loathing and strode past. Max entered the room to find Chiral sitting with her face in her hands.

"Everything alright?" He wanted to ask her about the conversation he'd overheard but she looked exhausted and miserable. He held her fingers in his and kissed her diamond nails. She managed a laugh. Questions could wait until the morning. He took her to bed and they fell asleep in a damp tangle half an hour later.

Cool lips on his forehead woke him but when he surfaced from his dreams Chiral was gone and he faced the dawn alone. *They've left for the palace. To argue about Pell.* He cursed himself for not having a chance to say a proper farewell to Chiral. He dressed and ate, gazing out of the window at a couple of servants tending to the sculptures in Count Xix's garden. Today he would meet a Machine Man with the news that Bassandis was dead and the only hope for humanity lay in the fragment of the giant's mind buried deep within his own. He searched his thoughts. No fear, just a steady inevitability as he prepared to walk a white-walled path through this strange world of ceramic tiles and burnished steel. What should he do? Write a letter to Chiral? To Abby? To the universe? Saying what? He couldn't think of anything that wouldn't be jejune or self-serving. He wasn't hoping for monuments or condemnation. *Go and talk to An-*

selm, tell the truth and ask the simple question. Can you take this remnant of the giant from my head and with it save us all? Will I die in the process? He remembered the row he'd heard last night. Part of him felt disquiet at the implications in the back and forth between the two Philosophers. Virasoro wanted to use Pell in their project, Chiral thought he was insane. Set against his own quest it could hardly be so important.

Persephone hadn't given him an exact time. He grew bored with the apartments and decided to wander the garden. When he descended into the hall he spotted Abby standing by the entrance with a pack on her back and a small blue case in her hand.

"Saves me sending for you to say goodbye," she said as he approached. "I'm leaving."

Leaving? He saw no anger in her eyes, no malice, just the plain truth. Somewhere in the back of his head another Max fell to his knees and wept and begged her to stay. He pushed it into the shadows of his mind.

"You've found your Machine Man so I guess this is the end of the road. I'm not going to watch you die, sorry. Lady Porcelain can do that instead."

"I haven't told her," said Max. Abby gave him a *I hope you know what you're doing* look followed by a smile that said all was forgiven.

"Where will you go?" he asked.

"To the theatre," she said with a crazy grin. He recognised the tussle between excitement and sadness in her eyes. She hefted the blue case up to show him.

"A typewriter." Max couldn't help but laugh.

"Athangild gave it to me as a present on condition I never ever tell the Queen a poem ever again. Peshon the theatre manager wants to see my plays. If he likes them, I'll have a job. Can you believe it? Me, a job," she laughed.

So this was it. Max looked at Abby Fabrice and a thousand memories crowded through his mind. Her screaming, yelling, laughing, falling over drunk, thumping enemies, hanging from the underside of colliding flyers, swinging between temple towers, picking off a hundred creatures with pistols, ray guns, throwing knives, bows and arrows, those damned hairpins. He remembered the scent of her hair, the feel of her breasts on his chest, his fingers on her bony ribs, her teeth sinking into his shoulder for the umpteenth time. Despite himself his nose prickled. *You knew this was coming.*

"Take care Abby," was all he could manage.

"Good luck among those Machine Men," she said. "If you survive come back and watch one of my plays. I've got an idea for a comedy just about you."

She tailed off and silence dropped between them. She put the typewriter down, reached up and hugged him. Part of him wanted to crush her in his arms and never let her go, but in the end the embrace was brief and awkward, punctuated by a swift kiss on his cheek.

"Goodbye Max, watch yourself," she said. Crazy Abby Fabrice - red hair, green eyes, freckles and that endless lippy insolence.

"Goodbye Abby."

She walked along the drive to the distant gates, her figure turning into a dark squiggle against the pale landscape. She didn't once look back. Long after she'd vanished Max stood and gazed in the direction she'd gone, sifting and resifting through his feelings. *One by one it all fades away. Father, Ruth, Abby, Odilon, Berthold, Theuderic, Metacarpi, the Carceral Archipelago, all replaced by this empty white world and a single path that leads to where?* In answer to his question a silver teardrop glided over the perimeter wall, swooped towards the house and settled in a puddle of dust on the flagstones in front of the entrance. A door slid open and Max saw Persephone sitting on a cushioned bench.

Max clambered into the flyer. It rose above the mansion and angled across the fields. Persephone smiled and nodded once before turning to look out of the window. Max glanced around the inside of the craft. He guessed a machine mind flew it. The compartment held nothing but cushioned seats and a couple of windows.

After a few hours Max was surprised to see they sped over hills. He'd assumed the interior of the sphere was uniformly flat but here the creators of this world had attempted to sculpt a landscape. A few moments later they hovered over a metropolis of lead-coloured blocks studded with mirror windows. Max noticed low-slung, sleek vehicles thread the streets among the tall buildings, but no people. Another of the dark double-walled trenches cut through the centre, curving into the distant mist.

"This is a city of machines," said Persephone, answering his unspoken question. *A fitting place for a Machine Man then,* thought Max. The woman's mouth twitched in amusement. "They are exceedingly primitive."

"The Queen made these?" asked Max, trying to make sense of the movements in the streets below.

Persephone nodded. "She is ambitious."

Max waited for further explanation but his escort was maddeningly enigmatic. Either that or too much time in the company of machines had rendered her incapable of a normal conversation with another human being. He gamely tried again.

"Is there anything I should know before I meet Anselm the Machine Man?" asked Max. "How do I address him, it?" Persephone pondered the question.

"Hello Anselm?" she said. *Great*, thought Max. At least he wouldn't have to worry about being polite.

The vessel landed in front of a windowless tower sitting on a hill above the rest of the city. Max forced himself to climb out and stand looking up at the blunt metal finger rising up towards the white sky. A door rolled open in the wall and Persephone entered. Max guessed he was supposed to follow. He found himself in a monochrome corridor winding upwards into the building. Persephone strode on ahead, her spindly figure tapping out crisp footfalls on the ridged metal floor. She stopped outside a set of double doors, pushed them open and gestured for Max to enter. He hesitated, a sudden wave of fear catching him unawares. Was this it? Was this the point of his death? Would he walk into the presence of a monster waiting to tear his mind apart, regardless of the terror and the pain? His legs grew weak. The walls curled around him. *Come on you bastard*, he thought. *Stone duty will bring you through this*. He tried a couple of deep breaths. *What if it doesn't*? To his surprise he felt Persephone's hand on his shoulder. He looked into her eyes at those bizarre barred pupils and saw his own reflection imprisoned within them.

"It's alright, Max," she said. "There's nothing to fear."

He nodded and stepped through the door. It closed behind him and he was on his own. He stood in a tall white room devoid of any furniture.

"Come in Max," said a voice, so low Max thought he felt the floor rumble under his boots. He saw an archway in the distance.

"Come and tell me about Ragaleis the Giant."

Max summoned up every last scrap of his courage and walked forwards into the presence of Anselm the Machine Man.

CHAPTER TWENTY-THREE

WHEN MAX ENTERED the house Ragaleis built in the Wilderness and saw the vision of the eight giants seated round the table in the centre of God's mind, Machine Men crawled over his hands like silver ants, glittering motes of delicate beauty and intelligence. In the eyes of a titan thousands of years ago they looked bright, precise and full of busy hope. Not any more. This hulking beast of rusted iron, copper, wood and glass bulked up against the white hall, carving a heart-stopping cloud of darkness out of the surrounding plaster. Beside it Theuderic was nothing more than a doll. Max's stomach twisted in fear.

It still held the outlines of an insect, though this was a parody flung together from the leftovers of the Great Task. Max counted six legs, three on each side, but there the symmetry ended. Two chains of steel cylinders sprawled across the floor, yellow fluid oozing from the joints to leave crusted smears on the ground. Another limb looked crafted out of wood in imitation of human bones, far too thin and delicate to support any of the creature's weight. The others were tentacles fashioned from oil-glistening slabs of metal linked by pistons the thickness of Max's torso. They finished in flat-bladed claws. A body made of crushed scrap trailed cables and ropes matted and tangled with lumps of debris. Max wondered if this was the detritus of thousands of years of crawling through God's body. He looked for a head. Did it even have a head? There, just below the apex of this hulking creature, a cluttered mess of pipes, valves and what looked like the guts of a clock. In the middle he spotted a man-sized cylinder of green glass, capped and tailed by copper domes, shining with a febrile light. Max didn't know if it was the face of the Machine Man, a random nutrient tank bolted to its front or a purposeless lump of junk. *It's dying*, thought Max in despair. *If they're all like this we're doomed.*

"Max, come closer," said Anselm. The voice filled the whole tower. It made him think of air swirling through the empty spaces of God's body, the lightless caverns reverberating like flutes. Fighting hard against fear and dismay he stepped forward until he stood between a scarred claw of yellow steel and a puddle of blood red oil seeping from the creature's body.

"Closer."

How much closer could he get? His toes pressed against Anselm's plated skin. He looked for winking lights signifying sensors or any power running through the inert mountain of wood and metal towering over him. Nothing. He glanced upwards and saw, with a start, a pale shape in the green tube. Were those hands pressed against the glass? Shadows that might be eyes returned his gaze.

"Up here, that's right."

Hardly able to credit what he was doing Max clambered up the front of the Machine Man, finding hand and footholds in the gaps between rusting sheets, splintering wood and sharp edges of broken copper. He balanced on a tilted platform beside the cylinder. The floor looked far away. The glass was thick and spattered with flaws and air bubbles. Cracks and dirt obscured his view. He made out a form that looked like a cross between a fish and a human foetus drifting in the eddies of whatever liquid filled the tube. Fingerless discs of flesh pressed against the inside of the container. The domed head was featureless save for two shadowed pits that he guessed were the creature's eyes. Was this the mind of Anselm, the true Machine Man? Were they organic creatures entombed in mad clusters of scrap bolted together to create metal bodies that were as much chaotic works of art as actual walking machines? It looked trapped. Did symbiotic monsters like this build something as delicate as the Mind of God? Max peered further into the tank. The glass distorted the light but it seemed as though he looked into a tunnel of darkness and the creature darted back and forth in an ivy-green ocean that stretched for miles.

"Max. You bring a message from Ragaleis the Giant."

The mind of Anselm, if that's what it was, swam towards him and pressed its half-formed face against the glass six inches away from Max's own fascinated gaze.

"Bassandis is dead. The Black Roses don't want humanity to enter the next universe and so they conspired with a traitor from the Empire of the Ear. They attacked Metacarpi and fought and killed Bassandis. We tried to save him, Ragaleis tried to save him, but we were too late. There are seven giants left and Ragaleis is filled with rage."

He paused. He could have left it there, told the creature his message, turned and walked out of the hall. They might even have let him go, allowed him to return to Count Xix's mansion. He'd track Abby down, ask her to forgive him, tell her he loved her and wanted to spend the rest of his life listening to her hammer away on her new typewriter and watching her plays and humanity could go perish for all he cared.

"Part of Bassandis's mind survived inside my head. Ragaleis thought this would give us hope, that you could use the fragment of his brother to remake the giant."

He closed his eyes and rested his forehead against the cool glass. *There, you've said it. No going back. The Machine Men know you're the key to God's awakening.*

"Why did Bassandis fight the Empire of the Ear?" asked Anselm.

Max opened his eyes. The shape hovered in the cylinder. If it had an expression on that smooth face Max couldn't read it.

"My father didn't understand what Bassandis was. He imprisoned him because he thought he was a weapon to defend our city. When the dreadnoughts from the Empire of the Ear arrived he sent Bassandis to attack them. That's how he died."

Anselm swam back into the depths of that impossible ocean. He became a distant speck, black upon deepest cyan. *If I run now I can make it to the door before this thing heaves into life.*

Too late. A light sped towards him out of the liquid depths, growing into a ball of fire that burst through the glass. He flung his arms up and cried out, tumbling backwards off the platform as it filled his mind and body with its roaring heat.

He stood in the garden under the burning clouds. Bassandis sat at the iron table, picking through wooden animals and placing them in holes on a board.

"There he is, come on."

The oldest human he'd ever seen leaned on a walking stick beside him. He wore a powder blue suit and an open-necked check shirt. His skin was semi-transparent silver and Max could have sworn it was made of a patchwork of tiny metal plates beneath which organs, veins and arteries of copper and gold shimmered in the carmine light from the coals above their head. Max thought he saw the echo of Persephone in that bird head with its sharp nose and liquid eyes. Perhaps the creature sought to give himself the semblance of humanity in Max's dreams by aping his assistant. Anselm hooked an arm through Max's and pointed at Bassandis with his cane.

"Give me your arm to lean on," said Anselm. "I'm not as steady as I was."

They walked over to the table and sat. Max noticed Bassandis seemed slower. The toys looked heavier in his hand, his movements clumsier and more laboured. The ghost of the giant looked at him with tired eyes.

"Max," he sounded drugged or drunk. "Look who's come to see you." A chill rippled over Max's skin as he heard his mother's words in the mouth of the titan. Anselm took the giant's hand in his own and examined the palm. He reached forward and pulled Bassandis's lower eyelid down.

"Say aaaah."

Bassandis gave a weary *aaah*, struggling to open his lips. Anselm ran hands through the giant's hair, feeling the texture. The Machine Man sat back and tapped his fingers against the steel lacework of the table.

"He's dying," he said. "Slowly. The remnant of his mind in your head is fading. It will take a while but if we don't act there will be insufficient for us to save him."

"Can you save him?" asked Max. Half of him wanted Anselm to say no.

"Possibly." His heart sank. The ancient creature looked at him. Max saw the machinery under his translucent skin whir and ripple. Tiny cogs, pistons and circuits shimmered in the gloom, a stark contrast to that grotesque mountain of scrap in the tower. It reminded Max of the Brittle Hag's beach, a lithified shoreline accreted from a million years of broken engines, given life and moulded into the shape of someone's great-great-grandfather.

"I will contact my brothers and sisters in the Heart. By rights this is a matter for Lord Theuderic himself in the Head. But he's too far away and I fear Bassandis will not survive the journey. If we take him to the Heart we can at least stabilise him."

"What about me?" asked Max.

Anselm looked at him. *What about you?* his eyes said.

"If you stabilise Bassandis and rebuild him in his original form, as a giant, what will happen to me?"

The Machine Man didn't answer. He seemed lost in thought, his hands over the end of his cane. After what felt like an age he reached forward and placed his hand on Bassandis's forehead once more. The titan folded his arms on the table, rested his head on them and closed his eyes.

"He will sleep now, and conserve his energy," said Anselm, struggling to his feet, holding onto Max's shoulder. "That will give us more time."

"What about me?" repeated Max. Anselm looked at him with eyes the same colour as the ocean beyond the cylinder.

"I don't know what will happen to you," he said. "I don't know how to remove Bassandis from your head. This world he's created is in your mind, I can't tell where it starts and where it ends. Can you?"

Max looked over the walls at the distant hills. Everywhere the same dull grey faded into hatched shadows. It was like standing in an illustration from an old book. He understood dreams echoed daytime thoughts mixed with deeper, errant desires. If he could unravel the landscape, understand the symbols that underlay this world, he'd see what belonged to him and what came from Bassandis. It was impossible. He'd no idea where to start. Those burning clouds above - what did they mean? Were they his or did they come from the depths of the giant's mind, a cypher for his own titanic fears?

"Who's that?" asked Anselm, nodding at the distant hills. Miles away Max spotted a silhouette standing on top of the domed skyline, the black cutout of a woman in a dress and broad hat. A memory of his mother perhaps but it suggested something far more disturbing. *The Brittle Hag.* But how and why? To his surprise he found himself raising his right hand in greeting. The figure glided out of sight over the far horizon. Anselm peered into the distance, deep in thought. *She's bothered him as well. Maybe she's not just the echo of my own memories. It's getting crowded in here, I want my mind back.* Anselm grunted as if to dismiss his own concerns.

"We have to get you and Bassandis away from the Kingdom of the Steel Queen," continued the Machine Man. "I'll contact the Heart so we can work out a way."

Max assumed they'd leave immediately, that once Anselm discovered Bassandis he'd want to bring Max to the others as quickly as possible. Having summoned up his courage to come here and reveal the giant in his head the last thing he wanted to do was hang around. Journey to the Kingdom of Theuderic in the Head, or wherever else he needed to be, and get it over with.

"Why can't we go now?" he asked.

"We can't," said Anselm. "I have to stay here."

Despite the bizarre otherness of that translucent face and the seething of tiny machinery beneath it, Max recognised worry in the creature's expression. He began to understand.

"What's going on? Why are you here? It's not just diplomacy, is it? Ever since I started on my journey here people have been telling me of the Queen and this project of hers. That's why you don't want to leave. You're watching her. What's so important that it stops you tearing him out of my mind right now and repairing the Mind of God?" He pointed at Bassandis who still slept with his head on his arms.

Anselm planted both hands over the head of his cane and stared at them for what felt like an eternity.

"You came here with the Philosophers *Transition to R*. What do you know about them?"

"Walking calculators designed by a pervert hundreds of thousands of years ago," said Max. "They glow in the dark, among other things." Fear and the disorienting experience of talking to a Machine Man inside his own head made him facetious. Either that or he'd be over the walls and running away screaming.

"Do you know what type of calculations *Transition to R* specialise in?" asked Anselm. This was getting infuriating. He reminded Max of the senile idiot of a schoolmaster his father cursed him with as a child. He shook his head.

"*Transition to R, Quotient Orbifold, Scheme to Stack* - the Philosophers who are here in the Kingdom of the Steel Queen study the structure of Space and Time. Leontine has gathered every Philosopher who has those functions in his or her head, who can look into the very fabric of this dead cosmos, to take part in her project."

Max remembered Pell flicking through dimensions as she stalked Theuderic five miles above the Glass City, her hand curling round his arm as she talked of bones and forces, the universe rotating around her as they plunged towards wicked pointed polyhedra as big as mountains. His mouth was dry. He could hear his heart hammering against the base of his skull. All his life the Body of God had filled the cosmos, immovable, remorseless, the foundation upon which the sum total of humanity had built its last desperate hope. As he looked into Anselm's filigree eyes he felt as if he stood on a doll made of tissue paper and any second now it would crumple like a paper toy in the rain.

"And what do they plan to do?"

"God is held together by a cage woven out of the forces that bind reality," said Anselm. "How else could we build a colossus half a million miles from head to toe, one that will stand and walk and carry humanity into a new universe?" said Anselm. "We think the Queen and her Philosophers are studying the space time nexus upon which God and the singularity rest. Can they do anything to affect it? I doubt it. Philosophers observe and analyse. In the long history of our dealings with them they have never betrayed any desire to change the structure of existence, merely to understand it. Even so, Leontine makes us nervous. She's hinted at an alliance with the Machine Men but won't say why. I hope they'll come to us with nothing more than a few interesting experiments and some good advice."

"So you're here to spy on her," said Max. Anselm laughed.

"You've seen what I have become out there," he pointed at the sky with his cane. "I'm hardly capable of creeping through the shadows of her Majesty's laboratories, am I? Persephone keeps the lines of communication open but she is watched at every turn and can learn little more than what common diplomatic courtesy allows her access to."

Anselm shook his head.

"In any case, as far as you are concerned this is academic. What you have here is far, far more important than the Queen's eccentric hobbies." He gestured at the garden and its white-haired occupant.

"You must stay in my tower until we can arrange your journey to the Heart. Persephone will return with you to Count Xix's mansion to gather your personal effects and so you can bid farewell to your human friends."

Anselm tapped Max on the forehead with his cane. White fire enveloped him once more.

He awoke on the tiles of the atrium. Persephone helped him to his feet and handed him a glass of water. Close up she could be dream-Anselm's great-great-grandchild and Max wondered whether she'd somehow overheard their conversation in Bassandis's garden. He looked through the arch at the hill of junk forming the Machine Man's body in the real world - a heap of rusting shapes against immaculate walls. He wondered how he'd be comfortable in this sterile tower. Persephone smiled.

"There are more accommodating rooms elsewhere." It did nothing to reassure him. He thought they probably wanted to ease the wait before they wrenched his head off or stuffed him into some horrendous engine.

During the return flight Max brooded on Anselm's explanation about the Steel Queen's project. Leontine had gathered Philosophers whose wisdom focussed on the nature of space and time and the flat singularity the Black Roses had beaten out for mankind to use as its workbench. From the argument he'd overheard between Virasoro and Chiral he knew Pell's brain held unique functions and routines developed by a group of clandestine Philosophers eradicated long ago by their horrified kin. She saw into the future, navigated the curves in space spiralling around the bones and forces holding God together and she transformed the dimensions of her own body. *Space and Time*. Did she merely observe the topography of the universe with her monstrous, weaponised mind? If she lacked the power to change reality what happened if she passed her discoveries onto those who could?

Max noticed the ship was no longer moving. Persephone peered out of the window beside her. They hovered above one of the walled trenches they'd spotted when they first arrived. He realised it had grown a roof of transparent metal, extruded from the sides.

"What's happening, why have we stopped?" he asked.

Persephone didn't reply. Max guessed it was because she didn't have a clue and wanted to see for herself. He gasped. Alternating red and yellow light blazed between the walls, creeping along the trench, heading away from them into the mist-shrouded distance. Long after the grey metal faded into fog the flickering radiance illuminated the clouds as it followed the inner surface of the sphere. The coloured bands sped up, merging into a single line of pale orange fire and lighting up the interior of the craft. Max squinted in the glare. From what he could make out, despite the energies suggested by the fireworks below, nothing outside seemed affected. Fields cut by precise roads lay undisturbed on either side.

The lights flicked off so suddenly he cried out. The transparent scales bridging the walls slid back into their sockets. He glanced at Persephone.

"Testing," she said. Acting on an unspoken command the flyer continued on its journey.

"Testing what?" asked Max. Persephone watched him with her cell window eyes.

"The sphere," she said.

"The sphere?" Max gawped at her.

"This entire world is a machine." A thousand mile wide engine, and one that worked?

"Made to do what?" said Max, aghast at the implied power he'd just witnessed.

"We don't know," said Persephone, turning back to stare out of the window.

When they landed in the courtyard of Count Xix's mansion Athangild hurried down the steps to meet them. He shot Max an exasperated *what did I warn you about?* look and a less chagrined one at Persephone.

"Honourable Persephone, if we knew you'd intended to visit us we would have prepared. You catch us at a disadvantage."

"I'm an escort, Athangild. Anselm the Machine Man wishes Max Ocel to stay with him. He is here to gather his possessions. We will return shortly."

"Max is Count Xix's guest," said Athangild.

"Count Xix is ever a friend to the Heart and Mind of God," said Persephone. Max swore he heard a hint of reproach in that flat, machine delivery. Athangild allowed himself an embarrassed laugh and a bow.

"Forgive me, Honourable Persephone. Count Xix's disappointment will be far outweighed by the joy at hearing a long and valued relationship so elegantly reaffirmed." *God almighty*, thought Max, reminded of the bizarre verbal jousting between his father and Hathus aboard the *Beatrice* just before the traitor's men cut Theodore's throat.

"A glass of wine while the servants help Max gather his things?" said Athangild.

Persephone nodded. The overseer guided her across the atrium, not before shooting Max another wary glance. He sensed the worry in the man's eyes. *He thinks I'm in this way over my head. He has no idea.*

Without waiting for help Max returned to his suite. He found Chiral standing at the window, looking out over the twisted groves of the garden. A cloud of black smoke rose from a bonfire in the distance. She turned and Max saw the tears on her paper-white cheeks. Before he reacted she ran to him and buried her face in his chest. He put his arms round her and felt her shaking.

"What is it, Chiral?"

"Where were you? I came back and you'd gone and Athangild said you'd left with the Machine Men." This wasn't right. She was acting as if they'd been lovers for years and he'd abandoned her, or was it something else? He eased her head up and peered into her blank eyes.

"What is it? What's happened?" She looked furious, pushing him away to march back and forth in front of the window, spider hands writhing over each other.

"Is it Pell?" She glared at him. That was it. Despite her misgivings the other Philosophers had voted to use the girl's knowledge in their project. But what did that mean?

"Take me to meet the Machine Man," she said. Grabbing his hands in hers she looked up at him, desperation tussling with fury. "That's where you're going, isn't it? I saw the flyer land and it's waiting for you downstairs. Take me with you. I must speak to him, urgently."

Max opened his mouth to reply but at that second a hideous wail of fear echoed through corridors behind him, followed by a word shrieked over and over again.

"Murder. Murder. Murder."

CHAPTER TWENTY-FOUR

THIS WASN'T MURDER, it was butchery. Whoever or whatever killed the Philosopher wanted to make sure nothing could be stitched back together. The headless, eviscerated corpse lay slumped in the corner. The head itself, half-crushed, sat in the centre of the bed. *White, everything's white.* Body, entrails, flesh, blood - it made it worse. Max fought the urge to be sick while outside the servant who'd found the victim shrieked and sobbed in the arms of her horrified colleagues. Chiral stood in the entrance, her hands over her mouth as other Philosophers gathered around her. Most reeled away but a couple tried to push forward. Max stopped them. From where he stood the dead woman was beyond help and her killer no longer in the room. Crowds of people barging into it would destroy any lingering evidence. To his relief Athangild appeared with a dozen armed guards. He took the scene in with one glance, his face turning pale, the laconic diffidence replaced by fury.

More shouting, this time from the floor above. Athangild ordered two soldiers to secure the chamber against intruders and ran upstairs with the remainder. Max followed. He'd grabbed his revolver as soon as the screaming started. A terrified servant pointed along the corridor with a shaking hand. The squad crouched into a defensive position, creeping swiftly down the passageway. Max kept pace. Athangild shot him a questioning glance but he ignored it. Through the entrance Max saw a second white body sprawled across a table. It looked as if someone had upended a crate of milk over a pile of bleached guts. Count Xix appeared, hurrying towards them in the company of Virasoro.

"Two dead," said Athangild. Count Xix's face creased into a mask of black anger.

"Find the scum who did this and bring them to me," he said. Max had pegged him as a harmless buffoon when they first arrived at the villa but now the set of the man's voice scared even him. Before he could prevent it Virasoro walked into the room, his expression immobile. He bent over and peered at the blood dripping from the table's edge, extruding thin strands as it fell.

"He died thirteen minutes ago," he said. *That's impossible*, thought Max. *We'd have heard or seen something*.

"Seal the house and raise the shields," said Athangild. "The killer must still be here. Virasoro, get all the Philosophers into the Great Hall. Captain, I want two armed squads to watch over them, none of them moves without an escort of three guards."

"Where's Pell?" asked Virasoro, a sudden look of murderous panic on his face. "Where's Pell?" he shouted.

"Here," the girl appeared among them causing two of the servants to scream out loud. Athangild jumped. Count Xix glared at her.

"Athangild, she must be protected at all costs," Virasoro said, a *fuck the others* tone in his voice that caused Chiral to flash him a look of hatred. Athangild gestured and four guards surrounded the girl.

"Search the estate. I want everyone accounted for. Seal both rooms and notify the palace. Send word to the other Lords and warn them that two Philosophers have been murdered. Everyone else downstairs, that means you too," he said to Max who knew better than to argue.

Persephone stood in the atrium watching them descend.

"What has happened?" she asked.

"Two Philosophers are dead," said Athangild. "We think the killer is still on the estate. You must accompany us so you'll be safe."

Persephone paused a second. *She's telling Anselm.*

"I will return to my master now and he will come with me," she said, pointing at Max. Athangild looked thunderstruck.

"No-one's going anywhere. I've got a murderer at loose and he's a witness," he said. *If not a suspect. No, I was still with Persephone when it happened.* A sudden thought struck him. Had she slaughtered the victims? No, ludicrous. Not in so short a time and not without drenching herself in white blood.

"Max Ocel is under the protection of Anselm the Machine Man. He is not to be placed in any danger whatsoever and it is imperative that he returns with me to ensure his safety."

"Persephone, I'm not interested in diplomacy right now," said Athangild. "Two guests in my care have been slaughtered. If you want to leave, fine - you're not a suspect at the moment - but he stays. I'll guarantee his wellbeing as best I can. If you have a problem with that then take it up with the Steel Queen, and I'd do it quickly because the second she gets wind of this a storm will fill this sphere the like of which none of us has seen."

Persephone went dead eyed again. Max sensed the tension, realising he stood in the centre of a standoff between the Machine Men and the last humans left alive. After a few more seconds she placed her empty glass on a steel table beside her.

"Athangild. Lord Anselm holds you personally responsible for the safety of Maximilian Ocel. I will petition the Queen. Prepare to release him into our care within twenty-four hours."

She glided out of the door. Max watched her step into the flyer. Whatever shields surrounded the house showed nothing more than a flash of static as the silver teardrop passed straight through them. Max heard Athangild swear behind him. Either she was going to the Queen or returning to Anselm. Part of him wanted to go with her to get his journey over with while part of him was relieved to see her leave. It was in everyone's interests to keep him alive and healthy, if only to prevent a major diplomatic incident between the Queen and the Machine Men. But on the other hand he was stuck in a sealed mansion with a murderer at loose and he didn't want to imagine what would happen when the Queen found out.

Max hated being a passive witness to danger. It went against his nature. Normally he'd be padding the corridors, gun in hand, Abby next to him, hunting whatever creature had slaughtered the defenceless Philosophers. Now he found himself in the uncomfortable position of someone so valuable they had to be protected at all costs. He noticed guards marking him as he joined the Philosophers and staff in the Great Hall. Usually he shared an easy camaraderie with fighters, providing they were more or less on the same side. Here they viewed him as another potential victim. He couldn't do anything about it. As much as he wanted to help it wasn't even his fight.

He tracked down Chiral, who comforted an older man in tears. He'd got used to reading those empty eyes by now and knew that in a human they'd be red and swollen with grief.

"Are you alright?" he asked. She stood up and moved away to be out of earshot of the others. Max saw her looking around for Virasoro. He had his own knot of guards and Pell sat next to him, hands folded on her lap staring into the distance. Chiral's face showed a loathing that worried him.

"Who are the victims?"

"No one important," she spat, glaring across the room at the Guide.

"Any reason why those two?" Max tried again. She gave him a look of sharp anguish.

"No, they were redundant. Duplicate functions, nothing that any of us couldn't provide," her voice rose. Max heard it crack with fury. "No reason why they should be killed at all. They weren't important. You'd have to kill ten, twenty of us to make a difference, so why bother protecting us?" she was shouting now, aiming her desperate misery at Virasoro. Philosophers turned to stare at her, their faces a mix of fear and grief. Max took her in his arms, she pushed him away.

"Protect the one you need to protect, Virasoro," shouted Chiral. "Go on, look after that monstrous bitch and consign all the rest of us to death."

Virasoro whispered in one of the guards' ears. The woman nodded and walked towards Max and Chiral, un-slinging her gun. *Oh shit*, thought Max. The other Philosophers gathered around his weeping friend, trying to comfort her after an outburst they didn't understand. Max readied himself. He wasn't going to let anyone touch Chiral and he knew they'd harm him at their peril.

Athangild clattered into the room with Count Xix who wore the expression of a man whose political capital bumped along the bottom of the Umbilical Ocean. He looked like he contemplated ending it all there and then. Max noticed Athangild stand close to him and give his hand a surreptitious squeeze. The guard walking towards them stopped and re-slung her gun over her shoulder. Max used the opportunity to manhandle Chiral out of Virasoro's line of sight. She wept openly, her face buried in her strange hands.

"A battalion of her majesty's personal guard will be here within seconds," said Athangild. "All our guests are to leave for the palace where they will be under the direct protection of Her Majesty Queen Leontine XXIII."

He walked over to Max.

"You too. Persephone can argue it out with the Queen if she wants you handed over to Anselm."

"How do you know the murderer's not among this lot?" asked Max.

"Whatever it was forced a servant in the garden to open a perimeter gate just before the shields went up, then tore him apart." said Athangild.

Max remembered seeing the smoke from the bonfire through the window of their suite, the cloud hanging in the mist. *Poor old bastard.*

"The man burning the leaves?" asked Max. Athangild looked puzzled.

"Burning leaves?"

"I saw smoke over by the wall."

"The trees here are made of liquid rhodium, we don't burn leaves," Athangild clicked his fingers and summoned a soldier, telling her to check the perimeter once more. Max could tell he wasn't convinced of the wisdom of bundling his guests off to the palace. Max had no frame of reference for the politics of the sphere other than his dealings with the labyrinthine treachery of the Empire of the Ear. Despite the more civilised courtesies of this kingdom he didn't doubt that underneath it all the same old power wove the same old nets of cruelty and deceit. The thought of moving into the tower of Anselm became more appealing by the minute.

The sound of ships landing in the courtyard drowned out any further conversation and the hall filled with soldiers in the grey and orange livery of the court, carrying rifles and evil-looking short swords. They escorted the Philosophers and Max outside to where squat military flyers with bubble canopies and chain guns rested on the ground, their motors thundering and arcs of electricity skipping between their coils. Max kept Chiral beside him. He didn't think Virasoro meant her harm but the Guide clearly wanted to shut her up. Mercifully the leader of *Transition to R* and his twisted little charge took another vessel. The fleet rose into the air. The last thing Max saw was Count Xix standing by himself on a balcony, watching his destroyed reputation float away through the veils of mist hanging between the estate and the Queen's palace. *Even Athangild has abandoned him*, thought Max, catching sight of the steward in the cockpit of the lead vessel. No amount of dreadful poetry would salvage the Count's name now.

They arrived at the palace to be swamped by servants, aides and officials who fluttered around the shocked Philosophers with anxious solicitude. Max insisted on staying with Chiral and as soon as he could he navigated her away from the throng to follow a servant to new quarters. The woman put them in adjacent rooms with windows looking out onto a platinum-flagged courtyard. Max noticed guards at either end of the corridor. They wore muted uniforms and concealed weapons but their gaze swept the passageways relentlessly and he saw how they assessed him in seconds. These weren't his father's goons or the brutalised thugs of the Glass City. Their machine-like professionalism overshadowed even the crisp, sneering superiority of the men and women of the Empire of the Ear.

Max wanted to talk to Chiral. At first she ignored him, sitting in the corner with clenched fists, staring into nowhere with cold anguish. He teased her hands apart and took them in his.

"What's happening, Chiral? Anselm the Machine Man said that all the Philosophers the Queen has gathered here are specialists in the structure of time and space. Pell is the same but she moves through dimensions, sees into the future and navigates flaws in reality. None of the rest of you can do those things and Virasoro wants her as part of this project. What is it? What are you doing and why do you so desperately want to keep her out of it?"

Chiral looked into his eyes. He saw the beginnings of hope as she realised how much he knew. She wrapped her arms around his neck and kissed him.

"All of us here have dedicated our lives to studying the structures of space and time, looking for flaws. As the cosmos dies it grows threadbare, as tattered as old rags worn for too long."

"The universe is disintegrating?" asked Max. The vision of the empty sky teased apart like rotting cloth terrified him. What lay beyond?

"We're safe here. The singularity God lies on binds this part of reality together. It draws its power from the wormholes the Black Roses drilled through deep time. They're the slender branches of existence holding everything up."

Max thought of the hair-fine struts of the Olecranon Bridge, delicate yet strong enough to support cities and kingdoms. *So the wormholes don't merely provide the materials to make God, they're our supports, anchoring us to the past so we don't dissipate like mist in this threadbare void. But they're closing, one by one. Time is running out, unless...*

"Is that what you're trying to do, repair the old wormholes so all this doesn't disintegrate before God wakes up?" said Max.

Chiral gave a sad laugh that said *if only that were true*. She took several deep breaths, gearing herself up to speak.

"Maximilian Ocel?" An officer stood at the doorway.

"Not now," snapped Max. He could have cheerfully throttled the man.

"Her Majesty Queen Leontine XXIII has summoned you. Immediately." Max saw the two sentinels behind him. *Shit, Persephone's spoken to her.* Refusal was out of the question.

"I'll come back shortly." He kissed her marble lips. "You can tell me everything then." She nodded and squeezed his hands.

He told her to lock the door and followed the escort. Max expected to meet the Queen in a courtroom at the apex of her palace. Instead they threaded their way to the base of the structure, emerging at last in a series of vaulted halls filled with machinery. Max gawped as they strode across polished floors and lacework bridges slung between generators, valves and accumulators as big as Anselm's tower. He'd seen engines larger than these but always as rusting hulks crumpled under their own weight in the Wastelands or the forgotten spaces inside God's forearm. These were uniformly clean, bright and humming with a latency that hinted at immense power. He remembered the flickering lights in the trench. *Persephone said the sphere is a machine and these are its guts.*

They came to a cluster of buildings set high in a curving wall. After leading him up a spiral staircase the clerk showed Max into a low-ceilinged room cluttered with sofas, bookshelves and desks. Papers spilled onto the floor and out of wastepaper baskets. Max tried to read a couple upside down but he couldn't make any sense of the symbols and formulae etched on pages cut with mathematical precision. Leontine walked in, pulling ornate rings from her fingers and dropping them into a cobalt bowl on a desk.

"Fucking hell, look at this place. This is what happens when I command them not to tidy my notes away."

"Your Majesty," Max thought he ought to say. To his surprise Leontine sat opposite and rested her head momentarily on her hand.

"You wouldn't believe how tired I am right now. You want a drink? I need a drink." Max watched, stunned, as the Queen of the Steel Sphere scrambled over the back of the sofa to yank on a bell rope. A few moments later a servant wafted in with two glasses on a tray. Leontine took a mouthful and rolled her eyes up in appreciation, waving at Max with her free hand to take his and sit down.

"So, Maximilian Ocel. You are the most significant individual in the entire history of mankind according to the Machine Men." Her mouth twitched in amusement but the eyes were shards of ice.

"I don't think so," said Max. *Oh but you are, more important than this woman realises.*

"Your person is inviolate. You are not be harmed, harassed, distressed or alarmed. Your bath has to be the correct temperature and your food cooked to perfection. Otherwise fifty thousand big clumpy metal monsters will turn up on my doorstep to forcefully express their concerns," Leontine gave him a scatty grin. "Care to tell me why? Or is this between you and them and I'm just supposed to go along with it?"

Max said nothing. Leontine took another sip of wine and pressed her palm to her forehead as if she'd developed a headache.

"OK, well, it makes no odds to me in the end." She peered into his eyes.

"They're not listening to me now, are they? Hello? Hello Mr Machine Man, are you in there?" She grimaced in disappointment and shook her head.

"Apparently not. However let's assume that you are going to talk to them later on so I will frame my remarks as much to them as to you, Maximilian Ocel from Metacarpi by the Left Thumb of God." She looked at him oddly. "Aren't you supposed to be ruling over that city instead of pissing around in my shallows?"

She knows exactly who I am, where I come from and my lineage. Max chose his next words very carefully.

"Metacarpi was attacked by the Empire of the Ear, it was all but wiped out."

Leontine nodded slowly.

"I heard something to that effect but I don't know the details." Her face said she wasn't particularly interested either. If she did have a hand in Hathus's treachery it wasn't obvious. She wouldn't have made it to the throne without the ability to dissemble, but having seen the power of the Steel Queen Max didn't think she'd ally herself with a deranged idiot like the renegade captain of the *Beatrice*. She stretched her legs out and smoothed her dress.

"Ever stopped and wondered about all this? How utterly ridiculous it is?" she gestured at the walls around her. Max guessed she meant the universe.

"You haven't, have you? You're like all the rest, wandering in and around this immense corpse we've stitched together, telling each other how one day it will come to life and carry us all through the magic door to the next universe. Do you never pause to wonder on the strangeness of it all, that we're in thrall to a fairy tale? You, me, the Philosophers, the Machine Men."

She shook her head as if astounded at the stupidity of everyone else.

"You see, Max, at the dawn of time the men and women who lived on the first worlds stared out at the sky filled with lights and fires and because they didn't understand what they saw they invented gods. Famine, war, disease, natural disasters, death, the universe itself - everything's down to the gods. Then bit by bit we learned the true nature of the cosmos and science replaced the deities we'd created for ourselves. Not everyone was happy of course. Gods are very useful when you want to control people, but in the end we understood that the gods of old were nothing more than phantoms conjured up in the minds of cruel and stupid men.

"And yet here we are at the end of a million years during which humanity has dedicated the sum of all its skill, wisdom and knowledge to what? To making a god because the aliens tell us only gods can go through the doorway that leads to the next universe and without one we perish."

She finished off her drink and looked at Max with amused contempt.

"What are we doing, Max? We've come round in a full circle, idiocy to understanding and back to idiocy and no-one questions it. The aliens turn up and give us the singularity and the doorways into the past so we can get the materials we need. The Machine Men build a heart and a mind while the rest of us glue together limbs and torso and arse and even a fucking tummy button for God's sake. And here we are, you and I, sailing in it," she waved around her head again. "The Black Roses, or whatever they call themselves, must be pissing themselves laughing."

They're not laughing. They take this very seriously. They don't want us in the next universe and they will destroy God himself to stop us.

"What if?" Leontine leaned forward, her eyes locked on his and Max understood why so many fell in love with her.

"What if we can use science, knowledge, those powers that made us noble, made us what we are - rational, thinking, knowing creatures? What if we can use science to save us, to find a way to fill the sky with stars again, to journey to places we've never even dreamed of? Why do you think I gathered the Philosophers to me? They'd be happy to spend the remaining millennia traipsing over the Body of God musing on great thoughts about nothing in particular. I've brought them here because their knowledge and my science may hold the key to humanity's survival, not this ridiculous mannequin we're squatting on. The Machine Men have the tools and power. I have the knowledge. What couldn't we accomplish together?"

Her words carried a heady resonance. Making a god to take mankind to the next universe was a ludicrous gamble. Whatever the Black Roses had done to persuade or coerce the first builders was lost in the depths of time. Max could see science all around him in the Steel Queen's sphere. Elsewhere he came across little else than debris, wreckage and ruins inhabited by knots of frightened humans clinging to existence in the shadowed interstices of the deity. Here he could smell the knowledge and the power in the air. If the Queen's obsessions held the promise of another way to save humanity he wouldn't have to surrender himself to the

Machine Men so they could rip his head apart to get at a fragment of a dead giant.

Leontine leaned back and grinned. In a second she'd flipped into the unfocussed girlish mannerisms of a scatty debutante.

"Even clanky bug men that look like enormous iron turds on legs can't argue with that."

She sighed.

"I'm tired. If Anselm has been listening in then let him ponder on what I've said. If not, pass on the message the next time you communicate with him or that po-faced stick Persephone. I'm happy to talk face to face." She waved a dismissive hand at Max. Taking his cue he rose to go.

"And Max," he stopped, shocked to see two suited officials hovering by the Queen with documents and next to them a guard carrying a lethal-looking machine pistol.

"Help my investigators. I will find who murdered those Philosophers and whether human, alien, or machine I will make sure it begs for its death in the end."

CHAPTER TWENTY-FIVE

MAX DIDN'T NEED this. Carrying the hope of humanity in his head was bad enough, especially as Anselm had given him no words of comfort about his own fate when they extracted the fragment of Bassandis from his skull. Now Queen Leontine XXIII marked him as an envoy between herself and the Kingdom of the Machine Men. He wasn't a diplomat. He lacked the subtlety of mind to weave alliances, plots and betrayals out of allusions, hints and glances. *Do you want to help me do something with Space and Time? Shall we use science to save everyone and stop wasting energy building a big god?* Wasn't that what the Queen's request to Anselm boiled down to? Why couldn't she just say that to the creature's face? Why all this innuendo and verbal fencing? He needed to find Persephone, if she was still in the palace, tell her what Leontine said and leave it to her to figure out the meaning and the ramifications. Max walked back with a couple of attendants, his eyes on his boots, lost in thought and blind to the machines rearing up on either side.

He remembered Chiral and her unspoken promise to reveal the truth about the project on his return. If he learned the true nature of the Queen's experiments it might give him a clue as to what butchered the Philosophers in cold blood, why Virasoro wanted to use Pell and why Chiral opposed the idea so desperately. He knew they must be linked with the conversation he'd just had with the Queen.

He nodded to the guards at the end of the corridor and rapped on Chiral's door. No answer. It was open so he stepped inside and closed it behind him. She'd dimmed the lights and sat with her head resting on the desk. *She's fallen asleep, exhausted after the trauma of the killings and the move here.* Max stroked her shoulders. His thumb caught against a sharp edge and when he raised his fingers they came away wet. The floor lurched under him and he scrabbled for the light. A half gasp, half sob broke from his mouth when he saw the short sword buried in her spine to the hilt, the white cloud of blood under her chair. The point of the weapon projected from her stomach in the hollow of her folded body. Tears welled up at the sheer wretched misery of the sight. *Not Chiral, please, not Chiral.*

Instinct kicked in and he stepped away from the corpse. Grief could wait, there was nothing he could do. He sensed another presence. He felt it hovering beside him. Whatever it was he'd make the monster pay for this.

"Come on you piece of shit, show yourself," he said.

He saw a line drift across the room as if the two halves of the universe had slipped out of alignment. He recognised it immediately. This wasn't a hidden assassin. Hope made him catch his breath.

"Pell, help me, Chiral's stabbed." The girl had the skill to heal Chiral. Unlike the bloody destruction in Count Xix's mansion this looked like a clean murder, a single stab wound through her spine.

"I can't," Max heard Pell's voice. "She's been killed in this way to make sure she can't be mended. You don't have to rip us apart to consign us to death."

A chill settled on Max's heart. He fought to concentrate on the girl's words.

"What do you mean?" A hideous realisation gripped him. He clutched at the table to steady himself.

"Pell, you murdered Chiral." Silence. He tried to track the fracture in the air. Logic told him she'd be no match in the normal three-dimensional world where she was just a delicate girl. But she was also a weaponised Philosopher with access to at least four dimensions if not more. Whatever attack she planned, he doubted it involved coming at him with her fists. He'd no idea what to expect or how to meet it.

"Even if I wanted to, she's beyond my help now. Like my love, lying out there in the endless night. If you'd brought him to me I could have mended him as well but you left him in that oh so dead city where the ice will shroud him forever."

Berthold. Was that what this was about? Pell sought revenge for Berthold by murdering Chiral? Had his death driven her insane or was this the natural progression of her lethally engineered mind?

"I didn't kill Berthold. He tried to murder me after he slaughtered his brother but the Queen's soldiers stopped him." *They spitted him on a hook and flipped him into the sky.* What good would it do to tell her even if she did believe him?

"I was born in darkness and all my life men passed me hand to hand from shadow to shadow, from evil to evil, and the functions and procedures in my mind embraced every single wicked instance. I watched cruelty, engineered cruelty, told those around me how to be cruel. Every part of my body was a vessel for the foulness of others. Then he came. He rescued me and I loved him for it. That love was a spark that drove the shadows away so that I saw light for the first time in the hundreds of years I've been forced to walk the skin of this immense corpse, until you crushed it with another filthy boot."

He didn't love you, he wanted Abby. You were no different from the other whores. He just saw you as someone to empty himself into and discard when he got bored. But even he'd no idea what you were and in the end you drove him mad. Hundreds of years old, insane and trained to be evil. When Max first met Pell he'd seen her as a damaged child to be rescued in the hope those wiser than him could coax her back to normality or at least ease the misery eating at her heart. The truth was far worse. God knew what she could do. He guessed the death of Chiral was nothing compared to what she was ultimately capable of.

"Did you murder the others?" he asked. Where were the guards? Of course, they let her in, why wouldn't they? She was just another Philosopher, Virasoro's favourite in fact. Could he alert them before she fell upon him? He'd lost sight of the fracture. No, there she was, one-dimensional, a dislocation in the fabric of the universe between him and the door. If only he understood what he faced. Not knowing the extent of her powers made it impossible for him to match her tactics.

"No," she said.

"Who did?" He chanced the question.

"I don't know."

He glanced across at Chiral. Her face rested on the desk as if she'd just put her head down for a nap. She looked just the same in death as in life. A grinding rage took hold of Max that someone so beautiful and open-hearted could be snatched away for the sake of jealous revenge. No empire would fall because of her death, no tyrant perish. According to her she wasn't essential to the Queen's project. The only reason for her futile, ugly death was Pell's malevolence and even that was fake, programmed into her mind hundreds of years ago.

Pell switched into two dimensions, a paper cutout watching him from the far end of the room, her expression as blank and cold as ever. A second later she was three dimensional. She pointed at Max, her jaw opened and she screamed. Max would finish this once and for all. He remembered Chiral telling Virasoro the girl should be erased. He channeled his anger into purposeful fury, yanked the blade out of Chiral's back and went for her. Futile, Pell flipped sideways like a target at a funfair and the point smacked into the wall. Before he had chance to pull it free the chamber filled with guards, training their rifles on him and shouting for him to drop his weapon. They kicked his legs away and he fell, eyes still on the Philosopher's distorted face.

They took him to a steel cell. It felt so familiar. He half expected his father to walk in and perch on the edge of the table. After two hours Athangild came in and sat opposite. He looked at Max as if he was an interesting insect he'd found at the bottom of that garden of his.

"Why did you kill Chiral?"

"I didn't, Pell killed her," said Max. Athangild's expression showed he thought the idea ludicrous.

"Why?"

"For revenge. She blames me for the death of her lover, Berthold. Your patrol killed him in one of the fallen cities," explained Max but the other man clearly had more important things on his mind.

"When the Queen heard she was going to come here and gut you herself. You are this far away from death," Athangild held his finger and thumb a fraction apart. "Not to mention kicking off an unholy war between her Majesty and the Machine Men. Why?"

"Where's Persephone?"

"She's gone back to Anselm's tower."

Max fought the wrenching fear in his guts. She'd abandoned him. Who'd vouch for him now?

"Why did you kill the Philosophers in Count Xix's estate?" said Athangild.

"Come on, I was with Persephone when it happened, then Chiral," he said. Surely the man didn't believe he'd murdered them and the gardener as well?

"Pell killed them, is that it?" asked Athangild. He sounded like a doctor trying to tease out an embarrassing symptom. No, Max didn't. He remembered the cruel precision of that sword through Chiral's spine compared to the chaotic butchery in the mansion. Did she die instantly? She looked as if she'd just put her head down to rest. He shook his head.

"Here's where we are," said the steward, tapping out a cigarette on a gold case stamped with the sigil of the Queen. "Nothing will happen to Pell. She's crucial to her Majesty's project and from what I understand she could behead babies if she wanted to and no one would lift a finger. I reckon you murdered Chiral. I don't know why. I doubt you killed the others but may have been part of the plot. Right now everything suggests the Machine Men or at least Anselm. The Queen offered an alliance, asking them to join her in the great work about to unfold. Why she's chosen you to carry the message baffles me, although something's made you so significant to the Machine Men they've put you under their diplomatic protection. Perhaps the death of Chiral was their way of making a point though I confess it's too obscure for me."

We were lovers, friends. I'm not like you. I don't belong to worlds where diplomats murder women to score points.

"I intend to discover why your wellbeing is so important and what bizarre game your allies in the Heart and Head think they're playing." said Athangild. "You can cooperate or not but I'll find out."

He left the room and four soldiers came in. They kicked Max's chair away but took great care not to leave too many marks as they beat him senseless.

As he struggled awake Max heard gunfire. A rescue, fighting its way through the palace corridors? Idiot, fooling himself and besides it didn't really sound like shots. He recognised it from somewhere though. Tap tap tap. *Throw the bloody thing out of the window into the canal and have done with it*. Tap tap tap.

He opened his eyes. His body ached and he could taste dried blood on his teeth. *Anselm won't be pleased. My person is inviolate*. Max hoped fear of the Machine Man stopped him getting anything more severe than a beating. He tried to move but couldn't. He lay on a tilted surface, pinioned at the wrist and ankles. Across the room he saw a figure chained to another table - a naked woman. In the dim light he couldn't see who it was. She didn't glow in the dark. Not a Philosopher then.

Tap tap tap.

He blinked and his vision cleared. Two men hunched over a bench. One of them poked at a blue box with his fingers. A piece of paper curled out of the top.

"Thomas. That's not how you spell corkscrew," said the other.

"No?" said his companion.

"No."

"How do I go back? I've written it now," asked the man called Thomas. He looked sixteen. A burly man with a grey beard stood beside him with an expression of amused exasperation.

"Put a line through it so it looks like a mistake and then write the word again." Tap tap tap tap. *It's a typewriter*. Horror snapped Max awake in a second. *Abby*. He yanked at his arms and legs but metal and leather dug into his skin, binding him fast to the splintered wood. One glance took it in. *It's an interrogation room.* Heated brazier, knives, crocodile clips on wires, dozens of machines and instruments, and amid them Abby naked and strapped to a bench. *They've got her. They're going to hurt her to make me talk.*

"Ah ha, someone's awake, Casper. Toys away, time to play," said Thomas.

"I'm protected by Anselm the Machine Man, you cannot harm me," said Max. Casper gave a shrug as if Max stated the utterly obvious.

"We're not stupid. Those moronic bastards shouldn't have beaten you. Sorry."

"Let us go, please," said Max. Abby stirred, blinked and tried to sit up.

"What the fuck is this?" she said, yanking at the chains.

"Abby," yelled Max. The band across her forehead stopped her turning her head towards him.

"Max? Max, what's happening?" Fury mingled with growing fear. Max wrestled with his own despair. How could he reason with these men?

"Please let us go. If Anselm finds out we're here it'll start a war."

Casper looked at the ceiling as if in thought.

"No," he said.

Abby was yelling now. Casper picked up a knife as long as his thigh and wandered over to lay it across Abby's stomach. She gasped at the cold metal.

"If you don't stop that noise I'll slice your tits off and stuff them in your mouth, I mean it," he said. Abby had the sense to clamp her teeth shut. Casper withdrew the blade but as he did so he stroked her skin with the edge, just enough to leave a shallow cut across the bottom of her rib cage. Abby snarled with the pain as Max went berserk, slamming himself against his fetters, shouting and cursing the bastards to the foulest of hells. Casper held his finger up as if to say *shush*.

"You're protected by the agreement between Anselm the Machine Man and her Majesty." He pointed at Abby. Blood trickled down her flank. "She, on the other hand, is not." Sick terror almost drove Max mad.

"I'll tell you anything, I'll help you however you want me to, just don't hurt her."

Thomas poked through a heap of clothes. Max realised they were Abby's.

"None of these would suit me," Thomas said. "Hello?"

He picked out a hair pin, six inches long with an opal head. He rapped it on the edge of the table like a drummer practising a roll. Max recognised it at once.

"It's poisoned, please, please, if you stick it in her she'll die," he said. Thomas held the tip to the light and peered at it.

"Well bugger me on a rainy day," he said, pointing at the dried venom. The other man shrugged and nodded.

"Can't have that can we?"

He stuck it in the brazier for a few seconds. When he pulled it out Max saw the air shimmer around the glowing metal. He begged them not to hurt her, to do it to him instead, but before he could draw another breath the man thrust the point two inches into Abby's breast. She shrieked and Max howled with her, hurling himself time and time again against the straps, calling on Bassandis, the Brittle Hag, anyone to make the horror end. He smelt the sickening stench of burning flesh. Abby's scream turned into a bestial roar of fury as she struggled to attack the man even as he yanked the pin out. A thread of smoke curled up from her side. Abby snapped her teeth at the torturer's hand. He backhanded her across the jaw. Max heard a crack as a gout of blood poured out of her mouth. Something small and white fell into the bloody tangle of her hair. Abby's eyes rolled up into her head as the blow and the agony from the burn pushed her into shock. Max was weeping like a child now - he felt the tears and snot running down his face. He tried to form the words.

"Please, please don't hurt her anymore. I'll tell you everything you want to know," he managed to gasp.

"That's the problem you see," said Thomas. "You'll say any old bullshit to make this stop. But in truth we won't have broken you, will we? We have to keep going so you really, really understand there's no hope for her or you. So just let us get on with the job eh?"

"I'll do anything," sobbed Max. "Please, don't hurt her anymore."

But they weren't paying attention. Casper started to unbutton his trousers.

"You've knackered her face up," said Thomas. Casper gave a shrug.

"Makes no odds to me," he said and reached forward to wrench Abby's thighs apart with one hand while stroking his half-erect penis with the other. He had the disinterested expression of someone faced with an unexpected pile of paperwork. The door handle rattled.

"What? Already?" said Thomas in exasperation. "Don't mind an audience do you?"

"Maybe he wants to join in," said Casper, one knee on the end of the bench. Max writhed and strained at his bonds, feeling the leather and iron cut into his skin. Anselm put Bassandis to sleep to protect him. He had a vision of a pale man in a black suit, head pillowed on his hands in a grey garden, a peaceful smile on his sleeping face. *He can't help me, can't send these filthy bastards mad.* Insanity tore at him. He fought against the universe, that cold, miserable dead void that did nothing while the bloody and bruised body of the woman he knew he loved more than anything lay chained to splintered boards waiting to be raped.

"Bit early aren't you? We've hardly started," Thomas was saying to a thin man with golden eyes. Somewhere in the back of his mind Max recognised him. Where had he seen him before, that intense gaze, that serious brow creased in thought? It was the Sonian poet, the man who pulled Abby's poem apart in the court of the Steel Queen. Was he a torturer's clerk then? He held up a clipboard for Thomas to sign, pointing here and there as the other man scratched on the form with a chewed pencil. *He's an artist. He loves beauty. Surely he can't let this happen.*

"Save her, please, I beg you," he said. The man's eyes locked on Max's and he smiled.

"She's a bit smashed up but if you want a fuck get in line," said Thomas.

The newcomer exploded. Churning darkness enveloped both him and the torturer. It roared up to the ceiling in a geyser of tattered smoke, leaving the headless body of Thomas standing in the middle of the room. Something wet thudded into the far corner. The corpse's knees collapsed and the body crumpled, spraying blood over the floor like a garden sprinkler. Casper, trousers round his ankles, floundered away from the table where Abby lay unconscious. He scrabbled at his pants. The cloud dived, picked him up, whirled him through the air and rammed his head deep into the brazier. Casper made a hideous mewling noise from within the fire as his legs kicked and jerked, piss hissing against the side of the stove as he emptied his bladder. The sound went on forever, the stink making Max retch. At last silence fell.

The black vapour formed a vortex as tall as a man, fluttering shreds weaving in and out of each other in an endless dancing tornado. *It can't be*, thought Max. *It can't be*. One nightmare was about to replace another. The darkness snapped into human shape and Max found himself staring into the penny coloured eyes of Odilon the Watcher. *He can see Bassandis, he'll look into my mind and find the giant.*

But Odilon wasn't interested in him. The Black Rose strode to the bench where Abby lay unconscious and lifted her eyelid with his thumb. He touched the side of her breast. Max knew he was an alien disguised as a man, aping human emotions, but everything in the set of the creature's body spoke of an intense and overwhelming fury. Odilon pulled a jar out of his blue robes. He dabbed a blob of grey paste on the charred wound. He peered into her mouth, looked around, fished the tooth out of her hair and coated the roots in ointment before pressing it back into her gum. To Max's utter astonishment, the creature kissed her on the forehead.

Odilon turned to Max, his face an immovable mask. Only his eyes glittered with anything approaching humanity but their gaze was twisted with a hatred that Max guessed focussed on every living man and woman in the universe save Abby Fabrice.

"You will carry her and I will lead the way," said Odilon, wrenching Max's bonds away with his hands. *He's grown stronger since he murdered Father in the giant's prison.* He stumbled from the table, falling to one knee. Odilon placed a hand under his arm and jerked him to his feet. Max recoiled from the alien's grasp but Odilon pushed him towards Abby. Together they freed her.

Max found a coarse blanket and bundled up her as best he could. He slung her over his shoulder. A surge of hope filled him. Had they really been rescued, by a Black Rose? By their greatest enemy, the creature who lied to them, killed his mother and his father and condemned humanity to endless night? Abby stirred and moaned in his arms. Right now Max didn't give a shit. Abby still lived and they had a chance of escape. Odilon opened the door and strode along the corridor, not bothering with any pretence at stealth. Max staggered after him.

CHAPTER TWENTY-SIX

A GUARD CALLED out to them as they marched towards her. Odilon burst into a cloud without breaking stride, reforming a few steps further on to leave a ring of gore across the floor, walls and ceiling. It pattered sickeningly on Max and Abby. *Black smoke in Xix's garden. Of course. You butchered the Philosophers. Why?* Clearly he wanted to play the demon once more and strew bloody terror through the Queen's palace. Max feared he was chancing a dangerous game. Abby felt light enough in his arms but his strength ebbed as the effect of the beating and the trauma of the interrogation room took its toll. It looked as if the alien moved deeper into the citadel. Surely he wasn't thinking of carrying his rage to the boudoir of the Queen herself? They wouldn't get within a mile.

Two more guards sat in a glass-walled cubby hole next to an access hatch, one writing a report while the other ate from a metal can. Odilon walked inside, the windows turned black then red and he emerged with a ring of keys. He opened the door to show a flight of stairs leading upwards, lit every fifty yards by bulbs under grills. Odilon locked the portal behind them and they climbed in silence, emerging on a gantry that ran between towers of accumulators. Far below Max saw a squad of soldiers run towards an archway. The sight spurred him on. Once they triggered the alarm he'd no doubt they'd seal the complex and then it'd be just a case of hunting them down.

Sure enough, half a mile along the walkway he heard the wail of a siren in the distance and his heart sank. Odilon ignored it, forging ahead between ribbed mountains of glass and copper. Their route led to a staircase spiralling around one of the towers, ending at a hatch set in the ground. To Max's surprise it opened easily. Odilon lowered himself through the portal. Max followed and almost fell as gravity flipped ninety degrees. He found himself on a semi-circular platform in a vault. The underside of the floor he'd just stood on was the wall at his back. It disappeared into darkness above and below. He could see shapes in the gloom marked with a handful of scattered lights. How far away were they? Yards? Miles? He couldn't tell. The door clanged behind him and he waited in a circle of ridged metal lit by a guttering lamp. Odilon walked to the edge of the light, his eyes fixed on Max. He struggled to avoid the alien's gaze. He remembered the look on the Black Rose's face after his first meeting with Ragaleis the giant, when the titan sat in his thoughts and peered out on the world. The Watcher in the Tower recognised his enemy in Max's head. Now the last remaining fragments of Bassandis slept in the dream garden inside his skull. Would Odilon spot him too? Was the sleep Anselm had laid upon the weakened titan sufficient to keep him hidden? He knew full well what Odilon would do if he realised. Which was preferable, to be ripped apart in a bloody second, or to fall into that mind-reeling gulf behind?

"Give her to me," said Odilon.

"What are you going to do?" asked Max.

"Save her," said the alien. Gone were the rubber-faced fake emotions, the twinkle in the eye, the warm, avuncular tones. He couldn't see any recognisable humanity in those penny-coloured eyes and that unnatural curve in the body Odilon chose to wear looked taut with unstoppable rage. What could he do? He guessed the creature really did want to rescue Abby, why else go through this? But he'd no idea what the Black Rose intended to do with him.

He placed Abby in the alien's arms, noticing with surprise how the bruise from Casper's hand had faded. Odilon exploded into a cloud of petals. Max jumped back, nearly pitching over the rail as the creature vanished into the darkness, Abby nestled amid the writhing storm of its body. *Is that it?* thought Max. Maybe Odilon had no intention of killing him. Why bother? The Queen would save him the trouble. He wanted Max to carry Abby so his tentacles were free to pull apart any resistance, and he no longer needed help. What now? Wait here, or return to the palace and surrender? He glanced around, wondering where he was, trying to calculate the route they'd taken. He knew they'd more or less journeyed into the depths of the citadel, down to its base where the Queen sat among her monstrous engines. An idea struck him. Could he be standing inside the skin of the sphere itself, hence the gravity shift? When they'd first entered the kingdom on the catamaran they'd travelled several miles from the outer entrance to the inner hangar. For a few seconds he forgot danger and gazed in wonder at the shapes and lights beyond the ledge. More machines that worked - vast, bright, glistening with grease and power - the muscles of this world.

Something thumped onto the platform. Odilon stood behind him. *I can't fight him. I tried it on the chain of the Carceral Archipelago. He had a knife then. This time he has the strength to rip me to bits.* Max held his hands up and stepped back, thinking he'd jump and take his chances.

He wasn't fast enough. Fluttering tendrils encompassed him and his cry was choked by the sudden lurch as the Black Rose hurtled upwards. Max fought against the terror, remembering the uncontrollable vertigo when Odilon plucked him from his father's balcony. Then the creature had tried to kill him, but this felt different. *He's saving me too, he wants me alive. Why?* They landed on a second platform next to a flyer bearing the Queen's sigil on its fins - clearly stolen. They climbed inside and Max spotted Abby lying curled up at the back of the cabin. Max joined her, feeling safer with a wall behind him. Odilon took the controls without a word and the ship dropped into the vault, moving so swiftly the passing lights turned into faint streaks.

After a while Max summoned up the courage to look past Odilon at the scene outside. They followed the curve of the sphere, weaving between spires, columns, arches, coils of wire miles thick, valves filled with glowing lakes, spheres and tetrahedrons hanging in lacy nets of light. Several hours passed and Abby still slept. Max crawled over to her and teased apart the blanket. The burn on her breast had gone and he found nothing more than faint discolouration amid the freckles. *Odilon's magic.*

The alien brought the ship to a stop outside a cluster of houses sitting on a plain littered with twisted metal, detritus and discarded machinery. To Max it looked like an abandoned scrapyard. He saw no sign of life. Perhaps these buildings once housed the people who sifted through the cast-off wreckage from the machines in the sphere's walls. *The perfect place for Odilon to hide, in the shadows at the very bottom of this world.* He guessed they'd descended over a hundred miles below the surface of the Umbilical Ocean.

He carried Abby out of the ship and followed Odilon into one of the buildings. Max noticed all the rooms were empty save for one with a bed. He lay the sleeping woman beneath the sheets. Odilon pushed him out of the way and stooped over his companion. He examined the mark on her breast and peered into her mouth, grunting in satisfaction.

"You'll be safe here. She'll wake up shortly," he said. "It's not a good idea for her to meet me yet. Tell her what happened. I'll come back with food in two hours."

Odilon turned to Max who avoided his gaze. He hoped the creature just saw the fear and not the attempt to hide the giant in his mind.

"If you try and escape I'll kill you," said the Watcher. Max nodded.

"Odilon," he called out despite himself as the being reached the door. "Thank you for saving us." He thought the alien paused for a second but then he was gone.

Abby came round an hour later. She stuck her tongue in her cheek and felt her breast, puzzled at not finding a wound or any pain. Her face hardened and she put her hand under the blankets, reaching between her legs.

"They didn't have time," said Max. She looked at him, blinking as if he stood in front of a strong light.

"What happened? Where are we?" she asked.

"We're in an abandoned house in the skin of the sphere. We were rescued."

"Who by?"

Here we go.

"Odilon the Watcher," he said. She frowned as if hunting through her mind for something to hang the name on. Max wondered if the alien's medicine affected her memory but he realised she simply struggled to believe him. She mouthed the words a few times, frowning.

"Why would Odilon the Watcher rescue you and me from being tortured by the Steel Queen?" she asked eventually as if trying to decipher an incomprehensible phrase in an unknown language. Max hadn't a clue. The only thing he had to go on was the alien's tenderness seeing to her injuries and the bloody fury he'd visited on everyone they'd met on their way out. *He kissed you on the forehead. I think he cares about you.* Better to keep the idea in his own head for the time being. Abby would reckon he'd gone insane.

"So I'm here because of you," Abby said. "They were going to torture me for your benefit."

He described as best he could the encounter with the Machine Man and the protection laid upon him by Persephone. When he told her about the murders at Count Xix's mansion her mouth dropped open. She snapped it shut again when he described the death of Chiral and his last conversation with Pell.

"That porcelain bitch always was trouble," said Abby. She lay her head back on the pillow.

"We can't escape each other, can we? Just when I'd got a new typewriter to bang out plays and a theatre to dance around in, Fate decides I'd be better off being raped and branded instead of you so that no-one important gets offended."

Max sat on the edge of the bed and cradled her face in his hand, revelling in the touch of the rarest treasure in the dying universe. She read the message in his eyes and closed hers, pressing his fingers against her cheek with her own. Tears spilled from under her lashes.

"We are so stupid aren't we? We're our own worst enemies," she managed. "I thought I could survive without you but I can't, can I?"

Neither could he. He realised that now. He tried to speak but found it impossible. Instead he rested his forehead on hers and forgot everything in the universe except the touch of her skin and the scent of her hair. At last he sat back and Abby's eyes went wide. Odilon waited in the door, watching them. He held a tray with two steaming bowls and lumps of black bread torn onto a plate. He set it on the table at the foot of the bed.

"Hello Abby," he said.

Abby stood up, white faced, and limped towards him. Her unsteady steps told Max she still felt the effects of the medicine. She stopped in front of the Black Rose, naked against his blue robes, and spat in his face. Odilon didn't even blink.

"Abby," warned Max. *She'll get us killed* was his first thought but he saw an odd sadness in the creature's eyes that made him pause.

She slapped Odilon but his head broke apart like a night flower blossoming for a second as her hand passed through it. It reformed again. She tried to hit him, a fighter's punch that would have shattered an ordinary man's skull. The same thing happened. She turned to the table, tipped the bread on the floor and smashed the plate on the edge. Clutching a wicked shard she stabbed and slashed at the Black Rose, sobbing and swearing as each blow plucked brief gouts of darkness from his body and clothes. In the end she dropped the fragment, wrapped her arms around Odilon's neck and wept into his chest. He embraced her and rested his face in the nest of her hair. Max watched, stunned. It was the last thing he expected from either of them.

"You were a father to me, to Rebecca. We adored you but everything you taught us, everything you did for us was a lie. A miserable fucking lie."

"It wasn't, Abby, it wasn't at all," whispered Odilon. "Everything I did for you and your sister I did because I love you."

"Why did you betray us?" came the snotty mumble from Abby's buried face.

"I didn't betray you. I did what I had to do to protect the next universe from man."

"You betrayed my father, and my mother," said Max. This reconciliation was very touching but no amount of alien contrition, genuine or otherwise, would bring his own parents back to life. "I was two years old when you murdered her, Odilon. Two years old."

Abby disentangled herself and stepped away, embarrassed by her performance. Max suppressed his own feelings of rage. Fury and revenge wouldn't redress the past and he had more burning questions in his mind.

"Why are you here? Why did you kill those Philosophers?"

"Don't you know?" asked Odilon. He looked from Max to Abby. They shook their heads in unison.

"The Queen is trying to build a wormhole," he said. Abby let out a bark of disbelief.

"Why for God's sake? There's thousands of the buggers out in the singularity - the ones you lot made. Is that what this mess is about? Is that why I got my left tit skewered, for a fucking wormhole?"

"Chiral talked about the wormholes, said they hold reality together," said Max. "We know they're closing. Is the Queen trying make new ones to stop the singularity vanishing?"

It didn't sound right. If Odilon thought God's mind was wrecked why worry about the ground he lay on?

None of this warranted the cruel butchery of the Philosophers. The shadows in the room grew longer as an unexplained fear took hold of Max.

"What's this wormhole for?" he managed to ask.

"It's designed to reach into the next universe," answered Odilon. Silence fell like a hammer on the room. Max groped behind him until he fetched up against the edge of the bed. He sat, waiting for the walls to stop rotating.

"That's why the Philosophers are in the palace, to show Leontine's scientists how to break through time and space," he said at last. Odilon nodded.

"The Steel Queen plans to build a tunnel that will bypass the God Door. This sphere of hers is the generator. It will interact with the mercury sea to open a portal."

Extruding wormholes from the singularity was one thing, they were made of the same stuff weren't they? But what happened if you created it in the Umbilical Ocean, bang smack at the centre of the deity's body?

"It will destroy your god," said Odilon, reading his thoughts.

"But that's what you want, isn't it?" said Abby. "That's why you killed Bassandis, so God can't be finished."

"I don't want humans in the next universe, whether through a wormhole or carried in the hands of this monster you've made."

"Who are you to decide if we can go or not?" spat Abby. Odilon gestured at her.

"Man is evil, Abby. Look what he did to you in the name of power. Of the people you have met in your journeys, how many are good, how many are wicked?"

"Most are neither," said Max. "Most just cling on to the days hoping the Great Task is worthwhile, that their descendants won't live in lightless caverns and in a dead Wasteland under an empty sky."

Odilon shook his head.

"Your time is over, long over. We should never have given you hope. You taint everything you touch with your greed and your anger. I want you to die in the old universe, fade away in the shadow of this god you've made."

"You're no better than us. You're a murderer, and a liar," said Abby.

"What I do, I do for the greater good," said Odilon. Abby gave a bitter laugh.

"Never heard that one before."

"You decided to kill off the Philosophers so the functions in their head couldn't be used by Leontine's scientists to create this wormhole between universes." said Max.

Odilon watched him, bronze eyes glowing in the darkness. Max ran through the events of the last few days. At last it all made sense - Chiral's anger at Virasoro and her desperate refusal to accept Pell.

"It won't work," said Max. "You've been murdering the wrong ones." The alien gave him a curious look.

"All those Philosophers working in unison make one great big calculation that the Queen will use to craft this wormhole of hers," he continued, piecing together the puzzle in his mind.

"But they were missing something, a link in the chain. Some functions and procedures they didn't have so they couldn't complete the sum. It didn't matter if you killed one, two, half a dozen, because no single Philosopher was essential. Their groups have natural built-in redundancy. They had nearly everything they needed many times over." He remembered Chiral shouting at Virasoro across Count Xix's hall. *You'd have to kill*

*ten, twenty of us to make a difference, so why bother protect-
ing us?*

"Except Pell," he finished. Abby stared at him, *that
little bitch?* written on her face.

"Pell belonged to a rogue group of Philosophers
who were designed as weapons. The others wiped them
out hundreds of years ago because they were too dangerous but she survived. The functions and procedures
inside her head are to enhance combat - war, cruelty, violence, strategy, tactics, you name it. But she also sees
into the future. She understands flaws in space and time
and she moves through dimensions. She, and only she,
has the knowledge the Queen needs to complete the project. It's unique to her. That's why Virasoro got so excited when we brought her to the Philosophers and why
he's so desperate to protect her - even to the extent that
he'll sacrifice any number of his colleagues. It doesn't
matter if they perish in their dozens. But she's the only
one with the missing part of the equation."

It was an ugly conclusion and he still couldn't get
the image of that pale girl out of his head, all innocent
and lost when she wanted. He hated himself for telling
an alien who'd dedicated itself to barring mankind from
the next universe but he needed to protect God. Max
couldn't let Leontine destroy his body. He had to say it.

"Kill Pell and you stop the wormhole."

"I can't," said Odilon. "Not any more. The Queen's
citadel is sealed and all the Philosophers are inside, including this one of which you speak. Not even I can get
back in there now."

An age passed. Abby spoke, her voice tinged with
wonder.

"You've failed because you rescued us?"

Odilon nodded. Max could see how she struggled to
comprehend the implication of his words. *She realises*

that behind the betrayal and the lies this unholy feathered darkness thought of her and her sister as a human would think of its own mad, beautiful daughters. He'd rather save her and fail in his quest than let her die. She shook her head and buried her face in her hands, struggling with a mountain of doubts.

"If the Queen succeeds she'll destroy your god and mankind will find a way into the next universe, or at least the humans within this sphere," said Odilon. "I don't think she cares much about the rest." He looked at each of them in turn.

"Max, why are you here?" he asked.

Max panicked, fighting to keep his face in a frozen mask of concerned interest. *Guess what? We're here to re-build the giant you killed.*

"You destroyed our old home," said Abby, her voice still filled with bitterness. "Metacarpi burned in the battle between the giants and the dreadnoughts. The Carceral Archipelago fell into the Forbidden Sea. All that was left in the end was smoke and ashes. We didn't want to stay, did we?" she looked at Max. *No, the universe had changed. I didn't recognise my own birthplace any more.*

"So we came to the Body of God to see its wonders and this is one of them," she gestured at the ceiling. "You read me stories about the Kingdom of the Steel Queen, remember? You and Rebecca both, from the books in your wonderful library."

"Have you seen wonders?" asked Odilon gently. Was he looking for an answer that would ease his guilt? Did these aliens even feel guilt?

Abby conceded him a nod.

"What happens now?" said Max. "Having rescued us and brought us here what do you intend to do with us?"

"Nothing," said the alien.

"Nothing?" said Abby in disbelief. Odilon shrugged.

"Nothing. You are free to go or stay. Unless you want to take me up on my original promise. You can come with me to the God of the Black Roses, leave this dead puppet behind. If you need wonders, Abby, I will fill your days with wonders beyond comprehension."

A weariness fell across Max. Odilon's words were so seductive. He looked at his surroundings. Grey box on a scrap heap at the bottom of a mad woman's world. And beyond that? More darkness and shadows, tunnels and empty rooms, desperate men and women creeping through a million years of debris, lost in the impossible, labyrinthine vastness of God's body. What did Leontine say? *Idiocy to understanding, and back to idiocy.* And who's the biggest idiot? He rubbed his forehead without thinking. Somewhere behind that tired bone a white-haired giant slept with his head on a wrought metal table in a scribbled pencil garden with cardboard walls. He thought of the creatures telling him he must go to the Heart or Head to rebuild the Mind of God and save everyone, except himself - Ragaleis, the Brittle Hag, Ioam, Anselm. *You must go. You must go and die. Duty calls. The stone duty Father bred you for.* He grew conscious of Abby's gaze upon him. *Tell Odilon you just want a few moments alone with her to make your decision. Have a chat, look into each other's eyes, kiss, hold hands and bid farewell to this exhausted old cosmos and all the idiots and villains still left in it. Journey to the God Door in the arms of a black feathered angel.* He sighed and looked at Odilon.

CHAPTER TWENTY-SEVEN

"THERE IS ONE way to get back into the palace of Queen Leontine," he said. Odilon froze. His gaze glittered danger.

"There is one person who will be allowed in, no matter what." Max closed his eyes and bid future hopes goodbye yet again. "Anselm the Machine Man."

It was Odilon's turn to look scared. Max didn't know whether he just aped the emotion for effect or the body he'd fashioned caught him unawares but alarm sparked in his face. *Got you, not so condescending now are you? If the Machine Men find out you're responsible for the death of Bassandis then you can flutter and storm all you want. They'll snuff you out like a candle.*

"The Queen wants an alliance with the Machine Men. She seeks their co-operation on this wormhole of hers. They might have guessed what she intends to do and realised the consequences for the deity. I bet she's desperate to show them what she's planning, promise them first class tickets to the new cosmos so they won't wipe her and her pretty sphere out of existence. She tried to use me to communicate with them, to get them face to face. If we roll up with Anselm the Machine Man for a bit of diplomatic bargaining, they'll let us in."

"Max, why do you seek to stop the Queen?" asked Odilon. "If she fails then you're left here with a dead god and no hope."

Abby saved him.

"Maybe, unlike you, we don't want to condemn everyone else to death. Even if this invention of hers works what about the millions of people outside the sphere? If she destroys God they'll die. We won't abandon them while there might be hope left somewhere, despite what you did." Odilon said nothing. "Sorry if that doesn't fit with your 'humans are bastards' belief."

"Leontine doesn't realise what she's attempting, neither do the Philosophers," said Max, remembering the argument between Chiral and Virasoro. '*You have no idea what you're doing. She's a weapon, Virasoro, we have no clue of the extent of the poison in her mind*'. *Chiral found out too late in the end.*

"Whatever they think they're creating could destroy everything. The woman they're using to complete their calculation is dangerously insane and driven by hatred and jealousy." Odilon walked to the window and looked across the heaps of scrap stretching into the gloom.

"What have you got to lose, Odilon?" asked Max, gambling all. "If you fail you fail but this gives you one more chance to stop the project. We can't do it, neither can Anselm. He's too weak. I've seen him. He's a big rusting bug who hasn't moved in years. We'll be lucky if he makes it to the palace. But if he does we can get inside and you can try again."

Odilon's profile stamped a black shape against the window.

"Does this Machine Man know what I did?" he asked.

"He knows you don't want us in the next universe and that you conspired to kill the giant of Metacarpi. But we're after the same thing, to stop the Queen. You so that we're doomed to this universe forever, Anselm because he wants to preserve the Body of God in the hope that he may still wake. None of us can do it by ourselves."

The house shuddered. Outside dislodged metal rattled down the slopes. Odilon strode out of the room. Max and Abby followed him, Abby wrapping the bed sheet round herself. Miles away thunder rumbled in a darkness lit by acid blues and yellows. Max's first thought was lightning but these explosions were too regular. Behind and above him he heard the grumbling of mountainous gear teeth engaging. Abby grabbed his hand, clinging tightly to his fingers. A sudden breeze whipped at Odilon's robe and it billowed around him. The noise ended and the lights faded.

"They're testing the sphere," said Max, remembering the bands of orange and white light flickering along the trench. "They must be close to activating the wormhole."

"Where is the lair of this Anselm?" asked Odilon.

"In a machine city set in rolling hills." Max tried to read the back of the alien's head. It told him nothing but he could guess the argument raging in whatever passed for a heart amid those roiling petals.

"Max, the second I sense betrayal I will rip you apart in front of Abigail," he said. Max was quick witted enough to elbow Abby in the ribs before she said what was on her mind. Even so she dug her nails painfully into his palm.

"I won't betray you, I give you my word." Would he keep it? Abby clearly didn't think so. She was giving him a look he recognised. He was the biggest idiot in the universe and she was going to have to rescue him yet again.

393

They lingered long enough to find clothes for Abby - a grubby pair of dungarees three sizes too big. The straps kept falling off her shoulders until she tied them in a knot behind her neck. They had no weapons but Max knew that revolvers and shotguns were little match against an agitated battalion of the Queen's crack guard. With any luck, if carnage broke out, they'd have time to equip themselves with a couple of those smart looking machine pistols the soldiers carried.

They boarded Odilon's ship and set off through the space between the walls. After several hours he landed on a platform next to another access hatch. This opened onto a storm drain curling away on both sides, its concrete floor lit by grills of light from above. Max listened but heard nothing. Through one of the skylights he saw dull buildings rising into a white sky. *We're in the machine city, Anselm's tower must be nearby.*

They waited until nightfall. Odilon lifted them onto the roof of a building so they could get their bearings in the fading light. Max spotted the tower half a mile away. He saw lights scattered around the hill on which it stood, and the outlines of three flyers circling above. The Queen didn't waste time. Having locked down her own palace she took no chances by surrounding the ambassador from the Machine Men with troops. *She thinks we're inside.* He doubted she'd risk any direct hostilities against the Machine Man but she obviously wanted to put on a show of force and out here the three of them were horribly vulnerable. They may not harm him but he'd seen what her Majesty's servants would do to Abby.

"How do we get in?" she asked. Max racked his brains. Odilon could carry them to the tower one at a time but they'd alert the flyers.

"Can you imitate any human?" he asked Odilon.

"Half a dozen minor variations on a theme," said the Black Rose. Max stared dumbfounded as he flickered through them. They all looked like thinner or fatter versions of Odilon or the Sonian poet, even the women. He'd go unnoticed in the dark but Max would be recognised in an instant and Abby stood out like a sore thumb half naked in those baggy dungarees with a flaming nest on her head. A thought struck him. It had worked once before, it might work again if they could get close enough to the tower and it wasn't shielded. They'd have to distract Odilon.

The alien lifted them to within two blocks of the tower, moving low and swift amid the unlit buildings. He dropped them among a cluster of silent machines on top of a skyscraper.

"Odilon, can you scout the perimeter? Find if there's any way we can get in. There might even be access from underneath," he asked. That should keep the creature occupied. The alien, not suspecting, exploded once more into a cloud of black petals and disappeared into the sky.

"Hit me," said Max to Abby.

"What?" The penny dropped. "Again? You think it'll work?"

"Just hit me!"

It took two blows this time. Either Abby held back because of their rediscovered love or the effects of the medicine lingered. It still hurt. To his relief he stood in the garden. He spotted Bassandis, head on the table. *He looks like Chiral when I found her*, he thought with a twist of fear. Was the giant alive? He had to be, this was his dream world and the sky above roared with dull red fire glimpsed through rents in the clouds. He couldn't see anyone else. No Anselm, no Brittle Hag standing on the hills.

"Anselm," he shouted, running back and forth. He'd no idea how long he had before he woke up or Odilon returned to find him unconscious. Abby would have fun explaining that away. He searched with increasing desperation. Nothing, just dun walls and that solitary figure slumped at the table. How quickly did time pass here? Slower or faster than in the real world? He always seemed to skip through dreams, the morning coming swift on the heels of the creatures that wandered through the landscapes of his ordinary sleep. In the end he vaulted over a wall, feeling it wobble beneath him, and stood at the foot of the hills, their domes piling into the distance under the lowering sky. He put his hands to his mouth and yelled again. A shape flickered half way up the slope. The memory of the Brittle Hag? No, it was Persephone. He pelted towards her. She looked like she was searching for him through fog, her barred pupils enlarged to almost fill her eye sockets, turning her whole head into a madman's prison.

"Max, is that you?" she called.

"I'm here, on a building two blocks away from you but I can't get to the tower past the troops," he described their location as best he could. Her flickering image winked out and he woke up to find Abby and Odilon standing over him. He instinctively closed his eyes in case the Black Rose recognised any remnants of Bassandis in his mind.

"What happened?" asked the alien.

"We argued, I hit him," said Abby sweetly. "But it's alright now. We're friends again." She kissed him on his bruised jaw, causing him to wince and swear.

"The perimeter's sealed and there's nowhere in from beneath. Our only chance is to fight our way through. I think I can cause enough of a disruption for us to reach the base of the tower."

Max stopped listening, his eyes on the summit of Anselm's fortress. A beam of light as wide as the top lanced up into the night. It illuminated the underside of a sphere rising like a slow motion cannon ball from a mortar. A ring of orange portholes cut the vessel in half. Max saw them wink on and off as the frantic shapes of Leontine's machines flickered around the craft. Far below he heard shouting. Spotlights sliced upwards through the murk, their beams skittering across rooftops to splash against the hull of the Machine Man's ship. It drifted onwards, moving in an arc towards their building. The three of them hunkered in the shadows, hoping it would reach them before the troops realised where it headed and attacked them from above and below. Max watched it, his anxiety mounting. Why did it move so slowly? It paused above their skyscraper and a disc descended from the lower hemisphere, revealing a spiral staircase. Persephone stood on the platform, a poised quill the colour of midnight, her gaze sweeping back and forth over the roof.

Max, Abby and Odilon ran for the steps just as the three flyers pinned them in their own lights, one ahead and one on each side. Behind them boots kicked open an access door and soldiers swarmed into a semi-circle, all guns pointing at Max.

"That man is a murderer and a spy," shouted an officer against the wind generated by the combination of the sphere and the flyers' engines. "Release him into my custody by order of Queen Leontine XXIII or face her swift and decisive wrath."

"Maximilian Ocel is under the protection of Theuderic Lord of the Machine Men," bellowed Anselm's ship in a voice that sounded like God himself had woken up.

A gun fired. The bullet zinged past Max's ear.

"The next shot begins a war between your Queen and the Machine Men, drop your weapons now," roared the sphere. A hole irised open and a pellet of white fire sped over their heads. It impacted on a building a mile away which burst apart in a column of melting steel. Everyone staggered in the shock wave. The officer stepped forwards and signalled for the soldiers to lower their guns. He had a sick look on his face, realising what his surrender would mean when he returned to the palace. The flyers fell back and the three of them climbed onto the platform. It whisked them up into the ship. Max gasped as he saw the interior was nothing but a single hollow space, padded in pale orange. The windows ringed the wall twenty yards above his head. Persephone waited, as still as ever. Abby clung to Max and looked around in awe at the vessel. Odilon stood as far away from Persephone as he could, watching her every move with his amber gaze.

The walls of the tower masked the portholes. The ship came to rest and they disembarked. Persephone turned and before Max could react she placed her fingers on his forehead and white light erased the universe from his mind.

Anselm waited for him at the table next to the sleeping Bassandis, resting one hand on the giant's hair. He tapped the base of an upturned glass with the fingers of his other hand. Underneath an indigo-winged moth beat its wings desperately against the transparent walls of its prison.

"Who's this then?" asked Anselm as Max sat down beside him.

"A Black Rose," said Max.

"The one that killed Bassandis?" Max couldn't lie. Anselm smiled. His teeth were fashioned from thousands of tiny interlinked chains.

"Well done, you've brought the villain here," he said. "What to do with him? Machine Men have no notion of justice or punishment. We are builders, that's all. I'll have to look to you for guidance."

"Can he hear us?" asked Max. The insect Odilon hurled itself time and time again against the table top and the inside of the glass.

"No. At the moment the creature is incapable of understanding anything except utter terror and abasement."

"Don't hurt him, we need his help," said Max. Once he'd have cheerfully consigned the monster to an ugly, fearful death but he couldn't shake the image of the sage hugging Abby and her hands clutching at his robes as if he were her long-lost father.

"Really?" said Anselm, obviously fascinated to learn why.

"He knows what the Queen is doing. She's using the Philosophers to build a wormhole into the next universe."

"That's not possible," said Anselm, his voice contemptuous, though Max detected uncertainty. "She lacks the knowledge. Even all the Philosophers on God's body can't fashion the equations to tunnel through time and space to the new cosmos."

"They can. They have a rogue, weaponised Philosopher with the missing functions. If they open the wormhole it'll destroy God."

"So this sphere and all its inhabitants will fly away, and everyone else perishes in the endless night." Max had no idea what *furious* looked like on a Machine Man's face but he guessed he was seeing it right now. Anselm tapped a gnarled finger on the glass.

"And this?"

"The Black Rose wants to stop the wormhole to prevent humans entering the next universe. He doesn't know about Bassandis, he thinks God is dead already. He can shut down the project if we get him into the palace. Agree to meet the Queen to negotiate - say you want to help her, you'll surrender me to her, whatever it takes."

"How does it intend to sabotage the experiment?" asked Anselm. Max had a vision of bleached entrails in pools of milk, a rain of blood pattering on his head and shoulders as he carried Abby along a passageway. Anselm gave a dream sigh and placed his hands on the head of his cane.

"Let's see what the Queen has to say, shall we? I'm happy to meet her and we'll soon discover whether this tells the truth." He rapped the glass, causing the moth to flutter in desperation.

Max opened his eyes to find Persephone withdrawing her fingers. He stumbled.

"Are you OK?" asked Abby.

"How long was I out?"

"Out?" Abby gave him a quizzical frown. "She touched you and you staggered. She's half your size," she added as an accusatory afterthought. *No time passes in the giant's dream garden.* Max looked at Odilon. He stood completely still as if he too had just disembarked but Max saw his eyes flicker back and forth as though something bothered him deep down.

"Attend," bellowed a voice outside. Abby jumped.

"Anselm, Ambassador of the Machine Men, will meet Queen Leontine XXIII to discuss the recent events," the tower shouted. "He seeks a peaceful meeting with Her Majesty to ensure bonds between our kingdoms remain strong."

"That should do it," said Persephone. "We depart immediately." Abby stuck her arms out sideways as if to say *like this*? The servant of Anselm looked her up and down.

"Alright, ten minutes," she said, gesturing for Abby to go with her.

They gathered in the room with Anselm the Machine Man. Still Odilon hung back. He hadn't spoken since his brief imprisonment under the glass and Max suspected he realised he stood in the presence of a being more powerful than he'd imagined. Abby, on the other hand, was decidedly unimpressed by the decaying mountain in front of her. Persephone had lent her a simple white dress and fortunately they were more or less the same size. She'd tied her hair back with a piece of copper wire and stood with her hands on her hips staring up at the Machine Man with an expression of baffled dismay. Max thought he glimpsed a pale shape floating in the glass cylinder high above but he didn't want to climb up again to make sure.

As he watched the walls of the room moved back and above them he saw the underside of the sphere descending through the tower. Its lower quarter irised open and the entire vessel dropped around them, its walls passing through the floor on which the Machine Man sat. Shuddering beneath Max's feet told him the ship had sealed itself below. It ascended once more and in moments the windows turned black as they drifted into the night. Max had no idea who or what piloted the craft. Persephone just stood there in front of Anselm. Odilon waited on the opposite side of the chamber. Max approached him.

"The Philosopher who holds the key to the project is a woman called Pell. We only need to remove her. I don't want anyone else harmed," he said. Odilon nodded but he didn't know whether it meant *I agree* or just *I understand*. "If you love Abby and crave her forgiveness keep your butchery for another time."

Odilon shot him a quick glance that made Max turn away for fear of what the Black Rose might see. To be honest he'd no idea if Abby held any feelings for the creature but the last thing he wanted was to find himself in the middle of a bloodbath.

"So we get in, kill Pell, then what?" asked Abby. If she'd heard his comments to Odilon she didn't react. "We'll be in the Queen's palace surrounded by her entire army, no doubt bent on revenge. Has anyone thought of an exit strategy?"

"Not a problem," said Persephone. Everyone waited but the assistant just stared back with an expression of urbane indifference. In the end Anselm himself elaborated, his voice filling the room.

"Queen Leontine will find herself in the presence of a Machine Man and a representative of the Black Roses. Even in her wildest rage she won't be so stupid as to declare war on both. If she decides to try anything foolish one shot from my craft can punch a mile-wide hole through the skin of her kingdom."

Max shuddered at the thought of the world's atmosphere venting into the night. He wondered why Anselm didn't just use the weapon to force the Queen to surrender. He guessed the being was either curious to see Leontine's project for himself or had subtler plans beyond his understanding

Max saw Persephone watching Odilon with her barred eyes. High up in the green cylinder Anselm's mind pressed hands against the glass to peer at him. The Watcher froze like an image on a faltering screen. Max found the sight disorientating. He'd always associated him with a glib, patronising confidence yet here he was, transfixed by fear.

"Whatever you've done is unimportant right now," Anselm continued, addressing his remarks to the alien. "We agree this experiment must be stopped and will therefore work together to ensure that outcome."

Max wasn't sure how reassuring they found his words but the creature had a point. He hoped Leontine wouldn't be so foolish as to go head to head with the architects of God's mind and beings powerful enough to create the singularity.

"We have arrived," said Persephone. This was it. Max gave Abby's hand a *for God's sake control yourself* squeeze. The sphere was shouting something but Max couldn't make out the words. Lights swept across the portholes.

"They negotiate," said Persephone.

The walls of the sphere rolled upwards and the surface under their feet descended into a courtyard. A regiment of troops stood to attention in front of the vessel, pretending to be a guard of honour. Two court officials in grey suits shielded their eyes against the wind kicked up from the sphere's engines. Max could see their amazement at the spectacle of Anselm. He wondered how often anyone from the palace had stood in his presence. Leontine called him a big iron turd, suggesting she'd met him at least once.

"Anselm will walk into the presence of the Queen with myself, Maximilian Ocel, Abigail Fabrice and Odilon," said Persephone. "He is the Machine Man's engineer. Our lord is ancient and needs constant attention. As protocol dictates we are unarmed."

The men conferred and nodded. Max heard a low grinding sound. He turned to see Anselm heave to his feet. Of the seven legs that supported him, five still functioned - their cylinders hissed and spat drops of red oil. The wooden limb dangled uselessly. The last leg, an articulated knot of gears and joints as thick as a man's torso, dragged behind leaving trails of fluid flecked with fragments of rust. Anselm lurched and rocked as he limped towards the palace doors. Max caught a glimpse of the pale form inside the tank pressing fingerless hands against the glass to steady itself.

They passed down long corridors flanked on both sides by soldiers and the officials who'd greeted them. Max wondered if the ancient beast would make it but he struggled on, leaving cracked tiles and a trail of dirt. Leontine waited for them in a hall designed for ceremonial occasions. Mile high tapestries showing noble men and women pointing at skies filled with stars cascaded down cliff-sized walls. The Queen waved the troops away but Max noticed they merely faded back into the shadows at the side of the vault. A handful of nervous looking functionaries remained. Leontine's eyebrow went up at the sight of Max and Abby.

"Honoured guest," she peered up at the head of the Machine Man. "We are delighted by your offer of a meeting. It would have been nice if Max had brought you the invitation in a slightly less, er, messy way, but hey ho." She looked at Abby.

"You're the woman who trounced Xix at poetry aren't you?" she said with a happy grin at the memory.

"I'm the woman you tortured to get Max to speak," said Abby. Max ground her hand in his. She responded by gouging his palm with her nail.

"Did we?" asked Leontine, taken aback. She turned to her aides who shuffled their feet and looked embarrassed. Leontine pulled an *oops sorry* face and turned to Odilon. Abby muttered something under her breath involving the Queen in an act as obscene as it was physically impossible. Luckily only Max caught her words.

"And you are?" Leontine asked the Black Rose.

"My lord's personal engineer," cut in Persephone.

"Yes," said Leontine, running her gaze over the Machine Man's brooding hulk. "I'm not surprised. My Lord Anselm, when we have concluded our business my technicians, who are the best in the Body of God barring your own good selves, would be delighted to examine you and perform the necessary adjustments and repairs to bring you to full and vibrant health. Wouldn't you?" She turned to a couple of her companions who Max realised were scientists. They managed a pair of weak smiles but the horror in their eyes said it all.

"Good, that's settled then," continued Leontine.

"My Lord Anselm has come to discuss your project," said Persephone. "You are trying to create a wormhole to carry this sphere into the next universe. If you do this you will destroy the Body of God and doom all who remain behind to death in the final night."

Leontine pursed her lips. To her credit she didn't falter for a second.

"Can Lord Anselm speak for himself?" she asked.

"You must end this project. You cannot risk the deity and his people for this experiment," Odilon's voice filled the vault. Leontine allowed herself a chuckle.

"I tell you what. Why don't I show you what I've achieved? It'll help give this conversation a bit of perspective," she said.

CHAPTER TWENTY-EIGHT

MAX'S HEART THUDDED against his ribs. *She's taking us to the wormhole*. One of the scientists whispered something in Leontine's ear.

"Really? Ah," she looked perplexed. "Apparently the Honourable Ambassador is too big to fit where we're going." She turned to Odilon. "Is there anyway we can get that, thing, to, I don't know…" she gestured at Anselm's head. Odilon stared back at her. Max cursed under his breath. Would the Black Rose give them away?

With a teeth-jarring screech of metal the cylinder broke away from the rest of the body and descended in a cloud of steam, blood coloured oil spilling out of the hole it left behind. Max saw it moved on its own caterpillar tracks, caked with thick grease and dirt from years of disuse. He allowed himself to start breathing again. They were out of danger, for the moment.

Even though Anselm looked far less intimidating than before, reduced to a ten-foot-high green tube, the Queen took no chances. A squad of soldiers surrounded them as they walked. Judging by the sigil on their caps these were Leontine's own guard. After half an hour threading their way along corridors and across rooms that grew increasingly utilitarian they passed through weapon scanners. Leontine apologised but was sure they understood. What she was about to show them was the profoundest discovery in the history of humanity. If she still thought Anselm responsible for the murdered Philosophers she no longer cared. Max realised that despite her unfocused and hyperactively girlish mannerisms this woman was as unyielding and ruthless as the steel they walked over. What were a handful of white-haired eccentrics to her? Useful calculating engines and nothing more. Apart from Pell there were plenty more to go round. He suspected her anger at their deaths was more at the personal insult it implied.

Halfway along a corridor one of Anselm's tracks seized up and he turned into the wall, running over a scientist's foot. While the howling man was bundled away and Persephone apologised to the Queen in her clipped minimalist voice Max, Odilon and Abby gathered around the ambassador, bending to examine the jammed sprocket wheel. Above them the Machine Man's mind looked at them with those shadowy caverns in its head, pads pressed against the inside of his glass cylinder. Odilon had no idea what to do. *Just arrived and we're rumbled*, thought Max, getting ready to fight his way out if necessary. He sneaked a glance at the nearest guard, wondering how easy it would be to disarm the man and take Leontine hostage. Abby got on her hands and knees to peer under the machinery.

"Allow me," said one of the Queen's technicians. With his boss ferried off to hospital he obviously spotted an opportunity to make his mark. Busy superciliousness replaced the look of terror he'd shown when Leontine first suggested he help Anselm. He reached under the Machine Man, pulled a face, yanked something and stood up. Anselm rolled back and forth experimentally, both tracks working again.

"Shall we continue?" asked Leontine with an expression that said *so you are one of the unbelievably powerful be-*

ings who fashioned the Heart and Mind of God? Max shared her scepticism. He assumed long years away from the Kingdom of the Machine Men, creeping through the spaces of God's body to end up sitting in a white-roomed tower in the Queen's sphere, had brought the creature to this. Were the rest of the architects of God's mind decaying lumps of junk, feeble creatures swimming in nutrient fluid encased in what looked like nothing more than an enormous storm lantern? Yet in the garden of his mind Anselm, though ancient, appeared as a delicate, exquisite clockwork human, millions upon millions of cogs, springs, wires and jewelled circuits under skin like translucent ivory. *Everyone thinks they're better looking than the face they see in the mirror but God almighty that's taking it to extremes.*

He suspected the Queen's minions had run ahead to switch machines on so that when they walked across bridges huge engines thundered above and below, and in city-sized halls white, red and glass towers hurled bolts of energy, lighting up the distant ceiling and searing afterimages in Max's eyes. It was very impressive but after asking a scientist what was happening and not understanding the evasive reply he put the light show down to more politics and tried to avoid being dazzled.

At last they emerged into a domed room ringed with a bewildering variety of machines and control panels. In the centre a silver capsule hung suspended in a frame. *It's a ship*, realised Max. He guessed it was about sixty feet long and twenty foot in diameter. As they walked along the walkway hugging the wall Max noticed a single crystal porthole at each end. Five equally spaced rings of dull metal encircled the hull. Wheeled steps led up to a doorway opening onto an interior bathed in soft blue light. Abby gazed at it with longing. She'd realised its intended destination.

"It's called the *Leontine*," said the Queen. She held her hands up. "Wasn't my idea."

The capsule hung over a disc in the floor. To Max it looked like a hatch. *They're going to open it and we'll look through eternity to the next universe.* He ached to see skies filled with stars. He noticed the same hunger in Abby's eyes. They swapped glances and grinned as the old conspiracy of wonder pulled them closer together. He looked across at the others. Persephone leant close to the cylinder as if conferring with the mind of Anselm. Odilon stared at a shimmering blue ring hanging above an iron box on the other side of the room.

Between this artefact and the capsule danced the Philosophers. Max guessed there were at least a hundred. He watched them in confusion as they weaved around each other with an unceasing rhythm. As they flowed back and forth they whispered in each other's ears, their hands touching in the briefest of handshakes, before moving on. The drifting figures formed and re-formed pale flowers on the brushed steel floor, robes and hair flaring as they turned.

"What are they doing?" asked Abby.

"Calculating," said Leontine. "See, they listen to data from a partner, process it in their minds and whisper the result to the next dancer."

It looked gorgeous, a never-ending pavane of knowledge and science flowing through a hundred porcelain heads. Max remembered Chiral's beauty, the touch of her own cold lips on his ear in the middle of the night, and the spectacle hit him with an unexpected sadness.

"What is it?" asked Abby. He shook his head. *Where's Pell?*

He searched for her in the crowd, wondering when the pristine science forged in this stunning performance entered into the dark labyrinth of a weaponised mind, taking on its corruption to open a doorway between realities. There she was. She didn't dance. Instead she waited next to Virasoro. They stood in a semicircle of machines covered in thousands of dials and levers operated by three of the Queen's own scientists. Once in a while a dancer broke away to murmur something in Pell's ear. After a few seconds she would point and the surrounding humans flicked switches and calibrated needles. *The last one in the chain*, thought Max. *She adds her functions to the calculation like a poisoner sprinkling drops of venom on a feast.*

"Want a closer look at the *Leontine*?" asked the Queen, her voice giddy with pride. "No talking to the Philosophers, mind. We're about to run another test."

Max's stomach clenched.

"A test?" asked Persephone.

"Yes, we can open a temporary wormhole small enough to carry that ship. We've sent it through unmanned. The next stage is to put a volunteer in it and pack them off - see what they come back with. I'd go myself but the po-faced bastards in the court say 'O no, Queen Leontine, we can't have you gadding off, we've got too many things for you to do here'." She sniffed in disdain. Max expected Abby to start jumping up and down going *me me me*. Since they'd arrived he'd caught her shooting filthy glances at the Queen and realised she was battling against the temptation for revenge, but in here excitement eclipsed her anger.

"Can I have a peek inside?" she blurted out despite herself.

"Can she?" asked Leontine. Her scientists looked thunderstruck but she ignored them. "Go on then."

Abby clattered up the stairs, trailing a panicked technician and a guard. They disappeared into the hatch.

"God's cock, Max, you've got to see this!" came Abby's happy yell from inside the capsule. Max's mind was on other things. In the corner of his eye he spotted Odilon walking towards that shimmering blue ring. As concerned scientists moved to intercept the alien Max joined him. He hadn't had a chance to point Pell out yet though the Black Rose may already have guessed which one she was. The Queen hadn't noticed. She was next to the ship and locked in a conversation with Anselm and Persephone, trying to persuade the Machine Man of the wisdom of collaboration. The Machine Man's rich tones rumbled from speakers set above his caterpillar tracks while Persephone stared at the floor with those inhuman eyes of hers. Odilon stopped in front of the floating artefact.

"What is it?" asked Max.

"It's special material teased out from between the fibres of existence," said a snub-nosed man in goggles and heavy gloves. "It holds the mouth of the wormhole open, like an iron washer in a rubber pipe. We knew it existed but didn't know where to look. She showed us." He pointed at Pell. Odilon looked across at the girl, then at Max who answered his unspoken question with a nod. Odilon turned back to the shimmering band.

"It's flawed," he said. The three beside them spluttered in protest. Odilon had trodden on several very sensitive toes.

"With all due respect, sir," said a bald woman, "we are the Queen's top scientists and these ladies and gentlemen are the greatest Philosophers ever to walk the Skin of God. If this matter was debased in any way they would know."

"Without question," chipped in her companion.

"It's flawed," repeated Odilon. He reached forward and grasped the ring on either side. The woman gave a squeak of alarm and several mouths dropped open. *Shit, ordinary humans can't handle that stuff, can they?* Max saw the answer in their faces. Odilon had done the impossible in front of every person in the room. *We're dead.* The Black Rose pulled the sides. The band grew to the size of a bicycle tyre. He ran it through his fingers as if looking for a puncture, finally pointing to a section that, to Max, looked just the same as everywhere else.

"There. If you use this your wormhole will last a few days at best. It's already evaporating." He put the ring back in its stasis field. It shrank back to the width of a dinner plate.

"Why are these people here?" thundered the voice of Virasoro. "My Queen, that man is a murderer. He killed three of my valued friends and companions." Max felt all eyes upon him. Beside him Odilon remained as still as a blue-robed sculpture. Virasoro strode between the Philosophers who, remarkably, continued to dance, locked in the baroque complexity of their mathematics.

"Guide Virasoro, may I introduce His Most Noble Excellency, Anselm, the Ambassador of the Machine Men, and his honoured guests, who I think you have already met," said the Steel Queen in tones designed to slam the Philosopher into the floor. They almost succeeded. He huffed and steamed, his face working as arrogance battled with good sense. "The noble Anselm has suggested co-operation between Lord Theuderic and ourselves and we are exploring the first tentative steps. I brought them here for a demonstration."

"Your Majesty," said Virasoro. "With all due respect, he should not be here," he jabbed a finger at Max who fought the urge to break the pompous bastard's arm. "He killed three of my people."

"No he didn't," said Persephone. "He was with me when the first two died and meeting the Queen when the third was murdered."

"Please, friends," Leontine held up her hands. "I, Queen Leontine XXIII, pardon this man and he is under the protection of the Machine Men. La! It is done."

Several of the officials nearby applauded at her gracious generosity. The Queen fixed her eyes on Virasoro.

"Your dead comrades, as deeply as I appreciate your loss, were hardly essential to this were they?" She waved her hand at the dancers. Max remembered Chiral and pushed away the fury in his heart. "Now, as I said, we are here for a demonstration." Her face hardened and Max saw the real Steel Queen. "Indulge me."

Virasoro had the wisdom to recognise defeat. He bowed. In the corner of his eye Max noticed a couple of the scientists whispering to an officer of Leontine's troops, their eyes on Odilon. They should move now, and swiftly, but still the Philosophers danced and the surrounding technicians busied themselves with their tasks. Max realised why nothing had happened yet. *We all want to see the wormhole.*

"You'd better get your friend out of the ship," said the Queen as three scientists plucked the blue ring from its stasis field with pincers and lay it on the floor under the capsule. To Max's surprise it sank into the steel, shrinking to a disc no larger than a penny. A knot of soldiers made their way round the perimeter of the room. Odilon returned to position himself behind Anselm. An officer appeared next to Leontine and murmured in her ear. She nodded.

"Mr..., forgive me I can't remember your name," she said to Odilon. "Would you be so good as to accompany these fine gentlemen. They wish to ask you a couple of questions." A dozen guns swung towards the alien who looked across the room at Pell. She stared back, her face unreadable as she continued to point at dials and switches, her fingers precise despite her distracted gaze.

"He is my engineer," said Anselm.

"No he's not," said Leontine.

Odilon burst into a cloud of black petals and hurtled towards Pell who vanished as he landed amid the machines. *She can peer into the future*, thought Max. *The bitch knows his every move.* Virasoro tried to scramble out of the way but a loop of darkness caught him around the chest and he disappeared into the seething mass. A hideous wail of terror and pain faltered into desperate slobbering and a second later his corpse, trailing white blood and fragments of bone and flesh, collided with the control panels. Bullets filled the air. Max felt something grab him round the waist. In a blur of motion he found himself behind the iron cube that held the blue ring's stasis field, with no idea how he'd got there. He spotted Anselm retreating into the shadows. Rounds ricocheted off his cylinder leaving white scratches across the reinforced glass and flicking sparks from the metal frame. Persephone stood beside him, her arms spread out and her bird's head twitching back and forth. *What she's doing*? To Max's astonishment the gunfire missed her. The Philosophers dissolved into a screaming mob, flinging themselves to the ground and back against the walls as the first wave of bullets subsided.

"The Queen, the Queen, protect the Queen," someone shouted. Max saw Leontine crouching under the ship. In that instant two halves of a transparent hemisphere rose out of the tiles and snapped shut over the capsule. Leontine, trapped in the enclosure, scampered up the steps and climbed inside, pulling the door closed behind her. *Abby's in there too*. Max ran for the dome but a hail of bullets drove him back. Desperate terror seized him as the blue ring under the craft started to grow, revealing a churning silver vortex. As it opened the floor sagged as if the ring grew heavy enough to distort the thick steel. Max lunged forward once more but again he was snatched back and hurled into a corner. *What keeps doing that?*

It couldn't be Odilon - he flew back and forth, hunting for Pell. Every few seconds he dipped, yanked a Philosopher into the air and ripped them apart, showering white blood and body parts on the shrieking, cowering mass beneath. Max watched in horror. He'd unleashed a monster bent on unholy slaughter. It was all his fault and the woman he loved was trapped in a ship suspended over a flawed wormhole. He fought against the sick anguish and desperately racked his brains for a plan, anything to stop this hideous carnage. The room briefly slipped out of alignment with itself, fractured by a drifting line.

"Odilon," yelled Max. The creature landed beside him and grasped the flaw in a seething coil of smoking petals. A thin howl came from nowhere. Odilon became a man once again, a kindly grandfather in blue robes with a penny-coloured gaze and a friendly word for everyone. His arm twisted as the fracture strained against his fist, unable to break away. Max spotted the other Philosophers running for the exit, ushered out by terrified guards. In the middle of the chamber the base of the hemisphere rotated in a whirlpool of energy, the underside of the ship blazing as if on fire.

"Watch out," shouted Max as Pell switched into two dimensions, breaking Odilon's grip. Max glimpsed the sad, frightened expression of a tormented girl. *They made you bad*, he thought. *Functions and procedures. It wasn't your fault.* Her flat image wavered as she gathered strength to flip into normality but before she could Odilon grabbed Pell in his fists and ripped her in half like a piece of paper. Max tried to shut out the sight of her face distended in agony, the vision of her exploding body erupting into their reality. A hideous silence descended, broken only by the faint whine from the generators. Max forced himself to look at the Black Rose. His clothes were spattered white with blood and shreds of flesh.

"Abby's in the capsule, save her," he begged. Odilon exploded into his true form, sped across the room, picked up Anselm's tube and hurled it at the transparent shield. It burst apart and the entire hall sagged downwards as the freed wormhole yanked on the threadbare fabric of the universe. The scaffolding above the *Leontine* sparked, collapsed and the craft dropped into the rupture, carrying Abby and the Queen with it. Max yelled out in despair, started forward, lost his balance and slid towards the vortex. In the final second he clutched the edge of the wreckage, shards cutting into his fingers. He howled again but kept hold as a roaring wind plucked at his boots. He looked to either side, searching for a way to escape the remorseless gravity. A pale shape flopped and writhed in a pool of viscous green liquid. The mind of Anselm the Machine Man slapped at the tiles with its paddle hands. Max had a brief impression of a smooth lozenge marked by twin shadowed pits as the entity vanished into the maelstrom. Max tried to pull himself forwards. He knew this wormhole was nothing like the silent brick-lined voids carved out of the singularity by the Black Roses. This was a rent in the cosmos itself. One touch would rip him to atoms.

A roiling petalled band looped around his waist and lifted him up. Odilon, a smoke demon once more, seethed as the atmosphere rushed past him into the opening below. The sage's head formed in front of him, framed by sooty tendrils, a night flower from a fevered child's hallucination. The alien peered deep into his eyes and the soft smile froze.

"Bassandis," said Odilon in surprise, as if spotting an old friend in a crowd. *This is it, this is the end.* Odilon disappeared and Max fell, thudding into the ground with his feet wedged against the bottom of the wrecked dome. The Black Rose lay in a writhing heap next to the control panels and, to Max's utter amazement, Persephone stood before him, tiny, sharp and precise in contrast to the chaos of the alien. He'd assumed she'd escaped with the Philosophers or died in the firefight. She caught Max's eye and to his astonishment she winked. Odilon, clearly stunned, flickered through his human avatars before bursting into a cloud once more. Persephone waited for him. Her own torso blossomed into an exquisite filigree cage filled with movement. Six slender arms extruded from the centre, sapphire blades of force. Max remembered the glittering motes crawling over Bassandis's skin. *A Machine Man.* This was Anselm, not that collapsing pile of junk Leontine so graciously referred to as an iron turd on legs. The decaying monster with its stained copper and pitted glass was a decoy. Persephone was the real ambassador from the court of Theuderic.

Odilon vaulted upwards but Anselm sprang at the same time, winding her quarry in a delicate weave of metal. Odilon battered against it like the moth under the goblet in Bassandis's garden. Anselm jerked back and forth as she strove to contain the Black Rose's desperate lunges. She would have triumphed but the howling tempest claimed one of the power consoles. It broke free, span through the air and struck the duelling creatures a glancing blow. Machine Man, Black Rose and control panel tumbled into the pit. Max yelled in fear as his boots lost purchase and he too plummeted into the churning light. He snatched at a chain that flapped down from the remains of the *Leontine's* gantry, but his palm was slick where he'd cut it on the hemisphere's jagged rim and he couldn't get purchase. As it slipped through his hand he shouted out a last despairing word.

CHAPTER TWENTY-NINE

THE DISSOLUTION STARTED in his hand. Horror engulfed him. He'd anticipated an instant death, did he now face unimaginable torture as the wormhole unravelled him atom by atom? He closed his eyes and tried to scream again but no voice escaped. A rushing wind enveloped him and still his hand turned inside out, each cell shrieking its agony as it bled into the void. The pain stopped as suddenly as if someone had flicked a switch. Max scrambled to understand what was happening. He lived, though it seemed as if his wrist was locked in a metal band. After an age he forced himself to open his eyes, dreading what he would find.

He floated in a grey bubble. Silver and black streaks peppered with flashes of light curved away from a glowing blue circle ahead to a red disc behind. He looked at his hand. Curled shards encasing his wrist. Ahead of him drifted a cluster of shapes forged out of tortured shrapnel. He tried to make sense of what he saw. Had he got tangled up in the wreckage of the gantry? But that was pristine and angular - this thing tugging him along was more a madman's sculpture of a woman in a dress. His heart leaped and he cried out in wonder. *The Brittle Hag*. At the point of death she'd come to him. That tearing pain in his hand must have been her extruding herself from the fragment she'd embedded in his palm and now he hung in her displacement field, a nexus of space and time so powerful it forced open the wormhole itself, protecting both of them from the titanic forces that rippled across its contours.

But for how long? He wasn't sure if he imagined it but the sphere appeared smaller, as if it shrank by the minute. Was it evaporating like the flawed ring of matter built by Leontine's scientists? He felt a tug at his feet and pulled up his knees. Yes, the walls were closing in. He had no idea how much time they had. He called out to the Brittle Hag but she ignored him, her other arm extended in front. She resembled a swimmer forging her way through a stormy ocean.

Max heard a clang and they stopped with a jolt. Ahead of him the being clung to a smooth metal surface, polished and studded with rivets. *What in God's name?* As he watched a hole opened before her. Max remembered how reality warped around the alien. He closed his eyes and clamped his teeth together as the Hag pushed through the metal, pulling Max after her. He experienced the hideous sensation of a sharp knife scraping over every inch of skin and then he was inside. The Hag flicked him across the room like a bowling ball and he smacked into a metal strut, banging his head so that his eyes sparkled and his ears rang. Someone screamed in horror. Was that a gun clattering to the floor? Arms caught his neck in a vicious lock and a mouth fastened over his. *Abby Fabrice. God's cock. No matter how hard I try I just can't get away from you can I?*

When she finally let him come up for air he prised his eyes open. The gloomy interior of the capsule flickered with warning lights. Two shapes lay in a heap in the shadows.

"I killed them," said Abby, "I had to. When the dome closed they tried to shoot me."

Not the Queen as well? He looked past Abby to see another curled body, its back to the Brittle Hag. He detected a distant keening sound - the whimpering of an animal at the limits of terror.

"What is that thing?" asked Abby. She pressed herself against Max, pushing at the plates with her heels as if trying to get as far away from the creature as possible. The alien stood in the centre of the capsule, a cluster of shards spiralling out from a twisted cage of midnight black. Max waited to hear that unnatural voice in his head again but she remained silent and unmoving. She looked like gouges left by a demon clawing ragged holes in existence. With a shock he noticed level ground beneath her. Where was her distortion sphere?

"She's the Brittle Hag. She saved my life. I guess it was to preserve Bassandis," he said. But at what price? He had a sudden vision of the Abhumans huddled and fearful in the shadows, bereft of their guardian. Still the Brittle Hag didn't move. Red and blue light from the two observation ports splashed over her but nothing could take away her essential wrongness. Even though she'd rescued Max, and was driven by an unholy compassion for living things, part of him wanted to get as far away as he could from this shadow. He and Abby shuffled round her on their bottoms, moving back until they fetched up against the front of the vessel. They stood up together and looked out of the porthole. Max could sense the Brittle Hag behind him. *Please say something before you get any closer.* He didn't think his ripped nerves would stand it if she suddenly materialised beside him. He dared to look at his hand. Max's fingers, Max's palm. All there and all in the right place.

Abby stared through the window, her mouth open. Max had imagined they'd be looking down a tunnel, neat and orderly like the wormhole shafts they used to explore in the Wasteland - brick lined and conveniently supplied with stairs. The swirling chaos of light in front was a river of discoloured mercury pouring over the glass. Max tried to catch images in the constant torrent. Were those landscapes? Skies? Worlds? He couldn't make any sense of the hypnotic mess. Abby looked at the dials and levers. The *Leontine* had controls but he doubted they'd be of much help here. He guessed the Queen's scientists intended to use these to pilot through whatever alien atmosphere they found at the end of the journey, if it had an end.

"Are we really going to the next universe?" asked Abby. He recognised the tone in her voice and felt the same. What if this was it? What if the wormhole was compromised by the flaws Odilon spotted in the ring holding it open? They could be trapped here forever, spinning between realities in a place beyond time or crushed in a second if the walls collapsed.

"What happens next?" Max called out to the Brittle Hag. She didn't speak or move. *Is she dead? Can she survive without that unholy void around her?*

Abby took his hand and pressed against him. They watched the seething vortex splash over the crystal for what seemed ages.

"I wanted to leave you because I didn't want to see you die," said Abby eventually.

"It's OK," said Max. She leant her head against his arm.

"I was wrong. I'm sorry. I'll come with you to the end and whatever wants to harm you will have to go through me first. That's how it should be, how it always should have been." Anything Max wanted to say in return would sound trite and self-serving but with her words an unexpected feeling of deep peace settled on him. They stood in a runaway ship plummeting out of control between universes, with a hideous, implacable and unknowable alien standing a few yards behind them. Death could arrive at any second but it didn't matter. *This is where we belong isn't it? Two spare idiots on their merry way.* He lifted up that pointed chin and kissed her, tasting the salt on her lips.

After several hours boredom and tiredness caught up. The Brittle Hag hadn't shifted an inch from her position in the centre of the vessel. Queen Leontine stayed curled up against the wall, either sleeping or locked up in some private childhood nightmare. Max doubted she'd be coming round any time soon and if she decided to cause trouble he was sure the sight of the alien she feared would be enough of a deterrent. They slumped down with their backs against the bulkhead and fell asleep, using each other as pillows.

Max awoke to find the cabin darker. A pale glow replaced the red and blue light from the windows. It washed across the bulkheads leaving shadows as black as ink. A soft wind teased his face and stirred Abby's hair where she slept on the floor beside him. With a shock he realised the Brittle Hag had vanished, along with Queen Leontine. The bodies of the guard and the technician still lay at the back. The strange radiance left the darkness pooling in their mouths and eye sockets. A lozenge splattered with glowing motes stood in the far wall. Max struggled to understand what he looked at, then realised. *The door's open.* He shook Abby awake. She mumbled her way into irritated semi-consciousness, blinking like a new-born. She saw the door, gave Max a look of astonished delight and before he could stop her leaped through it. *Stupid maniac, God knows what's out there,* thought Max as he scrambled after her.

The ship rested on top of a hill covered in what looked like broad-leaved grass. Night rendered the whole landscape in muted silvers, golds, blues and yellows. A black mass crowned with spikes stood to their left, spilling down into the valley. A forest? Max ran through the quick mental checklist he'd always used when they'd stepped onto other worlds in the distant past. Normal gravity, breathable, a little rich in oxygen maybe, and an underlying coppery smell that drifted over the ridge behind them. How long did they have? He closed his eyes and listened to his body. Nothing - no burning, no sensation of energy leaching through his skin. He rubbed his hands together. No change. *This isn't deep time*, he realised in wonder. *I'm not dying. I can stay here*. He turned to Abby but her head was thrown back and her mouth open. He followed her gaze and almost stumbled with the shock of it.

That sky. My God, that sky. He'd seen stars before when they'd skipped in and out of ancient worlds at night - lights scattered through the darkness, even the occasional cloud of dust and fire, the few remaining sun factories drifting through the void. They were dead shrouds compared to this.

The first thing he noticed were the moons - one as big as his palm, the other the size of a penny. Clouds circled the blue surface of the larger satellite. Maybe it was another world. Max wondered whether it span round their planet or they orbited it. The smaller moon looked like an orange rock trailing streamers of debris. But that was only the beginning. Further up he saw the galaxies. Three hung above them, the closest an immense explosion of silver and blue, light cored, fading to tattered edges and filaments strung with thousands, no, millions of stars sinking below the horizon. The second and third discs stretched back into the void. It looked as if the universe itself skimmed them across space like stones skipping over a lake. Max's neck started to hurt but he rotated on the spot, following the arc of the largest galaxy down the other side of the sky. Despite himself he gasped again. A cluster of more stars spread across the night, red and blue giants flanked by white points of light burning so fiercely Max thought he heard them roar. It was a cosmos filled with colour pouring from the stars to wash over the landscape in relentless diaphanous swathes.

Something like a huge bird fluttered past him. He jumped back with a cry. The creature turned in an arc and scampered back towards them. Max's heart calmed a little as he recognised Leontine, her arms stuck out as she danced around them in circles, upturned face bathed in starlight.

"I did it, I did it, I did it. The next universe. We're here, can't you see?" she grabbed Max's hands and whirled him round in a circle. Her expression was that of an ecstatic child but Max glimpsed a worrying madness in her eyes. She let go of his fingers, staggered back and fell. For a few seconds she stared upwards, then kicked her arms and legs as if having a tantrum, laughing all the while. She jumped up and was gone. Beyond her, in the double moonlight, Max thought he spotted the Brittle Hag gliding over a distant hill top.

"Max?" said Abby, voice suddenly full of doubt. "What's that?"

He followed her arm as she pointed between the star cluster and the largest galaxy. A narrow black band reached up into the sky. *That shouldn't be there*. It looked too regular, artificial even. The immense shape dwindled to a point far above their heads. A couple of stars hung between it and their planet.

"I've no idea." he said. If only he had a pair of binoculars or a telescope. *Wait a second*. At the same time he peered forward he heard Abby gasp. A quarter of the way up an ochre coloured object projected out of the blackness. It was a flat, lobed shape curled like an opening flower, or a hand. *A hand.* The world around him rocked and he fell to his knees, gasping in the rich air as he struggled to gain control of his reeling mind. He looked again. It wasn't human, the arrangement was all wrong. He could make out two opposing thumbs on either side of three spade fingers, but there was no mistaking that hand reaching from the darkness.

"It's the God Door," said Abby. "We're seeing it from the other side. We're really here Max, we're in the next universe. The Queen's wormhole worked."

Max stood. Every child in Metacarpi knew of the God Door - the legend of the portal between universes and the line of patient deities waiting to step through it and scatter their people across a new existence. Every adult could repeat the tale verbatim and yet how many believed it was real? Max always suspected that most, like himself, regarded it as little more than a charming fairy story concocted amid the guttering embers of the old cosmos. He didn't doubt that something existed, some exit from their own long-dead creation. Why else build a god to carry them through it? Why else would Odilon try so desperately to destroy the giants destined to form that titan's mind? *It's not futile. God's not just a mad joke we've made at our own expense to prove to ourselves we are hopeless, lost fools. The door is here and the first gods are entering the universe.*

He took Abby's hand and together they walked up to the crest of the hill. On the other side an immense ocean stretched away from impossible cliffs to the horizon where structures like inverted mountains rose out of the sea, silhouetted against the star light. Every so often Max heard Leontine's happy screams from the hills behind and once he caught a glimpse of the Brittle Hag gliding swiftly in front of a setting moon. They paused and Abby reached up to kiss him. In one deft move she slipped out of Persephone's dress and started to unbutton his shirt. She was clearly out of her mind.

"Abby, we're on an alien planet in another universe for God's sake," he said, trying to push her hands away. He dreaded to think what might be watching from those jagged forests. But there was no stopping her and when she nibbled at his neck and ears all coherent thoughts exited from his head into the night.

"Don't you want to be the first humans to fuck in the new cosmos?" she mumbled around his earlobe as she gently chewed away. When he failed to come up with any intelligent reply she hooked one foot behind his knee, threw him onto his back and jumped on top of him.

The last time we made love was just before you said you were leaving, thought Max. Abby yanked his pants off and tossed them into the grass with a whoop. *Never again. I will never be so stupid as to let you do that again. I love you, Abigail Fabrice.* She must have sensed his thoughts because the grin faded into such a look of open adoration and longing that his heart soared. She lay her head on his chest and sighed. He ran his hands over her warm skin, feeling the muscles, the scars and the curve of her hips.

"Do you think the Gods are peeking through that door?" she said. He had to laugh, even as he fought to imprint every part of her into his mind forever. "Shall we give them something to remember?"

He saw stars through her hair, her body outlined in the roaring fires of new galaxies. They were gods themselves, and the entire universe cascaded from their passion. For the first time ever Abby yelled out when she came, a scream of joy echoing through the hills and distant forest. They collapsed laughing in a heap on the grass before falling asleep from sheer happy exhaustion.

Max woke to the sound of screaming and sobbing. He panicked and looked around wildly. Abby lay on her back, her head pillowed in her hands, fast asleep with her mouth open. In the night blossoms from the alien trees had drifted over her naked body, dappling her skin with their curling fronds. A sun blazed in the sky, filling the world with light the colour of pure water. For a second Max forgot the crying and closed his eyes to sense the star warming his skin. He held up his hand. No energy bleeding into the air, no burning sensation of life ebbing away. He could spend the rest of his days on this planet. The mere thought made him giddy with delight. Between his fingers he counted the crescents of two moons.

Abby put her hand around his waist and stood naked beside him, her hair tickling his skin. She closed her eyes and lifted her face to the sun. In that second she looked so beautiful to Max he could have watched her forever. She frowned.

"What's that god-awful noise?" she asked. Hand in hand they walked to the crest of the hill and looked into the valley. The Brittle Hag stood a few yards further down the slope. Beyond her the Steel Queen knelt with her hands over her eyes, howling and weeping, putting out her fingers to feel through the grass before slapping them back over her face and keening in desperate fear.

"She's blind," said Abby. Max heard the horror and pity in her tones. The Brittle Hag moved beside them, causing Abby to shrink against Max.

"She looked at the sun," said the alien, her words jagged, inhuman and sickening. Max realised what had happened. He and Abby had visited enough ancient worlds to understand the power of those long dead stars. *Don't stare at a sun, not even a dying red one let alone this fierce blue giant.* The Steel Queen had never set foot beyond the end of the universe, never looked up into a sky that was anything other than soft glowing mist or empty darkness. When the sun rose on this new world she gazed at it in wonder, not knowing what it was and not realising it would destroy her sight until it was too late.

"We'll have to take her back, get the Philosophers to cure her," said Abby.

"No, she cannot go back," said the Brittle Hag. "She will be killed for what she tried to do."

"She can't stay here alone," said Max. "How can she look after herself?" Maybe they should put her out of her misery now. He shuddered at the thought. Kill a blind woman in cold blood? He couldn't do it, nor Abby. Would the alien be so cruel?

"I will stay," said the Brittle Hag. "I will protect her as I protected the Abhumans so she will not be left in the darkness as they were."

Max stared at the creature. He understood it was driven by the guilt and loathing of what it had once been, and now sought atonement by serving and protecting others, but what about the Abhumans? Who would look after them?

"The wormhole destroyed the energy sphere that prevented me falling through the rotting fabric of the old cosmos. Without it I can't return," said the Brittle Hag as if it read his thoughts. "You must care for the Abhumans. You must help all of them, all the creatures we have left behind."

A curling shard of alien metal touched his forehead as the creature held up its nightmare hand.

"The salvation of those lives rests in your head. You can't stay in this universe. Go back and rebuild the Mind of God."

She unfurled a hand towards the capsule.

"I can reopen the wormhole but it's unstable and will dissolve swiftly behind you."

Max felt Abby's shoulders sag, sensed the crushing disappointment in her heart. To go back to the darkness, to return to walk among the remnants of humanity scrabbling out their lives on the body of a colossal rotting doll was too much to bear. If Max could have plucked Bassandis from his head and cast him away he would have done it - even if in doing so he condemned billions yet unborn. Maybe Odilon was right. Perhaps this new universe didn't need mankind after all. If so, why should he be the one to help bring them here?

Beyond the Brittle Hag he noticed shapes moving on the horizon - angular, stilted shadows loping towards them. The alien saw them and glided down the slope towards the crying queen to stand sentinel beside her.

"Do we have to go back, Max?" asked Abby. He wrapped his arms around her and held her close, her lips at his ear, whispering visions that were so, so tempting. "We could live here forever. It's perfect for us - a whole world of adventure and wonder, and to fuck under that sky every night, Max. What greater paradise will we find?" He eased her away and saw the tears on her face that told him she knew as well as he did what they had to do.

"Come on," he said and led her back to their heaped clothes. They dressed and stood once more to marvel at the beauty of the world around them before climbing back into the *Leontine*. After pushing out the bodies of the guard and the scientist they sealed the hatch. They should have buried the men but lingering here any longer was too painful. The Brittle Hag stood in front of the ship. She raised one claw in an uncannily human gesture of farewell and the capsule dropped once more into the seething maelstrom between universes.

THEY RE-EMERGED over the Umbilical Ocean. Once she'd realised they were returning Abby threw herself into learning how the ship worked and by the time the wormhole slid over the hull like retreating surf she'd figured out how to manoeuvre it. Max watched the roiling disc fade and vanish behind them. *Taking our hopes with it.*

It was a remarkable machine, not only built to withstand the trip between universes but a powerful flyer capable of jaw-dropping speeds. Max even glimpsed the hint of a smile on that disappointed face as she brought it out of a steep dive to skim over the mercury waves. They rose once more and Max spotted the sphere. His first instinct was to get as far away as possible but he noticed it rested on the edge of the sea like a forgotten ball washed up on a beach. Chains of light spread away from it, curving over and through the jumbled canyons of God's skin. Abby brought them closer and horror seized Max. A vast, ragged hole in the side of the world vented gases into the sky. The edges still glowed, dropping lazy clumps of fused metal as big as houses into the waves.

"The wormhole," said Abby. "It destroyed the Steel Queen's kingdom."

Through the gap Max saw an interior lit with flashes of red lightning and mountainous billows of smoke. The delicate green and blue tracery of the Queen's civilisation, forever bathed in that cool mist, was gone. He understood those rivers of light streaming over the darkness. Refugees. All the inhabitants who'd survived were abandoning the sphere, fleeing the wreckage of that moon-sized artefact to seek shelter across God's skin and deep in his body. He remembered Queen Leontine dancing with happy madness through alien grass. Would she have been so delighted if she'd realised the cost of her experiment? The sight sickened him.

"Let's go."

"Where?" asked Abby.

Max wanted to get away from this eternal night. The endless darkness, the cluttered debris of the skin, the unnatural ocean, the lights and half-glimpsed monsters filled him with fear and oppressed his soul.

"Down, into the air, somewhere where there's light," he said. Even if it was just a parody of the radiance that washed real planets under real suns he didn't care. Abby turned the ship north east and they sped away from the Umbilicus, soon losing it in the darkness.

Max pondered his next move. Though Bassandis slept in his brain, placed in stasis by Anselm, he had to be quick. With this ship it made more sense to aim for the Head and try to make contact with the Machine Men who'd designed the giants in the first place. But the shortest way into God's skull was through the Empire of the Ear. The Emperor Demetrius himself dwelled in the AntiHelix, that immense fortress at the entrance to the Meatus, far above the atmosphere. His experience with his subjects so far had left him with the impression of an ancient, etiolated race given to self-absorbed asceticism and indifferent cruelty. Did he have allies there? The no-doubt disgraced Captain Andagis? Ruth's lover, the General Crysanthe Uella? The last time he'd seen her she'd done nothing but utter haughty pronouncements via a Speaking Lens. Besides, Ruth died in the Battle for Metacarpi. *Hello, your girlfriend fell out of the back of the ship I was piloting and burnt to death. Any chance you could help me get to the Tympanic Membrane?*

"Max, we're being followed." said Abby, her voice tense. He hadn't been paying attention and saw, with a shock, that they skimmed over red ground under a blue and purple sky.

"Where are we?"

"East of the Upper Arm," said Abby. She gave a happy grin. "Swift, isn't it?"

Max looked out of the window at the oh so familiar sight of a cracked, shattered plain littered with the crumpled corpses of immense gantries and machines. Mountains as sharp as teeth cut shapes out of the air. They roared over the landscape at a stunning velocity. A cluster of warehouses around a wormhole slipped past before he had time to make sense of what he saw. He remembered Abby's words.

"Followed?"

She nodded.

"It's fast too. Maybe it's another of the Steel Queen's ships."

He'd been naive to think they could get away so easily. It was his fault Odilon got into the palace to wreak carnage and destroy the wormhole. It came as no surprise that others would chase after him with vengeance in their hearts. The only weapon they had was the dead guard's machine pistol. As far as he could tell the ship itself carried no armaments, though its hull was strong enough to withstand the pressures beyond the fabric of reality. Would that be sufficient? He walked to the rear of the ship and peered through the porthole. There, skimming towards them, weaving in and out of the rusting towers that flashed past on both sides. There was no denying it, that ship was faster than theirs.

Five minutes later he called to Abby.

"Land the ship, put us down! Now!"

"What? Where?"

"Anywhere."

She probably thought him mad but she slowed the craft, bringing it to a halt on top of a cliff overlooking a valley filled with rusted metal frames and wheels as big as hills. Max opened the hatch and jumped onto the ground. The familiar dry wind of the Wasteland ruffled his hair. Far to the west God's upper arm cut the sky in half. Abby climbed after him just as the other ship landed a few hundred yards away. She swore as she recognised it.

As Max walked towards the Brittle Hag's vessel the ramp dropped from underneath the flat metal disc with a loud clang. Max paused, waiting to see if the alien had somehow managed to return from the other universe. God, had she brought the blind Queen back with her? A grey shape crept down the slope, shielding its billiard ball eyes against the bright sky with a black taloned hand. An Abhuman. Max remembered his promise to the Brittle Hag. *You must care for them she said. Oh shit, I thought she was being metaphorical.* Another Abhuman followed, then another with a child holding onto its arm.

"Max?" said Abby, her voice filled with foreboding.

He watched aghast as the flat disc disgorged a crowd that grew larger by the minute. All those corridors and rooms spiralling off into other dimensions. How many Abhumans rode that ship? Hundreds? *Dear God, they're all here.* A wall of grey-furred creatures stared at him. Now what? Were they going to kill him? Punish him for snatching away their guardian? Sacrifice him to a strange Abhuman idol? One of the figures detached itself from the rest and loped towards him, long hands swinging back and forth and bread loaf head cocked to the side. He tensed. Behind him he heard the bolt on the machine pistol click. He gestured to Abby with his hand. *Keep it calm.*

The Abhuman stopped in front of Max. Its jaw hinged open to reveal dagger teeth. It blinked, spread its arms wide and, to Max's astonishment, gave him a deep bow. Beyond their herald every Abhuman followed suit, a murmuring sound like wind-blown leaves drifted over the landscape as they bent their monstrous heads in obeisance. Behind him Abby burst out laughing.

"I don't believe it. Maximilian Ocel, King of the Abhumans!"

John Guy Collick was born in Yorkshire, England. When he was 10 years old his grandfather gave him a copy of *A Princess of Mars* by Edgar Rice Burroughs, and from then on he was hooked on science fiction and fantasy. He worked for Scotland Yard before moving to Japan for ten years to lecture in literature and philosophy, teaching courses on Science Fiction and Futurology. *Ragged Claws* is his second novel. As well as writing SF he is the author of a book on Shakespeare, essays on literature and several screenplays.

Website: johnguycollick.com
Twitter: @johnguycollick